CHRONICLES
VOLUME TWO

DRAGONS OF A
WINTER NIGHT

Margaret Weis and Tracy Hickman

Poetry by Michael Williams
Cover Art by Matt Stawicki
Interior Art by Denis Beauvais

DRAGONS OF WINTER NIGHT

©1985 TSR, Inc.
©2003 Wizards of the Coast, Inc.

Distributed in the United States by Holtzbrinck Publishing. Distributed in Canada by Fenn Ltd.

Distributed to the hobby, toy, and comic trade in the United States and Canada by regional distributors.

Distributed worldwide by Wizards of the Coast, Inc. and regional distributors.

Printed in the U.S.A.

Cover art by Matt Stawicki
Interior art by Denis Beauvais
Cartography by Rob Lazzaretti and Dennis Kauth
First Printing: April 1985
Library of Congress Catalog Card Number: 2002114360

9 8 7 6 5 4 3 2 1

US ISBN: 0-7869-3067-5
UK ISBN: 0-7869-3068-3
620-96207-001-EN

U.S., CANADA,
ASIA, PACIFIC, & LATIN AMERICA
Wizards of the Coast, Inc.
P.O. Box 707
Renton, WA 98057-0707
+1-800-324-6496

EUROPEAN HEADQUARTERS
Wizards of the Coast, Belgium
T Hofveld 6d
1702 Groot-Bijgaarden
Belgium
+322 467 3360

Visit our web site at **www.wizards.com**

by Margaret Weis and Tracy Hickman

ANSALON

North Keep
Nordmaar
Karthay
Mithas
Kalaman
argaard
Keep
Estwilde
Kothas
Khallist Mtns.
Neraka
Sanction
Khur
Flotsam
Zhakar
Khuri-Khan
Balifor
Kendermore
Goodlund
Bloten
Bay of Balifor
Blood Sea of Istar
Courrain Ocean
Silvanesti
Silvanost

0   200
Miles

Dedication

To my parents,
Dr. and Mrs. Harold R. Hickman,
who taught me what true honor is
—Tracy Raye Hickman

To my parents, Frances and George Weis,
who gave me a gift more precious than life—
the love of books
—Margaret Weis

We gratefully acknowledge the help of the authors of the
ADVANCED DUNGEONS & DRAGONS® DRAGONLANCE®
roleplaying adventure game modules:
Douglas Niles, *Dragons of Ice*; Jeff Grubb, *Dragons of Light*, and
Laura Hickman, co-author, *Dragons of War*.

Finally, to Michael: Est Sularus oth Mithas

he winter winds raged outside, but within the caverns of the mountain dwarves beneath the Kharolis Mountains, the fury of the storm was not felt. As the Thane called for silence among the assembled dwarves and humans, a dwarven bard stepped forward to do homage to the companions.

SONG OF THE NINE HEROES

From the north came danger, as we knew it would:
In the vanguard of winter, a dragon's dance
Unraveled the land, until out of the forest,
Out of the plains they came, from the mothering earth,
The sky unreckoned before them.
Nine they were, under the three moons,
Under the autumn twilight:
As the world declined, they arose
Into the heart of the story.

One from a garden of stone arising,
From dwarf-halls, from weather and wisdom,
Where the heart and mind ride unquestioned
In the untapped vein of the hand.
In his fathering arms, the spirit gathered.
Nine they were, under the three moons,
Under the autumn twilight:
As the world declined, they arose
Into the heart of the story.

One from a haven of breezes descending,
Light in the handling air,
To the waving meadows, the kender's country,
Where the grain out of smallness arises itself
To grow green and golden and green again.
Nine they were, under the three moons,
Under the autumn twilight:
As the world declined, they arose
Into the heart of the story.
The next from the plains, the long land's keeping,
Nurtured in distance, horizons of nothing.
Bearing a staff she came, and a burden
Of mercy and light converged in her hand:

Bearing the wounds of the world, she came.
Nine they were, under the three moons,
Under the autumn twilight:
As the world declined, they arose
Into the heart of the story.

The next from the plains, in the moon's shadow,
Through custom, through ritual, trailing the moon
Where her phases, her wax and her wane, controlled
The tide of his blood, and his warrior's hand
Ascended through hierarchies of space into light.
Nine they were, under the three moons,
Under the autumn twilight:
As the world declined, they arose
Into the heart of the story.

One within absences, known by departures,
The dark swordswoman at the heart of fire:
Her glories the space between words,
The cradlesong recollected in age,
Recalled at the edge of awakening and thought.
Nine they were, under the three moons,
Under the autumn twilight:
As the world declined, they arose
Into the heart of the story.

One in the heart of honor, formed by the sword,
By the centuries' flight of the kingfisher over the land,
By Solamnia ruined and risen, rising again
When the heart ascends into duty.
As it dances, the sword is forever an heirloom.
Nine they were, under the three moons,
Under the autumn twilight:
As the world declined, they arose
Into the heart of the story.

The next in a simple light a brother to darkness,
Letting the sword hand try all subtleties,
Even the intricate webs of the heart. His thoughts
Are pools disrupted in changing wind—
He cannot see their bottom.
Nine they were, under the three moons,

Under the autumn twilight:
As the world declined, they arose
Into the heart of the story.

The next the leader, half-elven, betrayed
As the twining blood pulls asunder the land,
The forests, the worlds of elves and men.
Called into bravery, but fearing for love,
And fearing that, called into both, he does nothing.
Nine they were, under the three moons,
Under the autumn twilight:
As the world declined, they arose
Into the heart of the story.

The last from the darkness, breathing the night
Where the abstract stars hide a nest of words,
Where the body endures the wound of numbers,
Surrendered to knowledge, until, unable to bless,
His blessing falls on the low, the benighted.
Nine they were, under the three moons,
Under the autumn twilight:
As the world declined, they arose
Into the heart of the story.

Joined by others they were in the telling:
A graceless girl, graced beyond graces;
A princess of seeds and saplings, called to the forest;
An ancient weaver of accidents;
Nor can we say who the story will gather.
Nine they were, under the three moons,
Under the autumn twilight:
As the world declined, they arose
Into the heart of the story.

From the north came danger, as we knew it would:
In encampments of winter, the dragon's sleep
Has settled the land, but out of the forest,
Out of the plains they come, from the mothering earth
Defining the sky before them.
Nine they were, under the three moons,
Under the autumn twilight:
As the world declined, they arose
Into the heart of the story.

The Hammer

"The Hammer of Kharas!"

The great Hall of Audience of the King of the Mountain Dwarves echoed with the triumphal announcement. It was followed by wild cheering, the deep booming voices of the dwarves mingling with the slightly higher-pitched shouts of the humans as the huge doors at the rear of the Hall were thrown open and Elistan, cleric of Paladine, entered.

Although the bowl-shaped Hall was large, even by dwarven standards, it was crammed to capacity. Nearly all of the eight hundred refugees from Pax Tharkas lined the walls, while the dwarves packed onto the carved stone benches below.

Elistan appeared at the foot of a long central aisle, the giant warhammer held reverently in his hands. The shouts increased at the sight of the cleric of Paladine in his white robes, the sound booming against the great vault of the ceiling and reverberating through the hall until it seemed that the ground shook with the vibrations.

Tanis winced as the noise made his head throb. He was stifled in the crowd. He didn't like being underground anyway and, although the ceiling was so high that the top soared beyond the blazing torchlight and disappeared into shadow, the half-elf felt enclosed, trapped.

"I'll be glad when this is over," he muttered to Sturm, standing next to him.

Sturm, always melancholy, seemed even darker and more brooding than usual. "I don't approve of this, Tanis," he muttered, folding his arms across the bright metal of his antique breastplate.

"I know," said Tanis irritably. "You've said it—not once, but several times. It's too late now. There's nothing to be done but make the best of it."

The end of his sentence was lost in another resounding cheer as Elistan raised the Hammer above his head, showing it to the crowd before beginning the walk down the aisle. Tanis put his hand on his forehead. He was growing dizzy as the cool underground cavern heated up from the mass of bodies.

Elistan started to walk down the aisle. Rising to greet him on a dais in the center of the Hall was Hornfel, Thane of the Hylar dwarves. Spaced behind the dwarf were seven carved stone thrones, all of them now empty. Hornfel stood before the seventh throne—the most magnificent, the throne for the King of Thorbardin. Long empty, it would be occupied once more, as Hornfel accepted the Hammer of Kharas. The return of this ancient relic was a singular triumph for Hornfel. Since his thanedom was now in possession of the coveted Hammer, he could unite the rival dwarven thanes under his leadership.

"We fought to recover that Hammer," Sturm said slowly, his eyes upon the gleaming weapon. "The legendary Hammer of Kharas.Used to forge the dragonlances. Lost for hundreds of years, found again, and lost once more. And now given to the dwarves!" he said in disgust.

"It was given to the dwarves once before," Tanis reminded him wearily, feeling sweat trickle down his forehead. "Have Flint tell you the tale, if you've forgotten. At any rate, it is truly theirs now." Elistan had arrived at the foot of the stone dais where the Thane, dressed in the heavy robes and massive gold chains dwarves loved, awaited him. Elistan knelt at the foot of the dais, a politic gesture, for otherwise the tall, muscular cleric would stand face-to-face with the dwarf, despite the fact that the dais was a good three feet off the ground. The dwarves cheered mightily at this. The humans were, Tanis noticed, more subdued, some muttering among themselves, not liking the sight of their leader abasing himself.

"Accept this gift of our people—" Elistan's words were lost in another cheer from the dwarves.

"Gift!" Sturm snorted. "Ransom is nearer the mark."

"In return for which," Elistan continued when he could be heard, "we thank the dwarves for their generous gift of a place to live within their kingdom."

"For the right to be sealed in a tomb . . ." Sturm muttered.

"And we pledge our support to the dwarves if the war should come upon us!" Elistan shouted.

Cheering resounded throughout the chamber, increasing as Thane Hornfel bent to receive the Hammer. The dwarves stamped and whistled, most climbing up on the stone benches.

Tanis began to feel nauseated. He glanced around. They would never be missed. Hornfel would speak; so would each of the other six Thanes, not to mention the members of the Highseekers Council. The half-elf touched Sturm on the arm, motioning to the knight to follow him. The two walked silently from the Hall, bending low to get through a narrow archway. Although still underground in the massive dwarven city, at least they were away from the noise, out in the cool night air.

"Are you all right?" Sturm asked, noticing Tanis's pallor beneath his beard. The half-elf gulped draughts of cool air.

"I am now," Tanis said, flushing in shame at his weakness. "It was the heat . . . and the noise."

"Well, we'll be out of here soon," Sturm said. "Depending, of course, on whether or not the Council of Highseekers votes to let us go to Tarsis."

"Oh, there's no doubt how they'll vote," Tanis said, shrugging. "Elistan is clearly in control, now that he's led the people to a place of safety. None of the Highseekers dares oppose him—at least to his face. No, my friend, within a month's time perhaps, we'll be setting sail in one of the white-winged ships of Tarsis the Beautiful."

"Without the Hammer of Kharas," Sturm added bitterly. Softly, he began to quote. *"'And so it was told that the Knights took the golden Hammer, the Hammer blessed by the great god Paladine and given to the One of the Silver Arm so that he might forge the Dragonlance of Huma, Dragonbane, and gave the Hammer to the dwarf they called Kharas, or Knight, for his extraordinary valor and honor in battle. And he kept Kharas for his name. And the Hammer of Kharas passed into the dwarven kingdom with assurances from the dwarves that it should be brought forth again at need—"*

"It has been brought forth," Tanis said, struggling to contain his rising anger. He had heard that quotation entirely too many times!

"It has been brought forth and will be left behind!" Sturm bit the words. *"We might have taken it to Solamnia, used it to forge our own dragonlances—"*

"And you would be another Huma, riding to glory, the Dragonlance in your hand!" Tanis's control snapped. *"Meanwhile you'd let eight hundred people die—"*

"No, I would not have let them die!" Sturm shouted in a towering rage. *"The first clue we have to the dragonlances and you sell it for—"*

Both men stopped arguing abruptly, suddenly aware of a shadow creeping from the darker shadows surrounding them.

"Shirak," whispered a voice, and a bright light flared, gleaming from a crystal ball clutched in the golden, disembodied claw of a dragon atop a plain, wooden staff. The light illuminated the red robes of a magic-user. The young mage walked toward the two, leaning upon his staff, coughing slightly. The light from his staff shone upon a skeletal face, with glistening metallic gold skin drawn tightly over fine bones. His eyes gleamed golden.

"Raistlin," said Tanis, his voice tight. "Is there something you want?"

Raistlin did not seem at all bothered by the angry looks both men cast him, apparently well accustomed to the fact that few felt comfortable in his presence or wanted him around.

He stopped before the two. Stretching forth his frail hand, the mage spoke, *"Akular-alan suh Tagolann Jistrathar,"* and a pale image of a weapon shimmered into being as Tanis and Sturm watched in astonishment.

It was a footman's lance, nearly twelve feet long. The point was made of pure silver, barbed and gleaming, the shaft crafted of polished wood. The tip was steel, designed to be thrust into the ground.

"It's beautiful!" Tanis gasped. "What is it?"

"A dragonlance," Raistlin answered. Holding the lance in his hand, the mage stepped between the two, who stood aside to let him pass as if unwilling to be touched by him. Their eyes were on the lance. Then Raistlin turned and held it out to Sturm.

"There is your dragonlance, knight," Raistlin hissed, "without benefit of the Hammer or the Silver Arm. Will you ride with it into glory, remembering that, for Huma, with glory came death?"

Sturm's eyes flashed. He caught his breath in awe as he reached out to take hold of the dragonlance. To his amazement, his hand passed right through it! The dragonlance vanished, even as he touched it.

"More of your tricks!" he snarled. Spinning on his heel, he stalked away, choking in anger.

"If you meant that as a joke, Raistlin," Tanis said quietly, "it wasn't funny."

"A joke?" the mage whispered. His strange golden eyes followed the knight as Sturm walked into the thick blackness of the dwarven city beneath the mountain. "You should know me better, Tanis."

The mage laughed—the weird laughter Tanis had heard only once before. Then, bowing sardonically to the half-elf, Raistlin disappeared, following the knight into the shadows.

BOOK I

I

White-winged ships.

Hope lies across the Plains of Dust.

anis Half-Elven sat in the meeting of the Council of Highseekers and listened, frowning. Though officially the false religion of the Seekers was now dead, the group that made up the political leadership of the eight hundred refugees from Pax Tharkas was still called that.

"It isn't that we're not grateful to the dwarves for allowing us to live here," stated Hederick expansively, waving his scarred hand. "We are all grateful, I'm certain. Just as we're grateful to those whose heroism in recovering the Hammer of Kharas made our move here possible." Hederick bowed to Tanis, who returned the bow with a brief nod of his head. "But we are not dwarves!" This emphatic statement brought murmurs of approval, causing Hederick to warm to his audience.

"We *humans* were never meant to live underground!" Loud calls of approval and some clapping of hands.

"We are farmers. We cannot grow food on the side of a mountain! We want lands like the ones we were forced to leave behind. And I say that those who forced us to leave our old homeland should provide us with new!"

"Does he mean the Dragon Highlords?" Sturm whispered sarcastically to Tanis. "I'm certain they'd be happy to oblige."

"The fools ought to be thankful they're alive!" Tanis muttered. "Look at them, turning to Elistan—as if it were *his* doing!" The cleric of Paladine—and leader of the refugees—rose to his feet to answer Hederick.

"It is because we need new homes," Elistan said, his strong baritone resounding through the cavern, "that I propose we send a delegation south, to the city of Tarsis the Beautiful."

Tanis had heard Elistan's plan before. His mind wandered over the month since he and his companions had returned from Derkin's Tomb with the sacred Hammer.

The dwarven Thanes, now consolidated under the leadership of Hornfel, were preparing to battle the evil coming from the north. The dwarves did not greatly fear this evil. Their mountain kingdom seemed impregnable. And they had kept the promise they made Tanis in return for the Hammer: the refugees from Pax Tharkas could settle in Southgate, the southernmost part of the mountain kingdom of Thorbardin.

Elistan brought the refugees to Thorbardin. They began trying to rebuild their lives, but the arrangement was not totally satisfactory.

They were safe, to be sure, but the refugees, mostly farmers, were not happy living underground in the huge dwarven caverns. In the spring they could plant crops on the mountainside, but the rocky soil would produce only a bare living. The people wanted to live in the sunshine and fresh air. They did not want to be dependent on the dwarves.

It was Elistan who recalled the ancient legends of Tarsis the Beautiful and its gull-winged ships. But that's all they were—legends, as Tanis had pointed out when Elistan first mentioned his idea. No one on this part of Ansalon had heard anything about the city of Tarsis since the Cataclysm three hundred years ago. At that time, the dwarves had closed off the mountain kingdom of Thorbardin, effectively shutting off all communication between the south and north, since the only way through the Kharolis Mountains was through Thorbardin.

Tanis listened gloomily as the Council of Highseekers voted unanimously to approve Elistan's suggestion. They proposed sending a small group of people to Tarsis with instructions to find what ships came into port, where they were bound, and how much it would cost to book passage—or even to buy a ship.

"And who's going to lead this group?" Tanis asked himself silently, though he already knew the answer.

All eyes now turned to him. Before Tanis could speak, Raistlin, who had been listening to all that was said without comment, walked forward to stand before the Council. He stared around at them, his strange eyes glittering golden.

"You are fools," Raistlin said, his whispering voice soft with scorn, "and you are living in a fool's dream. How often must I repeat myself? How often must I remind you of the portent of the stars? What do you say to yourselves when you look into the night sky and see the gaping black holes where the two constellations are missing?"

The Council members shifted in their seats, several exchanging long-suffering glances indicative of boredom.

Raistlin noticed this and continued, his voice growing more and more contemptuous. "Yes, I have heard some of you saying that it is nothing more than a natural phenomenon—a thing that happens, perhaps, like the falling of leaves from the trees."

Several Council members muttered among themselves, nodding. Raistlin watched silently for a moment, his lip curled in derision. Then he spoke once more. "I repeat, you are fools. The constellation known as the Queen of Darkness is missing from the sky because the Queen is present here upon Krynn. The Warrior constellation, which represents the ancient God Paladine, as we are told in the Disks of Mishakal, has also returned to Krynn to fight her."

Raistlin paused. Elistan, who stood among them, was a prophet of Paladine, and many here were converts to this new religion. He could sense the growing anger at what some considered his blasphemy. The idea that gods would become personally involved in the affairs of men! Shocking! But being considered blasphemous had never bothered Raistlin.

His voice rose to a high pitch. "Mark well my words! With the Queen of Darkness have come her 'shrieking hosts,' as it says in the Canticle. And the shrieking hosts are dragons!" Raistlin drew out the last word into a hiss that, as Flint said, "shivered the skin."

"We know all this," Hederick snapped in impatience. It was past time for the Theocrat's nightly glass of mulled wine, and his thirst gave him courage to speak. He immediately regretted it, however, when Raistlin's hourglass eyes seemed to pierce the Theocrat like black arrows. "W-what are you driving at?"

"That peace no longer exists anywhere on Krynn," the mage whispered. He waved a frail hand. "Find ships, travel where you will. Wherever you go, whenever you look up into the night sky, you will see those gaping black holes. Wherever you go, there will be dragons!" Raistlin began to cough. His body twisted with the spasms, and he seemed likely to fall, but his twin brother, Caramon, ran forward and caught him in his strong arms.

After Caramon led the mage out of the Council meeting, it seemed as if a dark cloud had been lifted. The Council members shook themselves and laughed—if somewhat shakily—and talked of children's tales. To think that war had spread to all of Krynn was comic. Why, the war was near an end here in Ansalon already. The Dragon Highlord, Verminaard, had been defeated, his draconian armies driven back.

The Council members stood and stretched and left the chamber to head for the alehouse or their homes.

They forgot they had never asked Tanis if he would lead the group to Tarsis. They simply assumed he would.

Tanis, exchanging grim glances with Sturm, left the cavern. It was his night to stand watch. Even though the dwarves might consider themselves safe in their mountain fortress, Tanis and Sturm insisted that a watch be kept upon the walls leading into Southgate. They had come to respect the Dragon Highlords too much to sleep in peace without it—even underground.

Tanis leaned against the outer wall of Southgate, his face thoughtful and serious. Before him spread a meadow covered by smooth, powdery snow. The night was calm and still. Behind him was the great mass of the Kharolis Mountains. The gate of Southgate was, in fact, a gigantic plug in the side of the mountains. It was part of the dwarven defenses that had kept the world out for three hundred years following the Cataclysm and the destructive Dwarven Wars.

Sixty feet wide at the base and almost half again as high, the gate was operated by a huge mechanism that forced it in and out of the mountain. At least forty feet thick in its center, the gate was as indestructible as any known on Krynn, except for the one matching it in the north. Once shut, they could not be distinguished from the faces of the mountain, such was the craftsmanship of the ancient dwarven masons.

Yet, since the arrival of the humans at Southgate, torches had been set about the opening, allowing the men, women, and children access to the outside air—a human need that seemed an unaccountable weakness to the subterranean dwarves.

As Tanis stood there, staring into the woods beyond the meadow and finding no peace in their quiet beauty, Sturm, Elistan, and Laurana joined him. The three had been talking—obviously of him—and fell into an uncomfortable silence.

"How solemn you are," Laurana said to Tanis softly, coming near and putting her hand on his arm. "You believe Raistlin is right, don't you, Tanthal—Tanis?" Laurana blushed. His human name still came clumsily to her lips, yet she knew him well enough now to understand that his elven name only brought him pain.

Tanis looked down at the small, slender hand on his arm and gently put his own over it. Only a few months earlier the touch of that hand would have irritated him, causing confusion and guilt as he wrestled with love for a human woman against what he told himself was a childhood infatuation with this elfmaiden. But now the touch of Laurana's hand filled him with warmth and peace, even as it stirred his blood. He pondered these new, disturbing feelings as he responded to her question.

"I have long found Raistlin's advice sound," he said, knowing how this would upset them. Sure enough, Sturm's face darkened. Elistan frowned. "And I think he is right this time. We have won a battle, but we are a long way from winning the war. We know it is being fought far north, in Solamnia. I think we may safely assume that it is not for the conquest of Abanasinia alone that the forces of darkness are fighting."

"But you are only speculating!" Elistan argued. "Do not let the darkness that hangs around the young mage cloud your thinking. He may be right, but that is no reason to give up hope, to give up trying! Tarsis is a large seaport city—at least according to all we know of it. There we'll find those who can tell us if the war encompasses the world. If so, then surely there still must be havens where we can find peace."

"Listen to Elistan, Tanis," Laurana said gently. "He is wise. When our people left Qualinesti, they did not flee blindly. They traveled to a peaceful haven. My father had a plan, though he dared not reveal it—"

Laurana broke off, startled to see the effect of her speech. Abruptly Tanis snatched his arm from her touch and turned his gaze on Elistan, his eyes filled with anger.

"Raistlin says hope is the denial of reality," Tanis stated coldly. Then, seeing Elistan's care-worn face regard him with sorrow, the half-elf smiled wearily. "I apologize, Elistan. I am tired, that's all. Forgive me. Your suggestion is good. We'll travel to Tarsis with hope, if nothing else."

Elistan nodded and turned to leave. "Are you coming, Laurana? I know you are tired, my dear, but we have a great deal to do before I can turn the leadership over to the Council in my absence."

"I'll be with you presently, Elistan," Laurana said, flushing. "I—I want to speak a moment with Tanis."

Elistan gave them both an appraising, understanding look, then walked through the darkened gateway with Sturm. Tanis began dousing the torches, preparatory to the closing of the gate. Laurana stood near the entrance, her expression growing cold as it became obvious Tanis was ignoring her.

"What is the matter with you?" she said finally. "It almost sounds as if you are taking that dark-souled mage's part against Elistan, one of the best and wisest humans I have ever met!"

"Don't judge Raistlin, Laurana," Tanis said harshly, thrusting a torch into a bucket of water. The light vanished with a hiss. "Things aren't always black and white, as you elves are inclined to believe. The mage has saved our lives more than once. I have come to rely upon his thinking—which, I admit, I find easier to rely on than blind faith!"

"*You* elves!" Laurana cried. "How typically human that sounds! There is more elven in you than you care to admit, Tanthalas! You used to say you didn't wear the beard to hide your heritage, and I believed you. But now I'm not so certain. I've lived around humans long enough to know how they feel about elves! But I'm proud of my heritage. You're not! You're ashamed of it. Why? Because of that human woman you're in love with! What's her name, Kitiara?"

"Stop it, Laurana!" Tanis shouted. Hurling down a torch to the ground, he strode to the elven maiden standing in the doorway. "If you want to discuss relationships, what about you and Elistan? He may be a cleric of Paladine, but he's a man, a fact to which you can, no doubt, testify! All I hear from you," he mimicked her voice," is 'Elistan is so wise,' 'Ask Elistan, he'll know what to do,' 'Listen to Elistan, Tanis—' "

"How dare you accuse me of your own failings?" Laurana returned. "I love Elistan. I reverence him. He is the wisest man I have known, and the gentlest. He is self-sacrificing—his entire life is wrapped up in serving others. But there is only one man I love, only one man I have ever loved—though now I am beginning to ask myself if perhaps I haven't made a mistake! You said, in that awful place, the Sla-Mori, that I was behaving like a little girl and I had better grow up. Well, I have grown, Tanis Half-Elven. In these past few bitter months, I have seen suffering and death. I have been afraid as I never knew fear existed! I have learned to fight, and I have dealt death to my enemies. All of that hurt me inside until I'm so numb I can't feel the pain anymore. But what hurts worse is to see you with clear eyes."

"I never claimed to be perfect, Laurana," Tanis said quietly.

The silver moon and the red had risen, neither of them full yet, but shining brightly enough for Tanis to see tears in Laurana's luminous eyes. He reached out his hands to take her in his arms, but she took a step backwards.

"You may never claim it," she said scornfully, "but you certainly enjoy allowing us to think it!"

Ignoring his outstretched hands, she grabbed a torch from the wall and walked into the darkness beyond the gate of Thorbardin. Tanis watched her leave, watched the light shine on her honey-colored hair, watched her walk, as graceful as the slender aspens of their elven homeland of Qualinesti.

Tanis stood for a moment, staring after her, scratching the thick, reddish beard that no elf on Krynn could grow. Pondering Laurana's last statement, he thought, incongruously, of Kitiara. He conjured up pictures in his mind of Kit's cropped, curly black hair, her crooked smile, her fiery, impetuous temper, and her strong, sensual body—the body of a trained swordswoman, but he discovered to his amazement that now the picture dissolved, pierced by the calm, clear gaze of two slightly slanted, luminous, elven eyes.

Thunder rolled out from the mountain. The shaft that moved the huge stone gate began to turn, grinding the door shut. Tanis, watching it shut, decided he would not go in. "Sealed in a tomb." He smiled, recalling Sturm's words, but there was a shiver in his soul as well. He stood for long moments, staring at the door, feeling its weight settle between him and Laurana. The door sealed shut with a dull boom. The face of the mountain was blank, cold, forbidding.

With a sigh, Tanis pulled his cloak about him and started toward the woods. Even sleeping in the snow was better than sleeping underground. He had better get used to it anyway. The Plains of Dust they would be traveling through to reach Tarsis would probably be choked with snow, even this early in the winter.

Thinking of the journey as he walked, Tanis looked up into the night sky. It was beautiful, glittering with stars. But two gaping black holes marred the beauty. Raistlin's missing constellations.

Holes in the sky. Holes in himself.

After his fight with Laurana, Tanis was almost glad to start on the journey. All the companions had agreed to go. Tanis knew that none of them felt truly at home among the refugees.

Preparations for the journey gave him plenty to think about. He was able to tell himself he didn't care that Laurana avoided him. And, at the beginning, the journey itself was enjoyable. It seemed as if they were back in the early days of fall instead of the beginning of winter. The sun shone, warming the air. Only Raistlin wore his heaviest cloak.

Conversation as the companions walked through the northern part of the Plains was light-hearted and merry, filled with teasing and bantering and reminding each other of the fun they had shared in earlier, happier days in Solace. No one spoke of the dark and evil things they had seen in the recent past. It was as if, in the contemplation of a brighter future, they willed these things never to have existed.

At night, Elistan explained to them what he was learning of the ancient gods from the Disks of Mishakal, which he carried with him. His stories filled their souls with peace and reinforced their faith. Even Tanis—who had spent a lifetime searching for something to believe in and now that they had found it viewed it with skepticism—felt deep in his soul that he could believe in this if he believed in anything. He wanted to believe in it, but something held him back, and every time he looked at Laurana, he knew what it was. Until he could resolve his own inner turmoil, the raging division between the elven and human inside of him, he would never know peace.

Only Raistlin did not share in the conversations, the merriment, the pranks and jokes, the campfire talks. The mage spent his days studying his spellbook. If interrupted, he would answer with a snarl. After dinner, of which he ate little, he sat by himself, his eyes on the night sky, staring at the two gaping black holes that were mirrored in the mage's black hourglass-shaped pupils.

It was only after several days that spirits began to flag. The sun was obscured by clouds and the wind blew chill from the north. Snow fell so thickly that one day they could not travel at all but were forced to seek shelter in a cave until the blizzard blew itself out. They set double watch at night, though no one could say exactly why, only that they felt a grow-ing sense of threat and menace. Riverwind stared uneasily at the trail they left in the snow behind them. As Flint said, a blind gully dwarf could follow it. The sense of menace grew, the sense of eyes watching and ears listening.

Yet who could it be, out here in the Plains of Dust where nothing and no one had lived for three hundred years?

2

BETWEEN MASTER AND DRAGON.

DISMAL JOURNEY.

 he dragon sighed, flexed his huge wings, and lifted his ponderous body from the warm, soothing waters of the hot springs. Emerging from a billowing cloud of vapor, he braced himself to step into the chill air. The clear winter air stung his delicate nostrils and bit into his throat. Swallowing painfully, he firmly resisted the temptation to return to the warm pools and began to climb to the high rocky ledge above him.

The dragon stamped irritably upon rocks slick with ice from the hot springs' vapor, which cooled almost instantly in the freezing air. The stones cracked and broke beneath his clawed feet, bounding and tumbling down into the valley below.

Once he slipped, causing him momentarily to lose his balance. Spreading his great wings, he recovered easily, but the incident only served to increase his irritation further.

The morning sun lit the mountain peaks, touching the dragon, causing his blue scales to shimmer golden in the clear light but doing little to warm his blood. The dragon shivered again, stamping his feet upon the chill ground. Winter was not for the blue dragons, nor was traveling this abysmal country. With that thought in mind, as it had been in his mind all the long, bitter night, Skie looked about for his master.

He found the Dragon Highlord standing upon an outcropping of rock, an imposing figure in horned dragonhelm and blue dragon-scale armor. The Highlord, cape whipping in the chill wind, was gazing within tense interest across the great flat plain far below.

"Come, Lord, return to your tent." And let me return to the hot springs, Skie added mentally. "This chill wind cuts to the bone. Why are you out here anyway?"

Skie might have supposed the Highlord was reconnoitering, planning the disposition of troops, the attacks of the dragonflights. But that was not the case. The occupation of Tarsis had long been planned—planned, in fact, by another Dragon Highlord, for this land was under the command of the red dragons.

The blue dragons and their Dragon Highlords controlled the north, yet here I stand, in these frigid southlands, Skie thought irritably. And behind me is an entire flight of blue dragons. He turned his head slightly, looking down upon his fellows beating their wings in the early morning, grateful for the hot springs' warmth which took the chill from their tendons.

Fools, Skie thought scornfully. All they're waiting for is a signal from the Highlord to attack. To light the skies and burn the cities with their deadly bolts of lightning are all they care about. Their faith in the Dragon Highlord is implicit. As well it might be, Skie admitted, their master had led them to victory after victory in the north, and they had not lost one of their number.

They leave it to me to ask the questions—because I am the Highlord's mount, because I am closest to the Highlord. Well, so be it. We understand each other, the Highlord and I.

"We have no reason to be in Tarsis." Skie spoke his feelings plainly. He did not fear the Highlord. Unlike many of the dragons in Krynn, who served their masters with grudging reluctance, knowing themselves to be the true rulers, Skie served his master out of respect—and love. "The reds don't want us here, that's certain. And we're not needed. That soft city that beckons you so strangely will fall easily. No army. They swallowed the bait and marched off to the frontier."

"We are here because my spies tell me they are here, or will be shortly," was the Highlord's answer. The voice was low but carried even over the biting wind.

"They . . . they . . ." grumbled the dragon, shivering and moving restlessly along the ridge. "We leave the war in the north, waste valuable time, lose a fortune in steel. And for what—a handful of itinerant adventurers."

"The wealth is nothing to me, you know that. I could buy Tarsis if it pleased me." The Dragon Highlord stroked the dragon's neck with an ice-caked leather glove that creaked with the powerful movements."The war in the north is going well. Lord Ariakas did not mind my leaving. Bakaris is a skilled young commander and knows my armies nearly as well as I do.

And do not forget, Skie, these are more than vagabonds. These 'itinerant adventurers' killed Verminaard."

"Bah! The man had already dug his own grave. He was obsessed, lost sight of the true purpose." The dragon flicked a glance at his master. "The same might be said of others."

"Obsessed? Yes, Verminaard was obsessed, and there are those who should be taking that obsession more seriously. He was a cleric, he knew what damage the knowledge of the true gods, once spread among the people, can do us," answered the Highlord. "Now, according to reports, the people have a leader in this human called Elistan, who has become a cleric of Paladine. Worshipers of Mishakal bring true healing back to the land. No, Verminaard was farseeing. There is great danger here. We should recognize and move to stop it—not scoff at it."

The dragon snorted derisively. "This priest—Elistan—doesn't lead *the people*. He leads eight hundred wretched humans, former slaves of Verminaard's in Pax Tharkas. Now they're holed up in Southgate with the mountain dwarves." The dragon settled down on the rock, feeling the morning sun finally bringing a modicum of warmth to his scaled skin. "Besides, our spies report they are traveling to Tarsis even as we speak. By tonight, this Elistan will be ours and that will be that. So much for the servant of Paladine!"

"Elistan is of no use to me." The Dragon Highlord shrugged without interest. "He is not the one I seek."

"No?" Skie raised his head, startled. "Who, then?"

"There are three in whom I have particular interest. But I will provide you with descriptions of all of them"—the Dragon Highlord moved closer to Skie—"because it is to capture them that we participate in the destruction of Tarsis tomorrow. Here are those whom we seek. . . ."

Tanis strode across the frozen plains, his booted footsteps punching noisily through the crust of wind-swept snow. The sun rose at his back, bringing a great deal of light but little warmth. He clutched his cloak about him and glanced around to make certain no one was lagging behind. The companions' line stretched out single-file. They trod in each other's tracks, the heavier, stronger people in front clearing the way for the weaker ones behind them.

Tanis led them. Sturm walked beside him, steadfast and faithful as ever, though still upset over leaving behind the Hammer of Kharas, which had taken on an almost mystical quality for the knight. He appeared more careworn and tired than usual, but he never failed to keep step with Tanis. This was not an easy feat, since the knight insisted on traveling in his full, antique battle armor, the weight of which forced Sturm's feet deep into the crusted snow.

Behind Sturm and Tanis came Caramon, trudging through the snow like a great bear, his arsenal of weapons clanking around him, carrying his armor and his share of supplies, as well as those of his twin brother, Raistlin, on his back. Just watching Caramon made Tanis weary, for the big warrior was not only walking through the deep snow with ease but was also managing to widen the trail for the others behind him.

Of all of the companions the one Tanis might have felt closest to, since they had been raised together as brothers, was the next, Gilthanas. But Gilthanas was an elflord, younger son of the Speaker of the Suns, ruler of the Qualinesti elves, while Tanis was a bastard and only half elven, product of a brutal rape by a human warrior. Worse, Tanis had dared to find himself attracted—even if in a childish, immature fashion—to Gilthanas's sister, Laurana. And so, far from being friends, Tanis always had the uneasy impression that Gilthanas might well be pleased to see him dead.

Riverwind and Goldmoon walked together behind the elflord. Cloaked in their furskin capes, the cold was little to the Plainsmen. Certainly the cold was nothing compared to the flame in their hearts.They had been married only a little over a month, and the deep love and compassion each felt for the other, a self-sacrificing love that had led the world to the discovery of the ancient gods, now achieved greater depths as they discovered new ways to express it.

Then came Elistan and Laurana. Elistan and Laurana. Tanis found it odd that, thinking enviously of the happiness of Riverwind and Goldmoon, his eyes should encounter these two. Elistan and Laurana. Always together. Always deeply involved in serious conversation. Elistan, cleric of Paladine, resplendent in white robes that gleamed even against the snow. White-bearded, his hair thinning, he was still an imposing figure. The kind of man who might well attract a young girl. Few men or women could look into Elistan's ice-blue eyes and not feel stirred, awed in the presence of one who had walked the realms of death and found a new and stronger faith.

With him walked his faithful 'assistant,' Laurana. The young elfmaid had run away from her home in Qualinesti to follow Tanis in childish infatuation. She had been forced to grow up rapidly, her eyes opened to the pain and suffering in the world. Knowing that many of the party—Tanis among them—considered her a nuisance, Laurana struggled to prove her worth. With Elistan she found her chance. Daughter to the Speaker of the Suns of the Qualinesti, she had been born and bred to politics. When Elistan was foundering among the rocks of trying to feed and clothe and control eight hundred men, women, and children, it was Laurana who stepped in and eased his burden. She had become indispensable to him, a fact Tanis found difficult to deal with. The half-elf gritted his teeth, letting his glance flick over Laurana to fall on Tika.

The barmaid turned adventuress walked through the snow with Raistlin, having been asked by his brother to stay near the frail mage, since Caramon was needed up front. Neither Tika nor Raistlin seemed happy with this arrangement. The red-robed mage walked along sullenly, his head bowed against the wind. He was often forced to stop, coughing until he nearly fell. At these times, Tika would start to put her arm around him hesitantly, her eyes seeing Caramon's worry. But Raistlin always pulled away from her with a snarl.

The ancient dwarf came next, bowling along through the snow; the tip of his helm and the tassel "from the mane of a griffon" were all that were visible above the snow. Tanis had tried to tell him that griffons had no manes, that the tassel was horsehair. But Flint, stoutly maintaining that his hatred of horses stemmed from the fact that they made him sneeze violently, believed none of it. Tanis smiled, shaking his head. Flint had insisted on being at the front of the line. It was only after Caramon had pulled him out of three snow drifts that Flint agreed, grumbling, to walk "rear guard."

Skipping along beside Flint was Tasslehoff Burrfoot, his shrill, piping voice audible to Tanis in the front of the line. Tas was regaling the dwarf with a marvelous tale about the time he found a woolly mammoth—whatever that was—being held prisoner by two deranged wizards. Tanis sighed. Tas was getting on his nerves. He had already sternly reprimanded the kender for hitting Sturm in the head with a snowball. But he knew it was useless. Kender lived for adventure and new experiences. Tas was enjoying every minute of this dismal journey.

Yes, they were all there. They were all still following him.

Tanis turned around abruptly, facing south. Why follow me? He asked resentfully. I hardly know where my life is going, yet I'm expected to lead others. I don't have Sturm's driving quest to rid the land of dragons, as did his hero Huma. I don't have Elistan's holy quest to bring knowledge of the true gods to the people. I don't even have Raistlin's burning quest for power.

Sturm nudged him and pointed ahead. A line of small hills stood on the horizon. If the kender's map was correct, the city of Tarsis lay just beyond them. Tarsis, and white-winged ships, and spires of glittering white.

3

Tarsis the Beautiful.

anis spread out the kender's map. They had arrived at the foot of the range of barren and treeless hills which, according to the map, must overlook the city of Tarsis.

"We don't dare climb those in daylight," Sturm said, drawing his scarf down from his mouth. "We'd be visible to everything within a hundred miles."

"No," Tanis agreed. "We'll make camp here at the base. I'll climb, though, to get a look at the city."

"I don't like this, not one bit!" Sturm muttered gloomily. "Something's wrong. Do you want me to go with you?"

Tanis, seeing the weariness in the knight's face, shook his head. "You get the others organized." Dressed in a winter traveling cloak of white, he prepared to climb the snow-covered, rock-strewn hills. Ready to start, he felt a cold hand on his arm. He turned and looked into the eyes of the mage.

"I will come with you," Raistlin whispered.

Tanis stared at him in astonishment, then glanced up at the hills. The climb would not be an easy one, and he knew the mage's dislike of extreme physical exertion. Raistlin saw his glance and understood.

"My brother will help me," he said, beckoning to Caramon, who appeared startled but stood up immediately and came over to stand beside his brother. "I would look upon the city of Tarsis the Beautiful."

Tanis regarded him uneasily, but Raistlin's face was as impassive and cold as the metal it resembled.

"Very well," the half-elf said, studying Raistlin. "But you'll show up on the face of that mountain like a blood stain. Cover yourself with a white robe." The half-elf's sardonic smile was an almost perfect imitation of Raistlin's own. "Borrow one from Elistan."

Tanis, standing on the top of the hill overlooking the legendary seaport city of Tarsis the Beautiful, began to swear softly. Wispy clouds of steam floated from his lips with the hot words. Drawing the hood of his heavy cloak over his head, he stared down into the city in bitter disappointment.

Caramon nudged his twin. "Raist," he said. "What's the matter? I don't understand."

Raistlin coughed. "Your brains are in your sword-arm, my brother," the mage whispered caustically. "Look upon Tarsis, legendary seaport city. What do you see?"

"Well . . ." Caramon squinted. "It's one of the biggest cities I've seen. And there are ships—just like we heard—"

"'The white-winged ships of Tarsis the Beautiful,'" Raistlin quoted bitterly. "You look upon the ships, my brother. Do you notice anything peculiar about them?"

"They're not in very good shape. The sails are ragged and—" Caramon blinked. Then he gasped. "There's no water!"

"Most observant."

"But the kender's map—"

"Dated before the Cataclysm," Tanis interrupted. "Damn it, I should have known! I should have considered this possibility! Tarsis the Beautiful—legendary seaport, now landlocked!"

"And has been for three hundred years, undoubtedly," Raistlin whispered.

"When the fiery mountain fell from the sky, it created seas—as we saw in Xak Tsaroth—but it also destroyed them. What do we do with the refugees now, Half-Elf?"

"I don't know," Tanis snapped irritably. He stared down at the city, then turned away. "It's no good standing around here. The sea isn't going to come back just for our benefit." He turned away and walked slowly down the cliff.

"What *will* we do?" Caramon asked his brother. "We can't go back to Southgate. I know something or someone was dogging our footsteps." He glanced around worriedly. "I feel eyes watching—even now."

Raistlin put his hand through his brother's arm. For a rare instant, the two looked remarkably alike. Light and darkness were not more different than the twins.

"You are wise to trust your feelings, my brother," Raistlin said softly."Great danger and great evil surround us. I have felt it growing on me since the people arrived in Southgate. I tried to warn them—" He broke off in a fit of coughing.

"How do you know?" Caramon asked.

Raistlin shook his head, unable to answer for long moments. Then, when the spasm had passed, he drew a shuddering breath and glanced at his brother irritably. "Haven't you learned yet?" he said bitterly. "I *know!* Put it at that. I paid for my knowledge in the Towers of High Sorcery. I paid for it with my body and very nearly my reason. I paid for it with—" Raistlin stopped, looking at his twin.

Caramon was pale and silent as always whenever the Testing was mentioned. He started to say something, choked, then cleared his throat. "It's just that I don't understand—"

Raistlin sighed and shook his head, withdrawing his arm from his brother's. Then, leaning on his staff, he began to walk down the hill. "Nor will you," he murmured. "Ever."

Three hundred years ago, Tarsis the Beautiful was Lordcity of the lands of Abanasinia. From here set sail the white-winged ships for all the known lands of Krynn. Here they returned, bearing all manner of objects, precious and curious, hideous and delicate. The Tarsian marketplace was a thing of wonder. Sailors swaggered the streets, their golden earrings flashing as brightly as their knives. The ships brought exotic peoples from distant lands to sell their wares. Some dressed in gaily colored, flowing silks, bedizened with jewels. They sold spices and teas, oranges and pearls, and bright-colored birds in cages. Others, dressed in crude skins, sold luxuriant furs from strange animals as grotesque as those who hunted them.

Of course, there were buyers at the Tarsian market as well; almost as strange and exotic and dangerous as the sellers. Wizards dressed in robes of white, red, or black strode the bazaars, searching for rare spell components to make their magic. Distrusted even then, they walked through the crowds, isolated and alone. Few spoke even to those wearing the white robes, and no one ever cheated them.

Clerics, too, sought ingredients for their healing potions. For there were clerics in Krynn before the Cataclysm. Some worshiped the gods of good, some the gods of neutrality, some the gods of evil. All had great power. Their prayers, for good or for evil, were answered.

And always, walking among all the strange and exotic peoples gathered in the bazaar of Tarsis the Beautiful, were the Knights of Solamnia: keeping order, guarding the land, living their disciplined lives in strict observance of the Code and the Measure. The Knights were followers of Paladine, and were noted for their pious obedience to the gods.

The walled city of Tarsis had its own army and—so it was said—had never fallen to an invading force. The city was ruled, under the watchful eyes of the Knights—by a Lordfamily and had the good fortune to fall to the care of a family possessing sense, sensitivity, and justice. Tarsis became a center of learning; sages from lands all around came here to share their wisdom. Schools and a great library were established, temples were built to the gods. Young men and women eager for knowledge came to Tarsis to study.

The early dragon wars had not affected Tarsis. The huge walled city, its formidable army, its fleets of white-winged ships, and its vigilant Knights of Solamnia daunted even the Queen of Darkness. Before she could consolidate her power and strike the Lordcity, Huma drove her dragons from the skies. Thus Tarsis prospered and became, during the Age of Might, one of the wealthiest and proudest cities of Krynn.

And, as with so many other cities in Krynn, with its pride grew its conceit. Tarsis began seeking more and more from the gods: wealth, power, glory. The people worshiped the Kingpriest of Istar who, seeing suffering in the land, demanded of the gods in his arrogance what they had granted Huma in humility. Even the Knights of Solamnia—bound by the strict laws of the Measure, encased in a religion that had become all ritual with little depth—fell under the sway of the mighty Kingpriest.

Then came the Cataclysm—a night of terror, when it rained fire. The ground heaved and cracked as the gods in their righteous anger hurled a mountain of rock down upon Krynn, punishing the Kingpriest of Istar and the people for their pride.

The people turned to the Knights of Solamnia. "You who are righteous, help us!" they cried. "Placate the gods!"

But the Knights could do nothing. The fire fell from the heavens, the land split asunder. The seawaters fled, the ships foundered and toppled, the wall of the city crumbled.

When the night of horror ended, Tarsis was landlocked. The white-winged ships lay upon the sand like wounded birds. Dazed and bleeding, the survivors tried to rebuild their city, expecting any moment to see the Knights of Solamnia come marching from their great fortresses in the north, marching from Palanthas, Solanthus, Vingaard Keep, Thelgaard, marching south to Tarsis to help them and protect them once more.

But the Knights did not come. They had their own troubles and could not leave Solamnia. Even if they had been able to march, a new sea split the lands of Abanasinia. The dwarves in their mountain kingdom of Thorbardin shut their gates, refusing admittance to anyone, and so the mountain passes were blocked. The elves withdrew into Qualinesti, nursing their wounds, blaming humans for the catastrophe. Soon, Tarsis lost all contact with the world to the north.

And so, following the Cataclysm, when it became apparent that the city had been abandoned by the Knights, came the Day of Banishment. The lord of the city was placed in an awkward position. He did not truly believe in the corruption of the Knights, but he knew the people needed something or someone to blame. If he sided with the Knights, he would lose control of the city, and so he was forced to close his eyes to angry mobs that attacked the few Knights remaining in Tarsis. They were driven from the city—or murdered.

After a time, order was restored in Tarsis. The lord and his family established a new army. But much was changed. The people believed the ancient gods they had worshiped for so long had turned away from them. They found new gods to worship, even though these new gods rarely answered prayers. All clerical powers that had been present in the land before the Cataclysm were lost. Clerics with false promises and false hopes proliferated. Charlatan healers walked the land, selling their phony cure-alls.

After a time, many of the people drifted away from Tarsis. No longer did sailors walk the marketplace; elves, dwarves, and other races came no more. The people remaining in Tarsis liked it this way. They began to fear and mistrust the outside world. Strangers were not encouraged.

But Tarsis had been a trade center for so long that those people in the outlying countryside who could still reach Tarsis continued to do so. The outer hub of the city was rebuilt. The inner part—the temples, the schools, the great library—was left in ruins. The bazaar was reopened, only now it was a market for farmers and a forum for false clerics preaching new religions. Peace settled over the town like a blanket. Former days of glory were as a dream and might not have even been believed, but for the evidence in the center of town.

Now, of course, Tarsis heard rumors of war, but these were generally discounted, although the lord did send his army out to guard the plains to the south. If anyone asked why, he said it was a field exercise, nothing more. These rumors, after all, had come out of the north, and all knew the Knights of Solamnia were trying desperately to reestablish their power. It was amazing what lengths the traitorous Knights would go to—even spreading stories of the return of dragons!

This was Tarsis the Beautiful, the city the companions entered that morning, just a short time after sunrise.

4

Arrested!

The heroes are separated.
An ominous farewell.

he few sleepy guards upon the city walls that morning woke up at the sight of the sword-bearing, travel-worn group seeking entry. They did not deny them. They did not even question them—much. A red-bearded, soft-spoken half-elf, the like of which had not been seen in Tarsis in decades, said they had traveled far and sought shelter. His companions stood quietly behind him, making no threatening gestures. Yawning, the guards directed them to the Red Dragon Inn.

This might have ended the matter. Tarsis, after all, was beginning to see more and more strange characters as rumors of war spread. But the cloak of one of the humans blew aside as he stepped through the gate, and a guard caught a flash of bright armor in the morning sun. The guard saw the hated and reviled symbol of the Knights of Solamnia on the antique breastplate. Scowling, the guard melted into the shadows, slinking after the group as it walked through the streets of the waking town.

The guard watched them enter the Red Dragon. He waited outside in the cold until he was sure they must be in their rooms. Then, slipping inside, he spoke a few words to the innkeeper. The guard peeped inside the common room and, seeing the group seated and apparently settled for some time, ran off to make his report.

"This is what comes of trusting a kender's map!" said the dwarf irritably, shoving away his empty plate and wiping his hand across his mouth. "Takes us to a seaport city with no sea!"

"It's not my fault," Tas protested. "I told Tanis when I gave him the map that it dated before the Cataclysm. 'Tas,' Tanis said before we left, 'do you have a map that shows us how to get to Tarsis?' I said I did and I gave him this one. It shows Thorbardin, the dwarven Kingdom under the Mountain, and Southgate, and here it shows Tarsis, and everything else was right where the map said it was supposed to be. I can't help it if something happened to the ocean! I—"

"That's enough, Tas." Tanis sighed. "Nobody's blaming you. It isn't anybody's fault. We just let our hopes get too high."

The kender, his feelings mollified, retrieved his map, rolled it up, and slid it into his mapcase with all his other precious maps of Krynn. Then he put his small chin in his hands and sat staring around the table at his gloomy companions. They began to discuss what to do next, talking half-heartedly.

Tas grew bored. He wanted to explore this city. There were all kinds of unusual sights and sounds—Flint had been forced to practically drag him along as they entered Tarsis. There was a fabulous marketplace with wonderful things just lying around, waiting to be admired. He had even spotted some other kenders, too, and he wanted to talk to them. He was worried about his homeland. Flint kicked him under the table. Sighing, Tas turned his attention back to Tanis.

"We'll spend the night here, rest, and learn what we can, then send word back to Southgate," Tanis was saying. "Perhaps there is another port city farther south. Some of us might go on and investigate. What do you think, Elistan?"

The cleric pushed away a plate of uneaten food. "I suppose it is our only choice," he said sadly. "But I will return to Southgate. I cannot be away from the people long. You should come with me, too, my dear." He laid his hand over Laurana's. "I cannot dispense with your help."

Laurana smiled at Elistan. Then, her gaze moving to Tanis, the smile vanished as she saw the half-elf scowl.

"Riverwind and I have discussed this already. We will return with Elistan," Goldmoon said. Her silver-gold hair gleamed in the sunlight streaming through the window. "The people need my healing skills."

"Besides which, the bridal couple misses the privacy of their tent," Caramon said in an audible undertone. Goldmoon flushed a dusky rose color as her husband smiled.

Sturm glanced at Caramon in disgust and turned to Tanis. "I will go with you, my friend," he offered.

"Us, too, of course," said Caramon promptly.

Sturm frowned, looking at Raistlin, who sat huddled in his red robes near the fire, drinking the strange herbal concoction that eased his cough.

"I do not think your brother is fit to travel, Caramon—" Sturm began.

"You are suddenly very solicitous of my health, knight," Raistlin whispered sarcastically. "But then, it is not my health that concerns you, is it, Sturm Brightblade? It is my growing power. You fear me—"

"That's enough!" said Tanis as Sturm's face darkened.

"The mage goes back, or I do," Sturm said coldly.

"Sturm—" Tanis began.

Tasslehoff took this opportunity to leave the table very quietly. Everyone was focused on the argument between the knight, the half-elf, and the magic-user. Tasslehoff skipped out the front door of the Red Dragon, a name he thought particularly funny. But Tanis had not laughed.

Tas thought about that as he walked along, looking at the new sights in delight. Tanis didn't laugh at anything anymore. The half-elf was certainly carrying the weight of the world on his shoulders, it seemed. Tasslehoff suspected he knew what was wrong with Tanis. The kender took a ring out of one of his pouches and studied it. The ring was golden, of elven make, carved in the form of clinging ivy leaves. He had picked it up in Qualinesti. This time, the ring was not something the kender had "acquired." It had been thrown at his feet by a heart-broken Laurana after Tanis had returned it to her.

The kender considered all this and decided that splitting up and going off after new adventure was just what everyone needed. He, of course, would go with Tanis and Flint—the kender firmly believed neither could get along without him. But first, he'd get a glimpse of this interesting city.

Tasslehoff reached the end of the street. Glancing back, he could see the Red Dragon Inn. Good. No one was out looking for him yet. He was just about to ask a passing street peddler how to get to the marketplace when he saw something that promised to make this interesting city a whole lot more interesting. . . .

Tanis settled the argument between Sturm and Raistlin, for the time being at least. The mage decided to stay in Tarsis to hunt for the remains of the old library. Caramon and Tika offered to stay with him, while Tanis, Sturm, and Flint (and Tas) would push southward, picking up the brothers on their way back. The rest of the group would take the disappointing news back to Southgate.

That being settled, Tanis went to the innkeeper to pay for their night's lodging. He was counting out silver coins when he felt a hand touch his arm.

"I want you to ask to have my room changed to one near Elistan's," Laurana said. Tanis glanced at her sharply.

"Why is that?" he asked, trying to keep the harshness out of his voice.

Laurana sighed. "We're not going to go through this again, are we?"

"I have no idea what you mean," Tanis said coldly, turning away from the grinning innkeeper.

"For the first time in my life, I'm doing something meaningful and useful," Laurana said, catching hold of his arm. "And you want me to quit because of some jealous notion you have about me and Elistan—"

"I am not jealous," Tanis retorted, flushing. "I told you in Qualinesti that what was between us when we were younger is over now. I—" He paused, wondering if that were true. Even as he spoke, his soul trembled at her beauty. Yes, that youthful infatuation was gone, but was it being replaced by something else, something stronger and more enduring? And was he losing it? Had he already lost it, through his own indecisiveness and stubbornness? He was acting typically human, the half-elf thought. Refusing that which was in easy reach, only to cry for it when it was gone. He shook his head in confusion.

"If you're not jealous, then why don't you leave me alone and let me continue my work for Elistan in peace?" Laurana asked coldly "You—"

"Hush!" Tanis held up his hand. Laurana, annoyed, started to talk, but Tanis glared at her so fiercely, she fell silent.

Tanis listened. Yes, he'd been right. He could hear clearly now the shrill, high-pitched, screaming whine of the leather sling on the end of Tas's hoopak staff. It was a peculiar sound, produced by the kender swinging the sling in a circle over his head, and it raised the hair on the back of the neck. It was also a kender signal for danger.

"Trouble," Tanis said softly. "Get the others." Taking one look at his grim face, Laurana obeyed without question. Tanis turned abruptly to face the innkeeper, who was sidling around the desk. "Where are you going?" he asked sharply.

"Just leaving to check your rooms, sir," the innkeeper said smoothly, and he vanished precipitously into the kitchen. Just then, Tasslehoff burst through the door of the inn.

"Guards, Tanis! Guards! Coming this way!"

"Surely they can't be here because of us," Tanis said. He stopped, eyeing the light-fingered kender, struck by a sudden thought. "Tas—"

"It wasn't me, honest!" Tas protested. "I never even reached the market-place! I just got to the bottom of the street when I saw a whole troop of guards coming this direction."

"What's this about guards?" Sturm asked as he entered from the common room. "Is this one of the kender's stories?"

"No. Listen," Tanis said. Everyone hushed. They could hear the tramp of booted feet coming their direction and glanced at each other in apprehension and concern. "The innkeeper's disappeared. I thought we got into the city a bit too easily. I should have expected trouble." Tanis scratched his beard, well aware that everyone was looking to him for orders.

"Laurana, you and Elistan go upstairs. Sturm, you and Gilthanas remain with me. The rest of you go to your rooms. Riverwind, you're in command. You, Caramon, and Raistlin protect them. Use your magic, Raistlin, if necessary. Flint—"

"I'm staying with you," the dwarf stated firmly.

Tanis smiled and put his hand on Flint's shoulder. "Of course, old friend. I didn't even think you needed telling."

Grinning, Flint pulled his battle-axe out of its holder on his back. "Take this," he said to Caramon. "Better you have it than any scurvy, lice-ridden city guards."

"That's a good idea," Tanis said. Unbuckling his swordbelt, he handed Caramon Wyrmslayer the magical sword given to him by the skeleton of Kith-Kanan, the Elven King.

Gilthanas silently handed over his sword and his elven bow.

"Yours, too, knight," Caramon said, holding out his hand.

Sturm frowned. His antique, two-handed sword and its scabbard were the only legacy he had left of his father, a great Knight of Solamnia, who had vanished after sending his wife and young son into exile. Slowly Sturm unbuckled his swordbelt and handed it to Caramon.

The jovial warrior, seeing the knight's obvious concern, grew serious. "I'll guard it carefully, you know that, Sturm."

"I know," Sturm said, smiling sadly. He glanced up at Raistlin, who was standing on the stairs. "Besides, there is always the great worm, Catyrpelius, to protect it, isn't there, mage?"

Raistlin started at this unexpected reminder of a time in the burned-out city of Solace when he had tricked some hobgoblins into believing Sturm's sword was cursed. It was the closest to an expression of gratitude that the knight had ever made to the mage. Raistlin smiled briefly.

"Yes," he whispered. "There is always the Worm. Do not fear, knight. Your weapon is safe, as are the lives of those you leave in our care . . . if any are safe. . . . Farewell, my friends," he hissed, his strange, hourglass eyes gleaming. "And a long farewell it will be. Some of us are not destined to meet again in this world!" With that, he bowed and, gathering his red robes around him, began to climb the stairs.

Trust Raistlin to exit with a flourish, Tanis thought irritably, hearing booted feet near the door. "Go on!" he ordered. "If he's right, there's nothing we can do about it now."

After a hesitant look at Tanis, the others did as he ordered, climbing the stairs quickly. Only Laurana cast a fearful glance back at Tanis as Elistan took her arm. Caramon, sword drawn, waited behind until the last was past.

"Don't worry," the big warrior said uneasily. "We'll be all right. If you're not back by night-fall—"

"Don't come looking for us!" Tanis said, guessing Caramon's intention. The half-elf was more disturbed than he cared to admit by Raistlin's ominous statement. He had known the mage many years and had seen his power grow, even as the shadows seemed to gather more thickly around him. "If we're not back, get Elistan, Goldmoon, and the others back to Southgate."

Caramon nodded reluctantly, then he walked ponderously up the stairs, his weapons clanking around him.

"It's probably just a routine check," Sturm said hurriedly in a low voice as the guards could be seen through the window now. "They'll ask us a few questions, then release us. But they've undoubtedly got a description of *all* of us!"

"I have a feeling it isn't routine. Not the way everyone's vanished. And they're going to have to settle for some of us," Tanis said softly as the guards entered the door, led by the constable and accompanied by he guard from the wall.

"That's them!" the guard cried, pointing. "There's the knight, like I told you. And the bearded elf, the dwarf, and the kender, and an elflord."

"Right," the constable said briskly. "Now, where are the others?" At his gesture, his guards leveled their hauberks, pointing them at the companions.

"I don't understand what all this is about," Tanis said mildly. "We are strangers in Tarsis, simply passing through on our way south. Is this how you welcome strangers to your city?"

"We don't welcome strangers to our city," the constable replied. His gaze shifted to Sturm and he sneered. "Especially a Knight of Solamnia. If you're innocent as you say you are, you won't mind answering some questions from the Lord and his council. Where's the rest of your party?"

"My friends are tired and have gone to their rooms to rest. Our journey has been long and tiring. But we do not want to cause trouble. The four of us will come with you and answer your questions. ('Five,' said Tasslehoff indignantly, but everyone ignored him.) There is no need to disturb our companions."

"Go get the others," the constable ordered his men.

Two guards headed for the stairs, which suddenly burst into flame! Smoke billowed into the room, driving the guards back. Everyone ran for the door. Tanis grabbed Tasslehoff, who was staring with wide-eyed interest, and dragged him outside.

The constable was frantically blowing on his whistle, while several of his men prepared to dash off through the streets, raising the alarm. But the flames died as quickly as they had been born.

"Eeep—" The constable choked off his whistle. His face pale, he stepped warily back inside the inn. Tanis, peering over his shoulder, shook his head in awe. There was not a whisper of smoke, not a bit of varnish had so much as peeled. From the top of the stairs, he could hear faintly the sound of Raistlin's voice. As the constable glanced apprehensively up the stairs, the chanting stopped. Tanis swallowed, then drew a deep breath.

He knew he must be as pale as the constable, and he glanced at Sturm and Flint. Raistlin's power was growing. . . .

"The magician must be up there," the constable muttered.

"Very good, Birdwhistle, and how long'd it take you to figure that one out—" Tas began in a tone of voice Tanis knew meant trouble. He trod upon the kender's foot, and Tas subsided into silence with a reproachful glance.

Fortunately, the constable didn't appear to have heard. He glared at Sturm. "You'll come with us peacefully?"

"Yes," answered Sturm. "You have my word of honor," the knight added, "and no matter what you may think of the Knights, you know that my honor is my life."

The constable's eyes went to the dark stairway. "Very well," he said finally. "Two of you guards stay here at the stair. The rest cover the other exits. Check anyone coming in and out. You all have the descriptions of the strangers?" The guards nodded, exchanging uneasy glances. The two slated for guard duty inside the inn gave the staircase a frightened look and stood as far from it as possible. Tanis smiled grimly to himself.

The five companions, the kender grinning with excitement, followed the constable out of the building. As they walked into the street, Tanis caught sight of movement at an upstairs window. Looking up, he saw Laurana watching, her face drawn with fear. She raised her hand, he saw her lips form the words, "I'm sorry," in elven. Raistlin's words came to his mind and he felt chilled. His heart ached. The thought that he might never see her again made the world seem suddenly bleak and empty and desolate. He realized what Laurana had come to mean to him in these last few dark months when even hope had died as he saw the evil armies of the Dragon Highlords overrun the land. Her steadfast faith, her courage, her unfailing, undying hope! How different from Kitiara!

The guard poked Tanis in the back. "Face forward! Quit signaling to those friends of yourn!" he snarled. The half-elf's thoughts returned to Kitiara. No, the warrior woman could never have acted so selflessly. She never could have helped the people as Laurana had helped them. Kit would have grown impatient and angry and left them to live or die as they chose. She detested and despised those weaker than herself.

Tanis thought of Kitiara and he thought of Laurana, but he was interested to note that the old painful thrill didn't knot his soul anymore when he said Kitiara's name to himself. No, now it was Laurana—the silly little girl who had been no more than a spoiled and irritating child only months before—who made his blood burn and his hands search for excuses to touch her. And now, perhaps, it was too late.

When he reached the end of the street, he glanced back again, hoping to give her some sort of sign. Let her know he understood. Let her know he'd been a fool. Let her know he—

But the curtain was drawn.

5

The Riot. Tas disappears.

Alhana Starbreeze.

Foul knight . . ."

A rock struck Sturm on the shoulder. The knight flinched, though the stone could have caused him little pain through his armor. Tanis, looking at his pale face and quivering moustache, knew the pain was deeper than a weapon could inflict.

The crowds grew as the companions were marched through the street and word of their coming spread. Sturm walked with dignity, his head held proudly, ignoring the taunts and jeers. Although their guards shoved the crowd back time and again, they did it half-heartedly and the crowd knew it. More rocks were thrown, as were other objects even less pleasant. Soon all of the companions were cut and bleeding and covered with garbage and filth.

Tanis knew Sturm would never stoop to retaliation, not on this rabble, but the half-elf had to keep a firm grip on Flint. Even then, he was in constant fear the angry dwarf would charge past the guards and start breaking heads. But in watching Flint, Tanis had forgotten Tasslehoff.

Besides being quite casual in respect to other people's property, kenders have another unendearing characteristic known as the "taunt." All kenders possess this talent to a greater or lesser degree. It is how their diminutive race has managed to thrive and survive in a world of knights and warriors, trolls and hobgoblins. The taunt is the ability to insult an enemy and work him into such a fever pitch of rage that he loses his head and begins fighting wildly and erratically. Tas was a master at the taunt, though he rarely found a need to use it when traveling with his warrior friends. But Tas decided to take full advantage of this opportunity.

He began to shout insults back.

Too late Tanis realized what was happening. In vain he tried to shut him up. Tas was at the front of the line, the half-elf at the back, and there was no way to gag the kender.

Such insults as "foul knight" and "elven scum" lacked imagination, Tas felt. He decided to show these people exactly how much range and scope for variety were available in the Common language. Tasslehoff's insults were masterpieces of creativity and ingenuity. Unfortunately, they also tended to be extremely personal and occasionally rather crude, delivered with an air of charming innocence.

"Is that your nose or a disease? Can those fleas crawling on your body do tricks? Was your mother a gully dwarf?" were only the beginning. Matters went rapidly down hill from there.

The guards began eyeing the angry crowd in alarm, while the constable gave the order to hurry the prisoners' march. What he had seen as a victory procession exhibiting trophies of conquest appeared to be disintegrating into a full-scale riot.

"Shut that kender up!" he yelled furiously.

Tanis tried desperately to reach Tasslehoff, but the struggling guards and the surging crowd made it impossible. Gilthanas was knocked off his feet. Sturm bent over the elf, trying to protect him. Flint was kicking and flailing about in a rage. Tanis had just neared Tasslehoff when he was hit in the face with a tomato and momentarily blinded.

"Hey, constable, you know what you could do with that whistle?You could—"

Tasslehoff never got a chance to tell the constable what he might do with the whistle, because at that instant a large hand plucked him up out of the center of the melee. A hand clapped itself over Tas's mouth, while two more pairs of hands gripped the kender's wildly kicking feet. A sack was popped over his head, and all Tas saw or smelled from that point on was burlap as he felt himself being carried away.

Tanis, wiping tomato from his stinging eyes, heard the sound of booted feet and more shouts and yells. The crowd hooted and jeered, then broke and ran. When he could finally see again, the half-elf glanced around quickly to make certain everyone was all right. Sturm was helping Gilthanas rise, wiping blood from a cut on the elf's forehead. Flint, swearing fluently, plucked cabbage from his beard.

"Where's that blasted kender!" the dwarf roared. "I'll—" He stopped and stared, turning this way and that. "Where *is* that blasted kender? Tas? So help me—"

"Hush!" Tanis ordered, realizing Tas had managed to escape.

Flint turned purple. "Why that little bastard!" he swore. "He was the one got us into this and he left us to—"

"Shhh!" Tanis said, glaring at the dwarf. Flint choked and fell silent. The constable hustled his prisoners into the Hall of Justice. It was only when they were safely inside the ugly brick building that he realized one of them was missing.

"Shall we go after him, sir?" asked a guard. The constable thought a moment, then shook his head in anger.

"Don't waste your time," he said bitterly. "Do you know what it's like trying to find a kender who doesn't want to be found? No, let him go. We've still got the important ones. Have them wait here while I inform the Council."

The constable entered a plain wooden door, leaving the companions and their guards standing in a dark, smelly hallway. A tinker lay in a corner, snoring noisily, obviously having taken too much wine. The guards wiped pumpkin rind off their uniforms and grimly divested themselves of carrot tops and other garbage that clung to them. Gilthanas dabbed at the blood on his face. Sturm tried to clean his cloak as best he could.

The constable returned, beckoning from the doorway.

"Bring them along."

As the guards shoved their prisoners forward, Tanis managed to get near Sturm. "Who's in charge here?" he whispered.

"If we are fortunate, the Lord is still in control of the city," the knight replied softly. "The Tarsian lords always had the reputation for being noble and honorable." He shrugged. "Besides, what charges do they have against us? We've done nothing. At the worst, an armed escort will make us leave the city."

Tanis shook his head dubiously as he entered the courtroom. It took some time for his eyes to adjust to the dimness of the dingy chambers that smelled even worse than the hallway. Two of the Tarsian council members held oranges studded with cloves up to their noses.

The six members of the council were seated at the bench, which stood upon a tall platform, three upon either side of their Lord, whose tall chair sat in the center. The Lord glanced up as they entered. His eyebrows raised slightly at the sight of Sturm, and it seemed to Tanis that his face softened. The Lord even nodded in a gesture of polite greeting to the knight. Tanis's hopes rose. The companions walked forward to stand before the bench. There were no chairs. Supplicants or prisoners before the council stood to present their cases.

"What is the charge against these men?" the Lord asked. The constable gave the companions a baleful glance.

"Inciting a riot, milord," he said.

"Riot!" Flint exploded. "We had nothing to do with any riot! It was that rattle-brained—"

A figure in long robes crept forward from the shadows to whisper in his Lordship's ear. None of the companions had noticed the figure as they entered. They noticed it now.

Flint coughed and fell silent, giving Tanis a meaningful, grim look from beneath his thick, white eyebrows. The dwarf shook his head, his shoulders slumped. Tanis sighed wearily. Gilthanas wiped blood from his cut with a shaking hand, his elven features pale with hatred. Only Sturm stood outwardly calm and unmoved as he looked upon the twisted half-man, half-reptilian face of a draconian.

The companions remaining in the Inn sat together in Elistan's room for at least an hour after the others were taken away by the guards. Caramon remained on guard near the door, his sword drawn. Riverwind kept watch out the window. In the distance, they could hear the sounds of the angry mob and looked at each other with tense, strained faces. Then the noise faded. No one disturbed them. The Inn was deathly quiet.

The morning wore on without incident. The pale, cold sun climbed in the sky, doing little to warm the winter day. Caramon sheathed his sword and yawned. Tika dragged a chair over to sit beside him. Riverwind went to stand watchfully near Goldmoon, who was talking quietly to Elistan, making plans for the refugees.

Only Laurana remained standing by the window, though there was nothing to see. The guards had apparently grown tired of marching up and down the street and now huddled in doorways, trying to keep warm. Behind her, she could hear Tika and Caramon laugh softly together. Laurana glanced around at them. Talking too quietly to be heard, Caramon appeared to be describing a battle. Tika listened intently, her eyes gleaming with admiration.

The young barmaid had received a great deal of practice in fighting on their journey south to find the Hammer of Kharas and, though she would never be truly skilled with a sword, she had developed shield-bashing into an art. She wore her armor casually now. It was still mis-matched, but she kept adding to it, scrounging pieces left on battlefields. The sunlight glinted on her chain-mail vest, glistened in her red hair. Caramon's face was animated and relaxed as he talked with the young woman. They did not touch—not with the golden eyes of Caramon's twin on them—but they leaned very near each other.

Laurana sighed and turned away, feeling very lonely and—thinking of Raistlin's words—very frightened.

She heard her sigh echoed, but it was not a sigh of regret. It was a sigh of irritation. Turning slightly, she looked down at Raistlin. The mage had closed the spellbook he was trying to read, and moved into the little bit of sunlight that came through the glass. He had to study his spellbook daily. It is the curse of the magi that they must commit their spells to memory time and again, for the words of magic flicker and die like sparks from a fire. Each spell cast saps the mage's strength, leaving him physically weakened until he is finally exhausted and cannot work any magic at all without rest.

Raistlin's strength had been growing since the companions' meeting in Solace, as had his power. He had mastered several new spells taught to him by Fizban, the bumbling old magician who had died in Pax Tharkas. As his power grew, so did the misgivings of his companions. No one had any overt cause to mistrust him, indeed, his magic had saved their lives several times. But there was something disquieting about him—secret, silent, self-contained, and solitary as an oyster.

Absently caressing the night-blue cover of the strange spellbook he had acquired in Xak Tsaroth, Raistlin stared into the street. His golden eyes with their dark, hourglass-shaped pupils glittered coldly.

Although Laurana disliked speaking to the mage, she had to know! What had he meant—a long farewell?

"What do you see when you look far away like that?" she asked softly, sitting down next to him, feeling a sudden weakness of fear sweep over her.

"What do I see?" he repeated softly. There was great pain and sadness in his voice, not the bitterness she was accustomed to hearing. "I see time as it affects all things. Human flesh withers and dies before my eyes. Flowers bloom, only to fade. Trees drop green leaves, never to regain them. In my sight, it is always winter, always night."

"And—this was done to you in the Towers of High Sorcery?" Laurana asked, shocked beyond measure. "Why? To what end?"

Raistlin smiled his rare and twisted smile. "To remind me of my own mortality. To teach me compassion." His voice sank. "I was proud and arrogant in my youth. The youngest to take the Test, I was going to show them all!" His frail fist clenched. "Oh, I showed them. They shattered my body and devoured my mind until by the end I was capable of—" He stopped abruptly, his eyes shifting to Caramon.

"Of what?" Laurana asked, fearing to know, yet fascinated.

"Nothing," Raistlin whispered, lowering his eyes. "I am forbidden to speak of it."

Laurana saw his hands tremble. Sweat beaded on his forehead. His breath wheezed and he began to cough. Feeling guilty for having inadvertently caused such anguish, she flushed and shook her head, biting her lip. "I—I'm sorry to have given you pain. I didn't mean to." Confused, she looked down, letting her hair fall forward to hide her face, a girlish habit.

Raistlin leaned forward almost unconsciously, his hand stretching out, trembling, to touch the wondrous hair that seemed possessed of a life of its own, so vibrant and luxuriant was it. Then, seeing before his eyes his own dying flesh, he withdrew his hand quickly and sank back in his chair, a bitter smile on his lips. For what Laurana did not know, could not know, was that, in looking at her, Raistlin saw the only beauty he would ever see in his lifetime. Young, by elven standards, she was untouched by death or decay, even in the mage's cursed vision.

Laurana saw nothing of this. She was aware only that he moved slightly. She almost got up and left, but she felt drawn to him now, and he still had not answered her question. "I—I meant, can you see the future? Tanis told me your mother was—what do they call it—prescient? I know that Tanis comes to you for advice. . . ."

Raistlin regarded Laurana thoughtfully. "The half-elf comes to me for advice, not because I can see the future. I can't. I am no seer. He comes because I am able to think, which is something most of these other fools seem incapable of doing."

"But what you said. Some of us may not see each other again." Laurana looked up at him earnestly. "You must have foreseen something! What—I must know! Was it . . . Tanis?"

Raistlin pondered. When he spoke, it was more to himself than to Laurana. "I don't know," he whispered. "I don't even know why I said that. It's just that—for an instant—I knew—" He seemed to struggle to remember, then suddenly shrugged.

"Knew what?" Laurana persisted.

"Nothing. My overwrought imagination as the knight would say if he were here. So Tanis told you about my mother," he said, changing the subject abruptly.

Laurana, disappointed but hoping to find out more if she kept talking to him, nodded her head. "He said she had the gift of foresight. She could look into the future and see images of what would come to pass."

"That is true," Raistlin whispered, then smiled sardonically. "Much good it did her. The first man she married was a handsome warrior from the northland. Their passion died within months, and after that they made life miserable for each other. My mother was fragile of health and given to slipping into strange trances from which she might not wake for hours. They were poor, living off what her husband could earn with his sword. Though he was clearly of noble blood, he never spoke of his family. I do not believe he even told her his real name."

Raistlin's eyes narrowed. "He told Kitiara, though. I'm sure of it. That is why she traveled north, to find his family."

"Kitiara . . ." Laurana said in a strained voice. She touched the name as one touches an aching tooth, eager to understand more of this human woman Tanis loved. "Then, that man—the noble warrior—was Kitiara's father?" she said in a husky voice.

Raistlin regarded her with a penetrating gaze. "Yes," he whispered. "She is my elder half-sister. Older than Caramon and I by about eight years. She is very much like her father, I believe. As beautiful as he was handsome. Resolute and impetuous, warlike, strong and fearless. Her father taught her the only thing he knew—the art of warfare. He began going on longer and longer trips, and one day vanished completely. My mother convinced the Highseekers to declare him legally dead. She then remarried the man who became our father. He was a simple man, a wood-cutter by trade. Once again, her farsight did not serve her."

"Why?" Laurana asked gently, caught up in the story, amazed that the usually taciturn mage was so voluble, not knowing that he was drawing more out of her simply by watching her expressive face than he was giving in return.

"The birth of my brother and I for one thing," Raistlin said. Then, overcome by a fit of coughing, he stopped talking and motioned to his brother. "Caramon! It is time for my drink," he said in the hissing whisper that pierced through the loudest talk. "Or have you forgotten me in the pleasure of other company?"

Caramon fell silent in mid-laugh. "No, Raist," he said guiltily, hur-riedly rising from his seat to hang a kettle of water over the fire. Tika, sub-dued, lowered her head, unwilling to meet the mage's gaze.

After staring at her a moment, Raistlin turned back to Laurana, who had watched all this with a cold feeling in the pit of her stomach. He began to speak again as if there had been no interruption. "My mother never really recovered from the childbirth. The midwife gave me up for dead, and I would have died, too, if it hadn't been for Kitiara. Her first battle, she used to say, was against death with me as the prize. She raised us. My mother was incapable of taking care of children, and my father was forced to work day and night simply to keep us fed. He died in an accident when Caramon and I were in our teens. My mother went into one of her trances that day"—Raistlin's voice dropped—"and never came out. She died of starvation."

"How awful!" Laurana murmured, shivering.

Raistlin did not speak for long moments, his strange eyes staring out into the chill, gray winter sky. Then his mouth twisted. "It taught me a valuable lesson—learn to control the power. Never let it control you!"

Laurana did not seem to have heard him. Her hands in her lap twisted nervously. This was the perfect opportunity to ask the questions she longed to ask, but it would mean giving up a part of her inner self to this man she feared and distrusted. But her curiosity—and her love—were too great. She never realized she was falling into a cunningly baited trap. For Raistlin delighted in discovering the secrets of people's souls, knowing he might find them useful.

"What did you do then?" she asked, swallowing. "Did Kit-Kitiara . . ."

Trying to appear natural, she stumbled over the name and flushed in embarrassment.

Raistlin watched Laurana's inner struggle with interest. "Kitiara was gone by then," he answered. "She left home when she was fifteen, earning her living by her sword. She is an expert—so Caramon tells me—and had no trouble finding mercenary work. Oh, she returned every so often, to see how we were getting along. When we were older, and more skilled, she took us with her. That was where Caramon and I learned to fight together— I using my magic, my brother his sword. Then, after she met Tanis"— Raistlin's eyes glittered at Laurana's discomfiture—"she traveled with us more often."

"Traveled with whom? Where did you go?"

"There was Sturm Brightblade, already dreaming of knighthood, the kender, Tanis, Caramon, and I. We traveled with Flint, before he retired from metalsmithing. The roads grew so dangerous that Flint gave up traveling. And by this time, we had all learned as much as we could from our friends. We were growing restless. It was time to separate, Tanis said."

"And you did as he said? He was your leader, even then?" She looked back to remember him as she had known him before he left Qualinost, beardless and lacking the lines of care and worry she saw now on his face. But even then he was withdrawn and brooding, tormented by his feelings of belonging to both races—and to neither. She hadn't understood him then. Only now, after living in a world of humans, was she beginning to.

"He has the qualities we are told are essential for leadership. He is quick-thinking, intelligent, creative. But most of us possess these—in greater or lesser degree. Why do the others follow Tanis? Sturm is of noble blood, member of an order whose roots go back to ancient times. Why does he obey a bastard half-elf? And Riverwind? He distrusts all who are not human and half who are. Yet he and Goldmoon both would follow Tanis to the Abyss and back. Why?"

"I *have* wondered," Laurana began, "and I think—"

But Raistlin, ignoring her, answered his own question. "Tanis listens to his feelings. He does not suppress them, as does the knight, or hide them, as does the Plainsman. Tanis realizes that sometimes a leader must think with his heart and not his head." Raistlin glanced at her. "Remember that."

Laurana blinked, confused for a moment, then, sensing a tone of superiority in the mage which irritated her, she said loftily, "I notice you leave out yourself. If you are as intelligent and powerful as you claim, why do you follow Tanis?"

Raistlin's hourglass eyes were dark and hooded. He stopped talking as Caramon brought his twin a cup and carefully poured water from the kettle. The warrior glanced at Laurana, his face dark, embarrassed and uncomfortable as always whenever his brother went on like this.

Raistlin did not seem to notice. Pulling a pouch from his pack, he sprinkled some green leaves into the hot water. A pungent, acrid smell filled the room. "I do not follow him." The young mage looked up at Laurana. "For the time being, Tanis and I simply happen to be traveling in the same direction."

"The Knights of Solamnia are not welcome in our city," the Lord said sternly, his face serious. His dark gaze swept the rest of the company. "Nor are elves, kender, or dwarves, or those who travel in their company. I understand you also have a magic-user with you, one who wears the red robes. You wear armor. Your weapons are blood-stained and come quickly and readily to your hands. Obviously you are skilled warriors."

"Mercenaries, undoubtedly, milord," the constable said.

"We are not mercenaries," Sturm said, coming to stand before the bench, his bearing proud and noble. "We come out of the northern Plains of Abanasinia. We freed eight hundred men, women, and children from the Dragon Highlord, Verminaard, in Pax Tharkas. Fleeing the wrath of the dragonarmies, we left the people hidden in a valley in the mountains and traveled south, hoping to find ships in the legendary city of Tarsis. We did not know it was landlocked, or we would not have bothered."

The Lord frowned. "You say you came from the north? That is impossible. No one has ever come safely through the mountain kingdom of the dwarves in Thorbardin."

"If you know aught of the Knights of Solamnia, you know we would die sooner than tell a lie—even to our enemies," Sturm said. "We entered the dwarven kingdom and won safe passage by finding and restoring to them the lost Hammer of Kharas."

The Lord shifted uncomfortably, glancing at the draconian who sat behind him. "I do know somewhat of the knights," he said reluctantly."And therefore I must believe your story, though it sounds more a child's bedtime tale than—"

Suddenly the doors banged open and two guards strode in, roughly dragging a prisoner between them. They thrust the companions aside as they flung their prisoner to the floor. The prisoner was a woman. Heavily veiled, she was dressed in long skirts and a heavy cape. She lay for a moment on the floor, as if too tired or defeated to rise. Then, seeming to make a supreme effort of will, she started to push herself up. Obviously no one was going to assist her. The Lord stared at her, his face grim and scowling. The draconian behind him had risen to its feet and was looking down at her with interest. The woman struggled, entangled in her cape and her long, flowing skirts.

Then Sturm was at her side.

The knight had watched in horror, appalled at this callous treatment of a woman. He glanced at Tanis, saw the ever-cautious half-elf shake his head, but the sight of the woman making a gallant effort to rise proved too much for the knight. He took a step forward, and found a hauberk thrust in front of him.

"Kill me if you will," the knight said to the guard, "but I am going to the aid of the lady."

The guard blinked and stepped back, his eyes looking up at the Lord for orders. The Lord shook his head slightly. Tanis, watching closely, held his breath. Then he thought he saw the Lord smile, quickly covering it with his hand.

"My lady, allow me to assist you," Sturm said with the courtly, old-fashioned politeness long lost in the world. His strong hands gently raised her to her feet.

"You had better leave me, sir knight," the woman said, her words barely audible from behind her veil. But at the sound of her voice, Tanis and Gilthanas gasped softly, glancing at each other. "You do not know what you do," she said. "You risk your life—"

"It is my privilege to do so," Sturm said, bowing. Then he stood near her protectively, his eyes on the guards.

"She is Silvanesti elven!" Gilthanas whispered to Tanis. "Does Sturm know?"

"Of course not," Tanis said softly. "How could he? I barely recognized her accent myself."

"What could she be doing here? Silvanesti is far away—"

"I—" Tanis began, but one of the guards shoved him in the back. He fell silent just as the Lord started to speak.

"Lady Alhana," he said in a cold voice, "you were warned to leave this city. I was merciful last time you came before me because you were on a diplomatic mission from your people, and protocol is still honored in Tarsis. I told you then, however, you could expect no help from us and gave you twenty-four hours to depart. Now I find you still here." He looked over at the guards. "What is the charge?"

"Trying to buy mercenaries, milord," the constable replied. "She was picked up in an inn along the Old Waterfront, milord." The constable gave Sturm a scathing glance. "It was a good thing she didn't meet up with this lot. Of course, no one in Tarsis would aid an elf."

"Alhana," Tanis muttered to himself. He edged over to Gilthanas. "Why is that name familiar?"

"Have you been gone from your people so long you do not recognize the name?" the elf answered softly in elven. "There was only one among our Silvanesti cousins called Alhana. Alhana Starbreeze, daughter of the Speaker of the Stars, princess of her people, ruler when her father dies, for she has no brothers."

"Alhana!" Tanis said, memories coming back to him. The elven people were split hundreds of years before, when Kith-Kanan led many of the elves to the land of Qualinesti following the bitter Kinslayer Wars. But the elven leaders still kept in contact in the mysterious manner of the elflords who, it is said, can read messages in the wind and speak the language of the silver moon. Now he remembered Alhana—of all elfmaidens reputed to be the most beautiful, and distant as the silver moon that shone on her birth.

The draconian leaned down to confer with the Lord. Tanis saw the man's face darken, and it seemed as if he was about to disagree, then he bit his lip and, sighing, nodded his head. The draconian melted back into the shadows once more.

"You are under arrest, Lady Alhana," the Lord said heavily. Sturm took a step nearer the woman as the guards closed in around her. Sturm threw back his head and cast them all a warning glance. So confident and noble did he appear, even unarmed, that the guards hesitated. Still, their Lord had given them an order.

"You better do something," Flint growled. "I'm all for chivalry, but there's a time and a place and this isn't either!"

"Have you got any suggestions?" Tanis snapped.

Flint didn't answer. There wasn't a damn thing any of them could do and they knew it. Sturm would die before one of those guards laid a hand on the woman again, even though he had no idea who this woman was. It didn't matter. Feeling himself torn with frustration and admiration for his friend, Tanis gauged the distance between himself and the nearest guard, knowing he could put at least one out of action. He saw Gilthanas close his eyes, his lips moving. The elf was a magic-user, though he rarely treated it seriously. Seeing the look on Tanis's face, Flint heaved a sigh and turned toward another guard, lowering his helmeted head like a battering ram.

Then suddenly the Lord spoke, his voice grating. "Hold, knight!" he said with the authority that had been bred in him for generations. Sturm, recognizing this, relaxed, and Tanis breathed a sigh of relief. "I will not have blood shed in this Council chamber. The lady has disobeyed a law of the land, laws which, in days gone by, you, sir knight, were sworn to uphold. But I agree, there is no reason to treat her disrespectfully. Guards, you will escort the lady to prison but with the same courtesy you show me. And you, sir knight, will accompany her, since you are so interested in her welfare."

Tanis nudged Gilthanas who came out of his trance with a start. "Truly, as Sturm said, this Lord comes from a noble and honorable line," Tanis whispered.

"I don't see what you're so pleased about, Half-elf." Flint grunted, overhearing them. "First the kender gets us charged with inciting a riot, then he disappears. Now the knight gets us thrown into prison. Next time, remind me to stick with the mage. I *know* he's crazed!"

As the guards started to herd their prisoners away from the bench, Alhana appeared to be hunting for something within the folds of her long skirt.

"I beg a favor, sir knight," she said to Sturm. "I seem to have dropped something. A trifle but precious. Could you look—"

Sturm knelt swiftly and immediately saw the object where it lay, sparkling, on the floor, hidden by the folds of her dress. It was a pin, shaped like a star, glittering with diamonds. He drew in his breath. A trifle! Its value must be incalculable. No wonder she did not want it found by these worthless guards. Quickly he wrapped his fingers around it, then feigned to look about. Finally, still kneeling, he looked up at the woman.

Sturm caught his breath as the woman removed the hood of her cloak and drew the veil from her face. For the first time, human eyes looked upon the face of Alhana Starbreeze.

Muralasa, the elves called her, Princess of the Night. Her hair, black and soft as the night wind, was held in place by a net as fine as cobweb, twinkling with tiny jewels like stars. Her skin was the pale hue of the silver moon, her eyes the deep, dark purple of the night sky and her lips the color of the red moon's shadows.

The knight's first thought was to give thanks to Paladine that he was already on his knees. His second was that death would be a paltry price to pay to serve her, and his third that he must say something, but he seemed to have forgotten the words of any known language.

"Thank you for searching, noble knight," Alhana said softly, staring intently into Sturm's eyes. "As I said, it was a trifle. Please rise. I am very weary and, since it seems we are going to the same place, you could do me a great favor by giving me your assistance."

"I am yours to command," Sturm said fervently, and he rose to his feet, swiftly tucking the jewel inside his belt. He held out his arm, and Alhana put her slender, white hand on his forearm. His arm trembled at her touch.

It seemed to the knight as if a cloud had covered the light of the stars when she veiled her face again. Sturm saw Tanis fall into line behind them, but so enraptured was the knight with the beautiful face burning in his memory that he stared straight at the half-elf without a flicker of recognition.

Tanis had seen Alhana's face and felt his own heart stir with her beauty. But he had seen Sturm's face as well. He had seen that beauty enter the knight's heart, doing more damage than a goblin's poisoned arrowtip. For this love must turn to poison, he knew. The Silvanesti were a proud and haughty race. Fearing contamination and the loss of their way of life, they refused to have even the slightest contact with humans. Thus the Kinslayer Wars had been fought.

No, thought Tanis sadly, the silver moon itself was not higher or farther out of Sturm's reach. The half-elf sighed. This was all they needed.

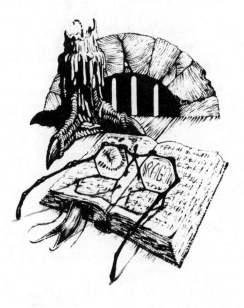

6

Knights of Solamnia.

Tasslehoff's glasses of true seeing.

s the guards led the prisoners from the Hall of Justice, they passed two figures standing outside in the shadows. Both were so swathed in clothing it was difficult to tell to what race they belonged. Hoods covered their heads, their faces were wrapped in cloth. Long robes shrouded their bodies. Even their hands were wrapped in strips of white, like bandages. They spoke together in low tones.

"See!" one said in great excitement. "There they are. They match the descriptions."

"Not all of them," said the other dubiously.

"But the half-elf, the dwarf, the knight! I tell you, it is them! And I know where the others are," the figure added smugly. "I questioned one of the guards."

The other, taller figure considered, watching the group being led off down the street. "You are right. We should report this to the Highlord at once." The shrouded figure turned, then stopped as it saw the other hesitate. "What are you waiting for?"

"But shouldn't one of us follow? Look at those puny guards. You know the prisoners will try and escape."

The other laughed unpleasantly. "Of course they'll escape. And we know where they'll go—to rejoin their friends." The shrouded figure squinted up at the afternoon sun. "Besides, in a few hours it won't make any difference." The tall figure strode away, the shorter hurrying after.

It was snowing when the companions left the Hall of Justice. This time, the constable knew better than to march his prisoners through the main city streets. He led them into a dark and gloomy alleyway that ran behind the Hall of Justice.

Tanis and Sturm were just exchanging glances, and Gilthanas and Flint were just tensing to attack when the half-elf saw the shadows in the alley begin to move. Three hooded and cloaked figures leaped out in front of the guards, their steel blades gleaming in the bright sunlight.

The constable put his whistle to his lips, but he never made a sound. One of the figures knocked him unconscious with the hilt of his sword, while the other two rushed the guards, who immediately fled. The hooded figures faced the companions.

"Who are you?" Tanis asked, astounded at his sudden freedom. The hooded and cloaked figures reminded him of the hooded draconians they had fought outside of Solace. Sturm pulled Alhana behind him.

"Have we escaped one danger only to find a worse?" Tanis demanded. "Unmask yourselves!"

But one of the hooded men turned to Sturm, his hands raised in the air. *"Oth Tsarthon e Paran,"* he said.

Sturm gasped. *"Est Tsarthai en Paranaith,"* he replied, then he turned to Tanis. "Knights of Solamnia," he said, gesturing at the three men.

"Knights?" Tanis asked in astonishment. "Why—"

"There is no time for explanation, Sturm Brightblade," one of the knights said in Common, his accent thick. "The guards will return soon. Come with us."

"Not so fast!" Flint growled, his feet planted firmly in the street, his hands breaking off the handle of a hauberk so that it suited his short stature. "You'll find time for explanations or I'm not going! How'd you know the knight's name and how came you to be waiting for us—"

"Oh, just run him through!" sang a shrill voice out of the shadows. "Leave his body to feed the crows. Not that they'll bother; there's few in this world who can stomach dwarf—"

"Satisfied?" Tanis turned to Flint, who was red-faced with rage.

"Someday," vowed the dwarf, "I'll kill that kender."

Whistles sounded from the street behind them. With no more hesitation, the companions followed the knights through twisting, rat infested alleys. Saying he had business to attend to, Tas disappeared before Tanis could catch hold of him. The half-elf noticed that the knights didn't seem at all surprised by this, nor did they try to stop Tas. They refused, however, to answer any questions, just kept hurrying the group along until they entered the ruins—the old city of Tarsis the Beautiful.

Here the knights stopped. They had brought the companions to a part of the city where no one ever came now. The streets were broken and empty, reminding Tanis strongly of the ancient city of Xak Tsaroth. Taking Sturm by the arm, the knights led him a short distance from his friends and began to confer in Solamnic, leaving the others to rest.

Tanis, leaning against a building, looked around with interest. What remained standing of the buildings on this street was impressive, much more beautiful than the modern city. He saw that Tarsis the Beautiful must have deserved its name before the Cataclysm. Now nothing but huge blocks of granite lay tumbled about. Vast courtyards were choked and overgrown with weeds turned brown by the biting winter winds.

He walked over to sit down on a bench with Gilthanas, who was talking to Alhana. The elflord introduced him.

"Alhana Starbreeze, Tanis Half-Elven," Gilthanas said. "Tanis lived among the Qualinesti for many years. He is the son of my uncle's wife." Alhana drew back the veil from her face and regarded Tanis coldly. *Son of my uncle's wife* was a polite way of saying Tanis was illegitimate, otherwise Gilthanas would have introduced him as the "son of my uncle." The half-elf flushed, the old pain returning forcibly, hurting as much now as it had fifty years before. He wondered if he would ever be free of it.

Scratching his beard, Tanis said harshly, "My mother was raped by human warriors during years of darkness following the Cataclysm. The Speaker kindly took me in following her death and raised me as his own."

Alhana's dark eyes grew darker until they were pools of night. She raised her eyebrows. "Do you see a need to apologize for your heritage?" she asked in a chill voice.

"N-no . . ." Tanis stammered, his face burning. "I—"

"Then do not," she said, and she turned away from him to Gilthanas. "You asked why I came to Tarsis? I came seeking aid. I must return to Silvanesti to search for my father."

"Return to Silvanesti?" Gilthanas repeated. "We—my people did not know the Silvanesti elves had left their ancient homeland. No wonder we lost contact—"

"Yes," Alhana's voice grew sad. "The evil that forced you, our cousins, to leave Qualinesti came to us as well." She bowed her head, then looked up, her own voice soft and low. "Long we fought this evil. But in the end we were forced to flee or perish utterly. My father sent the people, under my leadership, to Southern Ergoth. He stayed in Silvanesti to fight the evil alone. I opposed this decision, but he said he had the power to prevent the evil from destroying our homeland.With a heavy heart, I led my people to safety and there they remain.But I came back to seek my father, for the days have been long and we have heard no word of him."

"But had you no warriors, lady, to accompany you on such a dangerous journey?" Tanis asked.

Alhana, turning, glanced at Tanis as if amazed that he had intruded upon their conversation. At first she seemed about to refuse to answer him, then—looking longer at his face—she changed her mind.

"There were many warriors who offered to escort me," she said proudly. "But when I said I led my people to safety, I spoke rashly. Safety no longer exists in this world. The warriors stayed behind to guard the people. I came to Tarsis hoping to find warriors to travel into Silvanesti with me. I presented myself to the Lord and the Council, as protocol demands—"

Tanis shook his head, frowning darkly. "That was stupid," he said bluntly. "You should have known how they feel about elves, even before the draconians came! You were damn lucky they only ordered you tossed out of the city."

Alhana's pale face became—if possible—paler. Her dark eyes glittered. "I did as protocol demands," she replied, too well bred to show her anger beyond the cool tones of her voice. "To do otherwise would have been to come as a barbarian. When the Lord refused to aid me, I told him I intended to seek help on my own. To do less would have not been honorable."

Flint, who had been able to follow only bits and pieces of the conversation in elven, nudged Tanis. "She and the knight will get on perfectly." He snorted. "Unless their honor gets them killed first." Before Tanis could reply, Sturm rejoined the group.

"Tanis," Sturm said in excitement, "the knights have found the ancient library! That's why they're here. They discovered records in Palanthas saying that in ancient times knowledge of dragons was kept in the library here, at Tarsis. The Knights Council sent them to see if the library still survived."

Sturm gestured for the knights to come forward. "This is Brian Donner, Knight of the Sword," he said. "Aran Tallbow, Knight of the Crown, and Derek Crownguard, Knight of the Rose." The knights bowed.

"And this is Tanis Half-Elven, our leader," Sturm said. The half-elf saw Alhana start and look at him in wonder, glancing at Sturm to see if she had heard correctly.

Sturm introduced Gilthanas and Flint, then he turned to Alhana. "Lady Alhana," he began, then stopped, embarrassed, realizing he knew nothing more about her.

"Alhana Starbreeze," Gilthanas finished. "Daughter of the Speaker of the Stars. Princess of the Silvanesti elves."

The knights bowed again, lower this time.

"Accept my heartfelt gratitude for rescuing me," Alhana said coolly. Her gaze encompassed all the group but lingered longest on Sturm. Then she turned to Derek, whom she knew from his Order of the Rose to be the leader. "Have you discovered the records the Council sent you to find?"

As she spoke, Tanis examined the knights, now unhooded, with interest. He, too, knew enough to know that the Knights Council—the ruling body of the Solamnic knights—had sent the best. In particular he studied Derek, the elder and the highest in rank. Few knights attained the Order of the Rose. The tests were dangerous and difficult, and only knights of pure bloodline could belong.

"We have found a book, my lady," Derek said, "written in an ancient language we could not understand. There were pictures of dragons, however, so we were planning to copy it and return to Sancrist where, we hoped, scholars would be able to translate it. But instead we have found one who can read it. The kender—"

"Tasslehoff!" Flint exploded.

Tanis's mouth gaped open. "Tasslehoff?" he repeated incredulously. "He can barely read Common. He doesn't know any ancient languages. The only one among us who might possibly be able to translate an ancient language is Raistlin."

Derek shrugged. "The kender has a pair of glasses he says are 'magical glasses of true seeing.' He put them on and he has been able to read the book. It says—"

"I can imagine what it says!" Tanis snapped. "Stories about automatons and magic rings of teleporting and plants that live off air. Where is he? I'm going to have a little talk with Tasslehoff Burrfoot."

"Magical glasses of true seeing," Flint grumbled. "And I'm a gully dwarf!"

The companions entered a shattered building. Climbing over rubble, they followed Derek's lead through a low archway. The smell of must and mildew was strong. The darkness was intense after the brightness of the afternoon sun outside and for a moment, everyone was blinded. Then Derek lit a torch, and they saw narrow, winding stairs leading down into more darkness.

"The library was built below ground," Derek explained. "Probably the only reason it survived the Cataclysm so well."

The companions descended the stairs rapidly and soon found themselves inside a huge room. Tanis caught his breath and even Alhana's eyes widened in the flickering torchlight. The gigantic room was filled from ceiling to floor with tall, wooden shelves, stretching as far as the eye could see. On the shelves were books. Books of all kinds. Books with leather bindings, books bound in wood, books bound in what looked like leaves from some exotic tree. Many were not bound at all but were simply sheaves of parchment, held together with black ribbons. Several shelves had toppled over, spilling the books to the floor until it was ankle-deep in parchment.

"There must be thousands!" Tanis said in awe. "How did you ever find one among these?"

Derek shook his head. "It was not easy," he said. "Long days we have spent down here, searching. When we discovered it at last, we felt more despair than triumph, for it was obvious that the book cannot be moved. Even as we touched the pages, they crumbled to dust. We feared we would spend long, weary hours copying it. But the kender—"

"Right, the kender," Tanis said grimly. "Where is he?"

"Over here!" piped a shrill voice.

Tanis peered through the dimly lit room to see a candle burning on a table. Tasslehoff, seated on a high wooden chair, was bent over a thick book. As the companions neared him, they could see a pair of small glasses perched on his nose.

"All right, Tas," Tanis said. "Where did you get them?"

"Get what?" the kender asked innocently. He saw Tanis's eyes narrow and put his hand to the small wire-rimmed glasses. "Oh, uh, these? I had them in a pouch . . . and, well, if you must know, I found them in the dwarven kingdom—"

Flint groaned and put his hand over his face.

"They were just lying on a table!" Tas protested, seeing Tanis scowl. "Honest! There was no one around. I thought perhaps someone misplaced them. I only took them for safekeeping. Good thing, too. Some thief might have come along and stolen them, and they're very valuable! I meant to return them, but after that we were so busy, what with fighting dark dwarves and draconians and finding the Hammer, and I—sort of—forgot I had them. When I remembered them, we were miles away from the dwarves, on our way to Tarsis, and I didn't think you'd want me to go back, just to return them, so—"

"What do they do?" Tanis interrupted the kender, knowing they'd be here until the day after tomorrow if he didn't.

"They're wonderful," Tas said hastily, relieved that Tanis wasn't going to yell at him. "I left them lying on a map one day." Tas patted his map-case. "I looked down and what do you suppose? I could read the writing on the map through the glasses! Now, that doesn't sound very wonderful," Tas said hurriedly, seeing Tanis start to frown again, "but this was a map written in a language I'd never been able to understand before. So I tried them on all my maps and I could read them, Tanis! Every one! Even the real, real old ones!"

"And you never mentioned this to us?" Sturm glared at Tas.

"Well, the subject just never came up," Tas said apologetically. "Now, if you had asked me directly—'Tasslehoff, do you have a pair of magical seeing glasses?—' I would have told you the truth straight off. But you never did, Sturm Brightblade, so don't look at me like that. Anyway, I can read this old book. Let me tell you what I—"

"How do you know they're magic and not just some mechanical device of the dwarves?" Tanis asked, sensing that Tas was hiding something.

Tas gulped. He had been hoping Tanis wouldn't ask him *that* question.

"Uh," Tas stammered, "I—I guess I did sort of, happened to, uh, mention them to Raistlin one night when you were all busy doing something else. He told me they might be magic. To find out, he said one of those weird spells of his and they—uh—began to glow. That meant they were enchanted. He asked me what they did and I demonstrated and he said they were 'glasses of true seeing.' The dwarven magic-users of old made them to read books written in other languages and—" Tas stopped.

"And?" Tanis pursued.

"And—uh—magic spellbooks." Tas's voice was a whisper.

"And what else did Raistlin say?"

"That if I touched his spellbooks or even looked at them sideways, he'd turn me into a cricket and s-swallow m-me whole," Tasslehoff stammered. He looked up at Tanis with wide eyes. "I believed him, too."

Tanis shook his head. Trust Raistlin to come up with a threat awful enough to quench the curiosity of a kender. "Anything else?" he asked.

"No, Tanis," Tas said innocently. Actually Raistlin had mentioned something else about the glasses, but Tas hadn't been able to understand it very well. Something about the glasses seeing things too truly, which didn't make any sense, so he figured it probably wasn't worth bringing up. Besides, Tanis was mad enough already.

"Well, what have you discovered?" Tanis asked grudgingly.

"Oh, Tanis, it's so interesting!" Tas said, thankful the ordeal was over. He carefully turned a page and, even as he did so, it split and cracked beneath his small fingers. He shook his head sadly. "That happens almost every time. But you can see here"—the others leaned around to stare beneath the kender's finger—"pictures of dragons. Blue dragons, red dragons, black dragons, green dragons. I didn't know there were so many. Now, see this thing?" He turned another page. "Oops. Well, you can't see it now, but it was a huge ball of glass. And—so the book says—if you have one of these glass balls, you can gain control over the dragons and they'll do what you say!"

"Glass ball!" Flint sniffed, then sneezed. "Don't believe him, Tanis. I think the only thing those glasses have done is magnify his tall stories."

"I am so telling the truth!" Tas said indignantly. "They're called dragon orbs, and you can ask Raistlin about them! He must know because, according to this, they were made by the great wizards, long ago."

"I believe you," Tanis said gravely, seeing that Tasslehoff was really upset. "But I'm afraid it won't do us much good. They were probably all destroyed in the Cataclysm and we wouldn't know where to look anyway—"

"Yes, we do," Tas said excitedly. "There's a list here, of where they were kept. See—" He stopped, cocking his head. "Shhhh," he said, listening. The others fell silent. For a moment they heard nothing, then their ears caught what the kender's quicker hearing had already detected.

Tanis felt his hands grow cold; the dry, bitter taste of fear filled his mouth. Now he could hear, in the distance, the sound of hundreds of horns braying, horns all of them had heard before. The bellowing, brass horns that heralded the approach of the draconian armies—and the approach of the dragons.

The horns of death.

7

"—not destined to meet again

in this world."

he companions had just reached the marketplace when the first flight of dragons struck Tarsis.

The group had separated from the knights, not a pleasant parting. The knights had tried to convince them to escape with them into the hills. When the companions refused, Derek demanded that Tasslehoff accompany them, since the kender alone knew the location of the dragon orbs. Tanis knew Tas would only run away from the knights and was forced to refuse again.

"Bring the kender, Sturm, and come with us," Derek commanded, ignoring Tanis.

"I cannot, sir," Sturm replied, laying his hand on Tanis's arm. "He is my leader, and my first loyalty is to my friends."

Derek's voice was cold with anger. "If that is your decision," he answered, "I cannot stop you. But this is a black mark against you, Sturm Brightblade. Remember that you are not a knight. Not yet. Pray that I am not there when the question of your knighthood comes before the Council."

Sturm became as pale as death. He cast a sideways glance at Tanis, who tried to hide his astonishment at this startling news. But there was no time to think about it. The sound of the horns, screaming discordantly on the chill air, was coming closer and closer each second. The knights and the companions parted; the knights heading for their camp in the hills, the companions returning to town.

They found the townspeople outside their houses, speculating on the strange horn calls, which they had never heard before and did not understand. One Tarsian alone heard and understood. The Lord in the council chamber rose to his feet at the sound. Whirling, he turned upon the smug-looking draconian seated in the shadows behind him.

"You said we would be spared!" the Lord said through clenched teeth. "We're still negotiating—"

"The Dragon Highlord grew weary of negotiation," the draconian said, stifling a yawn. "And the city *will* be spared—after it has been taught a lesson, of course."

The Lord's head sank into his hands. The other council members, not fully comprehending what was happening, stared at each other in horrified awareness as they saw tears trickle through the Lord's fingers.

Outside, the red dragons were visible in the skies, hundreds of them. Flying in regimented groups of three to five, their wings glistened flame red in the setting sun. The people of Tarsis knew one thing and one thing only: death flew overhead.

As the dragons swooped low, making their first passes over the town, the dragonfear flowed from them, spreading panic more deadly than fire. The people had one thought in their minds as the shadows of the wings blotted out the dying light of day—escape.

But there was no escape.

After the first pass, knowing now that they would meet no resistance, the dragons struck. One after the other, they circled, then dropped from the sky like red-hot shot, their fiery breath engulfing building after building with flame. The spreading fires created their own windstorms. Choking smoke filled the street, turning twilight into midnight. Ash poured down like black rain. Screams of terror changed to screams of agony as people died in the blazing abyss that was Tarsis.

And as the dragons struck, a sea of fear-crazed humanity surged through the flame-lit streets. Few had any clear idea of where they were going. Some shouted they would be safe in the hills, others ran down by the old waterfront, still others tried to reach the city gates. Above them flew the dragons, burning at their discretion, killing at their leisure.

The human sea broke over Tanis and the companions, crushing them into the street, swirling them apart, smashing them up against buildings. The smoke choked them and stung their eyes, tears blinded them as they fought to control the dragon fear that threatened to destroy their reason.

The heat was so intense that whole buildings blew apart. Tanis caught Gilthanas as the elf was hurled into the side of a building. Holding onto him, the half-elf could only watch helplessly as the rest of his friends were swept away by the mob.

"Back to the Inn!" Tanis shouted. "Meet at the Inn!" But whether they heard him or not, he could not say. He could only trust that they would all try to head in that direction.

Sturm caught hold of Alhana in his strong arms, half-carrying, half-dragging her through the death-filled streets. Peering through the ash, he tried to see the others, but it was hopeless. And then began the most desperate battle he had ever fought, striving to keep his feet and support Alhana as time and again the dreadful waves of humanity broke over them.

Then Alhana was ripped from his arms by the shrieking mob, whose booted feet trampled all that lived. Sturm flung himself into the crowd, shoving and bashing with his armored arms and body, and caught Alhana's wrists. Deathly pale, she was shaking with fright. She hung onto his hands with all her strength, and finally he was able to pull her close. A shadow swept over them. A dragon, screaming cruelly, bore down upon the street that heaved and surged with men, women, and children. Sturm ducked into a doorway, dragging Alhana with him, and shielded her with his body as the dragon swooped low overhead. Flame filled the street; the screams of the dying were heart-rending.

"Don't look!" Sturm whispered to Alhana, pressing her against him, tears streaming down his own face. The dragon passed, and suddenly the streets were horribly, unbearably still. Nothing moved.

"Let's go, while we can," Sturm said, his voice shaking. Clinging to each other, the two stumbled out of the doorway, their senses numbed, moving only by instinct. Finally, sickened and dizzy from the smell of charred flesh and smoke, they were forced to seek shelter in another doorway.

For a moment, they could do nothing but hold onto each other, thankful for the brief respite, yet haunted by the knowledge that in seconds they must return to the deadly streets.

Alhana rested her head against Sturm's chest. The ancient, old fashioned armor felt cool against her skin. Its hard metal surface was reassuring, and beneath it she could feel his heart beat, rapid, steady, and soothing. The arms that held her were strong, hard, well-muscled. His hand stroked her black hair.

Alhana, chaste maiden of a stern and rigid people, had long known when, where, and whom she would marry. He was an elflord, and it was a mark of their understanding that, in all the years since this had been arranged they had never touched. He had stayed behind with the people, while Alhana returned to find her father. She had strayed into this world of humans, and her senses reeled from the shock. She detested them, yet was fascinated by them. They were so powerful, their emotions raw and untamed. And just when she thought she would hate and despise them forever, one stepped apart from the others.

Alhana looked up into Sturm's grieved face and saw etched there pride, nobility, strict inflexible discipline, constant striving for perfection—

perfection unattainable. And thus the deep sorrow in his eyes. Alhana felt herself drawn to this man, this human. Yielding to his strength, comforted by his presence, she felt a sweet, searing warmth steal over her, and suddenly she realized she was in more danger from this fire than from the fire of a thousand dragons.

"We'd better go," Sturm whispered gently, but to his amazement Alhana pushed herself away from him.

"Here we part," she said, her voice cold as the night wind. "I must return to my lodging. Thank you for escorting me."

"What?" Sturm said. "Go by yourself? That's madness." He reached out and gripped her arm. "I cannot allow—" The wrong thing to do, he realized, feeling her stiffen. She did not move but simply stared at him imperiously until he released her.

"I have friends of my own," she said, "as you do. Your loyalty is to them. My loyalty is to mine. We must go our separate ways." Her voice faltered at the look of intense pain on Sturm's face, still wet with tears. For a moment Alhana could not bear it and wondered if she would have the strength to continue. Then she thought of her people—depending on her. She found the strength. "I thank you for your kindness and your help, but now I must go, while the streets are empty."

Sturm stared at her, hurt and puzzled. Then his face hardened. "I was happy to be of service, Lady Alhana. But you are still in danger. Allow me to take you to your lodgings, then I will trouble you no more."

"That is quite impossible," Alhana said, gritting her teeth to keep her jaw set firmly. "My lodgings are not far, and my friends wait for me. We have a way out of the city. Forgive me for not taking you, but I am never certain about trusting humans."

Sturm's brown eyes flashed. Alhana, standing close, could feel his body tremble. Once more she nearly lost her resolve.

"I know where you are staying," she said, swallowing. "The Red Dragon Inn. Perhaps, if I find my friends—we could offer you help—"

"Do not concern yourself." Sturm's voice echoed her coldness. "And do not thank me. I did nothing more than my Code required of me. Farewell," he said, and started to walk away.

Then, remembering, he turned back. Drawing the sparkling diamond pin from his belt, he placed it in Alhana's hand. "Here," he said. Looking into her dark eyes, he suddenly saw the pain she tried to hide. His voice softened, though he could not understand. "I am pleased you trusted me with this gem," he said gently, "even for a few moments."

The elfmaid stared at the jewel for an instant, then she began to shake. Her eyes lifted to Sturm's eyes and she saw in them not scorn, as she expected, but compassion. Once more, she wondered at humans. Alhana dropped her head, unable to meet his gaze, and took his hand in hers. Then she laid the jewel in his palm and closed his fingers over it.

"Keep this," she said softly. "When you look at it, think of Alhana Star-breeze and know that, somewhere, she thinks of you."

Sudden tears flooded the knight's eyes. He bowed his head, unable to speak. Then, kissing the gem, he placed it carefully back into his belt and he reached out his hands, but Alhana drew back into the doorway, her pale face averted.

"Please go," she said. Sturm stood for a moment, irresolute, but he could not—in honor—refuse to obey her request. The knight turned and plunged back into the nightmarish street. Alhana watched him from the doorway for a moment, a protective shell hardening around her. "Forgive me, Sturm," she whispered to herself. Then she stopped. "No, do not forgive me," she said harshly. "Thank me."

Closing her eyes, she conjured up an image in her mind and sent a message speeding to the outskirts of the city where her friends waited to carry her from this world of humans. Receiving their telepathic answer in reply, Alhana sighed and began anxiously to scan the smoke-filled skies, waiting.

"Ah," said Raistlin calmly as the first horn calls shattered the stillness of the afternoon, "I told you so."

Riverwind cast an irritated glance at the mage, even as he tried to think what to do. It was all very well for Tanis to say protect the group from the town guards, but to protect them from armies of draconians, from dragons! Riverwind's dark eyes went over the group. Tika rose to her feet, her hand on her sword. The young girl was brave and steady, but unskilled. The Plainsman could still see the scars on her hand where she had cut herself.

"What is it?" Elistan asked, looking bewildered.

"The Dragon Highlord, attacking the city," Riverwind answered harshly, trying to think.

He heard a clanking sound. Caramon was getting up, the big warrior appearing calm and unperturbed. Thank goodness for that. Even though Riverwind detested Raistlin, he had to admit that the mage and his warrior brother combined steel and magic effectively. Laurana, too, he saw, appeared cool and resolute, but then she was an elf—Riverwind had never really learned to trust elves.

"Get out of the city, if we don't return," Tanis had told him. But Tanis hadn't foreseen this! They would get out of the city only to meet the armies of the Dragon Highlords on the Plains. Riverwind now had an excellent idea who had been watching them as they traveled to this doomed place. He swore to himself in his own language, then—even as the first dragons swept down over the city—he felt Goldmoon's arm around him. Looking down, he saw her smile—the smile of Chieftain's Daughter—and he saw the faith in her eyes. Faith in the gods, and faith in him. He relaxed, his brief moment of panic gone.

A shock wave hit the building. They could hear the screams in the streets below, the roaring whoosh of the fires.

"We've got to get off this floor, back to ground level," Riverwind said. "Caramon, bring the knight's sword and the other weapons. If Tanis and the others are—" He stopped. He had been about to say "still alive," then saw Laurana's face. "If Tanis and the others escape, they'll return here. We'll wait for them."

"Excellent decision!" hissed the mage caustically, "especially as we have nowhere else to go!"

Riverwind ignored him. "Elistan, take the others downstairs. Caramon and Raistlin, stay with me a moment." After they were gone, he said swiftly, "Our best chance, the way I see it, is to stay inside, barricade ourselves in the Inn. The streets will be deadly."

"How long do you think we can hold out?" Caramon asked.

Riverwind shook his head. "Hours, maybe," he said briefly.

The brothers looked at him, each of them thinking about the tortured bodies they had seen in the village of Qué-Shu, of what they had heard about the destruction of Solace.

"We cannot be taken alive," Raistlin whispered.

Riverwind took a deep breath. "We'll hold out as long as we can," he said, his voice shaking slightly, "but when we know we can last no longer—"

He stopped, unable to continue, his hand on his knife, thinking of what he must do.

"There will be no need for that," Raistlin said softly. "I have herbs. A tiny bit in a glass of wine. Very quick, painless."

"Are you certain?" Riverwind asked.

"Trust me," Raistlin replied. "I am skilled in the art. The art of herblore," he amended smoothly, seeing the Plainsman shudder.

"If I am alive," Riverwind said softly, "I will give her, them—the drink myself. If not—"

"I understand. You may trust me," the mage repeated.

"What about Laurana?" Caramon asked. "You know elves. She won't—"

"Leave it to me," Raistlin repeated softly.

The Plainsman stared at the mage, feeling horror creep over him. Raistlin stood before him coolly, his arms folded in the sleeves of his robe, his hood pulled up over his head. Riverwind looked at his dagger, considering the alternative. No, he couldn't do it. Not that way.

"Very well," he said, swallowing. He paused, dreading to go downstairs and face the others. But the sounds of death in the street were growing louder. Riverwind turned abruptly and left the brothers alone.

"I will die fighting," Caramon said to Raistlin, trying to speak in a matter-of-fact tone. After the first few words, though, the big warrior's voice broke. "Promise me, Raist, you'll take this stuff if I'm . . . not there. . . ."

"There will be no need," Raistlin said simply. "I have not the strength to survive a battle of this magnitude. I will die within my magic."

Tanis and Gilthanas fought their way through the crowd, the stronger half-elf holding onto the elf as they shoved and clawed and pushed through the panicked masses. Time and again, they ducked for shelter from the dragons. Gilthanas wrenched his knee, fell into a doorway, and was forced to limp in agony, leaning on Tanis's shoulder.

The half-elf breathed a prayer of thankfulness when he saw the Red Dragon Inn, a prayer that changed to a curse when he saw the black reptilian forms surging around the front. He dragged Gilthanas, who had been stumbling along blindly, exhausted by pain, back into a recessed doorway.

"Gilthanas!" Tanis shouted. "The Inn! It's under attack!"

Gilthanas raised glassy eyes and stared uncomprehendingly. Then, apparently understanding, he sighed and shook his head. "Laurana," he gasped, and he pushed himself forward, trying to stagger out of the doorway. "We've got to reach them." He collapsed in Tanis's arms.

"Stay here," the half-elf said, helping him sit down. "You're not capable of moving. I'll try and get through. I'll go around the block and come in from the back."

Tanis ran forward, darting in and out of doorways, hiding in the wreckage. He was about a block from the Inn when he heard a hoarse shout. Turning to look, he saw Flint gesturing wildly. Tanis dashed across the street.

"What is it?" he asked.

"Why aren't you with the others—" The half-elf stopped. "Oh, no," he whispered.

The dwarf, his face smudged with ash and streaked with tears, knelt beside Tasslehoff. The kender was pinned beneath a beam that had fallen in the street. Tas's face, looking like the face of a wise child, was ashen, his skin clammy.

"Blasted, rattle-brained kender," Flint moaned. "Had to go and let a house fall on him." The dwarf's hands were torn and bleeding from trying to lift a beam that would take three men or one Caramon to get off the kender. Tanis put his hand to Tas's neck. The lifebeat was very weak.

"Stay with him!" Tanis said unnecessarily. "I'm going to the Inn. I'll bring Caramon!"

Flint looked up at him grimly, then glanced over at the Inn. Both could hear the yells of the draconians, see their weapons flash in the glare of the firelight. Occasionally an unnatural light flared from the Inn—Raistlin's magic. The dwarf shook his head. He knew Tanis was about as capable of returning with Caramon as he was of flying.

But Flint managed to smile. "Sure, lad, I'll stay with him. Farewell, Tanis."

Tanis swallowed, tried to answer, then gave up and ran on down the street.

Raistlin, coughing until he could barely stand, wiped blood from his lips and drew a small, black leather pouch from the innermost pockets of his robes. He had just one spell left and barely energy enough to cast it. Now, his hands shaking with fatigue, he tried to scatter the contents of the little pouch into a pitcher of wine he had ordered Caramon to bring him before the battle started. But his hand trembled violently, and his coughing spasms doubled him over.

Then he felt another hand grasp his own. Looking up, he saw Laurana. She took the pouch from his frail fingers. Her own hand was stained with the dark green draconian blood.

"What's this?" she asked.

"Ingredients for a spell." The mage choked. "Pour it into the wine." Laurana nodded and poured in the mixture as instructed. It vanished instantly.

"Don't drink it," the mage warned when the coughing spasm passed. Laurana looked at him. "What is it?"

"A sleeping potion," Raistlin whispered, his eyes glittering.

Laurana smiled wryly. "You don't think we're going to be able to get to sleep tonight?"

"Not that kind," Raistlin answered, staring at her intently. "This one feigns death. The heartbeat slows to almost nothing, the breathing nearly stops, the skin grows cold and pale, the limbs stiffen."

Laurana's eyes opened wide. "Why—" she began.

"To be used as a last resort. The enemy thinks you are dead, leaves you on the field—if you are lucky. If not—"

"If not?" she prompted, her face pale.

"Well, a few have been known to waken on their own funeral pyres," Raistlin said coolly. "I don't believe that is likely to happen to us, however."

Breathing more easily, he sat down, ducking involuntarily as a spent arrow fluttered overhead and fell to the floor behind him. He saw Laurana's hand tremble then and realized she was not as calm as she was forcing herself to appear.

"Are you intending that we take this?" she asked.

"It will save us from being tortured by draconians."

"How do you know that?"

"Trust me," the mage said with a slight smile.

Laurana glanced at him and shivered. Absently, she wiped blood-stained fingers on her leather armor. The blood did not come off, but she didn't notice. An arrow thudded next to her. She didn't even start, just stared at it dully.

Caramon appeared, stumbling out of the smoke of the burning common room. He was bleeding from an arrow wound in the shoulder, his own red blood mingling oddly with the green blood of his enemy.

"They're breaking down the front door," he said, breathing heavily."Riverwind ordered us back here."

"Listen!" Raistlin warned. "That's not the only place they're breaking in!" There was a splintering crash at the door leading from the kitchen to the back alley.

Ready to defend themselves, Caramon and Laurana whirled just as the door shattered. A tall, dark figure entered.

"Tanis!" Laurana cried. Sheathing her weapon, she ran toward him.

"Laurana!" he breathed. Catching her in his arms, he held her close, nearly sobbing in his relief. Then Caramon flung his huge arms around both of them.

"How is everyone?" Tanis asked, when he could talk.

"So far, so good," Caramon said, peering behind Tanis. His face fell when he saw he was alone. "Where's—"

"Sturm's lost," Tanis said wearily. "Flint and Tas are across the street. The kender's pinned under a beam. Gilthanas is about two blocks away. He's hurt," Tanis told Laurana, "not badly, but he couldn't make it any farther."

"Welcome, Tanis," Raistlin whispered, coughing. "You have come in time to die with us."

Tanis looked at the pitcher, saw the black pouch lying near it, and stared at Raistlin in sudden shock.

"No," he said firmly. "We're not going to die. At least not like th—" he broke off abruptly. "Get everyone together."

Caramon lumbered off, yelling at the top of his lungs. Riverwind ran in from the common room where he had been firing the enemy's arrows back at them, his own having run out long ago. The others followed him, smiling hopefully at Tanis.

The sight of their faith in him infuriated the half-elf. Someday, he thought, I'm going to fail them. Maybe I already have. He shook his head angrily.

"Listen!" he shouted, trying to make himself heard over the noise of the draconians outside. "We can try and escape out the back! Only a small force is attacking the Inn. The main part of the army isn't in the city yet."

"Somebody's after us," Raistlin murmured.

Tanis nodded. "So it would appear. We haven't much time. If we can make it into the hills—"

He suddenly fell silent, raising his head. They all fell silent, listening, recognizing the shrill scream, the creak of giant leather wings, coming nearer and nearer.

"Take cover!" Riverwind yelled. But it was too late.

There was a screaming whine and a boom. The Inn, three stories tall and built of stone and wood, shook as if it were made of sand and sticks. The air exploded with dust and debris. Flames erupted outside. Above them, they could hear the sound of wood splitting and breaking, the thud of falling timber. The building began to collapse in on itself.

The companions watched in stunned fascination, paralyzed by the sight of the gigantic ceiling beams shuddering beneath the strain as the roof caved in onto the upper floors.

"Get out!" Tanis shouted. "The whole place is—"

The beam directly above the half-elf gave a great groan, then split and cracked. Gripping Laurana around the waist, Tanis flung her as far from him as he could and saw Elistan, standing near the front of the Inn, catch her in his arms.

As the huge beam above Tanis gave way with a shuddering snap, he heard the mage shriek strange words. Then he was falling, falling into blackness—and it seemed that the world fell on top of him.

Sturm rounded a corner to see the Inn of the Red Dragon collapse in a cloud of flame and smoke as a dragon soared in the sky above it. The knight's heart beat wildly with grief and fear.

He ducked into a doorway, hiding in the shadows as some draconians passed him—laughing and talking in their cold, guttural language. Apparently they assumed this job was finished and were seeking other amusement. Three others, he noticed—dressed in blue uniforms, not red—appeared extremely upset at the Inn's destruction, shaking their fist at the red dragon overhead.

Sturm felt the weakness of despair sweep over him. He sagged against the door, watching the draconians dully, wondering what to do next. Were they all still in there? Perhaps they had escaped. Then his heart gave a painful bound. He saw a flash of white.

"Elistan!" he cried, watching the cleric emerge from the rubble, dragging someone with him. The draconians, swords drawn, ran toward the cleric, calling out in Common for him to surrender. Sturm yelled the challenge of a Solamnic knight to an enemy and ran out from his doorway. The draconians whirled about, considerably disconcerted to see the knight.

Sturm became dimly aware that another figure was running with him. Glancing to his side, he saw the flash of firelight off a metal helm and heard the dwarf roaring. Then, from a doorway, he heard words of magic.

Gilthanas, unable to stand without help, had crawled out and was pointing at the draconians, reciting his spell. Flaming darts leaped from his hands. One of the creatures fell over, clutching its burning chest. Flint leaped on another, beating it over the head with a rock, while Sturm felled the other draconian with a blow from his fists. Sturm caught Elistan in his arms as the man staggered forward. The cleric was carrying a woman.

"Laurana!" Gilthanas cried from the doorway.

Dazed and sick from the smoke, the elfmaid lifted her glazed eyes. "Gilthanas?" she murmured. Then, looking up, she saw the knight.

"Sturm," she said confusedly, pointing behind her vaguely. "Your sword, it's here. I saw it—"

Sure enough, Sturm saw a flash of silver, barely visible beneath the rubble. His sword, and next to it was Tanis's sword, the elven blade of Kith-Kanan. Moving aside piles of stone, Sturm reverently lifted the swords that lay like artifacts within a hideous, gigantic cairn. The knight listened for movement, calls, cries. There was only a dreadful silence.

"We've got to get out of here," he said slowly, without moving. He looked at Elistan, who was staring back at the wreckage, his face deathly pale. "The others?"

"They were all in there," Elistan said in a trembling voice. "And the half-elf . . ."

"Tanis?"

"Yes. He came through the back door, just before the dragon hit the Inn. They were all together, in the very center. I was standing beneath a doorway. Tanis saw the beam breaking. He threw Laurana. I caught her, then the ceiling collapsed on top of them. There's no way they could have—"

"I don't believe it!" Flint said fiercely, leaping into the rubble. Sturm grasped hold of him, yanked him back.

"Where's Tas?" the knight asked the dwarf sternly.

The dwarf's face fell. "Pinned under a beam," he said, his face gray with grief and sorrow. He clutched at his hair wildly, knocking off his helm. "I've got to go back to him. But I can't leave them—Caramon—" The dwarf began to cry, tears streaming into his beard. "That big, dumb ox! I need him. He can't do this to me! And Tanis, too!" The dwarf swore. "Damn it, I need them!"

Sturm put his hand on Flint's shoulder. "Go back to Tas. He needs you now. There are draconians roaming the streets. We'll be all—"

Laurana screamed, a terrifying, pitiful sound that pierced Sturm like a spear. Turning, he caught hold of her just as she started to rush into the debris.

"Laurana!" he cried. "Look at that! Look at it!" He shook her in his own anguish. "Nothing could be alive in there!"

"You don't know that!" she screamed at him in fury, tearing away from his grasp. Falling onto her hands and knees, she tried to lift one of the blackened stones. "Tanis!" she cried. The stone was so heavy, she could only move it a few inches.

Sturm watched, heartsick, uncertain what to do. Then he had his answer. Horns! Nearer and nearer. Hundreds, thousands of horns. The armies were invading. He looked at Elistan, who nodded in sorrowful understanding. Both men hurried over to Laurana.

"My dear," Elistan began gently, "there is nothing you can do for them. The living need you. Your brother is hurt, so is the kender. The draconians are invading. We must either escape now, and keep fighting these horrible monsters, or waste our lives in useless grief. Tanis gave his life for you, Laurana. Don't let it be a needless sacrifice."

Laurana stared up at him, her face black with soot and filth, streaked with tears and blood. She heard the horns, she heard Gilthanas calling, she heard Flint shouting something about Tasslehoff dying, she heard Elistan's words. And then the rain began, dripping from the skies as the heat of the dragonfire melted the snow, changing it to water.

The rain ran down her face, cooling her feverish skin.

"Help me, Sturm," she whispered through lips almost too numb to shape the words. He put his arm around her. She stood up, dizzy and sick with shock.

"Laurana!" her brother called. Elistan was right. The living needed her. She must go to him. Though she would rather lie down on this pile of rocks and die, she must go on. That was what Tanis would do. They needed her. She must go on.

"Farewell, Tanthalas," she whispered.

The rain increased, pouring down gently, as if the gods themselves wept for Tarsis the Beautiful.

Water dripped on his head. It was irritating, cold. Raistlin tried to roll over, out of the way of the water. But he couldn't move. There was a heavy weight pressing down on top of him. Panicking, he tried desperately to escape. As fear surged through his body, he came fully to consciousness. With knowledge, panic vanished. Raistlin was in control once more and, as he had been taught, he forced himself to relax and study the situation.

He could see nothing. It was intensely dark, so he was forced to rely on his other senses. First, he had to get this weight off. He was being smothered and crushed. Cautiously he moved his arms. There was no pain, nothing appeared broken. Reaching up, he touched a body. Caramon, by the armor—and the smell. He sighed. He might have known. Using all his strength, Raistlin shoved his brother aside and crawled out from under him.

The mage breathed more easily, wiping water from his face. He located his brother's neck in the darkness and felt for the lifebeat. It was strong, the man's flesh was warm, his breathing regular. Raistlin lay back down on the floor in relief. At least, wherever he was, he wasn't alone.

Where was he? Raistlin reconstructed those last few terrifying moments. He remembered the beam splitting and Tanis throwing Laurana out from under it. He remembered casting a spell, the last one he had strength enough to manage. The magic coursed through his body, creating around him and those near him a force capable of shielding them from physical objects. He remembered Caramon hurling himself on top of him, the building collapsing around them, and a falling sensation.

Falling . . .

Ah, Raistlin understood. We must have crashed through the floor into the Inn's cellar. Groping around the stone floor, the mage suddenly realized he was soaked through. Finally, however, he found what he had been searching for—the Staff of Magius. Its crystal was unbroken; only dragonfire could damage the Staff given him by Par-Salian in the Towers of High Sorcery.

"*Shirak*," whispered Raistlin, and the Staff flared into light. Sitting up, he glanced around. Yes, he was right. They were in the cellar of the Inn. Broken bottles of wine spilled their contents onto the floor. Casks of ale were split in two. It wasn't all water he had been lying in.

The mage flashed the light around the floor. There were Tanis, Riverwind, Goldmoon, and Tika, all huddled near Caramon. They seemed all right, he thought, giving them a quick inspection. Around them lay scattered debris. Half of the beam slanted down through the rubble to rest on the stone floor. Raistlin smiled. A nice bit of work, that spell. Once more they were in his debt.

If we don't perish from the cold, he reminded himself bitterly. His body was shaking so he could barely hold the staff. He began to cough. This would be the death of him. They had to get out.

"Tanis," he called, reaching out to shake the half-elf.

Tanis lay crumpled at the very edge of Raistlin's magic, protective circle. He murmured and stirred. Raistlin shook him again. The half-elf cried out, reflexively covering his head with his arm.

"Tanis, you're safe," Raistlin whispered, coughing. "Wake up."

"What?" Tanis sat bolt upright, staring around him. "Where—" Then he remembered. "Laurana?"

"Gone." Raistlin shrugged. "You threw her out of danger—"

"Yes . . ." Tanis said, sinking back down. "And I heard you say words, magic—"

"That's why we're not crushed." Raistlin clutched his sopping wet robes around him, shivering, and drew nearer Tanis, who was staring around as if he'd fallen onto a moon.

"Where in the name of the Abyss—"

"We're in the cellar of the Inn," the mage said. "The floor gave way and dropped us down here." Tanis looked up. "By all the gods," he whispered in awe.

"Yes," Raistlin said, his gaze following Tanis's. "We're buried alive."

Beneath the ruins of the Red Dragon Inn, the companions took stock of their situation. It did not look hopeful. Goldmoon treated their injuries, which were not serious, thanks to Raistlin's spell. But they had no idea how long they had been unconscious or what was happening above them. Worse still, they had no idea how they could escape.

Caramon tried cautiously to move some of the rocks above their heads, but the whole structure creaked and groaned. Raistlin reminded him sharply that he had no energy to cast more spells, and Tanis wearily told the big man to forget it. They sat in the water that was growing deeper all the time.

As Riverwind stated, it seemed to be a matter of what killed them first: lack of air, freezing to death, the Inn falling down on top of them, or drowning.

"We could shout for help," suggested Tika, trying to keep her voice steady.

"Add draconians to the list, then," Raistlin snapped. "They're the only creatures up there liable to hear you."

Tika's face flushed, and she brushed her hand quickly across her eyes. Caramon cast a reproachful glance at his brother, then put his arm around Tika and held her close. Raistlin gave them both a look of disgust.

"I haven't heard a sound up there," Tanis said, puzzled. "You'd think the dragons and the armies—" He stopped, his glance meeting Caramon's, both soldiers nodding slowly in sudden grim understanding.

"What?" asked Goldmoon, looking at them.

"We're behind enemy lines," Caramon said. "The armies of draconians occupy the town. And probably the land for miles and miles around. There's no way out, and nowhere to go if there were a way out."

As if to emphasize his words, the companions heard sounds above them. Guttural draconian voices that they had come to know all too well drifted down through to them.

"I tell you, this is a waste of time," whined another voice, goblin by the sound, speaking in Common. "There's no one alive in this mess."

"Tell that to the Dragon Highlord, you miserable dog-eaters," snarled the draconian. "I'm sure his lordship'll be interested in your opinion. Or rather, his dragon'll be interested. You have your orders. Now dig, all of you."

There were sounds of scraping, sounds of stones being dragged aside. Rivulets of dirt and dust started to sift down through the cracks. The big beam shivered slightly but held.

The companions stared at each other, almost holding their breaths, each remembering the strange draconians who had attacked the Inn. "Somebody's after us," Raistlin had said.

"What are we looking for in this rubble?" croaked a goblin in the goblin tongue. "Silver? Jewels?"

Tanis and Caramon, who spoke a little goblin, strained to hear.

"Naw," said the first goblin, who had grumbled about orders. "Spies or some such wanted personally by the Dragon Highlord for questioning."

"In here?" the goblin asked in amazement.

"That's what *I* said," snarled his companion. "You saw how far I got. The lizardmen say they had them trapped in the Inn when the dragon hit it. Said none of them escaped, and so the Highlord figures they must still be here. If you ask me—the dracos screwed up and now we've got to pay for their mistakes."

The sounds of digging and of rock moving grew louder, as did the sound of goblin voices, occasionally punctuated by a sharp order in the guttural voice of the draconians. There must be fifty of them up there! Tanis thought, stunned.

Riverwind quietly lifted his sword out of the water and began wiping it dry. Caramon, his usually cheerful face somber, released Tika and found his sword. Tanis didn't have a sword, Riverwind tossed him his dagger. Tika started to draw her sword, but Tanis shook his head. They would be fighting in close quarters, and Tika needed lots of room. The half-elf looked questioningly at Raistlin.

The mage shook his head. "I will try, Tanis," he whispered. "But I am very tired. Very tired. And I can't think, I can't concentrate." He bowed his head, shivering violently in his wet robes. He was exerting all his effort not to cough and give them away, muffling his choking in his sleeve.

One spell will finish him, if he gets that off, Tanis realized. Still, he may be luckier than the rest of us. At least he won't be taken alive.

The sounds above them grew louder and louder. Goblins are strong, tireless workers. They wanted to finish this job quickly, then get back to looting Tarsis. The companions waited in grim silence below. An almost steady stream of dirt and crushed rock dropped down upon them, along with fresh rainwater. They gripped their weapons. It was only a matter of minutes, maybe, before they were discovered.

Then, suddenly, there were new sounds. They heard the goblins yell in fear, the draconians shout to them, ordering them back to work. But they could hear the sounds of shovels and picks being dropped down onto the rocks above them, then the cursing of the draconians as they tried to stop what was apparently a full-scale goblin revolt.

And above the noise of the shrieking goblins rose a loud, clear, high pitched call, which was answered by another call farther away. It was like the call of an eagle, soaring above the plains at sunset. But this call was right above them.

There was a scream—a draconian. Then a rending sound—as if the body of the creature were being ripped apart. More screams, the clash of steel being drawn, another call and another answer—this one much nearer.

"What is that?" Caramon asked, his eyes wide. "It isn't a dragon. It sounds like—like some gigantic bird of prey!"

"Whatever it is, it's tearing the draconians to shreds!" Goldmoon said in awe as they listened. The screaming sounds stopped abruptly, leaving a silence behind that was almost worse. What new evil replaced the old?

Then came the sound of rocks and stones, mortar and timber being lifted and sent crashing to the streets. Whatever was up there was intent on reaching them!

"It's eaten all the draconians," whispered Caramon gruffly, "and now it's after us!"

Tika turned deathly white, clutching at Caramon's arm. Goldmoon gasped softly and even Riverwind appeared to lose some of his stoic composure, staring intently upward.

"Caramon," Raistlin said, shivering, "shut up!"

Tanis felt inclined to agree with the mage. "We're all scaring ourselves over noth—" he began. Suddenly there was a rending crash. Stone and rubble, mortar and timber clattered down around them. They scrambled for cover as a huge, clawed foot plunged through the debris, its talons gleaming in the light of Raistlin's staff.

Helplessly seeking shelter beneath broken beams or under the casks of ale, the companions watched in wonder as the gigantic claw extricated itself from the rubble and withdrew, leaving behind it a wide, gaping hole.

All was silent. For a few moments, none of the companions dared move. But the silence remained unbroken.

"This is our chance," Tanis whispered loudly. "Caramon, see what's up there."

But the big warrior was already creeping out of his hiding place, moving across the rubble-strewn floor as best he could. Riverwind followed behind, his sword drawn.

"Nothing," said Caramon, puzzled, peering up.

Tanis, feeling naked without his sword, came over to stand beneath the hole, gazing upward. Then, to his amazement, a dark figure appeared above them, silhouetted against the burning sky. Behind the figure towered a large beast. They could just make out the head of a gigantic eagle, its eyes glittering in the firelight, its wickedly curved beak gleaming in the flames.

The companions shrank back, but it was too late. Obviously the figure had seen them. It stepped nearer. Riverwind thought—too late—of his bow. Caramon pulled Tika close with one hand, holding his sword in his other.

The figure, however, simply knelt down near the edge of the hole, being careful of its footing among the loose stones, and removed the hood covering its head.

"We meet again, Tanis Half-Elven," said a voice as cool and pure and distant as the stars.

8

Escape from Tarsis.

The story of the dragon orbs.

ragons flew on their leathery wings above the gutted city of
Tarsis as the draconian armies swarmed in to take possession.
The task of the dragons was completed. Soon the Dragon Highlord would call them back, holding them in readiness for the next strike.
But for now they could relax, drifting on the super-heated air currents
rising from the burning town, picking off the occasional human foolish
enough to come out of hiding. The red dragons floated in the sky, keeping in their well-organized flights, gliding and dipping in a wheeling
dance of death.

No power on Krynn existed now that could stop them. They knew this
and exulted in their victory. But occasionally something would occur to
interrupt their dance. One flight leader, for example, received a report of
fighting near the wreckage of an inn. A young male red dragon, he led his
flight to the site, muttering to himself about the inefficiency of the troop
commanders. What could you expect, though, when the Dragon Highlord
was a bloated hobgoblin who hadn't even courage enough to watch the
takeover of a soft town like Tarsis?

The male red sighed, recalling the days of glory when Verminaard
had led them personally, sitting astride the back of Pyros. He had been a

Dragon Highlord! The red shook his head disconsolately. Ah, there was the battle. He could see it clearly now. Ordering his flight to stay airborne, he swooped in low for a better look.

"I command you! Stop!"

The red halted in his flight, staring upward in astonishment. The voice was strong and clear, and it came from the figure of a Dragon Highlord. But the Dragon Highlord was certainly not Toede! This Dragon Highlord, although heavily cloaked and dressed in the shining mask and dragon-scale armor of the Highlords, was human, to judge by the voice, not hobgoblin. But where had this Highlord come from? And why? For, to the red dragon's amazement, he saw that the Highlord rode upon a huge blue dragon and was attended by several flights of blues.

"What is your bidding, Highlord?" the red asked sternly. "And by what right do you stop us, you who have no business in this part of Krynn?"

"The fate of mankind is my business, whether it be in this part of Krynn or another," the Dragon Highlord returned. "And the might of my sword-arm gives me all the right I need to command you, gallant red. As for my bidding, I ask that you capture these pitiful humans, do not kill them. They are wanted for questioning. Bring them to me. You will be well rewarded."

"Look!" called a young female red. "Griffons!"

The Dragon Highlord gave an exclamation of astonishment and displeasure. The dragons looked down to see three griffons sweeping up out of the smoke. Not quite half the size of a red dragon, griffons were noted for their ferocity. Draconian troops scattered like ashes in the wind before the creatures, whose sharp talons and ripping beaks were tearing the heads from those reptile-men unlucky enough to have been caught in their path.

The red snarled in hatred and prepared to dive, his flight with him, but the Dragon Highlord swooped down in front of him, causing him to pull up.

"I tell you, they must not be killed!" the Dragon Highlord said sternly.

"But they're escaping!" the red hissed furiously.

"Let them," the Highlord said coldly. "They will not go far. I relieve you of your duty in this. Return to the main body. And if that idiot Toede mentions this, tell him that the secret of how he lost the blue crystal staff did not die with Lord Verminaard. The memory of Fewmaster Toede lives on—in *my* mind—and will become known to others if he dares to challenge me!"

The Dragon Highlord saluted, then wheeled the large blue dragon in the air to fly swiftly after the griffons, whose tremendous speed had allowed them to escape with their riders well past the city gates. The red watched the blues disappear through the night skies in pursuit.

"Shouldn't we give chase as well?" asked the female red.

"No," the red male replied thoughtfully, his fiery eyes on the figure of the Dragon Highlord dwindling in the distance. "I will not cross *that* one!"

"Your thanks are not necessary, or even wanted," Alhana Starbreeze cut off Tanis's halting, exhausted words in midsentence. The companions rode through the slashing rain on the backs of three griffons, clutching their feathered necks with their hands, peering apprehensively down at the dying city falling rapidly away beneath them.

"And you may not wish to extend them after you hear me out," Alhana stated coldly, glancing at Tanis, riding behind her. "I rescued you for my own purposes. I need warriors to help me find my father. We fly to Silvanesti."

"But that's impossible!" Tanis gasped. "We must meet our friends! Fly to the hills. We *can't* go to Silvanesti, Alhana. There's too much at stake! If we can find these dragon orbs, we have a chance to destroy these foul creatures and end this war. *Then* we can go to Silvanesti—"

"*Now* we are going to Silvanesti," Alhana retorted. "You have no choice in the matter, Half-Elven. My griffons obey my command and mine alone. They would tear you apart, as they did those dragonmen, if I gave the order."

"Someday the elves will wake up and find they are members of a vast family," Tanis said, his voice shaking with anger. "No longer can they be treated as the spoiled elder child who is given everything while the rest of us wait for the crumbs."

"What gifts we received from the gods we earned. You humans and *half*-humans"—the scorn in her voice cut like a dagger—"had these same gifts and threw them away in your greed for more. We are capable of fighting for our own survival without your help. As to your survival, that matters little to us."

"You seem willing enough to accept our help now!"

"For which you will be well-rewarded," Alhana returned.

"There is not steel nor jewels enough in Silvanesti to pay us—"

"You seek the dragon orbs," Alhana interrupted. "I know where one is located. It is in Silvanesti."

Tanis blinked. For a moment, he could think of nothing to say, but the mention of the dragon orb brought back thoughts of his friend. "Where's Sturm?" he asked Alhana. "The last I saw him, he was with you."

"I don't know," she replied. "We parted. He was going to the Inn, to find you. I called my griffons to me."

"Why didn't you let him take you to Silvanesti if you needed warriors?"

"That is none of your concern." Alhana turned her back to Tanis, who sat wordlessly, too tired to think clearly. Then he heard a voice shouting at him, barely distinguishable through the feathery rustle of the griffon's mighty wings.

It was Caramon. The warrior was shouting and pointing behind them. What now? Tanis thought wearily.

They had left behind the smoke and the storm clouds that covered Tarsis, flying out into the clear night sky. The stars gleamed above them, their sparkling lights shining as cold as diamonds, emphasizing the gaping black holes in the night sky where the two constellations had wheeled in their track above the world. The moons, silver and red, had set, but Tanis did not need their light to recognize the dark shapes blotting out the shining stars.

"Dragons," he said to Alhana. "Following us."

Tanis could never afterward clearly remember the nightmare flight from Tarsis. It was hours of chill, biting wind that made even death by a dragon's flaming breath seem appealing. It was hours of panic, staring behind to see the dark shapes gaining on them, staring until his eyes watered and the tears froze on his cheeks, yet unable to turn away. It was stopping at dusk, worn out from fear and fatigue, to sleep in a cave on a high rock cliff. It was waking at dawn only to see—as they soared through the air again, the dark, winged shapes still behind them.

Few living creatures can outfly the eagle-winged griffon. But the dragons—blue dragons, the first they had ever seen—were always on the horizon, always pursuing, allowing no rest during the day, forcing the companions into hiding at night when the exhausted griffons must sleep. There was little food, only quith-pa, a dried-fruit type of iron ration that sustains the body, but does little to ease hunger—which Alhana carried and shared. But even Caramon was too weary and dispirited to eat much.

The only thing Tanis remembered vividly occurred on the second night of their journey. He was telling the small group huddled around a fire in a damp and cheerless cave about the kender's discovery in the library at Tarsis. At the mention of the dragon orbs, Raistlin's eyes glittered, his thin face lit from within by an eager, intense glow.

"Dragon orbs?" he repeated softly.

"I thought you might know of them," Tanis said. "What are they?"

Raistlin did not answer immediately. Wrapped in both his own and his brother's cloak, he lay as near the fire as possible, and still his frail body shook with the chill. The mage's golden eyes stared at Alhana, who sat somewhat apart from the group, deigning to share the cave but not the conversation. Now, however, it seemed she half-turned her head, listening.

"You said there is a dragon orb in Silvanesti," the mage whispered, glancing at Tanis. "Surely I am not the one to ask."

"I know little about it," Alhana said, turning her pale face to the firelight. "We keep it as a relic of bygone days, more a curiosity than anything else. Who believed humans would once again wake this evil and bring the dragons back to Krynn?"

Before Raistlin could answer, Riverwind spoke angrily. "You have no proof it was humans!"

Alhana swept the Plainsman an imperious glance. She did not reply, considering it beneath her to argue with a barbarian.

Tanis sighed. The Plainsman had little use for elves. It had taken long days before he had come to trust Tanis, longer for Gilthanas and Laurana. Now, just as Riverwind seemed to be able to overcome his inherited prejudices, Alhana with her equal prejudices had inflicted new wounds.

"Very well, Raistlin," Tanis said quietly, "tell us what you know of the dragon orbs."

"Bring my drink, Caramon," the mage ordered. Bringing the cup of hot water as commanded, Caramon set it before his brother. Raistlin propped himself up on one elbow and mixed herbs into the water. The strange, acrid odor filled the air. Raistlin, grimacing, sipped the bitter mixture as he talked.

"During the Age of Dreams, when those of my order were respected and revered upon Krynn, there were five Towers of High Sorcery."The mage's voice sank, as if recalling painful memories. His brother sat staring at the rock floor of the cave, his face grave. Tanis, seeing the shadow fall across both twins, wondered again what had happened within the Tower of High Sorcery to change their lives so drastically. It was useless to ask, he knew. Both had been forbidden to discuss it.

Raistlin paused a moment before he continued, then drew a deep breath. "When the Second Dragon Wars came, the highest of my order met together in the greatest of the Towers—the Tower of Palanthas—and created the dragon orbs."

Raistlin's eyes grew unfocused, his whispering voice ceased a moment. When he spoke next, it was as if recounting a moment he was reliving in his mind. Even his voice changed, becoming stronger, deeper, clearer. He no longer coughed. Caramon looked at him in astonishment.

"Those of the White Robes entered the chamber at the top of the Tower first, as the silver moon, Solinari, rose. Then Lunitari appeared in the sky, dripping with blood, and those of the Red Robes entered. Finally the black disk, Nuitari, a hole of darkness among the stars, could be seen by those who sought it, and the Black Robes walked into the chamber.

"It was a strange moment in history, when all enmity between the Robes was suppressed. It would come but one more time in the world, when the wizards joined together in the Lost Battles, but that time could not be foreseen. It was enough to know that, for now, the great evil must be destroyed. For at last we had seen that evil was intent on destroying *all* the magic of the world, so that only its own would survive! Some there were among the Black Robes, who might have tried to ally with this great power"—Tanis saw Raistlin's eyes burn—"but soon realized they would not be masters of it, only its slaves. And so the dragon orbs were born, on a night when all three moons were full in the sky."

"*Three* moons?" Tanis asked softly, but Raistlin did not hear him and continued to speak in the voice not his own.

"Great and powerful magic was worked that night—so powerful that few could withstand it and they collapsed, their physical and mental strength drained. But that morning, five dragon orbs stood upon pedestals, glistening with light, dark with shadows. All but one were taken from Palanthas and carried, in great peril, to each of the other four Towers. Here they helped rid the world of the Queen of Darkness."

The feverish gleam faded from Raistlin's eyes. His shoulders slumped, his voice sank, and he began to cough, violently. The others stared at him in breathless silence.

Finally Tanis cleared his throat. "What do you mean, three moons?"

Raistlin looked up dully. "Three moons?" he whispered. "I know nothing of three moons. What were we discussing?"

"Dragon orbs. You told us how they were created. How did you—" Tanis stopped, seeing Raistlin sink onto his pallet.

"I have told you nothing," Raistlin said irritably. "What are you talking about?"

Tanis glanced at the others. Riverwind shook his head. Caramon bit his lip and looked away, his face drawn with worry.

"We were speaking of the dragon orbs," Goldmoon said. "You were going to tell us what you knew of them."

Raistlin wiped blood from his mouth. "I do not know much," he said wearily, shrugging. "The dragon orbs were created by the high mages. Only the most powerful of my order could use them. It was said that great evil would come to those not strong in magic who tried to command the orbs. Beyond that, I know nothing. All knowledge of the dragon orbs perished during the Lost Battles. Two, it was said, were destroyed in the Fall of the Towers of High Sorcery, destroyed rather than let the rabble have them. Knowledge of the other three died with their wizards." His voice died. Sinking back onto his pallet, exhausted, he fell asleep.

"The Lost Battles, three moons, Raistlin talking with a strange voice. None of this makes sense," Tanis muttered.

"I don't believe any of it!" Riverwind said coldly. He shook out their furs, preparing to sleep.

Tanis was starting to follow his example when he saw Alhana creep from the shadows of the cave and come to stand next to Raistlin. Staring down at the sleeping mage, her hands twisted together.

"Strong in magic!" she whispered in a voice filled with fear. "My father!"

Tanis looked at her in sudden understanding.

"You don't think your father tried to use the orb?"

"I am afraid," Alhana whispered, wringing her hands. "He said he

alone could fight the evil and keep it from our land. He must have meant—
" Swiftly she bent down near Raistlin. "Wake him!" she commanded, her
black eyes flaring. "I must know! Wake him and make him tell me what
the danger is!"

Caramon pulled her back, gently but firmly. Alhana glared at him, her
beautiful face twisted in fear and rage, and it seemed for a moment as if
she might strike him, but Tanis reached her side and caught hold of her
hand.

"Lady Alhana," he said calmly, "it would do no good to wake him. He
has told us everything *he* knows. As for that other voice, he obviously
remembers nothing about what it said."

"I've seen it happen to Raist before," Caramon said in low tones, "as
if he becomes someone else. But it always leaves him exhausted and he
never remembers."

Alhana jerked her hand away from Tanis's, her face resuming its cold,
pure, marble stillness. She whirled and walked to the front of the cave.
Catching hold of the blanket Riverwind had hung to hide the fire's light,
she nearly tore it down as she flung it aside and stalked outdoors.

"I'll stand first watch," Tanis told Caramon. "You get some sleep."

"I'll stay up with Raist awhile," the big man said, spreading out his
pallet next to his frail twin's. Tanis followed Alhana outside.

The griffons slept soundly, their heads buried on the soft feathers of
their necks, taloned front feet clutching the cliff edge securely. For a
moment he could not find Alhana in the darkness, then he saw her, leaning against a huge boulder, weeping bitterly, her head buried in her arms.

The proud Silvanesti woman would never forgive him if he saw her
weak and vulnerable. Tanis ducked back behind the blanket.

"I'll stand watch!" he called out loudly before he walked outside
again. Lifting the blanket, he saw, without seeming to, Alhana start up and
wipe her hands hurriedly across her face. She turned her back to him, and
he walked slowly toward her, giving her time to pull herself together.

"The cave was stifling," she said in a low voice. "I could not bear it. I
had to come out for a breath of air."

"I have first watch," Tanis said. He paused, then added, "You seem
afraid your father might have tried to use this dragon orb. Surely he would
know its history. If I remember what I know of your people, he was a
magic-user."

"He knew where the orb came from," Alhana said, her voice quivering
before she could regain control. "The young mage was right when he spoke
of the Lost Battles and the destruction of the Towers. But he was wrong
when he said the other three orbs were lost. One was brought to Silvanesti
by my father for safe-keeping."

"What were the Lost Battles?" Tanis asked, leaning on the rocks next
to Alhana.

"Is no lore at all kept in Qualinost?" she returned, regarding Tanis with scorn. "What barbarians you have become since mingling with humans!"

"Say the fault is my own," Tanis said, "that I did not pay enough heed to the Loremaster."

Alhana glanced at him, suspecting him of being sarcastic. Seeing his serious face and not particularly wanting him to leave her alone, she decided to answer his question. "As Istar rose during the Age of Might to greater and greater glories, the Kingpriest of Istar and his clerics became increasingly jealous of the magic-users' power. The clerics no longer saw the need for magic in the world, fearing it—of course—as something they could not control. Magic-users themselves, although respected, were never widely trusted, even those wearing the white robes. It was a simple matter for the priests to stir the people against the wizards. As times grew more and more evil, the priests placed the blame upon the magic-users. The Towers of High Sorcery, where the magicians must pass their final, grueling tests, were where the powers of the mages rested. The Towers became natural targets. Mobs attacked them, and it was as your young friend said: for only the second time in their history, the Robes came together to defend their last bastions of strength."

"But how could they be defeated?" Tanis said incredulously.

"Can you ask that, knowing what you do of your mage friend? Powerful he is, but he must have rest. Even the strongest must have time to renew their spells, recommit them to memory. Even the eldest of the order—wizards whose might has not been seen on Krynn since—had to sleep and spend hours reading their spellbooks. And then, too, as now, the number of magic-users was small. There are few who dare take the tests in the Towers of High Sorcery, knowing that to fail is to die."

"Failure means death?" Tanis said softly.

"Yes," Alhana replied. "Your friend is very brave, to have taken the Test so young. Very brave, or very ambitious. Didn't he ever tell you?"

"No," Tanis murmured. "He never speaks of it. But go on."

Alhana shrugged. "When it became clear that the battle was hopeless, the wizards themselves destroyed two of the Towers. The blasts devastated the countryside for miles around. Only three remained—the Tower of Istar, the Tower of Palanthas, and the Tower of Wayreth. But the terrible destruction of the other two Towers scared the Kingpriest. He granted the wizards in the Towers of Istar and Palanthas safe passage from these cities if they left the Towers undamaged, for the wizards could have destroyed the two cities, as the Kingpriest well knew.

"And so the mages traveled to the one Tower which was never threatened—the Tower of Wayreth in the Kharolis Mountains. To Wayreth they came to nurse their wounds and to nurture the small spark of magic still left in the world. Those spellbooks they could not take with them—for the number of books was vast and many were bound with spells of protection—were given to the great library at Palanthas, and there they still remain, according to the lore of my people."

The silver moon had risen, its moonbeams graced their daughter with a beauty that took Tanis's breath away, even as its coldness pierced his heart.

"What do you know of a third moon?" he asked, staring into the night sky, shivering. "A black moon . . ."

"Little," Alhana replied. "The magic-user draws power from the moons: the White Robes from Solinari, the Red Robes from Lunitari. There is, according to lore, a moon that gives the Black Robes their power, but only they know its name or how to find it in the sky."

Raistlin knew its name, Tanis thought, or at least that other voice knew it. But he did not speak this aloud.

"How did your father get the dragon orb?"

"My father, Lorac, was an apprentice," Alhana replied softly, turning her face to the silver moon. "He traveled to the Tower of High Sorcery at Istar for the Tests, which he took and survived. It was there he first saw the dragon orb." She fell silent for a moment. "I am going to tell you what I have never told anyone, and what he has never told, except to me. I tell you only because you have a right to know what—what to expect.

"During the Tests, the dragon orb . . ."—Alhana hesitated, seeming to search for the right words—"*spoke* to him, to his mind. It feared some terrible calamity was approaching. 'You must not leave me here in Istar,' it told him. 'If so, I will perish and the world will be lost.' My father—I suppose you could say he stole the dragon orb, although he saw himself as rescuing it.

"The Tower of Istar was abandoned. The Kingpriest moved in and used it for his own purposes. Finally the mages left the Tower of Palanthas." Alhana shivered. "Its story is a terrible one. The Regent of Palanthas, a disciple of the Kingpriest, arrived at the Tower to seal the gates shut—so he said. But all could see his eyes lingering on the beautiful Tower greedily, for legends of the wonders within—both fair and evil—had spread throughout the land.

"The Wizard of the White closed the Tower's slender gates of gold and locked them with a silver key. The Regent stretched out his hand, eager for the key, when one of the Black Robes appeared in a window in one of the upper stories.

"'The gates will remain closed and the halls empty until the day when the master of both the past and the present returns with power,' he cried. Then the evil mage leaped out, hurling himself down at the gates. As the barbs pierced the black robes, he cast a curse upon the Tower. His blood poured down on the ground, the silver and golden gates withered and twisted and turned to black. The shimmering tower of white and red faded to ice-gray stone, its black minarets crumbling to dust.

"The Regent and the people fled in terror. To this day, no one has dared enter the Tower of Palanthas—or even approach its gates. It was after the cursing of the Tower that my father brought the dragon orb to Silvanesti."

"But surely your father knew something about the orb before he took it," Tanis persisted. "How to use it—"

"If so, he did not speak of it," Alhana said wearily, "for that is all I know. I must rest now. Good-night," she said to Tanis without looking at him.

"Good-night, Lady Alhana," Tanis said gently. "Rest easily this night. And don't worry. Your father is wise and has lived through much. I'm certain everything is all right."

Alhana started to sweep past without a word, then, hearing the sympathy in his voice, she hesitated.

"Though he passed the Test," she said so softly Tanis had to step closer to hear, "he was not as powerful in his magic as your young friend is now. And if he thought the dragon orb was our only hope, I fear—" Her voice broke.

"The dwarves have a saying." Sensing for a moment that the barriers between them had been lowered, Tanis put his arm around Alhana's slender shoulders and drew her close. "'Trouble borrowed will be paid back with interest compounded on sorrow.' Don't worry. We're with you."

Alhana did not answer. She let herself be comforted for just an instant, then, slipping free of his grasp, walked to the entrance of the cave. There she stopped and looked back.

"You are worried about your friends," she said. "Do not be. They escaped the city and are safe. Though the kender was close to death for a time, he survived, and now they travel to Ice Wall in search of a dragon orb."

"How do you know this?" Tanis gasped.

"I have told you all I can." Alhana shook her head.

"Alhana! How do you know?" Tanis asked sternly.

Her pale cheeks stained with pink, Alhana murmured, "I—I gave the knight a Starjewel. He does not know its power, of course, nor how to use it. I don't know why I gave it to him, even, except—"

"Except what?" Tanis asked, amazed beyond belief.

"He was so gallant, so brave. He risked his life to help me, and he didn't even know who I was. He helped me because I was in trouble. And—" Her eyes glimmered. "And he wept, when the dragons killed the people. I've never seen an adult weep before. Even when the dragons came and drove us from our home, we did not weep. I think, perhaps, we've forgotten how."

Then, as if realizing she had said too much, she hastily pulled aside the blanket and entered the cave.

"In the name of the gods!" Tanis breathed. A Starjewel! What a rare and priceless gift! A gift exchanged by elven lovers forced to part, the jewel creates a bond between souls. Thus linked, they share the innermost emotions of the loved one and can grant strength to each other in times of need. But never before in Tanis's long life, had the half-elf heard of a Starjewel being given to a human. What would it do to a human? What kind of effect would it have? And Alhana—she could never love a human, never return love. This must be some sort of blind infatuation. She had been frightened, alone. No, this could only end in sorrow, unless something changed drastically among the elves or within Alhana herself.

Even as Tanis's heart expanded with relief to know Laurana and the others were safe, it contracted with fear and grief for Sturm.

9

Silvanesti. Entering the dream.

he third day, they continued their journey, flying into the sunrise. They had lost the dragons, apparently, although Tika, keeping watch behind, thought she could see black dots upon the horizon. And that afternoon, as the sun was sinking behind them, they neared the river known as Thon-Thalas—Lord's River—which divided the outside world from Silvanesti.

All of his life, Tanis had heard of the wonder and beauty of the ancient Elven Home, though the elves of Qualinesti spoke of it without regret. They did not miss the lost wonders of Silvanesti, for the wonders themselves became a symbol of the differences that had developed between the elven kin.

The elves in Qualinesti lived in harmony with nature, developing and enhancing its beauty. They built their homes among the aspens, magically gilding the trunks with silver and gold. They built their dwellings of shimmering rose quartz, and invited nature to come dwell with them.

The Silvanesti, however, loved uniqueness and diversity in all objects. Not seeing this uniqueness existing naturally, they reshaped nature to conform to their ideal. They had patience and they had time, for what were centuries to elves whose life spans measured in the hundreds of years?

And so they reformed entire forests, pruning and digging, forcing the trees and flowers into fantastic gardens of incredible beauty.

They did not 'build' dwellings, but carved and molded the marble rock that existed naturally in their land into such strange and wondrous shapes that—in the years before the races were estranged—dwarven craftsmen traveled thousands of miles to view them, and then could do nothing but weep at the rare beauty. And, it was said, a human who wandered into the gardens of Silvanesti could not leave, but stayed forever, enraptured, caught in a beautiful dream.

All this was known to Tanis only through legend, of course, for none of the Qualinesti had set foot in their ancient home since the Kinslayer wars. No human, it was believed, had been allowed in Silvanesti since a hundred years before that.

"What about the stories," Tanis asked Alhana as they flew above the aspens on the backs of the griffons, "the stories of humans trapped by the beauty of Silvanesti, unable to leave? Do my friends dare go to this land?"

Alhana glanced back at him.

"I knew humans were weak," she said coldly, "but I did not think they were *that* weak. It is true humans do not come to Silvanesti, but that is because we keep them out. We certainly wouldn't want to keep any in. If I thought there was danger of that, I would not allow you into my homeland."

"Not even Sturm?" he couldn't help asking wryly, nettled by her stinging tone.

But he was not prepared for the answer. Alhana twisted to face him, whipping around so fast her long black hair flailed his skin. Her face was so pale with anger, it seemed translucent and he could see the veins pulse beneath her skin. Her dark eyes seemed to swallow him in their black depths.

"Never speak of that to me!" she said through clenched teeth and white lips. "Never speak of him!"

"But last night—" Tanis faltered, astonished, putting his hand to his burning cheek.

"Last night never happened," Alhana said. "I was weak, tired, frightened. As I was when . . . when I met Sturm, the knight. I regret speaking of him to you. I regret telling you of the Starjewel."

"Do you regret giving it to him?" Tanis asked.

"I regret the day I set foot in Tarsis," Alhana said in a low, passionate voice. "I wish I had never gone there! Never!" She turned away abruptly, leaving Tanis to dark thoughts.

The companions had just reached the river, within sight of the tall Tower of the Stars, shining like a strand of pearls twisting into the sun, when the griffons suddenly halted their flight. Tanis, glancing ahead, could see no sign of danger. But their griffons continued to descend rapidly.

Indeed, it seemed hard to believe that Silvanesti had been under attack. There were no thin columns of campfire smoke rising into the air, as there would be if the draconians occupied the country. The land was not blackened and ruined. He could see, below him, the green of the aspens gleaming in the sunlight. Here and there, the marble buildings dotted the forest with their white splendor.

"No!" Alhana spoke to the griffons in elven. "I command you! Keep going! I must reach the Tower!"

But the griffons circled lower and lower, ignoring her.

"What is it?" Tanis asked. "Why are we stopping? We're in sight of the Tower. What's the matter?" He looked all around. "I see nothing to be concerned over."

"They refuse to go on," Alhana said, her face drawn with worry. "They won't tell me why, only that we must travel on our own from here. I don't understand this."

Tanis didn't like it. Griffons were known as fierce, independent creatures, but once their loyalty was gained, they served their masters with undying devotion. The elven royalty of Silvanesti have always tamed griffons for their use. Though smaller than dragons, the griffons' lightning speed, sharp talons, tearing beak, and lion-clawed hind feet made them enemies to be respected. There was little they feared on Krynn, so Tanis had heard. These griffons he remembered, had flown into Tarsis through swarms of dragons without apparent fear.

Yet now the griffons were obviously afraid. They landed on the banks of the river, refusing all of Alhana's angry, imperious commands to fly farther. Instead, they moodily preened themselves and steadfastly refused to obey.

Finally there was nothing for the companions to do but climb off the griffons' backs and unload their supplies. Then the bird-lion creatures, with fierce, apologetic dignity, spread their wings and soared away.

"Well, that is that," said Alhana sharply, ignoring the angry glances she felt cast at her. "We shall simply have to walk, that's all. The way is not far."

The companions stood stranded upon the riverbank, staring across the sparkling water into the forest beyond. None of them spoke. All of them were tense, alert, searching for trouble. But all they saw were the aspen trees glistening in the last, lingering rays of sunset. The river murmured as it lapped on the shore. Though the aspens were green still, the silence of winter blanketed the land.

"I thought you said your people fled because they were under siege?" Tanis said to Alhana finally.

"If this land is under control of dragons, I'm a gully dwarf!" Caramon snorted.

"We were!" Alhana answered, her eyes scanning the sunlit forest.

"Dragons filled the skies, as in Tarsis! The dragonmen entered our beloved woods, burning, destroying—" Her voice died.

Caramon leaned near Riverwind and muttered, "Wild goose chase!"

The Plainsman scowled. "If it's nothing more than that, we'll be fortunate," he said, his eyes on the elfmaid. "Why did she bring us here? Perhaps it's a trap."

Caramon considered this a moment, then glanced uneasily at his brother, who had not spoken or moved or taken his strange eyes from the forest since the griffons left. The big warrior loosened his sword in its scabbard and moved a step nearer Tika. Almost accidentally, it seemed, their two hands clasped. Tika cast a fearful look at Raistlin but held onto Caramon tightly.

The mage just stared fixedly into the wilderness.

"Tanis!" Alhana said suddenly, forgetting herself in her joy and putting her hand on his arm. "Maybe it worked! Maybe my father defeated them, and we can come home! Oh, Tanis—" She trembled with excitement. "We've got to cross the river and find out! Come! The ferry landing's down around the bend—"

"Alhana, wait!" Tanis called, but she was already running along the smooth, grassy bank, her long full skirts fluttering around her ankles. "Alhana! Damn it. Caramon and Riverwind, go after her. Goldmoon, try to talk some sense into her."

Riverwind and Caramon exchanged uneasy glances, but they did as Tanis ordered, running along the riverbank after Alhana. Goldmoon and Tika followed more slowly.

"Who knows what's in these woods?" Tanis muttered. "Raistlin—"

The mage did not seem to hear. Tanis moved closer. "Raistlin?" he repeated, seeing the mage's abstracted stare.

Raistlin stared at him blankly, as if waking from a dream. Then the mage became aware of someone speaking to him. He lowered his eyes.

"What is it, Raistlin?" Tanis asked. "What do you sense?"

"Nothing, Tanis," the mage replied.

Tanis blinked. "Nothing?" he repeated.

"It is like an impenetrable fog, a blank wall," Raistlin whispered. "I see nothing, sense nothing."

Tanis stared at him intently, and suddenly he knew Raistlin was lying. But why? The mage returned the half-elf's gaze with equanimity, even a small, twisted smile on his thin lips, as if he knew Tanis didn't believe him but really didn't care.

"Raistlin," Tanis said softly, "suppose Lorac, the elfking, tried to use the dragon orb—what would happen?"

The mage lifted his eyes to stare into the forest. "Do you think that is possible?" he asked.

"Yes," Tanis said, "from what little Alhana told me, during the Tests in the Tower of High Sorcery at Istar, a dragon orb spoke to Lorac, asking him to rescue it from the impending disaster."

"And he obeyed it?" Raistlin asked, his voice as soft as the murmuring water of the ancient river.

"Yes. He brought it to Silvanesti."

"So this is the dragon orb of Istar," Raistlin whispered. His eyes narrowed, and then he sighed, a sigh of longing. "I know nothing about the dragon orbs," he remarked, coolly, "except what I told you. But I know this, Half-Elf—none of us will come out of Silvanesti unscathed, if we come out at all."

"What do you mean? What danger is there?"

"What does it matter what danger I see?" Raistlin asked, folding his hands in the sleeves of his red robes. "We must enter Silvanesti. You know it as well as I. Or will you forego the chance to find a dragon orb?"

"But if you see danger, tell us! We could at least enter prepared—"Tanis began angrily.

"Then prepare," Raistlin whispered softly, and he turned away and began to walk slowly along the sandy beach after his brother.

The companions crossed the river just as the last rays of the sun flickered among the leaves of the aspens on the opposite bank. And then the fabled forest of Silvanesti was gradually swamped by darkness. The shadows of night flowed among the feet of the trees like the dark water flowing beneath the keel of the ferry boat.

Their journey was slow. The ferry—an ornately carved, flat-bottomed boat connected to both shores by an elaborate system of ropes and pulleys, seemed at first to be in good condition. But once they set foot on board and began to cross the ancient river, they discovered that the ropes were rotting. The boat began to decay before their eyes. The river itself seemed to change. Reddish-brown water seeped through the hull, tainted with the faint smell of blood.

They had just stepped out of the boat on the opposite bank and were unloading their supplies, when the frayed ropes sagged and gave way.

The river swept the ferry boat downstream in an instant. Twilight vanished at the same moment, and night swallowed them. Although the sky was clear, without a cloud to mar its dark surface, there were no stars visible. Neither the red nor the silver moon rose. The only light came from the river, which seemed to gleam with an unwholesome brilliance, like a ghoul.

"Raistlin, your staff," Tanis said. His voice echoed too loudly through the silent forest. Even Caramon cringed.

"Shirak." Raistlin spoke the word of command and the crystal globe clutched in the disembodied dragon's claw flared into light. But it was a cold, pale light. The only thing it seemed to illuminate were the mage's strange, hourglass eyes.

"We must enter the woods," Raistlin said in a shaking voice. Turning, he stumbled toward the dark wilderness.

No one else spoke or moved. They stood on the bank, fear overtaking them. There was no reason for it, and it was all the more frightening because it was illogical. Fear crept up on them from the ground. Fear flowed through their limbs, turning the bowels to water, sapping the strength of heart and muscle, eating into the brain.

Fear of what? There was nothing, nothing there! Nothing to be afraid of, yet all of them were more terrified of this nothing than they had been of anything before in their lives.

"Raistlin's right. We've—got to—get into the woods—find shelter . . ." Tanis spoke with an effort, his teeth chattering. "F-follow Raistlin."

Shaking, he staggered forward, not knowing if anyone followed, not caring. Behind him, he could hear Tika whimper and Goldmoon trying to pray through lips that would not form words. He heard Caramon shout for his brother to stop and Riverwind cry out in terror, but it didn't matter. He had to run, get away from here! His only guidance was the light of Raistlin's staff.

Desperately, he stumbled after the mage into the woods. But when Tanis reached the trees, he found his strength was gone. He was too scared to move. Trembling, he sank down on his knees, then pitched forward, his hands clutching at the ground.

"Raistlin!" His throat was torn by a ragged scream.

But the mage could not help. The last thing Tanis saw was the light from Raistlin's staff falling slowly to the ground, slowly, and more slowly, released by the young mage's limp, seemingly lifeless hand.

The trees. The beautiful trees of Silvanesti. Trees fashioned and coaxed through centuries into groves of wonder and enchantment. All around Tanis were the trees. But these trees now turned upon their masters, becoming living groves of horror. A noxious green light filtered through the shivering leaves.

Tanis stared about in horror. Many strange and terrible sights he had seen in his life, but nothing like this. This, he thought, might drive him insane. He turned this way and that, frantically, but there was no escape. All around were the trees—the trees of Silvanesti. Hideously changed.

The soul of every tree around him appeared trapped in torment, imprisoned within the trunk. The twisted branches of the tree were the limbs of its spirit, contorted in agony. The grasping roots clawed the ground in hopeless attempts to flee. The sap of the living trees flowed from huge gashes in the trunk. The rustling of its leaves were cries of pain and terror. The trees of Silvanesti wept blood.

Tanis had no idea where he was or how long he had been here. He remembered he had begun walking toward the Tower of the Stars that he could see rising above the branches of the aspens. He had walked and walked, and nothing had stopped him. Then he'd heard the kender shriek in terror, like the scream of some small animal being tortured. Turning, he saw Tasslehoff pointing at the trees. Tanis, staring horrified at the trees, only eventually comprehended that Tasslehoff wasn't supposed to be here. And there was Sturm, ashen with fear, and Laurana, weeping in despair, and Flint, his eyes wide and staring.

Tanis embraced Laurana, and his arms encompassed flesh and blood, but still he knew she *was not there*—even as he held her, and the knowledge was terrifying.

Then, as he stood there in the grove that was like a prison of the damned, the horror increased. Animals bounded out from among the tormented trees and fell upon the companions.

Tanis drew his sword to strike back, but the weapon shook in his trembling hand, and he was forced to avert his eyes for the living animals had themselves been twisted and misshapen into hideous aspects of undying death.

Riding among the misshapen beasts were legions of elven warriors, their skull-like features hideous to behold. No eyes glittered in the hollow sockets of their faces, no flesh covered the delicate bones of their hands. They rode among the companions with brightly burning swords that drew living blood. But when any weapon struck them, they disappeared into nothing.

The wounds they inflicted, however, were real. Caramon, battling a wolf with snakes growing out of its body, looked up to see one of the elven warriors bearing down on him, a shining spear in his fleshless hand. He screamed to his brother for help.

Raistlin spoke, *"Ast kiranann kair Soth-aran/Suh kali Jalaran."* A ball of flame flashed from the mage's hands to burst directly upon the elf—without effect. Its spear, driven by incredible force, pierced Caramon's armor, entering his body, nailing him to the tree behind.

The elven warrior yanked his weapon free from the big man's shoulder. Caramon slumped to the ground, his life's blood mingling with the tree's blood. Raistlin, with a fury that surprised him, drew the silver dagger from the leather thong he wore hidden on his arm and flung it at the elf. The blade pricked its undead spirit and the elven warrior, horse and all, vanished into air. Yet Caramon lay upon the ground, his arm hanging from his body by only a thin strip of flesh.

Goldmoon knelt to heal him, but she stumbled over her prayers, her faith failing her amid the horror.

"Help me, Mishakal," Goldmoon prayed. "Help me to help my friend."

The dreadful wound closed. Though blood still seeped from it, trickling down Caramon's arm, death loosed its grip on the warrior. Raistlin knelt beside his brother and started to speak to him. Then suddenly the mage fell silent. He stared past Caramon into the trees, his strange eyes widening with disbelief.

"*You!*" Raistlin whispered.

"Who is it?" Caramon asked weakly, hearing a thrill of horror and fear in Raistlin's voice. The big man peered into the green light but could see nothing. "Who do you mean?"

But Raistlin, intent upon another conversation, did not answer.

"I need your aid," the mage said sternly. "Now, as before."

Caramon saw his brother stretch out his hand, as though reaching across a great gap, and was consumed with fear without knowing why.

"No, Raist!" he cried, clutching at his brother in panic. Raistlin's hand dropped.

"Our bargain remains. What? You ask for more?" Raistlin was silent a moment, then he sighed. "Name it!"

For long moments, the mage listened, absorbing. Caramon, watching him with loving anxiety, saw his brother's thin metallic-tinged face grow deathly pale. Raistlin closed his eyes, swallowing as though drinking his bitter herbal brew. Finally he bowed his head.

"I accept."

Caramon cried out in horror as he saw Raistlin's robes, the red robes that marked his neutrality in the world, begin to deepen to crimson, then darken to a blood red, and then darken more—to black.

"I accept this,"Raistlin repeated more calmly, "with the understanding that the future can be changed. What must we do?"

He listened. Caramon clutched his arm, moaning in agony.

"How do we get through to the Tower alive?" Raistlin asked his unseen instructor. Once more he attended carefully, then nodded. "And I will be given what I need? Very well. Farewell then, if such a thing is possible for you on your dark journey."

Raistlin rose to his feet, his black robes rustling around him. Ignoring Caramon's sobs and Goldmoon's terrified gasp as she saw him, the mage went in search of Tanis. He found the half-elf, back against a tree, battling a host of elven warriors.

Calmly, Raistlin reached into his pouch and drew forth a bit of rabbit fur and a small amber rod. Rubbing these together in his left palm, he held forth his right hand and spoke. "*Ast kiranann kair Gadurm Sotharn/Suh kali Jalaran.*"

Bolts of lightning shot from his fingertips, streaking through the green-tinted air, striking the elven warriors. As before, they vanished. Tanis stumbled backward, exhausted.

Raistlin stood in the center of a clearing of the distorted, tormented trees.

"Come around me!" the mage commanded his companions.

Tanis hesitated. Elven warriors hovered on the fringes of the clearing.

They surged forward to attack, but Raistlin raised his hand, and they stopped as though crashing against an unseen wall.

"Come to stand near me." The companions were astonished to hear Raistlin speak—for the first time since his Tests—in a normal voice."Hurry," he added, "they will not attack now. They fear me. But I cannot hold them back long."

Tanis came forward, his face pale beneath the red beard, blood dribbling from a wound on his head. Goldmoon helped Caramon stagger forward. He clutched his bleeding arm as his face was twisted in pain. Slowly, one by one, the other companions crept forward. Finally, only Sturm stood outside the circle.

"I always knew it would come to this," the knight said slowly. "I will die before I place myself under your protection, Raistlin."

And with that, the knight turned and walked deeper into the forest. Tanis saw the leader of the elven undead make a gesture, detailing some of his ghastly band to follow. The half-elf started after, then stopped as he felt a surprisingly strong hand grip his arm.

"Let him go," the mage said sternly, "or we are all lost. I have information to impart and my time is limited. We must make our way through this forest to the Tower of the Stars. We must walk the way of death, for every hideous creature ever conceived in the twisted, tortured dreams of mortals will arise to stop us. But know this—we walk in a *dream*, Lorac's nightmare. And our own nightmares as well. Visions of the future can arise to help us, or hinder. Remember, that though our bodies are awake, our minds sleep. Death exists only in our minds—unless we believe otherwise."

"Then why can't we wake up?" Tanis demanded angrily.

"Because Lorac's belief in the dream is too strong and your belief too weak. When you are firmly convinced, beyond doubt, that this is a dream, you will return to reality."

"If this is true," Tanis said, "and you're convinced it is a dream, why don't you awaken?"

"Perhaps," Raistlin said, smiling, "I choose not to."

"I don't understand!" Tanis cried in bitter frustration.

"You will," Raistlin predicted grimly, "or you will die. In which case, it won't matter."

10

Waking dreams. Future visions.

gnoring the horrified stares of his companions, Raistlin walked to his brother, who stood clutching his bleeding arm.

"I will take care of him," Raistlin said to Goldmoon, putting his own black-robed arm around his twin.

"No," Caramon gasped, "you're not strong en—" His voice died as he felt his brother's arm support him.

"I am strong enough now, Caramon," Raistlin said gently, his very gentleness sending a shiver through the warrior's body. "Lean on me, my brother."

Weak from pain and fear, for the first time in his life Caramon leaned on Raistlin. The mage supported him as, together, they starting walking through the hideous forest.

"What's happening, Raist?" Caramon asked, choking. "Why do you wear the Black Robes? And your voice—"

"Save your breath, my brother," Raistlin advised softly.

The two traveled deeper into the forest, and the undead elven warriors stared menacingly at them from the trees. They could see the hatred the dead bear the living, see it flicker in the hollow eye sockets of the undead warriors. But none dared attack the black-robed mage. Caramon felt his life's blood well thick and warm from between his fingers. As he watched it drip upon the dead, slime-coated leaves beneath his feet, he grew weaker and weaker. He had the fevered impression that the black shadow of himself gained in strength even as he lost it.

Tanis hurried through the forest, searching for Sturm. He found him fighting off a group of shimmering elven warriors.

"It's a dream," Tanis shouted to Sturm, who stabbed and slashed at the undead creatures. Every time he struck one, it vanished, only to re-appear once more. The half-elf drew his sword, running to fight at Sturm's side.

"Bah!" the knight grunted, then gasped in pain as an arrow thudded into his arm. The wound was not deep, because the chain mail protected him, but it bled freely. "Is this dreaming?" Sturm said, yanking out the blood-stained shaft.

Tanis jumped in front of the knight, keeping their foes back until Sturm could stanch the flow of blood.

"Raistlin told us—" Tanis began.

"Raistlin! Hah! Look at his robes, Tanis!"

"But you're here! In Silvanesti!" Tanis protested in confusion. He had the strangest feeling he was arguing with himself. "Alhana said you were in Ice Wall!"

The knight shrugged. "Perhaps I was sent to help you."

All right. It's a dream, Tanis told himself. I *will* wake up.

But there was no change. The elves were still there, still fighting. Sturm must be right. Raistlin *had* lied. Just as he had lied before they entered the forest. But why? To what purpose?

Then Tanis knew. The dragon orb!

"We've got to reach the Tower before Raistlin!" Tanis cried to Sturm. "I know what the mage is after!"

The knight could do nothing more than nod. It seemed to Tanis that from then on they did nothing but fight for every inch of ground they gained. Time and again, the two warriors forced the elven undead back, only to be attacked in ever-increasing numbers. Time passed, they knew, but they had no conception of its passing. One moment the sun shone through the stifling green haze. Then night's shadows hovered over the land like the wings of dragons.

Then, just as the darkness deepened, Sturm and Tanis saw the Tower. Built of marble, the tall Tower glistened white. It stood alone in a clearing, reaching up to the heavens like a skeletal finger clawing up from the grave.

At sight of the Tower, both men began to run. Though weak and exhausted, neither wanted to be in these deadly woods after nightfall. The elven warriors—seeing their prey escaping—screamed in rage and charged after them.

Tanis ran until it seemed his lungs would burst with pain. Sturm ran ahead of him, slashing at the undead who appeared before them, trying to block their path. Just as Tanis neared the Tower, he felt a tree root twist itself around his boot. He pitched headlong onto the ground.

Frantically Tanis fought to free himself, but the root held him fast. Tanis struggled helplessly as an undead elf, his face twisted grotesquely, raised a spear to drive it through Tanis's body. Suddenly the elf's eyes widened, the spear fell from nerveless fingers as a sword punctured its transparent body. The elf vanished with a shriek.

Tanis looked up to see who had saved his life. It was a strange warrior, strange—yet familiar. The warrior removed his helm, and Tanis stared into bright brown eyes!

"Kitiara!" he gasped in shock. "You're here! How? Why?"

"I heard you needed some help," Kit said, her crooked smile as charming as ever. "Seems I was right." She reached out her hand. He grasped it, doubting as she pulled him to his feet. But she was flesh and blood. "Who's that ahead? Sturm? Wonderful! Like old times! Shall we go to the Tower?" she asked Tanis, laughing at the surprise on his face.

Riverwind fought alone, battling legions of undead elven warriors. He knew he could not take much more. Then he heard a clear call. Raising his eyes, he saw Qué-Shu tribesmen! He cried out joyfully. But, to his horror, he saw them turning their arrows upon him.

"No!" he shouted in Qué-Shu. "Don't you recognize me? I—"

The Qué-Shu warriors answered only with their bowstrings. Riverwind felt shaft after feathered shaft sink into his body.

"You brought the blue crystal staff among us!" they cried. "Your fault! The destruction of our village was your fault!"

"I didn't mean to," he whispered as he slumped to the ground. "I didn't know. Forgive me."

Tika hacked and slashed her way through elven warriors only to see them turn suddenly into draconians! Their reptile eyes gleamed red, their tongues licked their swords. Fear chilled the barmaid. Stumbling, she bumped into Sturm. Angrily the knight whirled, ordering her out of his way. She staggered back and jostled Flint. The dwarf impatiently shoved her aside.

Blinded by tears, panic-stricken at the sight of the draconians, who sprang back into battle full-grown from their own dead bodies, Tika lost control. In her fear, she stabbed wildly at anything that moved.

Only when she looked up and saw Raistlin standing before her in his black robes did she come to her senses. The mage said nothing, he simply pointed downward. Flint lay dead at her feet, pierced by her own sword.

I led them here, Flint thought. This is my responsibility. I'm the eldest. I'll get them out.

The dwarf hefted his battle-axe and yelled a challenge to the elven warriors before him. But they just laughed.

Angrily, Flint strode forward—only to find himself walking stiffly. His knee joints were swollen and hurt abominably. His gnarled fingers trembled with a palsy that made him lose his grip on the battle-axe. His breath came short. And then Flint knew why the elves weren't attacking: they were letting old age finish him.

Even as he realized this, Flint felt his mind begin to wander. His vision blurred. Patting his vest pocket, he wondered where he had put those confounded spectacles. A shape loomed before him, a familiar shape. Was it Tika? Without his glasses, he couldn't see—

Goldmoon ran among the twisted, tortured trees. Lost and alone, she searched desperately for her friends. Far away, she heard Riverwind calling for her above the ringing clash of swords. Then she heard his call cut off in a bubble of agony. Frantically she dashed forward, fighting her way through the brambles until her hands and face were bleeding. At last she found Riverwind. The warrior lay upon the ground, pierced by many arrows—arrows she recognized!

Running to him, she knelt beside him. "Heal him, Mishakal," she prayed, as she had prayed so often.

But nothing happened. The color did not return to Riverwind's ashen face. His eyes remained locked, staring fixedly into the green tinged sky.

"Why don't you answer? Heal him!" Goldmoon cried to the gods. And then she knew. "No!" she screamed. "Punish me! I am the one who has doubted. I am the one who has questioned! I saw Tarsis destroyed, children dying in agony! How could you allow that? I try to have faith, but I cannot help doubting when I see such horrors! Do not punish him." Weeping, she bent over the lifeless body of her husband. She did not see the elven warriors closing in around her.

Tasslehoff, fascinated by the horrible wonders around him, wandered off the path, and then discovered that—somehow—his friends had managed to lose him. The undead did not bother him. They who fed off fear felt no fear in his small body.

Finally, after roaming here and there for nearly a day, the kender reached the doors to the Tower of the Stars. Here his lighthearted journey came to a sudden halt, for he had found his friends—one of them at least.

Backed up against the closed doors, Tika fought for her life against a host of misshapen, nightmare-begotten foes. Tas saw that if she could get inside the Tower, she would be safe. Dashing forward, his small body flitting easily through the melee, he reached the door and began to examine the lock while Tika held the elves back with her wildly swinging sword.

"Hurry, Tas!" she cried breathlessly.

It was an easy lock to open; with such a simplistic trap to protect it, Tas was surprised that the elves even bothered.

"I should have this lock picked in seconds," he announced. Just as he set to work, however, something bumped him from behind, causing him to fumble.

"Hey!" he shouted at Tika irritably, turning around. "Be a little more careful—" He stopped short, horrified. Tika lay at his feet, blood flowing into her red curls.

"No, not Tika!" Tas whispered. Maybe she was only wounded! Maybe if he got her inside the Tower, someone could help her. Tears dimmed his vision, his hands shook.

I've got to hurry, Tas thought frantically. Why won't this open? It's so simple! Furious, he tore at the lock.

He felt a small prick in his finger just as the lock clicked. The door to the Tower began to swing open. But Tasslehoff just stared at his finger where a tiny spot of blood glistened. He looked back at the lock where a small, golden needle sparkled. A simple lock, a simple trap. He'd sprung them both. And, as the first effects of the poison surged with a terrible warmness through his body, he looked down to see he was too late. Tika was dead.

Raistlin and his brother made their way through the forest without injury. Caramon watched in growing amazement as Raistlin drove back the evil creatures that assailed them; sometimes with feats of incredible magic, sometimes through the sheer force of his will.

Raistlin was kind and gentle and solicitous. Caramon was forced to stop frequently as the day waned. By twilight, it was all Caramon could do to drag one foot in front of the other, even leaning upon his brother for support. And as Caramon grew ever weaker, Raistlin grew stronger.

Finally, when night's shadows fell, bringing a merciful end to the tortured green day, the twins reached the Tower. Here they stopped. Caramon was feverish and in pain.

"I've got to rest, Raist," he gasped. "Put me down."

"Certainly, my brother," Raistlin said gently. He helped Caramon lean against the pearl wall of the Tower, then regarded his brother with cool, glittering eyes.

"Farewell, Caramon," he said.

Caramon looked at his twin in disbelief. Within the shadows of the trees, the warrior could see the undead elves, who had followed them at a respectful distance, creep closer as they realized the mage who had warded them off was leaving.

"Raist," Caramon said slowly, "you can't leave me here! I can't fight them. I don't have the strength! I need you!"

"Perhaps, but you see, my brother, I no longer need you. I have gained your strength. Now, finally, I am as I was meant to be but for nature's cruel trick—one whole person."

As Caramon stared, uncomprehending, Raistlin turned to leave.

"Raist!"

Caramon's agonized cry halted him. Raistlin stopped and gazed back at his twin, his golden eyes all that were visible from within the depths of his black hood.

"How does it feel to be weak and afraid, my brother?" he asked softly. Turning, Raistlin walked to the Tower entrance where Tika and Tas lay dead. Raistlin stepped over the kender's body and vanished into the darkness.

Sturm and Tanis and Kitiara, reaching the Tower, saw a body lying on the grass at its base. Phantom shapes of undead elves were starting to surround it, shrieking and yelling, hacking at it with their cold swords.

"Caramon!" Tanis cried, heartsick.

"And where's his brother?" Sturm asked with a sidelong glance at Kitiara. "Left him to die, no doubt."

Tanis shook his head as they ran forward to aid the warrior. Wielding their swords, Sturm and Kitiara kept the elves at bay while Tanis knelt beside the mortally wounded warrior.

Caramon lifted his glazed eyes and met Tanis's, barely recognizing him through the bloody haze that dimmed his vision. He tried desperately to talk.

"Protect Raistlin, Tanis—" Caramon choked on his own blood—"since I won't be there now. Watch over him."

"Watch over *Raistlin?*" Tanis repeated furiously. "He left you here, to die!" Tanis held Caramon in his arms.

Caramon closed his eyes wearily. "No, you're wrong, Tanis. I sent him away. . . ." The warrior's head slumped forward.

Night's shadows closed over them. The elves had disappeared. Sturm and Kit came to stand beside the dead warrior.

"What did I tell you?" Sturm asked harshly.

"Poor Caramon," Kitiara whispered, bending down near him. "Somehow I always guessed it would end this way." She was silent for a moment, then spoke softly. "So my little Raistlin has become truly powerful," she mused, almost to herself.

"At the cost of your brother's life!"

Kitiara looked at Tanis as if perplexed at his meaning. Then, shrugging, she glanced down at Caramon, who lay in a pool of his own blood. "Poor kid," she said softly.

Sturm covered Caramon's body with his cloak, then they sought the entrance to the Tower.

"Tanis—" Sturm said, pointing.

"Oh, no. Not Tas," Tanis murmured. "And Tika."

The kender's body lay just inside the doorway, his small limbs twisted by convulsions from the poison. Near him lay the barmaid, her red curls matted with blood. Tanis knelt beside them. One of the kender's packs had opened in his death throes, its contents scattered. Tanis caught sight of a glint of gold. Reaching down, he picked up the ring of elven make, carved in the shape of ivy leaves. His vision blurred, tears filled his eyes as he covered his face with his hands.

"There's nothing we can do, Tanis." Sturm put his hand on his friend's shoulder. "We've got to keep going and put an end to this. If I do nothing else, I'll live to kill Raistlin."

Death is in the mind. This is a dream, Tanis repeated. But it was Raistlin's words he was remembering, and he'd seen what the mage had become.

I will wake up, he thought, bending the full force of his will to believing it was a dream. But when he opened his eyes, the kender's body still lay on the floor.

Clasping the ring in his hand, Tanis followed Kit and Sturm into a dank, slime-covered, marble hallway. Paintings hung in golden frames upon marble walls. Tall, stained-glass windows let in a lurid, ghastly light. The hallway might have been beautiful once, but now even the paintings on the walls appeared distorted, portraying horrifying visions of death. Gradually, as the three walked, they became aware of a brilliant green light emanating from a room at the end of the corridor.

They could feel a malevolence radiate from that green light, beating upon their faces with the warmth of a perverted sun.

"The center of the evil," Tanis said. Anger filled his heart—anger, grief, and a burning desire for revenge. He started to run forward, but the green-tainted air seemed to press upon him, holding him back until each step was an effort.

Next to him, Kitiara staggered. Tanis put his arm around her, though he could barely find the strength to move himself. Kit's face was drenched with sweat, the dark hair curled around her damp forehead. Her eyes were wide with fear—the first time Tanis ever saw her afraid. Sturm's breath came in gasps as the knight struggled forward, weighted down by his armor.

At first, they seemed to make no progress at all. Then slowly, they realized they were inching forward, drawing nearer and nearer the green-lit room. Its bright light was now painful to their eyes, and movement exacted a terrible toll. Exhaustion claimed them, muscles ached, lungs burned.

Just as Tanis realized he could not take another step, he heard a voice call his name. Lifting his aching head, he saw Laurana standing in front of him, her elven sword in her hand. The heaviness seemingly had no effect on her at all, for she ran to him with a glad cry.

"Tanthalas! You're all right! I've been waiting—"

She broke off, her eyes on the woman clasped in Tanis's arm.

"Who—" Laurana started to ask, then suddenly, somehow she knew. This was the human woman, Kitiara. The woman Tanis loved. Laurana's face went white, then red.

"Laurana—" Tanis began, feeling confusion and guilt sweep over him, hating himself for causing her pain.

"Tanis! Sturm!" Kitiara cried, pointing.

Startled by the fear in her voice, all of them turned, staring down the green-lit marble corridor.

"*Drakus Tsaro, deghnyah!*" Sturm intoned in Solamnic.

At the end of the corridor loomed a gigantic green dragon. His name was Cyan Bloodbane, and he was one of the largest dragons on Krynn. Only the Great Red herself was larger. Snaking his head through a doorway, he blotted out the blinding green light with his hulking body. Cyan smelled steel and human flesh and elven blood. He peered with fiery eyes at the group.

They could not move. Overcome with the dragon fear, they could only stand and stare as the dragon crashed through the doorway, shattering the marble wall as easily as if it had been baked mud. His mouth gaping wide, Cyan moved down the corridor.

There was nothing they could do. Their weapons dangled from hands gone nerveless. Their thoughts were of death. But, even as the dragon neared, a dark shadowy figure crept from the deeper shadows of an unseen doorway and came to stand before them, facing them.

"Raistlin!" Sturm said quietly. "By all the gods, you will pay for your brother's life!"

Forgetting the dragon, remembering only Caramon's lifeless body, the knight sprang toward the mage, his sword raised. Raistlin just stared at him coldly.

"Kill me, knight, and you doom yourself and the others to death, for through my magic—and my magic alone—will you be able to defeat Cyan Bloodbane!"

"Hold, Sturm!" Though his soul was filled with loathing, Tanis knew the mage was right. He could feel Raistlin's power radiate through the black robes. "We need his help."

"No," Sturm said, shaking his head and backing away as Raistlin neared the group. "I said before—I will not rely on his protection. Not now. Farewell, Tanis."

Before any of them could stop him, Sturm walked past Raistlin toward Cyan Bloodbane.The great dragon's head wove back and forth in eager anticipation of this first challenge to his power since he had conquered Silvanesti.

Tanis clutched Raistlin. "Do something!"

"The knight is in my way. Whatever spell I cast will destroy him, too," Raistlin answered.

"Sturm!" Tanis shouted, his voice echoing mournfully.

The knight hesitated. He was listening, but not to Tanis's voice. What he heard was the clear, clarion call of a trumpet, its music cold as the air from the snow-covered mountains of his homeland. Pure and crisp, the trumpet call rose bravely above the darkness and death and despair to pierce his heart.

Sturm answered the trumpet's call with a glad battle cry. He raised his sword—the sword of his father, its antique blade twined with the king-fisher and the rose. Silver moonlight streaming through a broken window caught the sword in a pure-white radiance that shredded the noxious green air.

Again the trumpet sounded, and again Sturm answered, but this time his voice faltered, for the trumpet call he heard had changed tone. No longer sweet and pure, it was braying and harsh and shrill.

No! thought Sturm in horror as he neared the dragon. Those were the horns of the enemy! He had been lured into a trap! Around him now he could see draconian soldiers, creeping from behind the dragon, laughing cruelly at his gullibility.

Sturm stopped, gripping his sword in a hand that was sweating inside its glove. The dragon loomed above him, a creature undefeatable, sur-rounded by masses of its troops, slavering and licking its jowls with its curled tongue.

Fear knotted Sturm's stomach; his skin grew cold and clammy. The horn call sounded a third time, terrible and evil. It was all over. It had all been for nothing. Death, ignominious defeat awaited him. Despair descend-ing, he looked around fearfully. Where was Tanis? He needed Tanis, but he could not find him. Desperately he repeated the code of the knights, *My Honor Is My Life*, but the words sounded hollow and meaningless in his ears. He was not a knight. What did the Code mean to him? He had been living a lie! Sturm's sword arm wavered, then dropped; his sword fell from his hand and he sank to his knees, shivering and weeping like a child, hiding his head from the terror before him.

With one swipe of his shining talons, Cyan Bloodbane ended Sturm's life, impaling the knight's body upon a bloodstained claw. Disdainfully, Cyan shook the wretched human to the floor while the draconians swept shrieking toward the knight's still-living body, intent upon hacking it to pieces.

But they found their way blocked. A bright figure, shining silver in the moonlight, ran to the knight's body. Reaching down swiftly, Laurana lifted Sturm's sword. Then, straightening, she faced the draconians.

"Touch him and you will die," she said through her tears.

"Laurana!" Tanis screamed and tried to run forward to help her. But draconians sprang at him. He slashed at them desperately, trying to reach the elfmaid. Just when he had won through, he heard Kitiara call his name. Whirling, he saw her being beaten back by four draconians. The half-elf stopped in agony, hesitating, and at that moment Laurana fell across Sturm's body, her own body pierced by draconian swords.

"No! Laurana!" Tanis shouted. Starting to go to her, he heard Kitiara cry out again. He stopped, turning. Clutching at his head, he stood irresolute and helpless, forced to watch as Kitiara fell beneath the enemy.

The half-elf sobbed in frenzy, feeling himself begin to sink into madness, longing for death to end this pain. He clutched the magic sword of Kith-Kanan and rushed toward the dragon, his one thought to kill and be killed.

But Raistlin blocked his path, standing in front of the dragon like a black obelisk.

Tanis fell to the floor, knowing his death was fixed. Clasping the small golden ring firmly in his hand, he waited to die.

Then he heard the mage chanting strange and powerful words. He heard the dragon roar in rage. The two were battling, but Tanis didn't care. With eyes closed fast, he blotted out the sounds around him, blotted out life. Only one thing remained real. The golden ring he held tightly in his hand.

Suddenly Tanis became acutely conscious of the ring pressing into his palm: the metal was cool, its edges rough. He could feel the golden twisted ivy leaves bite into his flesh.

Tanis closed his hand, squeezing the ring. The gold bit into his flesh, bit deeply. Pain . . . real pain . . .

I am dreaming!

Tanis opened his eyes. Solinari's silver moonlight flooded the Tower, mingled with the red beams of Lunitari. He was lying on a cold, marble floor. His hand was clasped tightly, so tightly that pain had wakened him. Pain! The ring. The dream! Remembering the dream, Tanis sat up in terror and looked around. But the hall was empty except for one other person. Raistlin slumped against a wall, coughing.

The half-elf staggered to his feet and walked shakily toward Raistlin. As he drew nearer, he could see blood on the mage's lips. The blood gleamed red in Lunitari's light—as red as the robes that covered Raistlin's frail, shivering body.

The dream.

Tanis opened his hand. It was empty.

II

Che dream ends.

Che nightmare begins.

he half-elf stared around the hallway. It was as empty as his hand. The bodies of his friends were gone. The dragon was gone. Wind blew through a shattered wall, fluttering Raistlin's red robes about him, scattering dead aspen leaves along the floor. The half-elf walked over to Raistlin, catching the young mage in his arms as he collapsed.

"Where are they?" Tanis asked, shaking Raistlin. "Laurana? Sturm? And the others, your brother? Are they dead?" He glanced around. "And the dragon—"

"The dragon is gone. The orb sent the dragon away when it realized it could not defeat me." Pushing himself from Tanis's grasp, Raistlin stood alone, huddled against the marble wall. "It could not defeat me as I was. A child could defeat me now," he said bitterly. "As for the others"—he shrugged—"I do not know." He turned his strange eyes on Tanis. "You lived, half-elf, because your love was strong. I lived because of my ambition. We clung to reality in the midst of the nightmare. Who can say with the others?"

"Caramon's alive, then," Tanis said. "Because of his love. With his last breath, he begged me to spare your life. Tell me, mage, was this future you say we saw irreversible?"

"Why ask?" Raistlin said wearily. "Would you kill me, Tanis? Now?"

"I don't know," Tanis said softly, thinking of Caramon's dying words. "Perhaps."

Raistlin smiled bitterly. "Save your energy," he said. "The future changes as we stand here, else we are the game pieces of the gods, not their heirs, as we have been promised. But"—the mage pushed himself away from the wall—"this is far from over. We must find Lorac, and the dragon orb."

Raistlin shuffled down the hall, leaning heavily upon the Staff of Magius, its crystal lighting the darkness now that the green light had died.

Green light. Tanis stood in the hallway, lost in confusion, trying to wake up, trying to separate the dream from reality—for the dream seemed much more real than any of this did now. He stared at the shattered wall. Surely there had been a dragon? And a blinding green light at the end of the corridor? But the hallway was dark. Night had fallen. It had been morning when they started. The moons had not been up, yet now they were full. How many nights had passed? How many days?

Then Tanis heard a booming voice at other end of the corridor, near the doorway.

"Raist!"

The mage stopped, his shoulder slumped. Then he turned slowly. "My brother," he whispered.

Caramon—alive and apparently uninjured—stood in the doorway, outlined against the starry night. He stared at his twin.

Then Tanis heard Raistlin sigh softly.

"I am tired, Caramon." The mage coughed, then drew a wheezing breath. "And there is still much to be done before this nightmare is ended, before the three moons set." Raistlin extended his thin arm. "I need your help, brother."

Tanis heard Caramon heave a shuddering sob. The big man ran into the room, his sword clanking at his thigh. Reaching his brother, he put his arm around him.

Raistlin leaned on Caramon's strong arm. Together, the twins walked down the cold hallway and through the shattered wall toward the room where Tanis had seen the green light and the dragon. His heart heavy with foreboding, Tanis followed them.

The three entered the audience room of the Tower of the Stars. Tanis looked at it curiously. He had heard of its beauty all his life. The Tower of the Sun in Qualinost had been built in remembrance of this Tower—the Tower of the Stars. The two were alike, yet not alike. One was filled with light, one filled with darkness. He stared around. The Tower soared above him in marble spirals that shimmered with a pearly radiance. It had been built to collect moonlight, as the Tower of the Sun collected sunlight. Windows carved into the Tower were faceted with gems that caught and magnified the light of the two moons, Solinari and Lunitari, making red and silver moon-beams dance in the chamber. But now the gems were broken. The moon-light that filtered in was distorted, the silver turning to the pale white of a corpse, the red to blood.

Tanis, shivering, looked straight up to the top. In Qualinost, there were murals on the ceiling, portraying the sun, the constellations, and the two moons. But here there was nothing but a carved hole in the top of the Tower. Through the hole, he could see only empty blackness. The stars did not shine. It was as if a perfectly round, black sphere had appeared in the starry darkness. Before he could ponder what this portended, he heard Raistlin speak softly, and he turned.

There, in the shadows at the front of the audience chamber was Alhana's father, Lorac, the elfking. His shrunken and cadaverous body almost disappeared in a huge stone throne, fancifully carved with birds and animals. It must once have been beautiful, but now the animals' heads were skulls.

Lorac sat motionless, his head thrown back, his mouth wide in a silent scream. His hand rested upon a round crystal globe.

"Is he alive?" Tanis asked in horror.

"Yes," Raistlin answered, "undoubtedly to his sorrow."

"What's wrong with him?"

"He is living a nightmare," Raistlin answered, pointing to Lorac's hand. "There is the dragon orb. Apparently he tried to take control of it. He was not strong enough, so the orb seized control of him. The orb called Cyan Bloodbane here to guard Silvanesti, and the dragon decided to destroy it by whispering nightmares into Lorac's ear. Lorac's belief in the nightmare was so strong, his empathy with his land so great, that the nightmare became reality. Thus, it was his dream we were living when we entered. His dream—and our own. For we too came under the dragon's control when we stepped into Silvanesti."

"You knew we faced this!" Tanis accused, grabbing Raistlin by the shoulder and spinning him around. "You knew what we were walking into, there on the shores of the river—"

"Tanis," Caramon said warningly, removing the half-elf's hand. "Leave him alone."

"Perhaps," Raistlin said, rubbing his shoulder, his eyes narrow. "Perhaps not. I need not reveal my knowledge or its source to you!"

Before he could reply, Tanis heard a moan. It sounded as if it came from the base of the throne. Casting Raistlin an angry glance, Tanis turned quickly from him and stared into the shadows. Warily he approached, his sword drawn.

"Alhana!" The elfmaid crouched at her father's feet, her head in his lap, weeping. She did not seem to hear Tanis. He went to her. "Alhana," he said gently.

She looked up at him without recognition.

"Alhana," he said again.

She blinked, then shuddered, and grabbed hold of his hand as if clutching at reality.

"Half—Elven!" she whispered.

"How did you get here? What happened?"

"I heard the mage say it was a dream," Alhana answered, shivering at the memory, "and I—I refused to believe in the dream. I woke, but only to find the nightmare was real! My beautiful land filled with horrors!" She hid her face in her hands. Tanis knelt beside her and held her close.

"I made my way here. It took—days. Through the nightmare." She gripped Tanis tightly. "When I entered the Tower, the dragon caught me. He brought me here, to my father, thinking to make Lorac murder me. But not even in his nightmare could my father harm his own child. So Cyan tortured him with visions, of what he would do to me."

"And you? You saw them, too?" Tanis whispered, stroking the woman's long, dark hair with a soothing hand.

After a moment, Alhana spoke. "It wasn't so bad. I knew it was nothing but a dream. But to my poor father it was reality—" She began to sob.

The half-elf motioned to Caramon. "Take Alhana to a room where she can lie down. We'll do what we can for her father."

"I will be all right, my brother," Raistlin said in answer to Caramon's look of concern. "Do as Tanis says."

"Come, Alhana," Tanis urged her, helping her stand. She staggered with weariness. "Is there a place you can rest? You'll need your strength."

At first she started to argue, then she realized how weak she was. "Take me to my father's room," she said. "I'll show you the way." Caramon put his arm around her, and slowly they began to walk from the chamber.

Tanis turned back to Lorac. Raistlin stood before the elf king. Tanis heard the mage speaking softly to himself.

"What is it?" the half-elf said quietly. "Is he dead?"

"Who?" Raistlin started, blinking. He saw Tanis looking at Lorac. "Oh, Lorac? No, I do not believe so. Not yet."

Tanis realized the mage had been staring at the dragon orb.

"Is the orb still in control?" Tanis asked nervously, his eyes on the object they had gone through so much to find.

The dragon orb was a huge globe of crystal, at least twenty-four inches across. It sat upon a stand of gold that had been carved in hideous, twisted designs, mirroring the twisted, tormented life of Silvanesti. Though the orb must have been the source of the brilliant green light, there was now only a faint, iridescent, pulsing glow at its heart.

Raistlin's hands hovered over the globe, but, Tanis noted, he was careful not to touch it as he chanted the spidery words of magic. A faint aura of red began to surround the globe. Tanis backed away.

"Do not fear," Raistlin whispered, watching as the aura died. "It is my spell. The globe is enchanted—still. Its magic has not died with the passing of the dragon, as I thought possible. It is still in control, however."

"Control of Lorac?"

"Control of itself. It has released Lorac."

"Did you do this?" Tanis murmured. "Did you defeat it?"

"The orb is not defeated!" Raistlin said sharply. "With help, I was able to defeat the dragon. Realizing Cyan Bloodbane was losing, the orb sent him away. It let go of Lorac because it could no longer use him. But the orb is still very powerful."

"Raistlin, tell me—"

"I have no more to say, Tanis." The young mage coughed. "I must conserve my energy."

Whose help had Raistlin received? What else did he know of this orb? Tanis opened his mouth to pursue the subject, then he saw Raistlin's golden eyes flicker. The half-elf fell silent.

"We can free Lorac now," Raistlin added. Walking to the elf king, he gently removed Lorac's hand from the dragon orb, then put his slender fingers to Lorac's neck. "He lives. For the time being. The lifebeat is weak. You may come closer."

But Tanis, his eyes on the dragon orb, held back. Raistlin glanced at the half-elf, amused, then beckoned.

Reluctantly, Tanis approached. "Tell me one more thing—can the orb still be of use to us?"

For long moments, Raistlin was silent. Then, faintly, he replied, "Yes, if we dare."

Lorac drew a shivering breath, then screamed, a thin, wailing scream horrible to hear. His hands—little more than living skeletal claws—twisted and writhed. His eyes were tightly closed. In vain, Tanis tried to calm him. Lorac screamed until he was out of breath, and then he screamed silently.

"Father!" Tanis heard Alhana cry. She reappeared in the doorway of the audience chamber and pushed Caramon aside. Running to her father, she grasped his bony hands in hers. Kissing his hands, she wept, pleading for him to be silent.

"Rest, Father," she repeated over and over. "The nightmare is ended. The dragon is gone. You can sleep, Father!"

But the man's screaming continued.

"In the name of the gods!" Caramon said as he came up to them, his face pale. "I can't take much of this."

"Father!" Alhana pleaded, calling to him again and again. Slowly her beloved voice penetrated the twisted dreams that lingered on in Lorac's tortured mind. Slowly his screams died to little more than horrified whimpers. Then, as if fearing what he might see, he opened his eyes.

"Alhana, my child. Alive!" He lifted a shaking hand to touch her cheek. "It cannot be! I saw you die, Alhana. I saw you die a hundred times, each time more horrifying than the last. He killed you, Alhana. He wanted *me* to kill you. But I could not. Though I know not why, as I have killed so many." Then he caught sight of Tanis. His eyes flared open, shining with hatred.

"You!" Lorac snarled, rising from his chair, his gnarled hands clutching the sides of the throne. "You, half-elf! I killed you—or tried to. I must protect Silvanesti! I killed you! I killed those with you." Then his eyes went to Raistlin. The look of hatred was replaced by one of fear. Trembling, he shrank away from the mage. "But you, you I could not kill!"

Lorac's look of terror changed to confusion. "No," he cried. "You are not he! Your robes are not black! Who are you?" His eyes went back to Tanis. "And you? You are not a threat? What have I done?" He moaned.

"Don't, Father," Alhana pleaded, soothing him, stroking his fevered face. "You must rest now. The nightmare is ended. Silvanesti is safe."

Caramon lifted Lorac in his strong arms and carried him to his chambers. Alhana walked next to him, her father's hand held fast in her own.

Safe, Tanis thought, glancing out the windows at the tormented trees. Although the undead elven warriors no longer stalked the woods, the tortured shapes Lorac had created in his nightmare still lived. The trees contorted in agony, still wept blood. Who will live here now? Tanis wondered sadly. The elves will not return. Evil things will enter this dark forest and Lorac's nightmare will become reality.

Thinking of the nightmarish forest, Tanis suddenly wondered where his other friends were. Were they all right? What if they had believed the nightmare—as Raistlin said? Would they have truly died? His heart sinking, he knew he would have to go back into that demented forest and search for them.

Just as the half-elf began to try and force his weary body to action, his friends entered the Tower room.

"I killed him!" Tika cried, catching sight of Tanis. Her eyes were wide with grief and terror. "No! Don't touch me, Tanis. You don't know what I've done. I killed Flint! I didn't mean to, Tanis, I swear!"

As Caramon entered the room, Tika turned to him, sobbing. "I killed Flint, Caramon. Don't come near me!"

"Hush," Caramon said, gently enfolding her in his big arms. "It was a dream, Tika. That's what Raist says. The dwarf was never here. Shhh." Stroking Tika's red curls, he kissed her. Tika clung to him, Caramon clung to her, each finding comfort with the other. Gradually Tika's sobs lessened.

"My friend," Goldmoon said, reaching out to embrace Tanis.

Seeing the grave, somber expression on her face, the half-elf held her tightly, glancing questioningly at Riverwind. What had each of them dreamed? But the Plainsman only shook his head, his own face pale and grieved.

Then it occurred to Tanis that each must have lived through his or her own dream, and he suddenly remembered Kitiara! How real she had been! And Laurana, dying. Closing his eyes, Tanis laid his head against Goldmoon's. He felt Riverwind's strong arms surround them both. Their love blessed him. The horror of the dream began to recede.

And then Tanis had a terrifying thought. Lorac's dream became reality! *Would theirs?*

Behind him, Tanis heard Raistlin begin to cough. Clutching his chest, the mage sank down onto the steps leading up to Lorac's throne. Tanis saw Caramon, still holding Tika, glance at his brother in concern. But Raistlin ignored his brother. Gathering his robes around him, the mage lay down on the cold floor and closed his eyes in exhaustion.

Sighing, Caramon pressed Tika closer. Tanis watched her small shadow become part of Caramon's larger one as they stood together, their bodies outlined in the distorted silver and red beams of the fractured moonlight.

We all must sleep, Tanis thought, feeling his own eyes burn. Yet how can we? How can we ever sleep again?

12

Visions shared.

The death of Lorac.

et finally they slept. Huddled on the stone floor of the Tower of the Stars, they kept as near each other as possible. While, as they slept, others in lands cold and hostile, lands far from Silvanesti, wakened.

Laurana woke first. Starting up from a deep sleep with a cry, at first she had no idea where she was. She spoke one word—"Silvanesti!"

Flint, trembling, woke to find that his fingers still moved, the pains in his legs were no worse than usual.

Sturm woke in panic. Shaking with terror, for long moments he could only crouch beneath his blankets, shuddering. Then he heard something outside his tent. Starting up, hand on his sword, he crept forward and threw open the tent flap.

"Oh!" Laurana gasped at the sight of his haggard face.

"I'm sorry," Sturm said. "I didn't mean—" Then he saw she was shaking so she could scarcely hold her candle. "What is it?" he asked, alarmed, drawing her out of the cold.

"I—I know this sounds silly," Laurana said, flushing, "but I had the most frightening dream and I couldn't sleep."

Shivering, she allowed Sturm to lead her inside the tent. The flame of

---

115

her candle cast leaping shadows around the tent. Sturm, afraid she might drop it, took it from her.

"I didn't mean to wake you, but I heard you call out. And my dream was so real! You were in it—I saw you—"

"What is Silvanesti like?" Sturm interrupted abruptly.

Laurana stared at him. "But that's where I dreamed we were! Why did you ask? Unless . . . you dreamed of Silvanesti, too!"

Sturm wrapped his cloak around him, nodding. "I—" he began, then heard another noise outside the tent. This time, he just opened the tent flap. "Come in, Flint," he said wearily.

The dwarf stumped inside, his face flushed. He seemed embarrassed to find Laurana there, however, and stammered and stamped until Laurana smiled at him.

"We know," she said. "You had a dream. Silvanesti?"

Flint coughed, clearing his throat and wiping his face with his hand. "Apparently I'm not the only one?" he asked, staring narrowly at the other two from beneath his bushy eyebrows. "I suppose you—you want me to tell you what I dreamed?"

"No!" Sturm said hurriedly, his face pale. "No, I do not want to talk about it—ever!"

"Nor I," Laurana said softly.

Hesitantly, Flint patted her shoulder. "I'm glad," he said gruffly. "I couldn't talk about mine either. I just wanted to see if it was a dream. It seemed so real I expected to find you both—"

The dwarf stopped. There was a rustling sound outside, then Tasslehoff burst excitedly through the tent flap.

"Did I hear you talking about a dream? I *never* dream, at least not that I remember. Kender don't, much. Oh, I suppose we do. Even animals dream, but—" He caught Flint's eye and came hurriedly back to the original subject. "Well! I had the most fantastic dream! Trees crying blood. Horrible dead elves going around killing people! Raistlin wearing black robes! It was the most incredible thing! And you were there, Sturm. Laurana and Flint. And everyone died! Well, almost everyone. Raistlin didn't. And there was a green dragon—"

Tasslehoff stopped. What was wrong with his friends? Their faces were deathly pale, their eyes wide. "G-green dragon," he stammered. "Raistlin, dressed in black. Did I mention that? Q-quite becoming, actually. Red always makes him look kind of jaundiced, if you know what I mean. You don't. Well, I g-guess I'll go back to bed. If you don't want to hear anymore?" He looked around hopefully. No one answered.

"Well, g-night," he mumbled. Backing out of the tent precipitously, he returned to his bed, shaking his head, puzzled. What was the matter with everyone? It was only a dream—

For long moments, no one spoke. Then Flint sighed.

"I don't mind having a nightmare," the dwarf said dourly. "But I object to sharing it with a kender. How do you suppose we all came to have the same dream? And what does it mean?"

"A strange land—Silvanesti," Laurana said. Taking her candle, she started to leave. Then she looked back. "Do you—do you think it was real? Did they die, as we saw?" Was Tanis with that human woman? she thought, but didn't ask aloud.

"We're here," said Sturm. "We didn't die. We can only trust the others didn't either. And"—he paused—"this seems funny, but somehow I *know* they're all right."

Laurana looked at the knight intently for a moment, saw his grave face calm after the initial shock and horror had worn off. She felt herself relax. Reaching out, she took Sturm's strong lean hand in her own and pressed it silently. Then she turned and left, slipping back into the starlit night.

The dwarf rose to his feet. "Well, so much for sleep. I'll take my turn at watch now."

"I'll join you," said Sturm, standing and buckling on his swordbelt.

"I suppose we'll never know," Flint said, "why or how we all dreamed the same dream."

"I suppose not," Sturm agreed.

The dwarf walked out of the tent. Sturm started to follow, then stopped as his eyes caught a glimpse of light. Thinking perhaps that a bit of wick had fallen from Laurana's candle, he bent down to put it out, only to find instead that the jewel Alhana had given him had slipped from his belt and lay upon the ground. Picking it up, he noticed it was gleaming with its own inner light, something he'd never seen it do before.

"I suppose not," Sturm repeated thoughtfully, turning the jewel over and over in his hand.

Morning dawned in Silvanesti for the first time in many long, horrifying months. But only one saw it. Lorac, watching from his bedchamber window, saw the sun rise above the glistening aspens. The others, worn out, slept soundly.

Alhana had not left her father's side all night. But exhaustion had overwhelmed her, and she fell asleep sitting in her chair. Lorac saw the pale sunlight light her face. Her long black hair fell across her face like cracks in white marble. Her skin was torn by thorns, caked with dried blood. He saw beauty, but that beauty was marred by arrogance. She was the epitome of her people. Turning back, he looked outside into Silvanesti, but found no comfort there. A green, noxious mist still hung over Silvanesti, as though the ground itself was rotting.

"This is my doing," he said to himself, his eyes lingering on the twisted, tortured trees, the pitiful misshapen beasts that roamed the land, seeking an end to their torment.

For over four hundred years, Lorac had lived in this land. He had watched it take shape and flower beneath his hands and the hands of his people.

There had been times of trouble, too. Lorac was one of the few still living on Krynn to remember the Cataclysm. But the Silvanesti elves had survived it far better than others in the world—being estranged from other races. They knew why the ancient gods left Krynn—they saw the evil in humankind—although they could not explain why the elven clerics vanished as well.

The elves of Silvanesti heard, of course, via the winds and birds and other mysterious ways, of the sufferings of their cousins, the Qualinesti, following the Cataclysm. And, though grieved at the tales of rapine and murder, the Silvanesti asked themselves what could one expect, living among humans? They withdrew into their forest, renouncing the outside world and caring little that the outside world renounced them.

Thus Lorac had found it impossible to understand this new evil sweeping out of the north, threatening his homeland. Why should they bother the Silvanesti? He met with the Dragon Highlords, explaining to them that the Silvanesti would give them no trouble. The elves believed everyone had the right to live upon Krynn, each in his own unique fashion, evil and good. He talked and they listened and, at first, all seemed well. Then the day came when Lorac realized he had been deceived—the day the skies erupted with dragons.

The elves were not, after all, caught unprepared. Lorac had lived too long for that. Ships waited to take the people to safety. Lorac ordered them to depart under his daughter's command. Then, when he was alone, he descended to the chambers beneath the Tower of the Stars where he had secreted the dragon orb.

Only his daughter and the long-lost elven clerics knew of the orb's existence. All others in the world believed it destroyed in the Cataclysm. Lorac sat beside it, staring at it for long days. He recalled the warnings of the High Mages, bringing to mind everything he could remember about the orb. Finally, though fully aware that he had no idea how it worked, Lorac decided he had to use it to try and save his land.

He remembered the globe vividly, remembered it burning with a swirling, fascinating green light that pulsed and strengthened as he looked at it. And he remembered knowing, almost from the first seconds he had rested his fingers on the globe, that he had made a terrible mistake. He had neither the strength nor the control to command the magic. But by then, it was too late. The orb had captured him and held him enthralled, and it had been the most hideous part of his nightmare to be constantly reminded that he *was* dreaming, yet unable to break free.

And now the nightmare had become waking reality. Lorac bowed his head, tasting bitter tears in his mouth. Then he felt gentle hands upon his shoulders.

"Father, I cannot bear to see you weep. Come away from the window. Come to bed. The land will be beautiful once more in time. You will help to shape it—"

But Alhana could not look out the window without a shudder. Lorac felt her tremble and he smiled sadly.

"Will our people return, Alhana?" He stared out into the green that was not the vibrant green of life but that of death and decay.

"Of course," Alhana said quickly.

Lorac patted her hand. "A lie, my child? Since when have the elves lied to each other?"

"I think perhaps we may have always lied to ourselves," Alhana murmured, recalling what she had learned of Goldmoon's teaching. "The ancient gods did not abandon Krynn, Father. A cleric of Mishakal the Healer traveled with us and told us of what she had learned. I—I did not want to believe, Father. I was jealous. She is a human, after all, and why should the gods come to the humans with this hope? But I see now, the gods are wise. They came to humans because we elves would not accept them. Through our grief, living in this place of desolation, we will learn—as you and I have learned—that we can no longer live within the world and live apart *from* the world. The elves will work to rebuild not only this land, but all lands ravaged by the evil."

Lorac listened. His eyes turned from the tortured landscape to his daughter's face, pale and radiant as the silver moon, and he reached out his hand to touch her.

"You will bring them back? Our people?"

"Yes, Father," she promised, taking his cold, fleshless hand in her own and holding it fast. "We will work and toil. We will ask forgiveness of the gods. We will go out among the peoples of Krynn and—" Tears flooded her eyes and choked her voice, for she saw Lorac could no longer hear her. His eyes dimmed, and he began to sink back in the chair.

"I give myself to the land," he whispered. "Bury my body in the soil, daughter. As my life brought this curse upon it, so, perhaps, my death will bring its blessing."

Lorac's hand slipped from his daughter's grasp. His lifeless eyes stared out into the tormented land of Silvanesti. But the look of horror on his face faded away, leaving it filled with peace.

And Alhana could not grieve.

That night, the companions prepared to leave Silvanesti. They were to travel under the cover of darkness for much of their journey north, since by now they knew the dragonarmies controlled the lands they must pass through. They had no maps to guide them. They feared trusting ancient maps anymore, after their experience with the landlocked seaport city, Tarsis. But the only maps that could be found in Silvanesti dated back thousands of years. The companions decided to travel north from Silvanesti blindly, with some hope of discovering a seaport where they could find passage to Sancrist.

They traveled lightly, so they could travel swiftly. Besides, there was little to take; the elves had stripped their country bare of food and supplies when they left.

The mage took possession of the dragon orb—a charge no one disputed him. Tanis at first despaired of how they could carry the massive crystal with them—it was nearly two feet in diameter and extraordinarily heavy. But the evening before they left—Alhana came to Raistlin, a small sack in her hand.

"My father carried the orb in this sack. I always thought it odd, considering the orb's size, but he said the sack was given to him in the Tower of High Sorcery. Perhaps this will help you."

The mage reached out his thin hand to grasp it eagerly.

"*Jistrah tagopar Ast moirparann Kini,*" he murmured and watched in satisfaction as the nondescript bag began to glow with a pale pink light.

"Yes, it is enchanted," he whispered. Then he lifted his gaze to Caramon. "Go and bring me the orb."

Caramon's eyes opened wide in horror. "Not for any treasure in this world!" the big man said with an oath.

"Bring me the orb!" Raistlin ordered, staring angrily at his brother, who still shook his head.

"Oh, don't be a fool, Caramon!" Raistlin snapped in exasperation. "The orb cannot hurt those who do not attempt to use it. Believe me, my dear brother, you do not have the power to control a cockroach, let alone a dragon orb!"

"But it might trap me," Caramon protested.

"Bah! It seeks those with—" Raistlin stopped suddenly.

"Yes?" Tanis said quietly. "Go on. Who does it seek?"

"People with intelligence," Raistlin snarled. "Therefore I believe the members of *this* party are safe. Bring me the orb, Caramon, or perhaps you want to carry it yourself? Or you, Half-Elf? Or you, cleric of Mishakal?"

Caramon glanced uncomfortably at Tanis, and the half-elf realized that the big man was seeking his approval. It was an odd move for the twin, who had always done what Raistlin commanded without question.

Tanis saw that he wasn't the only one who noticed Caramon's mute appeal. Raistlin's eyes glittered in rage.

Now more than ever, Tanis felt wary of the mage, distrusting Raistlin's strange and growing power. It's illogical, he argued with himself. A reaction to a nightmare, nothing more. But that didn't solve his problem. What should he do about the dragon orb? Actually, he realized ruefully, he had little choice.

"Raistlin's the only one with the knowledge and the skill and—let's face it—the guts to handle that thing," Tanis said grudgingly. "I say he should take it, unless one of you wants the responsibility?"

No one spoke, though Riverwind shook his head, frowning darkly. Tanis knew the Plainsman would leave the orb—and Raistlin as well— here in Silvanesti if he had the choice.

"Go ahead, Caramon," Tanis said. "You're the only one strong enough to lift it."

Reluctantly, Caramon went to fetch the orb from its golden stand. His hands shook as he reached out to touch it, but, when he laid his hands upon it, nothing happened. The globe did not change in appearance. Sighing in relief, Caramon lifted the orb, grunting from the weight, and carried it back to his brother, who held the sack open.

"Drop it in the bag," Raistlin ordered.

"What?" Caramon's jaw sagged as he stared from the giant orb to the small bag in the mage's frail hands. "I can't, Raist! It won't fit in there! It'll smash!"

The big man fell silent as Raistlin's eyes flared golden in the dying light of day.

"No! Caramon, wait!" Tanis leaped forward, but this time Caramon did as Raistlin commanded. Slowly, his eyes held fast by his brother's intense gaze, Caramon dropped the dragon orb.

The orb vanished!

"What? Where—" Tanis glared at Raistlin suspiciously.

"In the sack," the mage replied calmly, holding forth the small bag. "See for yourself, if you do not trust me."

Tanis peered into the bag. The orb was inside and it was the true dragon orb, all right. He had no doubt. He could see the swirling mist of green, as though some faint life stirred within. It must have shrunk, he thought in awe, but the orb appeared to be the same size as always, giving Tanis the fearful impression that it was *he* who had grown.

Shuddering, Tanis stepped back. Raistlin gave the drawstring on the top of the bag a quick jerk, snapping it shut. Then, glancing at them distrustfully, he slipped the bag within his robes, secreting it in one of his numerous hidden pockets, and began to turn away. But Tanis stopped him.

"Things can never again be the same between us, can they?" the half-elf asked quietly.

Raistlin looked at him for a moment, and Tanis saw a brief flicker of regret in the young mage's eyes, a longing for trust and friendship and a return to the days of youth.

"No," Raistlin whispered. "But such was the price I paid." He began to cough.

"Price? To whom? For what?"

"Do not question, Half-Elf." The mage's thin shoulders bent with coughing. Caramon put his strong arm around his brother and Raistlin leaned weakly against his twin. When he recovered from the spasm, he lifted his golden eyes. "I cannot tell you the answer, Tanis, because I do not know it myself."

Then, bowing his head, he let Caramon lead him away to find what rest he could before their journey.

"I wish you would reconsider and let us assist you in the funeral rites for your father," Tanis said to Alhana as she stood in the door of the Tower of the Stars to bid them farewell. "A day will not make a difference to us."

"Yes, let us," Goldmoon entreated earnestly. "I know much about this from our people, for our burial customs are similar to yours, if Tanis has told me correctly. I was priestess in my tribe, and I presided over the wrapping of the body in the spiced cloths that will preserve it—"

"No, my friends," Alhana said firmly, her face pale. "It was my father's wish that I—I do this alone."

This was not quite true, but Alhana knew how shocked these people would be at the sight of her father's body being consigned to the ground— a custom practiced only by goblins and other evil creatures. The thought appalled her. Involuntarily, her gaze was drawn to the tortured and twisted tree that was to mark his grave, standing over it like some fearful carrion bird. Quickly she looked away, her voice faltered.

"His tomb is—is long prepared and I have some experience of these things myself. Do not worry about me, please."

Tanis saw the agony in her face, but he could not refuse to honor her request.

"We understand," Goldmoon said. Then, on impulse, the Qué-Shu Plainswoman put her arms around the elven princess and held her as she might have held a lost and frightened child. Alhana stiffened at first, then relaxed in Goldmoon's compassionate embrace.

"Be at peace," Goldmoon whispered, stroking back Alhana's dark hair from her face. Then the Plainswoman left.

"After you bury your father, what then?" Tanis asked as he and Alhana stood alone together on the steps of the Tower.

"I will return to my people," Alhana replied gravely. "The griffons will come to me, now that the evil in this land is gone, and they will take me to Ergoth. We will do what we can to help defeat this evil, then we will come home."

Tanis glanced around Silvanesti. Horrifying as it was in the daytime, its terrors at night were beyond description.

"I know," Alhana said in answer to his unspoken thoughts. "This will be our penance."

Tanis raised his eyebrows skeptically, knowing the fight she had ahead of her to get her people to return. Then he saw the conviction on Alhana's face. He gave her even odds.

Smiling, he changed the subject. "And will you find time to go to Sancrist?" he asked. "The knights would be honored by your presence. Particularly one of them."

Alhana's pale face flushed. "Perhaps," she said, barely speaking above a whisper. "I cannot say yet. I have learned many things about myself. But it will take me a long time to make these things a part of me." She shook her head, sighing. "It may be I can never truly be comfortable with them."

"Like learning to love a human?"

Alhana lifted her head, her clear eyes looked into Tanis's. "Would he be happy, Tanis? Away from his homeland, for I must return to Silvanesti? And could I be happy, knowing that I must watch him age and die while I am still in my youth?"

"I asked myself these same questions, Alhana," Tanis said, thinking with pain of the decision he had reached concerning Kitiara. "If we deny love that is given to us, if we refuse to give love because we fear the pain of loss, then our lives will be empty, our loss greater."

"I wondered, when first we met, why these people follow you, Tanis Half-Elven," Alhana said softly. "Now I understand. I will consider your words. Farewell, until your life's journey's end."

"Farewell, Alhana," Tanis answered, taking the hand she extended to him. He could find nothing more to say, and so turned and left her.

But he could not help wondering, as he did, that if he was so damn wise, why was his life in such a mess?

Tanis joined the companions at the edge of the forest. For a moment they stood there, reluctant to enter the woods of Silvanesti. Although they knew the evil was gone, the thought of traveling for days among the twisted, tortured forest was a somber one. But they had no choice. Already they felt the sense of urgency that had driven them this far. Time was sifting through the hourglass, and they knew they could not let the sands run out, although they had no idea why.

"Come, my brother," said Raistlin finally. The mage led the way into the woods, the Staff of Magius shedding its pale light as he walked. Caramon followed, with a sigh. One by one the others trailed after. Tanis alone turned to look back.

They would not see the moons tonight. The land was covered with a heavy darkness as if it too mourned Lorac's death. Alhana stood in the doorway to the Tower of the Stars, her body framed by the Tower, which glimmered in the light of moon rays captured ages ago. Only Alhana's face was visible in the shadows, like the ghost of the silver moon. Tanis caught a glimpse of movement. She raised her hand and there was a brief, clear flash of pure white light—the Starjewel. And then she was gone.

BOOK II

he story of the companions' journey to Ice Wall Castle and their defeat of the evil Dragon Highlord, Feal-thas, became legend among the Ice Barbarians who inhabit that desolate land. It is still told by the village cleric on long winter nights when heroic deeds are remembered and songs are sung.

Song of the Ice Reaver

I am the one who brought them back.
I am Raggart I am telling you this.
Snow upon snow cancels the signals of ice
Over the snow the sun bleeds whiteness
In cold light forever unbearable.
And if I do not tell you this
The snow descends on the deeds of heroes
And their strength in my singing
Lies down in a core of frost rising no more
No more as the lost breath crumbles.

Seven they were from the hot lands
(I am the one who brought them back)
Four swordsmen sworn in the North
The elf-woman Laurana
The dwarf from the floes of stone
The kender small-boned as a hawk.
Riding three blades they came to the tunnel
To the throat of the only castle.

Down among Thanoi the old guardians
Where their swordsmen carved hot air
Finding tendon finding bone
As the tunnels melted red.
Down upon minotaur upon ice bear
And the swords whistled again
Bright on the corner of madness
The tunnel knee-high in arms
In claws in unspeakable things
As the swordsmen descended
Bright steam freezing behind them.

Then to the chambers at the castle heart
Where Feal-thas awaited lord of dragons and wolves
Armored in white that is nothing
That covers the ice as the sun bleeds whiteness.
And he called on the wolves the baby-stealers
Who suckled on murder in the lairs of ancestors.
Around the heroes a circle of knives of craving
As the wolves stalked in their master's eye.

And Aran the first to break the circle
Hot wind at the throat of Feal-thas
Brought down and unraveled
In the reel of the hunt perfected.
Brian the next when the sword of the wolf lord
Sent him seeking the warm lands.
All stood frozen in the wheel of razors
All stood frozen except for Laurana.
Blind in a hot light flashing the crown of the mind
Where death melts in a diving sun
She takes up the Ice Reaver
And over the boil of wolves over the slaughter
Bearing a blade of ice bearing darkness
She opened the throat of the wolf lord
And the wolves fell silent as the head collapsed.

The rest is short in the telling.
Destroying the eggs the violent get of the dragons
A tunnel of scales and ordure
Followed into the terrible larder
Followed further followed to treasure.
There the orb danced blue danced white
Swelled like a heart in its endless beating
(They let me hold it I brought them back).
Out from the tunnel blood on blood under the ice
Bearing their own incredible burden
The young knights silent and tattered
They came five now only
The kender last small pockets bulging.
I am Raggart I am telling you this.
I am the one who brought them back.

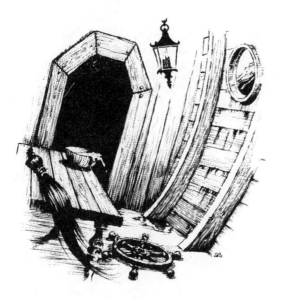

1

The flight from Ice Wall

he old dwarf lay dying.

His limbs would no longer support him. His bowels and stomach twisted together like snakes. Waves of nausea broke over him. He could not even raise his head from his bunk. He stared above him at an oil lamp swinging slowly overhead. The lamp's light seemed to be getting dimmer. This is it, thought the dwarf. The end. The darkness is creeping over my eyes. . . .

He heard a noise near him, a creaking of wooden planks as if someone were very quietly stealing up on him. Feebly, Flint managed to turn his head.

"Who is it?" he croaked.

"Tasslehoff," whispered a solicitous voice. Flint sighed and reached out a gnarled hand. Tas's hand closed over his own.

"Ah, lad. I'm glad you've come in time to say farewell," said the dwarf weakly. "I'm dying, lad. I'm going to Reorx—"

"What?" asked Tas, leaning closer.

"Reorx," repeated the dwarf irritably. "I'm going to the arms of Reorx."

"No, we're not," said Tas. "We're going to Sancrist. Unless you mean an inn. I'll ask Sturm. The Reorx Arms. Hmmm—"

"Reorx, the God of the Dwarves, you doorknob!" Flint roared.

129

"Oh," said Tas after a moment. "*That* Reorx."

"Listen, lad," Flint said more calmly, determined to leave no hard feelings behind. "I want you to have my helm. The one you brought me in Xak Tsaroth, with the griffon's mane."

"Do you really?" Tas asked, impressed. "That's awfully nice of you, Flint, but what will you do for a helm?"

"Ah, lad, I won't need a helm where I'm going."

"You might in Sancrist," Tas said dubiously. "Derek thinks the Dragon Highlords are preparing to launch a full-scaled attack, and I think a helm could come in handy—"

"I'm not talking about Sancrist!" Flint snarled, struggling to sit up. "I won't need a helm because I'm dying!"

"I nearly died once," Tas said solemnly. Setting a steaming bowl on a table, he settled back comfortably in a chair to relate his story. "It was that time in Tarsis when the dragon knocked the building down on top of me. Elistan said I was nearly a goner. Actually those weren't his exact words, but he said it was only through the inter . . . interces . . . oh well, inter-something-or-other of the gods that I'm here today."

Flint gave a mighty groan and fell back limply on his bunk. "Is it too much to ask," he said to the lamp swinging above his head, "that I be allowed to die in peace? Not surrounded by kenders!" This last was practically a shriek.

"Oh, come now. You're not dying, you know," Tas said. "You're only seasick."

"I'm dying," the dwarf said stubbornly. "I've been infected with a serious disease and now I'm dying. And on your heads be it. You dragged me onto this confounded boat—"

"Ship," interrupted Tas.

"Boat!" repeated Flint furiously. "You dragged me onto this confounded boat, then left me to perish of some terrible disease in a rat infested bedroom—"

"We could have left you back in Ice Wall, you know, with the walrus-men and—" Tasslehoff stopped.

Flint was once again struggling to sit up, but this time there was a wild look in his eyes. The kender rose to his feet and began edging his way toward the door. "Uh, I guess I better be going. I just came down here to—uh—see if you wanted anything to eat. The ship's cook made something he calls green pea soup—"

Laurana, huddled out of the wind on the foredeck, started as she heard the most frightful roaring sound come from below decks, followed by the cracking of smashed crockery. She glanced at Sturm, who was standing near her. The knight smiled.

"Flint," he said.

"Yes," Laurana said, worried. "Perhaps I should—"

She was interrupted by the appearance of Tasslehoff dripping with green pea soup.

"I think Flint's feeling better," Tasslehoff said solemnly. "But he's not quite ready to eat anything yet."

The journey from Ice Wall had been swift. Their small ship fairly flew through the sea waters, carried north by the currents and the strong, cold prevailing winds.

The companions had traveled to Ice Wall where, according to Tasslehoff, a dragon orb was kept in Ice Wall Castle. They found the orb and defeated its evil guardian, Feal-thas—a powerful Dragonlord. Escaping the destruction of the castle with the help of the Ice Barbarians, they were now on a ship bound for Sancrist. Although the precious dragon orb was stowed safely in a chest below decks, the horrors of their journey to Ice Wall still tormented their dreams at night.

But the nightmares of Ice Wall were nothing compared to that strange and vivid dream they had experienced well over a month ago. None of them referred to it, but Laurana occasionally saw a look of fear and loneliness, unusual to Sturm, that made her think he might be recalling the dream as well.

Other than that, the party was in good spirits—except the dwarf, who had been hauled on the ship bodily and was promptly seasick. The journey to Ice Wall had been an undoubted victory. Along with the dragon orb, they carried away with them the broken shaft of an ancient weapon, believed to be a dragonlance. And they carried something more important, though they did not realize it at the time they found it. . . .

The companions, accompanied by Derek Crownguard and the other two young knights who had joined them at Tarsis, had been searching Ice Wall castle for the dragon orb. The search had not gone well. Time and again they had fought off the evil walrus-men, winter wolves, and bears. The companions began to think they may have come here for nothing, but Tas swore that the book he read in Tarsis said there was an orb located here. So they kept looking.

It was during their search that they came upon a startling sight—a huge dragon, over forty feet long, its skin a shimmering silver, completely encased in a wall of ice. The dragon's wings were spread, poised for flight. The dragon's expression was fierce, but his head was noble, and he did not inspire them with the fear and loathing they remembered experiencing around the red dragons. Instead, they felt a great, overwhelming sorrow for this magnificent creature.

But strangest to them was the fact that this dragon had a rider! They had seen the Dragon Highlords ride their dragons, but this man appeared by his ancient armor to have been a Knight of Solamnia! Held tightly in his gloved hand was the broken shaft of what must have been a large lance.

"Why would a Knight of Solamnia be riding a dragon?" Laurana asked, thinking of the Dragon Highlords.

"There have been knights who turned to evil," Lord Derek Crownguard said harshly. "Though it shames me to admit it."

"I get no feeling of evil here," Elistan said. "Only a great sorrow. I wonder how they died. I see no wounds—"

"This seems familiar," Tasslehoff interrupted, frowning. "Like a picture. A knight riding a silver dragon. I've seen—"

"Bah!" Flint snorted. "You've seen furry elephant—"

"I'm serious," Tas protested.

"Where was it, Tas?" Laurana asked gently, seeing a hurt expression on the kender's face. "Can you remember?"

"I think . . ." Tasslehoff's eyes lost their focus. "It puts me in mind of Pax Tharkas and Fizban. . . ."

"Fizban!" Flint exploded. "That old mage was crazier than Raistlin, if that's possible."

"I don't know what Tas is talking about," Sturm said, gazing up at the dragon and its rider thoughtfully. "But I remember my mother telling me that Huma rode upon a Silver Dragon, carrying the Dragonlance, in his final battle."

"And I remember my mother telling me to leave sweetcakes for the white-robed Old One who came to our castle at Yuletime," scoffed Derek. "No, this is undoubtedly some renegade Knight, enslaved by evil."

Derek and the other two young knights turned to go, but the rest lingered, staring up at the figure on the dragon.

"You're right, Sturm. That's a dragonlance," Tas said wistfully. "I don't know how I know, but I'm sure of it."

"Did you see it in the book in Tarsis?" Sturm asked, exchanging glances with Laurana, each of them thinking that the kender's seriousness was unusual, even frightening.

Tas shrugged. "I don't know," he said in a small voice. "I'm sorry."

"Maybe we should take it with us," Laurana suggested uneasily. "It couldn't hurt."

"Come along, Brightblade!" Derek's voice came back to them, echoing sternly. "The Thanoi may have lost us for the moment, but they'll discover our trail before long."

"How can we get it?" Sturm asked, ignoring Derek's order. "It's encased in ice at least three feet thick!"

"I can," Gilthanas said.

Jumping up onto the huge cliff of ice that had formed around the dragon and its rider, the elf found a handhold and began to inch his way up the monument. From the dragon's frozen wing, he was able to crawl along on his hands and knees until he came to the lance, clutched in the rider's hand. Gilthanas pressed his hand against the ice wall covering the lance and spoke the strange, spidery language of magic.

A red glow spread from the elf's hand to the ice, melting it away rapidly. Within moments, he was able to reach his hand through the hole to grasp the lance. But it was held fast in the dead knight's hand.

Gilthanas tugged and even tried to pry the frozen fingers of the hand loose. Finally he could stand the cold of the ice no longer and dropped, shivering, back down to the ground. "There's no way," he said. "He's got it gripped tight."

"Break the fingers—" suggested Tas helpfully.

Sturm silenced the kender with a furious look. "I will not have his body desecrated," he snapped. "Maybe we can slide the lance out of his hand. I'll try—"

"No good," Gilthanas told his sister as they watched Sturm climb up the side of the ice. "It's as if the lance has become part of the hand. I—" The elf stopped.

As Sturm put his hand through the hole in the ice and took hold of the lance, the ice-bound figure of the knight seemed to move suddenly, just slightly. Its stiff and frozen hand relaxed its grip on the shattered lance. Sturm nearly fell in his amazement, and, letting go of the weapon hurriedly, he backed away along the dragon's ice-coated wing.

"He's giving it to you," cried Laurana. "Go ahead, Sturm! Take it! Don't you see, he's giving it to another knight."

"Which I'm not," Sturm said bitterly. "But perhaps that's indicative, perhaps it is evil—" Hesitantly, he slid back to the hole and grasped the lance once more. The stiff hand of the dead knight released its grip. Taking hold of the broken weapon, Sturm carefully brought it out of the ice. He jumped back to the ground and stood staring at the ancient shaft.

"That was wonderful!" Tas said in awe. "Flint, did you see the corpse come alive?"

"No!" snapped the dwarf. "And neither did you. Let's get out of here," he added, shivering.

Then Derek appeared. "I gave you an order, Sturm Brightblade! What's the delay?" Derek's face darkened with anger as he saw the lance.

"I asked him to get it for me," Laurana said, her voice as cool as the wall of ice behind her. Taking the lance, she began to wrap it swiftly in a fur cloak from her pack.

Derek regarded her angrily for a moment, then bowed stiffly and turned on his heel.

"Dead knights, live knights, I don't know who's worse," Flint grumbled, grabbing Tas and dragging him along after Derek.

"What if it is a weapon of evil?" Sturm asked Laurana in a low voice as they traveled the icy corridors of the castle.

Laurana looked back one final time at the dead knight mounted on the dragon. The cold pale sun of the southland was setting, its light casting watery shadows across the corpses, giving them a sinister aspect. Even as she watched, she thought she saw the body slump lifelessly.

"Do you believe the story of Huma?" Laurana asked softly.

"I don't know what to believe anymore," Sturm said, bitterness hardening his voice. "Everything used to be black and white for me, all things clear-cut and well-defined. I believed in the story of Huma. My mother taught it to me as the truth. Then I went to Solamnia." He paused, as if unwilling to continue. Finally, seeing Laurana's face filled with interest and compassion, he swallowed and went on. "I never told anyone this, not even Tanis. When I returned to my homeland, I found that the Knighthood was not the order of honorable, self-sacrificing men my mother had described. It was rife with political intrigue. The best of the men were like Derek, honorable, but strict and unbending, with little use for those they consider beneath them. The worst—" He shook his head. "When I spoke of Huma, they laughed. An itinerant knight, they called him. According to their story, he was cast out of the order for disobeying its laws. Huma roamed the countryside, they said, endearing himself to peasants, who thus began to create legends about him."

"But did he really exist?" Laurana persisted, saddened by the sorrow in Sturm's face.

"Oh, yes. Of that there can be no doubt. The records that survived the Cataclysm list his name among the lower orders of the knights. But the story of the Silver Dragon, the Final Battle, even the Dragonlance itself—no one believes anymore. Like Derek says, there is no proof. The tomb of Huma, according to the legend, was a towering structure—one of the wonders of the world. But you can find no one who has ever seen it. All we have are children's stories, as Raistlin would say." Sturm put his hand to his face, covering his eyes, and gave a deep, shuddering sigh.

"Do you know," he said softly, "I never thought I'd say it, but I miss Raistlin. I miss all of them. I feel as if a part of me's been cut off, and that's how I felt when I was in Solamnia. That's why I came back, instead of waiting and completing the tests for my knighthood. These people—my friends—were doing more to combat evil in the world than all the Knights lined up in a row. Even Raistlin, in some way I can't understand. He could tell us what all this means." He jerked his thumb back at the ice-encased knight. "At least he would believe in it. If he were here. If Tanis were here—" Sturm could not go on.

"Yes," Laurana said quietly. "If Tanis were here—"

Remembering her great sorrow, so much greater than his own, Sturm put his arm around Laurana and held her close. The two stood for a moment, each comforted for their losses by the other's presence. Then Derek's voice came sharply back to them, reprimanding them for lagging behind.

And now, the broken lance, wrapped in Laurana's fur cloak, lay in the chest with the dragon orb and Wyrmslayer, Tanis's sword, which Laurana and Sturm had carried with them from Tarsis. Beside the chest lay the bodies of the two young knights, who had given their lives in defense of the group, and who were being carried back to be buried in their homeland.

The strong southern wind, blowing swift and cold from the glaciers, propelled the ship across the Sirrion Sea. The captain said that, if the winds held, they might make Sancrist in two days.

"That way lies Southern Ergoth." The captain told Elistan, pointing off to starboard. "We'll be just coming up on the south end of it. This nightfall, you'll see the Isle of Cristyne. Then, with a fair wind, we'll be in Sancrist. Strange thing about Southern Ergoth," the captain added, glancing at Laurana, "it's filled with elves, they say, though I haven't been there to know if that's true."

"Elves!" said Laurana eagerly, coming forward to stand beside the captain, the early morning wind whipping her cloak.

"Fled their homeland, so I heard," the captain continued. "Driven off by the dragonarmies."

"Perhaps it's our people!" Laurana said, clutching at Gilthanas, who stood next to her. She gazed out over the bow of the ship intently, as if she could will the land to appear.

"Most likely the Silvanesti," Gilthanas said. "In fact, I think Lady Alhana may have mentioned something about Ergoth. Do you remember, Sturm?"

"No," the knight answered abruptly. Turning and walking over to the port side of the ship, he leaned against the railing, staring out across the pink-tinged sea. Laurana saw him pull something from his belt and run his fingers over it lovingly. There was a bright flash, as it caught the sun's rays, then he slipped it back into his belt. His head bowed. Laurana started to go to him when suddenly she stopped, catching a glimpse of movement.

"What kind of strange cloud is that to the south?"

The captain turned immediately, whipping his spyglass out of the pocket of his fur parka and placing it to his eye. "Send a man aloft," he snapped to his first mate.

Within moments, a sailor was scampering up the rigging. Clinging to the dizzying heights of the mast with one arm, he peered south through the spyglass.

"Can you make it out?" the captain called aloft.

"No, capt'n," the man bellowed. "If it's a cloud, it's like none I've seen afore."

"I'll look!" volunteered Tasslehoff eagerly. The kender began to climb the ropes as skillfully as the sailor. Reaching the mast, he clung to the rigging near the man and stared south.

It certainly seemed to be a cloud. It was huge and white and appeared to be floating above the water. But it was moving much more rapidly than any other cloud in the sky and—

Tasslehoff gasped. "Let me borrow that," he asked, holding out his hand for the watch's spyglass. Reluctantly, the man gave it to him. Tas put it to his eye, then he groaned softly. "Oh, dear," he muttered. Lowering the spyglass, he shut it up with a snap and absently stuffed it into his tunic. The sailor caught him by the collar as he was about to slide down.

"What?" Tas said, startled. "Oh! Is that yours? Sorry." Giving the spyglass a wistful pat, he handed it back to the sailor. Tas slid skillfully down the ropes, landed lightly on the deck, and came running over to Sturm.

"It's a dragon," he reported breathlessly.

2

The White Dragon.

Captured!

he dragon's name was Sleet. She was a white dragon, a species of dragon smaller than other dragons dwelling in Krynn. Born and bred in the arctic regions, these dragons were able to withstand extreme cold, and controlled the ice-bound southern regions of Ansalon.

Because of their smaller size, the white dragons were the swiftest flyers of all dragonkind. The Dragon Highlords often used them for scouting missions. Thus Sleet had been away from her lair in Ice Wall when the companions entered it in search of the dragon orb. The Dark Queen had received a report that Silvanesti had been invaded by a group of adventurers. They had managed, somehow, to defeat Cyan Bloodbane and were reportedly in possession of a dragon orb.

The Dark Queen guessed they might be traveling across the Plains of Dust, along the Kings Road, which was the most direct overland route to Sancrist where the Knights of Solamnia were reportedly trying to regroup. The Dark Queen ordered Sleet and her flight of white dragons to speed north to the Plains of Dust, now lying under a thick, heavy blanket of packed snow, to find the orb.

Seeing the snow glistening beneath her, Sleet doubted very much if even humans would be foolhardy enough to attempt to cross the wasteland. But she had her orders and she followed them. Scattering her flight, Sleet scoured every inch of land from the borders of Silvanesti on the east to the Kharolis Mountains on the west. A few of her dragons even flew as far north as New Coast, which was held by the blues.

The dragons met to report that they had seen no sign of any living being on the Plains when Sleet received word that danger had marched in the back door while she was out scouting the front.

Furious, Sleet flew back but arrived too late. Feal-thas was dead, the dragon orb missing. But her walrus-men allies, the Thanoi, were able to describe the group who had committed this heinous act. They even pointed out the direction their ship had sailed, although there was only one direction any ship could sail from Ice Wall—north.

Sleet reported the loss of the dragon orb to her Dark Queen, who was intensely angry and frightened. Now there were two orbs missing! Although secure in the knowledge that her force for evil was the strongest in Krynn, the Dark Queen knew with a nagging certainty that the forces of good still walked the land. One of these might prove strong and wise enough to figure out the secret of the orb.

Sleet, therefore, was ordered to find the orb and bring it not back to Ice Wall, but to the Queen herself. Under no circumstances was the dragon to lose it or allow it to be lost. The orbs were intelligent and imbued with a strong sense of survival. Thus they had lived this long when even those who created them were dead.

Sleet sped out over the Sirrion Sea, her strong white wings soon carrying her swiftly to within sight of the ship. But now Sleet was presented with an interesting intellectual problem, and she was not prepared to handle it.

Perhaps because of the inbreeding necessary to create a reptile that can tolerate cold weather, white dragons are the lowest in intelligence among dragonkind. Sleet had never needed to think much on her own. Feal-thas always told her what to do. Consequently, she was considerably perplexed over her current problem as she circled the ship: how could she get the orb?

At first she had just planned to freeze the ship with her icy breath. Then she realized this would simply enclose the orb in a frozen block of wood, making it extremely difficult to remove. There was also every probability the ship would sink before she could tear it apart. And if she did manage to take the ship apart, the orb might sink. The ship was too heavy to lift in her claws and fly to land. Sleet circled the ship and pondered, while down below she could see the pitiful humans racing around like scared mice.

The white dragon considered sending another telepathic message to her Queen, asking for help. But Sleet hesitated to remind the vengeful queen of either her presence or her ignorance. The dragon followed the ship all day, hanging just above it, pondering. Floating easily on the wind currents, she let her dragon fear stir the humans into a frenzy of panic. Then, just as the sun was setting, Sleet had an idea. Without stopping to think, she acted upon it at once.

Tasslehoff's report of the white dragon following the vessel sent waves of terror through the crew. They armed themselves with cutlasses and grimly prepared to fight the beast as long as they could, though all knew how such a contest must end. Gilthanas and Laurana, both skillful archers, fit arrows to their bows. Sturm and Derek held shield and sword. Tasslehoff grabbed his hoopak. Flint tried to get out of bed, but he couldn't even stand up. Elistan was calm, praying to Paladine.

"I have more faith in my sword than that old man and his god," Derek said to Sturm.

"The Knights have always honored Paladine," Sturm said in rebuke.

"I honor him—his memory," Derek said. "I find this talk of Paladine's 'return' disturbing, Brightblade. And so will the Council, when they hear of it. You would do well to consider that when the question of your knighthood arises."

Sturm bit his lip, swallowing his angry retort like bitter medicine.

Long minutes passed. Everyone's eyes were on the white-winged creature flying above them. But they could do nothing, and so they waited.

And waited. And waited. The dragon did not attack.

She circled above them endlessly, her shadow crossing and crisscrossing the deck with monotonous, chilling regularity. The sailors, who had been prepared to fight without question, soon began to mutter among themselves as the waiting grew unbearable. To make matters worse, the dragon seemed to be sucking up the wind, for the sails fluttered and drooped lifelessly. The ship lost its graceful forward momentum and began to flounder in the water. Storm clouds gathered on the northern horizon and slowly drifted over the water, casting a pall across the bright sea.

Laurana finally lowered her bow and rubbed her aching back and shoulder muscles. Her eyes, dazzled from staring into the sun, were blurred and watery.

"Put 'em in a lifeboat and cast 'em adrift," she overheard one old grizzled sailor suggest to a companion in a voice meant to carry. "Perhaps yon great beast will let us go. It's them she's after, not us."

It's not even us she's after, Laurana thought uneasily. It's probably the dragon orb. That's why she hasn't attacked. But Laurana couldn't tell this, even to the captain. The dragon orb must be kept secret.

The afternoon crept on, and still the dragon circled like a horrible seabird. The captain was growing more and more irritable. Not only did he have a dragon to contend with, but the likelihood of mutiny as well. Near dinnertime, he ordered the companions below decks.

Derek and Sturm both refused, and it appeared things might get out of hand when, "Land ho, off the starboard bow!"

"Southern Ergoth," the captain said grimly. "The current's carrying us toward the rocks." He glanced up at the circling dragon. "If a wind doesn't come soon, we'll smash up on them."

At that moment, the dragon quit circling. She hovered a moment, then soared upward. The sailors cheered, thinking she was flying away. But Laurana knew better, remembering Tarsis.

"She's going to dive!" she cried. "She's going to attack!"

"Get below!" Sturm shouted, and the sailors, after one hesitant look skyward, began to scramble for the hatches. The captain ran to the wheel.

"Get below," he ordered the helmsman, taking over.

"You can't stay up here!" Sturm shouted. Leaving the hatch, he ran back to the captain. "She'll kill you!"

"We'll founder if I don't," the captain cried angrily.

"We'll founder if you're dead!" Sturm said. Clenching his fist, he hit the captain in the jaw and dragged him below.

Laurana stumbled down the stairs with Gilthanas behind her. The elflord waited until Sturm brought the unconscious captain down, then he pulled the hatch cover shut.

At that moment, the dragon hit the ship with a blast that nearly sent the vessel under. The ship listed precariously. Everyone, even the most hardened sailor, lost his feet and went skidding into each other in the crowded quarters below deck. Flint rolled onto the floor with a curse.

"Now's the time to pray to your god," Derek said to Elistan.

"I am," Elistan replied coolly, helping the dwarf up.

Laurana, clinging to a post, waited fearfully for the flaring orange light, the heat, the flames. Instead, there was a sudden sharp and biting cold that took her breath away and chilled her blood. She could hear, above her, rigging snap and crack, the flapping of the sails cease. Then, as she stared upward, she saw white frost begin to sift down between the cracks in the wooden deck.

"The white dragons don't breathe flame!" Laurana said in awe. "They breathe ice! Elistan! Your prayers were answered!"

"Bah! It might as well be flame," the captain said, shaking his head and rubbing his jaw. "Ice'll freeze us up solid."

"A dragon breathing ice!" Tas said wistfully. "I wish I could see!"

"What will happen?" Laurana asked, as the ship slowly righted itself, creaking and groaning.

"We're helpless," the captain snarled. "The riggin'll snap beneath the weight of the ice, dragging the sails down. The mast'll break like a tree in an ice storm. With no steerage, the current will smash her upon the rocks, and that'll be an end of her. There's not a damn thing we can do!"

"We could try to shoot her as she flies past," Gilthanas said. But Sturm shook his head, pushing on the hatch.

"There must be a foot of ice on top of this," the knight reported. "We're sealed in."

This is how the dragon will get the orb, Laurana thought miserably. She'll drive the ship aground, kill us, then recover the orb where there's no danger of it sinking into the ocean.

"Another blast like that will send us to the bottom," the captain predicted, but there was not another blast like the first. The next blast was more gentle, and all of them realized the dragon was using her breath to blow them to shore.

It was an excellent plan, and one of which Sleet was rather proud. She skimmed after the ship, letting the current and the tide carry it to shore, giving it a little puff now and then. It was only when she saw the jagged rocks sticking up out of the moonlit water that the dragon suddenly saw the flaw in her scheme. Then the moon's light was gone, swept away by the storm clouds, and the dragon could see nothing. It was darker than her Queen's soul.

The dragon cursed the storm clouds, so well suited to the purposes of the Dragon Highlords in the north. But the clouds worked against her as they blotted out the two moons. Sleet could hear the rending and cracking sounds of splintering wood as the ship struck the rocks. She could even hear the cries and shouts of the sailors—but she couldn't see! Diving low over the water, she hoped to encase the miserable creatures in ice until daylight. Then she heard another, more frightening sound in the darkness—the twanging of bow strings.

An arrow whistled past her head. Another tore through the fragile membrane of her wing. Shrieking in pain, Sleet pulled up from her steep dive. There must be elves down there, she realized in a fury! More arrows zinged past her. Cursed, night-seeing elves! With their elvensight, they would find her an easy target, especially crippled in one wing.

Feeling her strength ebb, the dragon decided to return to Ice Wall. She was tired from flying all day, and the arrow wound hurt abominably. True, she would have to report another failure to the Dark Queen, but—as she came to think of it—it wasn't such a failure after all. She had kept the dragon orb from reaching Sancrist, and she had demolished the ship. She knew the location of the orb. The Queen, with her vast network of spies on Ergoth, could easily recover it.

Mollified, the white dragon fluttered south, traveling slowly. By morning she had reached her vast glacier home. Following her report, which was moderately well-received, Sleet was able to slip into her cavern of ice and nurse her injured wing back to health.

"She's gone!" said Gilthanas in astonishment.

"Of course," said Derek wearily as he helped salvage what supplies they could from the wrecked ship. "Her vision cannot match your elfsight. Besides, you hit her once."

"Laurana's shot, not mine," Gilthanas said, smiling at his sister, who stood on shore, her bow in her hand.

Derek sniffed doubtfully. Carefully setting down the box he carried, the knight started back out into the water. A figure looming out of the darkness stopped him.

"No use, Derek," Sturm said. "The ship sank."

Sturm carried Flint on his back. Seeing Sturm stagger with weariness, Laurana ran back into the water to help him. Between them, they got the dwarf to shore and stretched him on the sand. Out to sea, the sounds of cracking timber had ceased, replaced now by the endless breaking of the waves.

Then there was a splashing sound, Tasslehoff waded ashore after them, his teeth chattering, but his grin as wide as ever. He was followed by the captain, being helped by Elistan.

"What about the bodies of my men?" Derek demanded the moment he saw the captain. "Where are they?"

"We had more important things to carry," Elistan said sternly. "Things needed for the living, such as food and weapons."

"Many another good man has found his final home beneath the waves. Yours won't be the first—nor the last—I suppose, more's the pity," the captain added.

Derek seemed about to speak, but the captain, grief and exhaustion in his eyes, said, "I've left six of my own men there this night, sir. Unlike yours, they were alive when we started this voyage. To say nothing of the fact that my ship and my livelihood lies down there, too. I wouldn't consider adding anything further, if you take my meaning. Sir."

"I am sorry for your loss, captain," Derek answered stiffly. "And I commend you and your crew for all you tried to do."

The captain muttered something and stood looking aimlessly around the beach, as if lost.

"We sent your men north along the shore, captain," Laurana said, pointing. "There's shelter there, within those trees."

As if to verify her words, a bright light flared, the light of a huge bonfire.

"Fools!" Derek swore bitterly. "They'll have the dragon back on us."

"It's either that or catch our deaths of cold," the captain said bitterly over his shoulder. "Take your choice, sir knight. It matters little to me." He disappeared into the darkness.

Sturm stretched and groaned, trying to ease chilled, cramped muscles. Flint lay huddled in misery, shaking so the buckles on his armor jangled.

Laurana, leaning down to tuck her cloak around him, realized suddenly how cold she was.

In the excitement of trying to escape the ship and fighting the dragon, she had forgotten the chill. She couldn't even remember, in fact, any details of her escape. She remembered reaching the beach, seeing the dragon diving on them. She remembered fumbling for her bow with numb, shaking fingers. She wondered how anyone had presence of mind to save anything—

"The dragon orb!" she said fearfully.

"Here, in this chest," Derek answered. "Along with the lance and that elvish sword you call Wyrmslayer. And now, I suppose, we should take advantage of the fire—"

"I think not." A strange voice spoke out of the darkness as lighted torches flared around them, blinding them.

The companions started and immediately drew their weapons, gathering around the helpless dwarf. But Laurana, after an instant's fright, peered into the faces in the torchlight.

"Hold!" she cried. "These are our people! These are elves!"

"Silvanesti!" Gilthanas said heartily. Dropping his bow to the ground, he walked forward toward the elf who had spoken. "We have journeyed long through darkness," he said in elven, his hands outstretched. "Well met, my broth—"

He never finished his ancient greeting. The leader of the elven party stepped forward and slammed the end of his staff across Gilthanas's face, knocking him to the sand, unconscious.

Sturm and Derek immediately raised their swords, standing back to back. Steel flashed among the elves.

"Stop!" Laurana shouted in elven. Kneeling by her brother, she threw back the hood of her cloak so that the light fell upon her face. "We are your cousins. Qualinesti! These humans are Knights of Solamnia!"

"We know well enough who you are!" The elven leader spit the words, "Qualinesti spies! And we do not find it unusual that you travel in the company of humans. Your blood has long been polluted. Take them," he said, motioning to his men. "If they don't come peacefully, do what you must. And find out what they mean by this dragon orb they mentioned."

The elves stepped forward.

"No!" Derek cried, jumping to stand before the chest. "Sturm, they must not have the orb!"

Sturm had already given the Knight's salute to an enemy and was advancing, sword drawn.

"It appears they will fight. So be it," the leader of the elves said, raising his weapon.

"I tell you, this is madness!" Laurana cried angrily. She threw herself between the flashing swordblades. The elves halted uncertainly. Sturm grabbed hold of her to drag her back, but she jerked free of his restraining hand.

"Goblins and draconians, in all their hideous evil, do not sink to fighting among themselves"—her voice shook with rage—"while we elves, the ancient embodiment of good, try to kill each other! Look!"She lifted the lid of the chest with one hand and threw it open. "In here we have the hope of the world! A dragon orb, taken at great peril from Ice Wall. Our ship lies wrecked in the waters out there. We drove away the dragon that sought to recover this orb. And, after all this, we find our greatest peril among our own people! If this is true, if we have sunk so low, then kill us now, and I swear, not one person in this group will try to stop you."

Sturm, not understanding elven, watched for a moment, then saw the elves lower their weapons. "Well, whatever she said, it seems to have worked." Reluctantly, he sheathed his weapon. Derek, after a moment's hesitation, lowered his sword, but he did not put it back in its scabbard.

"We will consider your story," the elven leader began, speaking haltingly in Common. Then he stopped as shouts and cries were heard from down the beach. The companions saw dark shadows converge on the campfire. The elf glanced that direction, waited a moment until all had quieted, then turned back to the group. He looked particularly at Laurana, who was bending over her brother. "We may have acted in haste, but when you have lived here long, you will come to understand."

"I will never understand this!" Laurana said, tears choking her voice.

An elf appeared out of the darkness. "Humans, sir." Laurana heard him report in elven. "Sailors by their appearance. They say their ship was attacked by a dragon and wrecked on the rocks."

"Verification?"

"We found bits of wreckage floating ashore. We can search in the morning. The humans are wet and miserable and half-drowned. They offered no resistance. I don't think they've lied."

The elven leader turned to Laurana. "Your story appears to be true," he said, speaking once more in Common. "My men report that the humans they captured are sailors. Do not worry about them. We will take them prisoner, of course. We cannot have humans wandering around this island with all our other problems. But we will care for them well. We are not goblins," he added bitterly. "I regret striking your friend—"

"Brother," Laurana replied. "And younger son of the Speaker of the Suns. I am Lauralanthalasa, and this is Gilthanas. We are of the royal house of Qualinesti."

It seemed to her that the elf paled at this news, but he regained his composure immediately. "Your brother will be well tended. I will send for a healer—"

"We do not need your healer!" Laurana said. "This man"—she gestured toward Elistan—"is a cleric of Paladine. He will aid my brother—"

"A human?" the elf asked sternly.

"Yes, human!" Laurana cried impatiently. "Elves struck my brother down! I turn to humans to heal him. Elistan—"

The cleric started forward, but, at a sign from their leader, several elves quickly grabbed him and pinned his arms behind him. Sturm started to go to his aid, but Elistan stopped him with a look, glancing at Laurana meaningfully. Sturm fell back, understanding Elistan's silent warning. Their lives depended on her.

"Let him go!" Laurana demanded. "Let him treat my brother!"

"I find this news of a cleric of Paladine impossible to believe, Lady Laurana," the elf leader said. "All know the clerics vanished from Krynn when the gods turned their faces from us. I do not know who this charlatan is, or how he has tricked you into believing him, but we will not allow him to lay his human hands upon an elf!"

"Even an elf who is an enemy?" she cried furiously.

"Even if the elf had killed my own father," the elf said grimly. "And now, Lady Laurana, I must speak to you privately and try to explain what is transpiring on Southern Ergoth."

Seeing Laurana hesitate, Elistan spoke, "Go on, my dear. You are the only one who can save us now. I will stay near Gilthanas."

"Very well," Laurana said, rising to her feet. Her face pale, she walked apart with the elven leader.

"I don't like this," Derek said, scowling. "She told them of the dragon orb, which she should not have done."

"They heard us talking about it," Sturm said wearily.

"Yes, but she told them where it was! I don't trust her, or her people. Who knows what kind of deals they are making?" Derek added.

"That does it!" grated a voice.

Both men turned in astonishment to see Flint staggering to his feet. His teeth still chattered, but a cold light glinted in his eyes as he looked at Derek. "I—I've had a-about enough of y-you, S-Sir High and M-Mighty." The dwarf gritted his teeth to stop shivering long enough to speak.

Sturm started to intervene, but the dwarf shoved him aside to confront Derek. It was a ludicrous sight, and one Sturm often remembered with a smile, storing it up to share with Tanis. The dwarf, his long white beard wet and scraggly, water dripping from his clothes to form puddles at his feet, stood nearly level with Derek's belt buckle, scolding the tall, proud Solamnic knight as he might have scolded Tasslehoff.

"You knights have lived encased in metal so long it's shaken your brains to mush!" The dwarf snorted. "If you ever had any brains to begin with, which I doubt. I've seen that girl grow from a wee bit of a thing to the beautiful woman she is now. And I tell you there isn't a more courageous, nobler person on Krynn. What's got you is that she just saved your hide. And you can't handle that!"

Derek's face flushed dark in the torchlight.

"I need neither dwarves nor elves defending me—" Derek began angrily when Laurana came running back, her eyes glittering.

"As if there is not evil enough," she muttered through tight lips, "I find it brewing among my own kindred!"

"What's going on?" asked Sturm.

"The situation stands thus: There are now three races of elves living in Southern Ergoth—"

"Three races?" interrupted Tasslehoff, staring at Laurana with interest. "What's the third race? Where'd they come from? Can I see them? I never heard—"

Laurana had had enough. "Tas," she said, her voice taut. "Go stay with Gilthanas. And ask Elistan to come here."

"But—"

Sturm gave the kender a shove. "Go!" he ordered.

Wounded, Tasslehoff trailed off disconsolately to where Gilthanas still lay. The kender slumped down in the sand, pouting. Elistan patted him kindly as he went to join the others.

"The Kaganesti, known as Wilder Elves in the Common tongue, are the third race," Laurana continued. "They fought with us during the Kinslayer wars. In return for their loyalty, Kith-Kanan gave them the mountains of Ergoth—this was before Qualinesti and Ergoth were split apart by the Cataclysm. I am not surprised you have never heard of the Wilder Elves. They are a secretive people and keep to themselves. Once called the Border Elves, they are ferocious fighters and served Kith-Kanan well, but they have no love for cities. They mingled with Druids and learned their lore. They brought back the ways of the ancient elves. My people consider them barbarians—just as your people consider the Plainsmen barbaric.

"Some months ago, when the Silvanesti were driven from their ancient homeland, they fled here, seeking permission of the Kaganesti to dwell in Ergoth temporarily. Then came my people, the Qualinesti, from across the sea. And so they met, at last, kindred who had been separated for hundreds of years."

"I fail to see the relevance—" Derek interrupted.

"You will," she said, drawing a deep breath. "For your lives depend upon understanding what is happening on this sad isle." Her voice broke. Elistan moved near her and put his arm around her comfortingly.

"All started out peacefully enough. After all, the two exiled cousins had much in common—both driven from their beloved homelands by the evil in the world. They established homes upon the Isle—the Silvanesti upon the western shore, the Qualinesti upon the eastern, separated by a strait known as Thon-Tsalarian, which means the 'River of the Dead' in Kaganesti. The Kaganesti live in the hill country north of the river.

"For a time, there was even some attempt to establish friendships between the Silvanesti and the Qualinesti. And that is where the trouble began. For these elves could not meet, even after hundreds of years, without the old hatreds and misunderstandings beginning to surface." Laurana closed her eyes a moment. "The River of the Dead could very well be known as Thon-Tsalaroth—'River of Death.' "

"There now, lass," Flint said, touching her hand. "The dwarves have known it, too. You saw the way I was treated in Thorbardin—a hill dwarf among mountain dwarves. Of all the hatreds, the ones between families are the cruelest."

"There has been no killing yet, but so shocked were the elders at the thought of what might happen—elves killing their own kindred—that they decreed no one may cross the straits on penalty of arrest," Laurana continued. "And this is where we stand. Neither side trusts the other. There have even been charges of selling out to the Dragon Highlords! Spies have been captured on both sides."

"That explains why they attacked us," Elistan murmured.

"What about the Kag—Kag—" Sturm stammered over the unfamiliar elven word.

"Kaganesti." Laurana sighed wearily. "They, who allowed us to share their homeland, have been treated worst of all. The Kaganesti have always been poor in material wealth. Poor, by our standards, though not by theirs. They live in the forests and mountains, taking what they need from the land. They are gatherers, hunters. They raise no crops, they forge no metal. When we arrived, our people appeared rich to them with our golden jewelry and steel weapons. Many of their young people came to the Qualinesti and the Silvanesti, seeking to learn the secrets of making shining gold and silver—and steel."

Laurana bit her lip, her face hardened. "I say it to my shame, that my people have taken advantage of the Wilder Elves' poverty. The Kaganesti work as slaves among us. And, because of that, the Kaganesti elders grow more savage and warlike as they see their young people taken away and their old way of life threatened."

"Laurana!" called Tasslehoff.

She turned. "Look," she said to Elistan softly. "There is one of them now." The cleric followed her gaze to see a lithe young woman—at least he supposed it was a young woman by the long hair; she was dressed in male clothing—kneel down beside Gilthanas and stroke his forehead. The elflord stirred at her touch, groaning in pain. The Kaganesti reached into a pouch at her side and began busily to mix something in a small clay cup.

"What is she doing?" Elistan asked.

"She is apparently the 'healer' they sent for," Laurana said, watching the girl closely. "The Kaganesti are noted for their Druidic skills."

Wilder elf was a suitable name, Elistan decided, studying the girl intently. He had certainly never seen any intelligent being on Krynn quite so wild-looking. She was dressed in leather breeches tucked into leather boots. A shirt, obviously cast off by some elflord, hung from her shoulders. She was pale and too thin, undernourished. Her matted hair was so filthy it was impossible to distinguish its color. But the hand that touched Gilthanas was slender and shapely. Concern and compassion for him was apparent in her gentle face.

"Well," Sturm said, "what are we to do in the midst of all this?"

"The Silvanesti have agreed to escort us to my people," Laurana said, her face flushing. Evidently this had been a point of bitter contention. "At first they insisted that we go to their elders, but I said I would go nowhere without first bidding my father greeting and discussing the matter with him. There wasn't much they could say to that." Laurana smiled slightly, though there was a touch of bitterness in her voice. "Among all the kindred, a daughter is bound to her father's house until she comes of age. Keeping me here, against my will, would be viewed as kidnapping and would cause open hostility. Neither side is ready for that."

"They are letting us go, though they know we have the dragon orb?" Derek asked in astonishment.

"They are *not* letting us go," Laurana said sharply. "I said they are escorting us to my people."

"But there is a Solamnic outpost to the north," Derek argued. "We could get a ship there to take us to Sancrist—"

"You would never live to reach those trees if you tried to escape," Flint said, sneezing violently.

"He is right," Laurana said. "We must go to the Qualinesti and convince my father to help us get the orb to Sancrist." A small dark line appeared between her eyebrows which warned Sturm she didn't believe that was going to be as easy as it sounded. "And now, we've been talking long enough. They gave me leave to explain things to you, but they're getting restless to go. I must see to Gilthanas. Are we agreed?"

Laurana regarded each knight with a look that was not so much seeking approbation as simply waiting for an acknowledgement of her leadership. For a moment, she appeared so like Tanis in the firm set of her jaw and the calm, steady deliberation in her eyes that Sturm smiled. But Derek was not smiling. He was infuriated and frustrated, the more so because he knew there wasn't a thing he could do.

Finally, however, he snarled a muttered reply that he supposed they must make the best of it and angrily stalked over to pick up the chest. Flint and Sturm followed, the dwarf sneezing until he nearly sneezed himself off his feet.

Laurana walked back to her brother, moving quietly along the sand in her soft leather boots. But the Wilder elf heard her approach. Raising her head, she gave Laurana a fearful look and crept backward as an animal cringes at the sight of man. But Tas, who had been chatting with her in an odd mixture of Common and elven, gently caught hold of the Wilder elf's arm.

"Don't leave," said the kender cheerfully. "This is the elflord's sister. Look, Laurana. Gilthanas is coming around. It must be that mud stuff she stuck on his forehead. I could have sworn he'd be out for days." Tas stood up. "Laurana, this is my friend—what did you say your name was?"

The girl, her eyes on the ground, trembled violently. Her hands picked up bits of sand, then dropped them again. She murmured something none of them could hear.

"What was it, child?" Laurana asked in such a sweet and gentle voice that the girl raised her eyes shyly.

"Silvart," she said in a low voice.

"That means 'silver-haired' in the Kaganesti language, does it not?" Laurana asked. Kneeling down beside Gilthanas, she helped him sit up. Dizzily, he put his hand to his face where the girl had plastered a thick paste over his bleeding cheek.

"Don't touch," Silvart warned, clasping her hand over Gilthanas's hand quickly. "It will make you well." She spoke Common, not crudely, but clearly and concisely.

Gilthanas groaned in pain, shutting his eyes and letting his hand fall. Silvart gazed at him in deep concern. She started to stroke his face, then— glancing swiftly at Laurana—hurriedly withdrew her hand and started to rise.

"Wait," Laurana said. "Wait, Silvart."

The girl froze like a rabbit, staring at Laurana with such fear in her large eyes that Laurana was overcome with shame.

"Don't be frightened. I want to thank you for caring for my brother. Tasslehoff is right. I thought his injury was grave indeed, but you have aided him. Please stay with him, if you would."

Silvart stared at the ground. "I will stay with him, mistress, if such is your command."

"It is not my command, Silvart," Laurana said. "It is my wish. And my name is Laurana."

Silvart lifted her eyes. "Then I will stay with him gladly, mis—Laurana, if that is your wish." She lowered her head, and they could barely hear her words. "My true name, Silvara, means silver-haired. Silvart is what *they* call me." She glanced at the Silvanesti warriors, then her eyes went back to Laurana. "Please, I want you to call me Silvara."

The Silvanesti elves brought over a makeshift litter they had constructed of a blanket and tree limbs. They lifted the elflord—not ungently— onto the litter. Silvara walked beside it. Tasslehoff walked near her, still chattering, pleased to find someone who had not yet heard his stories. Laurana and Elistan walked on the other side of Gilthanas. Laurana held his hand in hers, watching over him tenderly. Behind them came Derek, his face dark and shadowed, the chest with the dragon orb on his shoulder. Behind them marched a guard of Silvanesti elves.

Day was just beginning to dawn, gray and dismal, when they reached the line of trees along the shore. Flint shivered. Twisting his head, he gazed out to sea. "What was that Derek said about a—a ship to Sancrist?"

"I am afraid so," Sturm replied. "It is also an island."

"And we've *got* to go there?"

"Yes."

"To use the dragon orb? We don't know anything about it!"

"The Knights will learn," Sturm said softly. "The future of the world rests on this."

"Humpf!" The dwarf sneezed. Casting a terrified glance at the night-dark waters, he shook his head gloomily. "All I know is I've been drowned twice, stricken with a deadly disease—"

"You were seasick."

"Stricken with a deadly disease," Flint repeated loudly, "and sunk. Mark my words, Sturm Brightblade—boats are bad luck to us. We've had nothing but trouble since we set foot in that blasted boat on Crystalmir Lake. That was where the crazed magician first saw the constellations had disappeared, and our luck's gone straight downhill from there. As long as we keep relying on boats, it's going to go from bad to worse."

Sturm smiled as he watched the dwarf squish through the sand. But his smile turned to a sigh. I wish it were all that simple, the knight thought.

3

The Speaker of the Suns.

Laurana's decision.

he Speaker of the Suns, leader of the Qualinesti elves, sat in the crude shelter of wood and mud the Kaganesti elves had built for his domicile. He considered it crude, the Kaganesti considered it a marvelously large and well-crafted dwelling, suitable for five or six families. They had, in fact, intended it as such and were shocked when the Speaker declared it barely adequate for his needs and moved in with his wife—alone.

Of course, what the Kaganesti could not know was that the Speaker's home in exile became the central headquarters for all the business of the Qualinesti. The ceremonial guards assumed exactly the same positions as they had in the sculptured halls of the palace in Qualinost. The Speaker held audience at the same time and in the same courtly manner, save that his ceiling was a mud-covered dome of thatched grass instead of glittering mosaic, his walls wood instead of crystal quartz.

The Speaker sat in state every day, his wife's sister's daughter by his side acting as his scribe. He wore the same robes, conducted business with the same cold aplomb. But there were differences. The Speaker had changed dramatically in the past few months. There were none in the Qualinesti who marveled at this, however. The Speaker had sent his younger son on a mission that most considered suicidal. Worse, his beloved daughter had run away to chase after her half-elven lover. The Speaker expected never to see either of these children again.

He could have accepted the loss of his son, Gilthanas. It was, after all, a heroic, noble act. The young man had led a group of adventurers into the mines of Pax Tharkas to free the humans imprisoned there and draw off the dragonarmies threatening Qualinesti. This plan had been a success—an unexpected success. The dragonarmies had been recalled to Pax Tharkas, giving the elves time to escape to the western shores of their land, and from there across the sea to Southern Ergoth.

The Speaker could not, however, accept his daughter's loss—or her dishonor.

It was the Speaker's elder son, Porthios, who had coldly explained the matter to him after Laurana had been discovered missing. She had run off after her childhood friend—Tanis Half-Elven. The Speaker was heartsick, consumed with grief. How could she do this? How could she bring disgrace upon their household? A princess of her people chasing after a bastard half-breed!

Laurana's flight quenched the light of the sun for her father. Fortunately, the need to lead his people gave him the strength to carry on. But there were times when the Speaker asked what was the use? He could retire, turn the throne over to his eldest son. Porthios ran almost everything anyway, deferring to his father in all that was proper, but making most decisions himself. The young elflord, serious beyond his years, was proving an excellent leader, although some considered him too harsh in his dealings with the Silvanesti and the Kaganesti.

The Speaker was among these, which was the main reason he did *not* turn things over to Porthios. Occasionally he tried to point out to his elder son that moderation and patience won more victories than threats and sword-rattling. But Porthios believed his father to be soft and sentimental. The Silvanesti, with their rigid caste structure, considered the Qualinesti barely part of the elven race and the Kaganesti no part of the elven race at all, viewing them as a subrace of elves, much as gully dwarves were seen as a subrace of the dwarves.Porthios firmly believed, although he did not tell his father, that it must end in bloodshed.

His views were matched on the other side of the Thon-Tsalarian by a stiff-necked, cold-blooded lord named Quinath, who, it was rumored, was the betrothed of the Princess Alhana Starbreeze. Lord Quinath was now leader of the Silvanesti in her unexplained absence, and it was he and Porthios who divided the isle between the two warring nations of elves, disregarding the third race entirely.

The borderlines were patronizingly communicated to the Kaganesti, as one might communicate to a dog that it is not to enter the kitchen. The Kaganesti, notable for their volatile tempers, were outraged to find their land being divided up and parceled out. Already the hunting was growing bad. The animals the Wilder elves depended on for their survival were being wiped out in great numbers to feed the refugees. As Laurana had said, the River of the Dead could, at any moment, run red with blood, and its name change tragically.

And so the Speaker found himself living in an armed camp. But if he grieved over this fact at all, it was lost in such a multitude of griefs that eventually he grew numb. Nothing touched him. He withdrew into his mud home and allowed Porthios to handle more and more.

The Speaker was up early the morning the companions arrived in what was now called Qualin-Mori. He always rose early. Not so much because he had a great deal to do, but because he had already spent most of the night staring at the ceiling. He was jotting down notes for the day's meetings with the Heads of Household—an unsatisfactory task, since the Heads of Household could do nothing but complain—when he heard a tumult outside his dwelling.

The Speaker's heart sank. What now? he wondered fearfully. It seemed these alarms came once or twice every day. Porthios had probably caught some hot-blooded Qualinesti and Silvanesti youths raiding or fighting. He kept writing, expecting the tumult to die down. But instead it increased, coming nearer and nearer. The Speaker could only suppose something more serious had happened. And not for the first time, he wondered what he would do if the elves went to war again.

Dropping the quill pen, he wrapped himself in his robes of state and waited with dread. Outside, he heard the guards snap to attention. He heard Porthios's voice perform the traditional rights of seeking entry, since it was before hours. The Speaker glanced fearfully at the door that led to his private chambers, fearing his wife might be disturbed. She had been in ill health since their departure from Qualinesti. Trembling, he rose to his feet, assuming the stern and cold look he had become accustomed to putting on as one might put on an article of clothing, and bade them come inside.

One of the guards opened the door, obviously intending to announce someone. But words failed him and, before he could speak, a tall, slender figure dressed in a heavy, hooded fur cloak, pushed past the guard and ran toward the Speaker. Startled, seeing only that the figure was armed with sword and bow, the Speaker shrank back in alarm.

The figure threw back the hood of her cloak. The Speaker saw honey-colored hair flow down around a woman's face—a face remarkable even among the elves for its delicate beauty.

"Father!" she cried, then Laurana was in his arms.

The return of Gilthanas, long mourned as dead by his people, was the occasion of the greatest celebration to be held by the Qualinesti since the night the companions had been feasted before setting off for the Sla-Mori.

Gilthanas had recovered sufficiently from his wounds to be able to attend the festivities, a small scar on his cheekbone the only sign of his injury. Laurana and her friends wondered at this, for they had seen the terrible blow inflicted upon him by the Silvanesti elf. But when Laurana mentioned it to her father, the Speaker only shrugged and said that the Kaganesti had befriended druids living in the forests; they had probably learned much in the way of healing arts from them.

This frustrated Laurana, who knew the rarity of true healing powers on Krynn. She longed to discuss it with Elistan, but the cleric was closeted for hours with her father, who was very soon impressed by the man's true clerical powers.

Laurana was pleased to see her father accept Elistan—remembering how the Speaker had treated Goldmoon when she first came to Qualinesti wearing the medallion of Mishakal, Goddess of Healing. But Laurana missed her wise mentor. Though overjoyed at being home, Laurana was beginning to realize that for her, home had changed and would never be the same again.

Everyone appeared very glad to see her, but they treated her with the same courtesy they gave Derek and Sturm, Flint and Tas. She was an outsider. Even her parents' manner was cool and distant after their initial emotional welcome. She might not have wondered at this, if they hadn't been so doting over Gilthanas. Why the difference? Laurana couldn't understand. It remained to her elder brother, Porthios, to open her eyes.

The incident began at the feast.

"You will find our lives much different from our lives in Qualinesti," her father told her brother that night as they sat at the banquet held indoors in a great log hall built by the Kaganesti. "But you will soon become accustomed to it." Turning to Laurana, he spoke formally. "I would be glad to have you back in your old place as my scribe, but I know you will be busy with other things around our household."

Laurana was startled. She had not intended to stay, of course, but she resented being replaced in what was a daughter's traditional role in the royal household. She also resented the fact that, though she had talked to her father about taking the orb to Sancrist, he had apparently ignored her.

"Speaker," she said slowly, trying to keep the irritation from her voice, "I have told you. We cannot stay. Haven't you been listening to me and to Elistan? We have discovered the dragon orb! Now we have the means to control dragons and bring an end to this war! We must take the orb to Sancrist—"

"Stop, Laurana!" her father said sharply, exchanging looks with Porthios. Her brother regarded her sternly. "You know nothing of what you speak, Laurana. The dragon orb is truly a great prize, and so should not be discussed here. As for taking it to Sancrist, that is out of the question."

"I beg your pardon, sir," Derek said, rising and bowing, "but you have no say in the matter. The dragon orb is not yours. I was sent by the Knights

Council to recover a dragon orb, if possible. I have succeeded and I intend to take it back as I was ordered. You have no right to stop me."

"Haven't I?" the Speaker's eyes glittered angrily. "My son, Gilthanas, brought it into this land which we, the Qualinesti, declare to be our homeland in exile. That makes it ours by right."

"I never claimed that, Father," Gilthanas said, flushing as he felt the companions' eyes turn to him. "It is not mine. It belongs to all of us—"

Porthios shot his younger brother a furious glance. Gilthanas stammered, then fell silent.

"If it is anyone's to claim, it is Laurana's," Flint Fireforge spoke up, not at all intimidated by the elves' glaring stares. "For it was she who killed Feal-thas, the evil elven magic-user."

"If it be hers," the Speaker said in a voice older than his hundreds of years, "then it is mine by right. For she is not of age, what is hers is mine, since I am her father. That is elven law and dwarven law, too, if I'm not mistaken."

Flint's face flushed. He opened his mouth to reply, but Tasslehoff beat him to it.

"Isn't that odd?" remarked the kender cheerfully, having missed the serious portent of the conversation. "According to kender law, if there is a kender law, everybody sort of owns everything." (This was quite true. The kenders' casual attitude toward the possessions of others extended to their own. Nothing in a kender house remained there long, unless it was nailed to the floor. Some neighbor was certain to wander in, admire it, and absentmindedly walk off with it. A family heirloom among kenders was defined as anything remaining in a house longer than three weeks.)

No one spoke after that. Flint kicked Tas under the table, and the kender subsided in hurt silence which lasted until he discovered his neighbor, an elvenlord, had been called from the table, leaving his purse behind. Rummaging through the elflord's possessions kept the kender happily occupied throughout the rest of the meal.

Flint, who ordinarily would have kept an eye on Tas, did not notice this in his other worries. It was obvious there was going to be trouble. Derek was furious. Only the rigid code of the Knights kept him seated at the table. Laurana sat in silence, not eating. Her face was pale beneath her tanned skin, and she was punching small holes in the finely woven table cloth with her fork. Flint nudged Sturm.

"We thought getting the dragon orb out of Ice Wall was tough," the dwarf said in an undertone. "There we only had to escape a crazed wizard and a few walrus-men. Now we're surrounded by three nations of elves!"

"We'll have to reason with them," Sturm said softly.

"Reason!" The dwarf snorted. "Two stones would have a better chance of reasoning with each other!"

That proved to be the case. By the Speaker's request, the companions remained seated after the other elves left, following dinner. Gilthanas and his sister sat side by side, their faces drawn and worried as Derek stood up before the Speaker to "reason" with him.

"The orb is ours," Derek stated coldly. "You have no right to it at all. It certainly does not belong to your daughter or to your son. They traveled with me only by my courtesy, after I rescued them from the destruction of Tarsis. I am happy to have been able to escort them back to their homeland, and I thank you for your hospitality. But I leave tomorrow for Sancrist, taking the orb with me."

Porthios stood up to face Derek. "The kender may say the dragon orb is his. It doesn't matter." The elflord spoke in a smooth, polite voice that slid through the night air like a knife. "The orb is in elven hands now, and here it will stay. Do you think we are foolish enough to let this prize be taken by humans to cause more trouble in this world?"

"More trouble!" Derek's face flushed deep red. "Do you realize the trouble this world is in now? The dragons drove you from your homeland. They are approaching our homeland now! Unlike you, we do not intend to run. We will stand and fight! This orb could be our only hope—"

"You have my leave to go back to your homeland and be burned to a crisp for all I care," Porthios returned. "It was you humans who stirred up this ancient evil. It is fitting that you fight it. The Dragon Highlords have what they want from us. They will undoubtedly leave us in peace. Here, on Ergoth, the orb will be kept safe."

"Fool!" Derek slammed his fist on the table. "The Dragon Highlords have only one thought and that is to conquer all of Ansalon! That includes this miserable isle! You may be safe here for a time, but if we fall, you will fall, too!"

"You know he speaks truly, Father," Laurana said, greatly daring. Elven women did not attend war meetings, much less speak. Laurana was present only because of her unique involvement. Rising to her feet, she faced her brother, who glowered at her disapprovingly. "Porthios, our father told us in Qualinesti that the Dragon Highlord wanted not only our lands but also the extermination of our race! Have you forgotten?"

"Bah! That was one Dragon Highlord, Verminaard. He is dead—"

"Yes, because of us," Laurana shouted angrily, "not you!"

"Laurana!" The Speaker of the Suns rose to his full height, taller even than his oldest son. His presence towered over them all. "You forget yourself, young woman. You have no right to speak to your elder brother like that. We faced perils of our own in our journey. *He* remembered his duty and his responsibility, as did Gilthanas. They did not go running off after a half-elven bastard like a brazen, human wh—" The Speaker stopped abruptly.

Laurana went white to the lips. She swayed, clutching the table for support. Gilthanas rose swiftly, coming to her side, but she pushed him away. "Father," she said in a voice she did not recognize as her own, "what were you about to say?"

"Come away, Laurana," Gilthanas begged. "He didn't mean it. We'll talk in the morning."

The Speaker said nothing, his face, gray and cold.

"You were about to say 'human whore!' " Laurana said softly, her words falling like pins on nerves stretched taut.

"Go to your lodgings, Laurana," the Speaker ordered in a tight voice.

"So that is what you think of me," Laurana whispered, her throat constricting. "That is why everyone stares and stops talking when I come near them. Human whore."

"Sister, do as your father commands," Porthios said. "As for what we think of you—remember, you brought this on yourself. What do you expect? Look at you, Laurana! You are dressed like a man. You proudly wear a sword stained with blood. You talk glibly of your 'adventures!' Traveling with men such as these, humans and dwarves! Spending the nights with them. Spending the nights with your half-breed lover. Where is he? Did he tire of you and—"

The firelight flared before Laurana's eyes. Its heat swept over her body, to be replaced by a terrible cold. She could see nothing and remembered only a horrifying sensation of falling without being able to catch herself. Voices came at her from a great distance, distorted faces bent over her.

"Laurana, my daughter . . ."

Then nothing.

"Mistress . . ."

"What? Where am I? Who are you? I—I can't see! Help me!"

"There, mistress. Take my hand. Shhhh. I am here. I am Silvara. Remember?"

Laurana felt gentle hands take her own as she sat up.

"Can you drink this, mistress?"

A cup was placed to her lips. Laurana sipped at it, tasting clear, cold water. She grasped it and drank eagerly, feeling it cool her fevered blood. Strength returned, she found she could see again. A small candle burned beside her bed. She was in her room, in her father's house. Her clothes lay on a crude wooden bench, her swordbelt and scabbard stood near, her pack was on the floor. At a table, across from her bed, sat a nursemaid, her head cradled in her arms, fast asleep.

Laurana turned to Silvara, who, seeing the question in her eyes, put her finger to her lips.

"Speak softly," the Wilder elf replied. "Oh, not for that one"—Silvara glanced at the nurse—"she will sleep peacefully for many, many hours before the potion wears off. But there are others in the house who may be wakeful. Do you feel better?"

"Yes," Laurana answered, confused. "I don't remember . . ."

"You fainted," Silvara answered. "I heard them talking about it when they carried you back here. Your father is truly grieved. He never meant to say those things. It is just that you hurt him so terribly—"

"How did you hear?"

"I was hiding, in the shadows in the corner there. An easy thing for my people to do. The old nurse said you were fine, you just needed rest, and they left. When she went to fetch a blanket, I put the sleep juice in her tea."

"Why?" Laurana asked. Looking at the girl closely, Laurana saw that the Wilder elf must be a beautiful woman—or would be if the layers of grime and filth were washed from her.

Silvara, aware of Laurana's scrutiny, flushed in embarrassment."I—I ran away from the Silvanesti, mistress, when they brought you across the river."

"Laurana. Please, child, call me Laurana."

"Laurana," Silvara corrected, blushing. "I—I came to ask you to take you with me when you leave."

"Leave?" Laurana said. "I'm not goi—" She stopped.

"Aren't you?" Silvara asked gently.

"I . . . I don't know," Laurana said in confusion.

"I can help," Silvara said eagerly. "I know the way through the mountains to reach the Knights' outpost where the ships with birds' wings sail. I will help you get away."

"Why would you do this for us?" Laurana asked. "I'm sorry, Silvara. I don't mean to be suspicious—but you don't know us, and what you're doing is very dangerous. Surely you could escape more easily on your own."

"I know you carry the dragon orb," Silvara whispered.

"How do you know about the orb?" Laurana asked, astounded.

"I heard the Silvanesti talking, after they left you at the river."

"And you knew what it was? How?"

"My . . . people have stories . . . about it," Silvara said, her hands twisting. "I—I know it is important to end this war. Your people and the Silvan elves will go back to their homes and let the Kaganesti live in peace. There is that reason and—" Silvara was silent for a moment, then she spoke so softly Laurana could barely hear her. "You are the first person who ever knew the meaning of my name."

Laurana looked at her, puzzled. The girl seemed sincere. But Laurana didn't believe her. Why would she risk her life to help them? Perhaps she was a Silvanesti spy, sent to get the orb? It seemed unlikely, but stranger things—

Laurana put her head in her hands, trying to think. Could they trust Silvara, at least enough to get them out of here? They apparently had no choice. If they were going into the mountains, they would have to pass through Kaganesti lands. Silvara's help would be invaluable.

"I must talk to Elistan," Laurana said. "Can you bring him here?"

"No need, Laurana," Silvara answered. "He has been waiting outside for you to awaken."

"And the others? Where are the rest of my friends?"

"Lord Gilthanas is within the house of your father, of course—" Was it Laurana's imagination, or did Silvara's pale cheek flush when she said that name? "The others have been given 'guest quarters.'"

"Yes," said Laurana grimly, "I can imagine."

Silvara left her side. Creeping quietly across the floor of the room, she went to the door, opened it, and beckoned.

"Laurana?"

"Elistan!" She flung her arms around the cleric. Laying her head on his chest, Laurana shut her eyes, feeling his strong arms embrace her tenderly. Everything will be fine now, she knew. Elistan will take charge. He'll know what to do.

"Are you feeling better?" the cleric asked. "Your father—"

"Yes, I know," Laurana interrupted him. She felt a dull ache in her heart whenever her father was mentioned. "You must decide what we are to do, Elistan. Silvara has offered to help us escape. We could take the orb and leave tonight."

"If that is what you must do, my dear, then you should waste no more time," Elistan said, sitting by her in a chair.

Laurana blinked. Reaching out, she grabbed hold of his arm. "Elistan, what do you mean? You must come with us—"

"No, Laurana," Elistan said, grasping her hand tightly in his own. "If you do this, you will have to leave on your own. I have sought help from Paladine, and I must stay here, with the elves. I believe if I stay, I will be able to convince your father that I am a cleric of the true gods. If I leave, he would always believe I am a charlatan, as your brother brands me."

"What about the dragon orb?"

"That is up to you, Laurana. The elves are wrong in this. Hopefully, in time, they will come to see it. But we do not have centuries to talk this over. I think you should take the orb to Sancrist."

"Me?" Laurana gasped. "I can't!"

"My dear," Elistan said firmly, "you must realize that if you make this decision, the burden of leadership will be upon you. Sturm and Derek are too caught up in their own quarrel and, besides, they are human. You will be dealing with elves, your own people and the Kaganesti. Gilthanas sides with your father. You are the only one who has a chance to succeed."

"But I'm not capable—"

"You are more capable than you give yourself credit for, Laurana. Perhaps everything you have been through up to now has been preparing you for this. You must waste no more time. Farewell, my dear." Elistan rose to his feet and laid his hand on her head. "May Paladine's blessing—and my own—go with you."

"Elistan!" Laurana whispered, but the cleric was gone. Silvara quietly shut the door.

Laurana sank back into her bed, trying to think. Elistan is right, of course. The dragon orb cannot stay here. And if we are going to escape, it must be tonight. But it's all happening so fast! And it's all up to me! Can I trust Silvara? But why ask? She's the only one who can guide us. Then all I have to do is get the orb and the lance and free my friends. I know how to get to the orb and the lance. But my friends—

Laurana knew, suddenly, what she would do. She realized she had been planning it in the back of her mind even as she talked to Elistan.

This commits me, she thought. There will be no turning back. Stealing the dragon orb, fleeing into the night, into strange and hostile country. And then, there is Gilthanas. We've been through too much together for me to leave him behind. But he will be appalled at the idea of stealing the orb and running away. And if he chooses not to go with me, would he betray us?

Laurana closed her eyes for a moment. She laid her head down wearily on her knees. Tanis, she thought, where are you? What should I do? Why is it up to me? I didn't want this.

And then, as she sat there, Laurana remembered seeing weariness and sorrow on Tanis's face that mirrored her own. Maybe he asked himself these same things. All the times I thought he was so strong, perhaps he really felt as lost and frightened as I do. Certainly he felt abandoned by his people. And we depended on him, whether he wanted us to or not. But he accepted it. He did what he believed was right.

And so must I.

Briskly, refusing to allow herself to think any further, Laurana lifted her head and beckoned for Silvara to come near.

Sturm paced the length of the crude cabin that had been given to them, unable to sleep. The dwarf lay stretched out on a bed, snoring loudly. Across the room, Tasslehoff lay curled in a ball of misery, chained by his foot to the bedpost. Sturm sighed. How much more trouble could they get into?

The evening had gone from bad to worse. After Laurana had fainted, it had been all Sturm could do to hold back the enraged dwarf. Flint vowed to tear Porthios limb from limb. Derek stated that he considered himself to be a prisoner held by the enemy and, as such, it was his duty to try and escape; then he would bring the Knights down to recover the dragon orb by force. Derek was immediately escorted away by the guards. Just when Sturm got Flint calmed down, an elflord appeared out of nowhere and accused Tasslehoff of stealing his purse.

Now they were being held under double guard, "guests" of the Speaker of the Suns.

"Must you pace about like that?" Derek asked coldly.

"Why? Am I keeping you awake?" snapped Sturm.

"Of course not. Only fools could sleep under these circumstances. You're breaking my concen—"

"Hsst!" Sturm said, raising his hand warningly.

Derek instantly fell silent. Sturm gestured. The older knight joined Sturm in the center of the room where he was staring up at the ceiling. The log house was rectangular, with one door, two windows, and a firepit in the center of the floor. A hole cut in the roof provided ventilation.

It was through this hole Sturm heard the odd sound that caught his attention. It was a shuffling, scraping sound. The wooden beams in the ceiling creaked as though something heavy was crawling over it.

"A wild beast of some sort," Derek muttered. "And we're weaponless!"

"No," Sturm said, listening closely. "It's not growling. It's moving too silently, as if it didn't want to be heard or seen. What are those guards doing out there?"

Derek went to the window and peered out. "Sitting around a fire. Two are asleep. They're not overly concerned about us, are they?" he asked bitterly.

"Why should they be?" Sturm said, keeping his eyes on the ceiling. "There's a couple of thousand elves within the sound of a whisper. What the—"

Sturm fell back in alarm as the stars he had been watching through the hole were suddenly blotted out by a dark, shapeless mass. Sturm reached down swiftly and grabbed a log from the smoldering fire, holding it by the end like a club.

"Sturm! Sturm Brightblade!" said the shapeless mass.

Sturm stared, trying to remember the voice. It was familiar. Thoughts of Solace flooded his mind. "Theros!" he gasped. "Theros Ironfeld! What are you doing here? The last I saw you, you were lying near death in the elven kingdom!"

The huge blacksmith of Solace struggled down through the opening in the ceiling, bringing part of the roof with him. He landed heavily, waking the dwarf, who sat up and peered, bleary-eyed, at the apparition in the center of the cabin.

"What—" the dwarf started up, fumbling for his battle-axe which was no longer by his side.

"Hush!" the smith commanded. "No time for questions. The Lady Laurana sent me to free you. We're to meet her in the woods beyond the camp. Make haste! We have only a few hours before dawn and we must be across the river by then." Theros strode over to look at Tasslehoff, who was trying without success to free himself. "Well, master thief, I see someone caught you at last."

"I'm not a thief!" Tas said indignantly. "You know me better than that, Theros. That purse was planted on me—"

The smith chuckled. Taking hold of the chain in his hands, he gave a sudden heave and it split apart. Tasslehoff, however, did not even notice. He was staring at the smith's arms. One arm, the left, was a dusky black, the color of the smith's skin. But the other arm, the right, was bright, shining silver!

"Theros," Tas said in a strangled voice. "Your arm—"

"Questions later, little thief," the smith said sternly. "Now we move swift and now we move silent."

"Across the river," Flint moaned, shaking his head. "More boats. More boats . . ."

"I want to see the Speaker," Laurana told the guard at the door to her father's suite of rooms.

"It is late," the guard said. "The Speaker is sleeping."

Laurana drew back her hood. The guard bowed. "Forgive me, Princess. I did not recognize you."

He glanced at Silvara suspiciously. "Who is that with you?"

"My maid. I would not travel at night by myself."

"No, of course not," the guard said hurriedly as he opened the door. "Go ahead. His sleeping room is the third one down the hall on your right."

"Thank you,"Laurana answered and brushed past the guard. Silvara, muffled in a voluminous cape, swept softly after her.

"The chest is in his room, at the foot of his bed," Laurana whispered to Silvara. "Are you sure you can carry the dragon orb? It is big and very heavy."

"It's not that big," Silvara murmured, staring perplexed at Laurana."Only about so—" She made a gesture with her hands roughly the shape of a child's ball.

"No," Laurana said, frowning. "You have not seen it. It is nearly two feet in diameter. That's why I had you wear that long cape."

Silvara stared at her in wonder. Laurana shrugged. "Well, we can't stand here arguing. We'll figure something out when the time comes."

The two crept down the hallway, silently as kender, until they came to the bedroom.

Holding her breath, fearing that even her heartbeat was too loud, Laurana pressed on the door. It opened with a creaking sound that made her grit her teeth. Next to her, Silvara shivered in fear. A figure in the bed stirred and turned over—her mother. Laurana saw her father, even in his sleep, put out his hand to pat her reassuringly. Tears dimmed Laurana's eyes. Tightening her lips resolutely, she gripped Silvara's hand and slipped inside the room.

The chest stood at the end of her father's bed. It was locked, but the companions all carried a copy of the small silver key. Swiftly Laurana unlocked the chest and lifted the lid. Then she nearly dropped it in her amazement. The dragon orb was there, still glowing with the soft white and blue light. But it wasn't the same orb! Or if it was, it had shrunk! As Silvara said, it was now no more than the size of a child's playing ball! Laurana reached in to take it. It was still heavy, but she could lift it easily. Gingerly grasping it, her hand shaking, she raised it from the box and handed it to Silvara. The Wilder elf immediately hid it beneath her cloak.

Laurana picked up the wood shaft of the broken dragonlance, wondering, as she did so, why she bothered taking the broken old weapon.

I'll take it because the knight handed it to Sturm, she thought. He wanted him to have it.

At the bottom of the chest lay Tanis's sword, Wyrmslayer, given him by Kith-Kanan. Laurana looked from the sword to the dragonlance. I can't carry both, she thought, and started to put the lance back. But Silvara grabbed her.

"What are you doing?" Her mouth formed the words, her eyes flashed. "Take it! Take it, too!"

Laurana stared at the girl in amazement. Then, hastily, she retrieved the lance, concealed it beneath her cloak, and carefully shut the chest, leaving the sword inside. Just as the lid left her cold fingers, her father rolled over in his bed, half-sitting up.

"What? Who is there?" he asked, starting to shake off his sleep in his alarm.

Laurana felt Silvara trembling and clutched the girl's hand reassuringly, warning her to be silent.

"It is I, Father," she said in a faint voice. "Laurana. I—I wanted to—to tell you I am sorry, Father. And I ask you to forgive me."

"Ah, Laurana." The Speaker lay back down on his pillows, closing his eyes. "I forgive you, my daughter. Now return to your bed. We'll talk in the morning."

Laurana waited until his breathing became quiet and regular. Then she led Silvara from the room, gripping the dragonlance firmly beneath her cloak.

"Who goes there?" softly called a human voice in elven.

"Who asks?" replied a clear elven voice.

"Gilthanas? Is that you?"

"Theros! My friend!" The young elflord stepped swiftly from the shadows to embrace the human blacksmith. For a moment Gilthanas was so overcome he could not speak. Then, startled, he pushed back from the smith's bearlike hug. "Theros! You have two arms! But the draconians in Solace cut off your right arm! You would have died, if Goldmoon hadn't healed you."

"Do you remember what that pig of a Fewmaster told me?" Theros asked in his rich, deep voice, whispering softly. " 'The only way you'll get a new arm, smith, is to forge it yourself!' Well, I did just that! The story of my adventures to find the Silver Arm I wear now is a long one—"

"And not for telling now," grumbled another voice behind him. "Unless you want to ask a couple of thousand elves to hear it with us."

"So you managed to escape, Gilthanas," said Derek's voice out of the shadows. "Did you bring the dragon orb?"

"I did not *escape*," Gilthanas returned coldly. "I left my father's house to accompany my sister and Silvara, her maid, through the darkness. Taking the orb is my sister's idea, not mine. There is still time to reconsider this madness, Laurana." Gilthanas turned to her. "Return the orb. Don't let Porthios's hasty words drive away your common sense. If we keep the orb here, we can use it to defend our people. We can find out how it works, we have magic-users among us."

"Let's just turn ourselves over to the guards now! Then we can get some sleep where it's warm!" Flint's words came out in explosive puffs of frost.

"Either sound the alarm now, elf, or let us go. At least give us time before you betray us," Derek said.

"I have no intention of betraying you," Gilthanas stated angrily. Ignoring the others, he turned once more to his sister. "Laurana?"

"I am determined on this course of action," she answered slowly. "I have thought about it and I believe we are doing the right thing. So does Elistan. Silvara will guide us through the mountains—"

"I, too, know the mountains," Theros spoke up. "I have had little to do here but wander them. And you'll need me to get you past the guards."

"Then we are resolved."

"Very well." Gilthanas sighed. "I am coming with you. If I stayed behind, Porthios would always suspect me of complicity."

"Fine," snapped Flint. "Can we escape now? Or do we need to wake up anyone else?"

"This way," Theros said. "The guards are accustomed to my late night rambles. Stay in the shadows, and let *me* do the talking." Reaching down, he caught hold of Tasslehoff by the collar of his heavy fur coat and lifted the kender off the ground to look him right in the eye."That means you, little thief," the big smith said sternly.

"Yes, Theros," the kender replied meekly, squirming in the man's silver hand until the smith set him down. Somewhat shaken, Tas readjusted his pouches and tried to regain his injured dignity.

The companions followed the tall, dark-skinned smith along the outskirts of the silent elven encampment, moving as quietly as possible for two armor-clad knights and a dwarf. To Laurana, they sounded as loud as a wedding party. She bit her lip to keep silent as the knights clanked and rattled in the darkness, while Flint fell over every tree root and splashed through every puddle.

But the elves lay wrapped in their complacency like a soft, fleecy blanket. They had safely fled the danger. None believed it would find them again. And so they slept as the companions escaped into the night.

Silvara, carrying the dragon orb, felt the cold crystal grow warm as she held it near her body, felt it stir and pulse with life.

"What am I to do?" she whispered to herself distractedly in Kaganesti, stumbling almost blindly through the darkness. "This came to *me*! Why? I don't understand? What am I to do?"

4

River of the Dead.

The Legend of the Silver Dragon.

he night was still and cold. Storm clouds blotted out the light of
the moons and stars. There was no rain, no wind, just an oppressive sense of waiting. Laurana felt that all of nature was alert,
wary, fearful. And behind her, the elves slept, cocooned in a web of their
own petty fears and hatreds. What horrible winged creature would burst
from that cocoon, she wondered.

The companions had little trouble slipping past the elven guards. Recognizing Theros, the guards stood and chatted amiably with him, while
the others crept through the woods around them. They reached the river
in the first chill light of dawn.

"And how are we to get across?" the dwarf asked, staring out at the
water gloomily. "I don't think much of boats, but they beat swimming."

"That should not be a problem." Theros turned to Laurana and said,
"Ask your little friend," nodding at Silvara.

Startled, Laurana looked at the Wilder elf, as did the others. Silvara,
embarrassed at so many eyes upon her, flushed deeply, bowing he head.
"Kargai Sargaron is right," she murmured. "Wait here, within the shadows
of the trees."

She left them and ran lightly to the riverbank with a wild, free grace, enchanting to watch. Laurana noticed that Gilthanas's gaze, in particular, lingered upon the Wilder elf.

Silvara put her fingers to her lips and whistled like the call of a bird. She waited a moment, then repeated the whistle three times. Within minutes, her call was answered, echoing across the water from the opposite bank of the river.

Satisfied, Silvara returned to the group. Laurana saw that, though Silvara spoke to Theros, the girl's eyes were drawn to Gilthanas. Finding him staring at her, she blushed and looked quickly back at Theros.

"Kargai Sargaron," she said hurriedly, "my people are coming, but you should be with me to meet them and explain things." Silvara's blue eyes—Laurana could see them clearly in the morning light—went to Sturm and Derek. The Wilder elf shook her head slightly. "They will not be happy about bringing these humans to our land, nor these elves either, I am afraid," she said, with an apologetic glance at Laurana and Gilthanas.

"I will talk to them," Theros said. Gazing across the lake, he gestured. "Here they come now."

Laurana saw two black shapes sliding across the sky-gray river. The Kaganesti must keep watch there constantly, she realized. They recognized Silvara's call. Odd—for a slave to have such freedom. If escape was this easy, why did Silvara stay among the Silvanesti? It didn't make any sense . . . unless escape was not her purpose.

"What does 'Kargai Sargaron' mean?" she asked Theros abruptly.

"He of the Silver Arm," Theros answered, smiling.

"They seem to trust you."

"Yes. I told you I spend a good part of my time wandering. That is not quite true. I spend much time among Silvara's people." The smith's dusky face creased in a scowl. "Meaning no disrespect, elflady, but you have no idea what hardships your people are causing these wild ones: shooting the game or driving it away, enslaving the young with gold and silver and steel." Theros heaved an angry sigh. "I have done what I could. I showed them how to forge hunting weapons and tools. But the winter will be long and hard, I fear. Already, game is becoming scarce. If it comes to starving or killing their elven kin—"

"Maybe if I stayed," Laurana murmured, "I could help—" Then she realized that was ridiculous. What could she do? She wasn't even accepted by her own people!

"You can't be in all places at the same time," Sturm said. "The elves must solve their problems, Laurana. You are doing the right thing."

"I know," she said, sighing. She turned her head, looking behind her, toward the Qualinesti camp. "I was just like them, Sturm," she said, shivering. "My beautiful tiny world had revolved around me for so long that I thought I was the center of the universe. I ran after Tanis because I was certain I could make him love me. Why shouldn't he? Everyone else did. And then I discovered the world didn't revolve around me. It didn't even care about me! I saw suffering and death. I was forced to kill"—she stared down at her hands—"or be killed. I saw real love. Love like Riverwind's and Goldmoon's, love that was willing to sacrifice everything—even life itself. I felt very petty and very small. And now that's how my people seem to me. Petty and small. I used to think they were perfect, but now I understand how Tanis felt—and why he left."

The boats of the Kaganesti had reached the shore. Silvara and Theros walked down to talk to the elves who paddled them. At a gesture from Theros, the companions stepped out of the shadows of the trees and stood upon the bank—hands well away from their weapons—so the Kaganesti could see them. At first, it seemed hopeless. The elves chattered in their strange, uncouth version of elven which Laurana had difficulty following. Apparently they refused outright to have anything to do with the group.

Then horn calls sounded from the woods behind them. Gilthanas and Laurana looked at each other in alarm. Theros, glancing back, stabbed his silver finger at the group urgently, then thumped himself on the chest—apparently pledging his word to answer for the companions. The horns sounded again. Silvara added her own pleas. Finally, the Kaganesti agreed, although with a marked lack of enthusiasm.

The companions hurried down to the water, all of them aware now that their absence had been discovered and that pursuit had started. One by one, they all stepped carefully into the boats that were no more than hollowed-out trunks of trees. All, that is, except Flint, who groaned and cast himself down on the ground, shaking his head and muttering in dwarven. Sturm eyed him in concern, fearing a repetition of the incident at Crystalmir when the dwarf had flatly refused to set foot in a boat. It was Tasslehoff, however, who tugged and pulled and finally dragged the grumbling dwarf to his feet.

"We'll make a sailor of you yet," the kender said cheerfully, prodding Flint in the back with his hoopak.

"You will not! And quit sticking me with that thing!" the dwarf snarled. Reaching the edge of the water, he stopped, nervously fumbling with a piece of wood. Tas hopped into a boat and stood waiting expectantly, his hand outstretched.

"Confound it, Flint, get in the boat!" Theros ordered.

"Just tell me one thing," the dwarf said, swallowing. "Why do they call it the 'River of the Dead'?"

"You'll see, soon enough," Theros grunted. Reaching out his strong black hand, he plucked the dwarf off the bank and plopped him like a sack of potatoes on to the seat. "Shove off," the smith told the Wilder elves, who needed no bidding. Their wooden oars were already biting deep into the water.

The log boat caught the current and floated swiftly downstream, heading west. The tree-shrouded banks fairly flew past, and the companions huddled down into the boats as the cold wind stung their faces and took away their breath. They saw no signs of life along the southern shore where the Qualinesti made their home. But Laurana caught glimpses of shadowy, darting figures ducking in and out of the trees on the northern shore. She realized then that the Kaganesti were not as naive as they seemed—they were keeping close watch upon their cousins. She wondered how many of the Kaganesti living as slaves were, in reality, spies. Her eyes went to Silvara.

The current carried them swiftly to a fork in the river where two streams joined together. One flowed from the north, the other—the stream they traveled—flowed into it from the east. Both merged into one wide river, flowing south into the sea. Suddenly Theros pointed.

"There, dwarf, is your answer," he said solemnly.

Drifting down the branch of the river that flowed from the north was another boat. At first, they thought it had slipped its moorings, for they could see no one inside. Then they saw that it rode too low in the water to be empty. The Wilder elves slowed their own boats, steering them into the shallow water, and held them steady, heads bowed in silent respect.

And then Laurana knew.

"A funeral boat," she murmured.

"Aye," said Theros, watching with sad eyes. The boat drifted past, carried near them by the current. Inside they could see the body of a young Wilder elf, a warrior to judge by his crude leather armor. His hands, folded across his chest, clasped an iron sword in cold fingers. A bow and quiver of arrows lay at his side. His eyes were closed in the peaceful sleep from which he would never waken.

"Now you know why it is called *Thon-Tsalarian*, the River of the Dead," Silvara said in her low, musical voice. "For centuries, my people have returned the dead to the sea where we were born. This ancient custom of my people has become a bitter point of contention between the Kaganesti and our cousins." Her eyes went to Gilthanas. "Your people consider this a desecration of the river. They try to force us to stop."

"Someday the body that floats down the river will be Qualinesti, or Silvanesti, with a Kaganesti arrow in his chest," Theros predicted. "And then there will be war."

"I think all the elves will have a much more deadly enemy to face," Sturm said, shaking his head. "Look!" He pointed.

At the feet of the dead warrior lay a shield, the shield of the enemy he had died fighting. Recognizing the foul symbol traced on the battered shield, Laurana drew in her breath.

"Draconian!"

The journey up the Thon-Tsalarian was long and arduous, for the river ran swift and strong. Even Tas was given an oar to help paddle, but he promptly lost it overboard, then nearly went in headfirst trying to retrieve it. Catching hold of Tas by his belt, Derek dragged him back as the Kaganesti indicated by sign language that if he caused any more trouble, they'd throw him out.

Tasslehoff soon grew bored and sat peering over the side, hoping to see a fish.

"Why, how odd!" the kender said suddenly. Reaching down, he put his small hand into the water. "Look," he said in excitement. His hand was coated in fine silver and sparkled in the early morning light. "The water glitters! Look, Flint," he called to the dwarf in the other boat."Look into the water—"

"I will *not*," said the dwarf through chattering teeth. Flint rowed grimly, though there was some question as to his effectiveness. He steadfastly refused to look into the water and consequently was out of time with everyone else.

"You are right, Kenderken," Silvara said, smiling. "In fact, the Silvanesti named the river *Thon-Sargon*, which means 'Silver Road.' It is too bad you have come here in such dismal weather. When the silver moon rises in its fullness, the river turns to molten silver and is truly beautiful."

"Why? What causes it?" the kender asked, studying his shimmering hand with delight.

"No one knows, though there is a legend among my people—" Silvara fell silent abruptly, her face flushed.

"What legend?" Gilthanas asked. The elflord sat facing Silvara, who was in the prow of the boat. His paddling was not much better than Flint's, Gilthanas being much more interested in Silvara's face than his work. Every time Silvara looked up, she found he was staring at her. She became more confused and flustered as the hours passed.

"Surely you are not interested," she said, gazing out across the silver-gray water, trying to avoid Gilthanas's gaze. "It is a child's tale about Huma—"

"Huma!" Sturm said from where he sat behind Gilthanas, his swift, strong oar strokes making up for the ineptness of both elf and dwarf."Tell us your legend of Huma, Wilder elf."

"Yes, tell us your legend," Gilthanas repeated smiling.

"Very well," she said, flushing. Clearing her throat, she began. "According to the Kaganesti, in the last days of the terrible dragon wars, Huma traveled through the land, seeking to help the people. But he realized, to his sorrow, that he was powerless to stop the desolation and destruction of the dragons. He prayed to the gods for an answer." Silvara glanced at Sturm, who nodded his head solemnly.

"True," the knight said. "And Paladine answered his prayer, sending the White Stag. But where it led him, none know."

"My people know," Silvara said softly, "because the Stag led Huma, after many trials and dangers, to a quiet grove, here, in the land of Ergoth. In the grove he met a woman, beautiful and virtuous, who eased his pain. Huma fell in love with her and she with him. But she refused his pledges of love for many months. Finally, unable to deny the burning fire within her, the woman returned Huma's love. Their happiness was like the silver moonlight in a night of terrible darkness."

Silvara fell silent a moment, her eyes staring far away. Absently she reached down to touch the coarse fabric of the cloak covering the dragon orb which lay at her feet.

"Go on," Gilthanas urged. The elflord had given up all pretext of paddling and sat still, enchanted by Silvara's beautiful eyes, her musical voice.

Silvara sighed. Dropping the fabric from her hands, she stared out over the water into the shadowy woods. "Their joy was brief," she said softly. "For the woman had a terrible secret—she was not born of woman, but of dragon. Only by her magic did she keep the shape of womankind. But she could no longer lie to Huma. She loved him too much. Fearfully she revealed to Huma what she was, appearing before him one night in her true shape—that of a silver dragon. She hoped he would hate her, even destroy her, for her pain was so great she did not want to live. But, looking at the radiant, magnificent creature before him, the knight saw within her eyes the noble spirit of the woman he loved. Her magic returned her to the shape of woman, and she prayed to Paladine that he give her woman's shape forever. She would give up her magic and the long life span of the dragons to live in the world with Huma."

Silvara closed her eyes, her face drawn with pain. Gilthanas, watching her, wondered why she was so affected by this legend. Reaching out, he touched her hand. She started like a wild animal, drawing back so suddenly the boat rocked.

"I'm sorry," Gilthanas said. "I didn't mean to scare you. What happened? What was Paladine's answer?"

Silvara drew a deep breath. "Paladine granted her wish, with a terrible condition. He showed them both the future. If she remained a dragon, she and Huma would be given the Dragonlance and the power to defeat the evil dragons. If she became mortal, she and Huma would live together as man and wife, but the evil dragons would remain in the land forever. Huma vowed he would give up everything—his knighthood, his honor—to remain with her. But she saw the light die in his eyes as he spoke, and, weeping, she knew the answer she must give. The evil dragons must not be allowed to stay in the world. And the silver river, it is said, was formed from the tears shed by the dragon when Huma left her to find the Dragonlance."

"Nice story. Kind of sad," said Tasslehoff, yawning. "Did old Huma come back? Does the story have a happy ending?"

"Huma's story does not end happily," Sturm said, frowning at the kender. "But he died most gloriously in battle, defeating the leader of the dragons, though he himself had sustained a mortal wound. I have heard, though," the knight added thoughtfully, "that he rode to battle upon a Silver Dragon."

"And we saw a knight on a silver dragon in Ice Wall," Tas said brightly. "He gave Sturm the—"

The knight gave the kender a swift poke in the back. Too late, Tas remembered that was supposed to be secret.

"I don't know about a Silver Dragon," Silvara said, shrugging. "My people know little about Huma. He was, after all, a human. I think they tell this legend only because it is about the river they love, the river who takes their dead."

At this point, one of the Kaganesti pointed at Gilthanas and said something sharply to Silvara. Gilthanas looked at her, not understanding. The elfmaid smiled. "He asks if you are too grand an elflord to paddle, because— if you are—he will allow your lordship to swim."

Gilthanas grinned at her, his face flushing. Quickly he picked up his paddle and set to work.

Despite all their efforts—and by the end of the day even Tasslehoff was paddling again—the journey upstream was slow and taxing. By the time they made landfall, their muscles ached with the strain, their hands were bloody and blistered. It was all they could do to drag the boats ashore and help hide them.

"Do you think we've thrown off the pursuit?" Laurana asked Theros wearily.

"Does that answer your question?" He pointed downstream.

In the deepening dusk, Laurana could barely make out several dark shapes upon the water. They were still far down river, but it was clear to Laurana that there would be little rest for the companions tonight. One of the Kaganesti, however, spoke to Theros, gesturing downstream. The big smith nodded.

"Do not worry. We are safe until morning. He says they will have to make landfall as well. None dare travel the river at night. Not even the Kaganesti, and they know every bend and every snag. He says he will make camp here, near the river. Strange creatures walk the forest at night— men with the heads of lizards. Tomorrow we will travel by water as far as we can, but soon we will have to leave the river and take to land."

"Ask him if his people will stop the Qualinesti from pursuing us if we enter his land," Sturm told Theros.

Theros turned to the Kaganesti elf, speaking the elven tongue clumsily but well enough to be understood. The Kaganesti elf shook his head. He was a wild, savage-looking creature. Laurana could see how her people thought them only one step removed from animals. His face revealed traces of distant human ancestry. Though he had no beard—the elven blood ran too purely in the veins of the Kaganesti to allow that—the elf reminded Laurana vividly of Tanis with his quick, decisive way of speaking, his strong, muscular build, and his emphatic gestures. Overcome with memories, she turned away.

Theros translated. "He says that the Qualinesti must follow protocol and ask permission from the elders to enter Kaganesti lands in search of you. The elders will likely grant permission, maybe even offer to help. They don't want humans in Southern Ergoth any more than their cousins. In fact," Theros added slowly, "he's made it plain that the only reason he and his friends are helping us now is to return favors I've done in the past and to help Silvara."

Laurana's gaze went to the girl. Silvara stood on the riverbank, talking to Gilthanas.

Theros saw Laurana's face harden. Looking at the Wilder elf and the elflord, he guessed her thoughts.

"Odd to see jealousy in the face of one who—according to rumor—ran away to become the lover of my friend, Tanis, the half-elf," Theros remarked. "I thought you were different from your people, Laurana."

"It's not that!" she said sharply, feeling her skin burn. "I'm not Tanis's lover. Not that it makes any difference. I simply don't trust the girl. She's—well—too eager to help us, if that makes any sense."

"Your brother might have something to do with that."

"He's an elflord—" Laurana began angrily. Then, realizing what she had been about to say, she broke off. "What do you know of Silvara?" she asked instead.

"Little," Theros answered, regarding Laurana with a disappointed look that made her unreasonably angry. "I know she is highly respected and much loved by her people, especially for her healing skills."

"And her spying skills?" Laurana asked coolly.

"These people are fighting for their own survival. They do what they must," Theros said sternly. "That was a fine talk you made back on the beach, Laurana. I almost believed it."

The blacksmith went to help the Kaganesti hide the boats. Laurana, angry and ashamed, bit her lip in frustration. Was Theros right? Was she jealous of Gilthanas's attention? Did she consider Silvara unworthy of him? It was how Gilthanas had always considered Tanis, certainly. Was this different?

Listen to your feelings, Raistlin had told her. That was all very well, but first she had to understand her feelings! Hadn't her love for Tanis taught her anything?

Yes, Laurana decided finally, her mind clearing. She'd meant what she'd said to Theros. If there was something about Silvara she didn't trust, it had nothing to do with the fact that Gilthanas was attracted to the girl. It was something indefinable. Laurana was sorry Theros had misunderstood her, but she would take Raistlin's advice and trust her instincts.

She would keep an eye on Silvara.

5

Silvara.

lthough every muscle in Gilthanas's body cried for rest and he thought he couldn't crawl into his bedroll soon enough, the elflord found himself wide awake, staring into the sky. Storm clouds still hung thickly overhead, but a breeze tinged with salt air was blowing from the west, breaking them up. Occasionally he caught a glimpse of stars, and once the red moon flickered in the sky like a candle flame, then was snuffed out by the clouds.

The elf tried to get comfortable, turning and twisting until his bedroll was a shambles, then he had to sit up and untangle himself. Finally he gave up, deciding it was impossible to sleep on the hard, frozen ground.

None of the rest of his companions seemed to be having any problems, he noticed bitterly. Laurana lay sleeping soundly, her cheek resting on her hand as was her habit from childhood. How strangely she'd been acting lately, Gilthanas thought. But then, he supposed he could hardly blame her. She had given up everything to do what she believed right and take the orb to Sancrist. Their father might have accepted her back into the family once, but now she was an outcast forever.

Gilthanas sighed. What about himself? He'd wanted to keep the orb in Qualin-Mori. He believed his father was right. . . . Or did he?

Apparently not, since I'm here, Gilthanas told himself. By the gods, his values were getting as muddled as Laurana's! First, his hatred for Tanis—a hatred he'd nurtured righteously for years—was starting to dwindle away, replaced by admiration, even affection. Next, he'd felt his hatred of other races beginning to die. He'd known few elves as noble or self-sacrificing as the human, Sturm Brightblade. And, though he didn't like Raistlin, he envied the young mage's skill. It was something Gilthanas, a dabbler in magic, had never had the patience or the courage to acquire. Finally, he had to admit he even liked the kender and the grumpy old dwarf. But he had never thought he would fall in love with a Wilder elf.

"There!" Gilthanas said aloud. "I've admitted it. I love her!" But was it love, he wondered, or simply physical attraction. At that, he grinned, thinking of Silvara with her dirt-streaked face, her filthy hair, her tattered clothes. My soul's eye must be seeing more clearly than my head, he thought, glancing fondly over at her bedroll.

To his astonishment, he saw it was empty! Startled, Gilthanas looked quickly around the camp. They had not dared light a fire—not only were the Qualinesti after them, but Theros had talked of groups of draconians roaming the land.

Thinking of this, Gilthanas rose to his feet quickly and began to search for Silvara. He moved silently, hoping to avoid the questions of Sturm and Derek, who were standing watch. A sudden chilling thought crossed his mind. Hurriedly, he looked for the dragon orb. But it was still where Silvara had put it. Beside it lay the broken shaft of the dragonlance.

Gilthanas breathed more easily. Then his quick ears caught the sound of water splashing. Listening carefully, he determined it wasn't a fish or a nightbird diving for its catch in the river. The elflord glanced at Derek and Sturm. The two stood apart from one another on a rock outcropping overlooking the camp. Gilthanas could hear them arguing with each other in fierce whispers. The elflord crept away from camp, heading toward the sound of softly splashing water.

Gilthanas walked through the dark forest with no more noise than the shadows of night itself would make. Occasionally he caught a glimpse of the river glistening faintly through the trees. Then he came to a place where the water, flowing among the rocks, had become trapped in a small pool. Here Gilthanas stopped, and here his heart almost stopped beating. He had found Silvara.

A dark circle of trees stood starkly outlined against the racing clouds. The silence of the night was broken only by the gentle murmurs of the silver river, which fell over rock steps into the pool, and by the splashing sounds that had caught Gilthanas's attention. Now he knew what they were.

Silvara was bathing. Oblivious to the chill in the air, the elfmaid was submerged in the water. Her clothes lay scattered on the bank next to a frayed blanket. Only her shoulders and arms were visible to Gilthanas's elvensight. Her head was thrown back as she washed the long hair that trailed out behind her, floating like a dark cobweb on the darker pool. The elflord held his breath, watching her. He knew he should leave, but he was held fast, entranced.

And then, the clouds parted. Solinari, the silver moon, though only half-full, burned in the night sky with a cold brilliance. The water in the pool turned to molten silver. Silvara rose up out of the pool. The silver water glistened on her skin, gleamed in her silver hair, ran in shining rivulets down her body that was painted in silver moonlight. Her beauty struck Gilthanas's heart with such intense pain that he gasped.

Silvara started, looking around her terrified. Her wild, abandoned grace added so much to her loveliness that Gilthanas, though he longed to speak to her reassuringly, couldn't force the words past the pain in his chest.

Silvara ran from the water to the bank where her clothes lay. But she did not touch them. Instead, she reached into a pocket. Grabbing a knife, she turned, ready to defend herself.

Gilthanas could see her body quivering in the silvery moonlight, and he was reminded vividly of a doe he had cornered after a long hunt. The creature's eyes sparkled with the same fear he now saw in Silvara's luminous eyes. The Wilder elf stared around, terrified. Why doesn't she see me? Gilthanas wondered briefly, feeling her eyes pass over him several times. With the elven sight, he should stand out to her like a—

Suddenly Silvara turned, starting to flee from the danger she could feel, yet could not see.

Gilthanas felt his voice freed. "No! Wait, Silvara! Don't be frightened. It's me, Gilthanas." He spoke in firm, yet hushed tones—as he had spoken to the cornered doe. "You shouldn't be out alone, it's dangerous. . . ."

Silvara paused, standing half in silver light, half in protecting shadows, her muscles tense, ready to spring. Gilthanas followed his huntsman's instinct, walking slowly, continuing to talk, holding her with his steady voice and his eyes.

"You shouldn't be out here alone. I'll stay with you. I want to talk to you anyway. I want you to listen to me for a moment. I need to talk to you, Silvara. I don't want to be here alone, either. Don't leave me, Silvara. So much has left me in this world. Don't leave. . . ."

Talking softly, continuously, Gilthanas moved with smooth, deliberate steps toward Silvara until he saw her take a step backward. Raising his hands, he sat down quickly on a boulder at the pool's edge, keeping the water between them. Silvara stopped, watching him. She made no move to clothe herself, apparently deciding that defense was more important than modesty. She still held the knife poised in her hand.

Gilthanas admired her determination, although he was ashamed for her nakedness. Any well-bred elven woman would have fainted dead away by now. He knew he should avert his eyes, but he was too awed by her beauty. His blood burned. With an effort, he kept talking, not even knowing what he was saying. Only gradually did he become aware that he was speaking the innermost thoughts of his heart.

"Silvara, what am I doing here? My father needs me, my people need me. Yet here I am, breaking the law of my lord. My people are in exile. I find the one thing that might help them—a dragon orb—but now I risk my life taking it from my people to give to humans to aid them in their war! It's not even my war, it's not my people's war." Gilthanas leaned toward her earnestly, noticing that she had not taken her eyes from him. "Why, Silvara? Why have I brought this dishonor on myself? Why have I done this to my people?"

He held his breath. Silvara glanced into the darkness and the safety of the woods, then looked back at him. She will flee, he thought, his heart pounding. Then, slowly, Silvara lowered her knife. There was such sadness and sorrow in her eyes that, finally, Gilthanas looked away, ashamed of himself.

"Silvara," he began, choking, "forgive me. I didn't mean to involve you in my trouble. I don't understand what it is that I must do. I only know . . ."

" . . . that you must do it," Silvara finished for him.

Gilthanas looked up. Silvara had covered herself with the frayed blanket. This modest effort served only to fan the flames of his desire. Her silver hair, hanging down past her waist, gleamed in the moonlight. The blanket eclipsed her silver skin.

Gilthanas rose slowly and began to walk along the shore toward her. She still stood at the edge of the forest's safety. He could still sense her coiled fear. But she had dropped the knife.

"Silvara," he said, "what I have done is against all elven custom. When my sister told me of her plot to steal the orb, I should have gone directly to my father. I should have sounded the alarm. I should have taken the orb myself—"

Silvara took a step toward him, still clutching the blanket around her. "Why didn't you?" she asked in a low voice.

Gilthanas was nearing the rock steps at the north end of the pond. The water flowing over them made a silver curtain in the moonlight."Because I know that my people are wrong. Laurana is right. Sturm is right. Taking the orb to the humans is right! We must fight this war. My people are wrong, their laws, their customs are wrong. I know this—in my heart! But I can't make my head believe it. It torments me—"

Silvara walked slowly along the pool's edge. She, too, was nearing the silver curtain of water from the opposite side.

"I understand," she said softly. "My own . . . people do not understand what I do or why I do it. But I understand. I know what is right and I believe in it."

"I envy you, Silvara," Gilthanas whispered.

Gilthanas stepped to the largest rock, a flat island in the glittering, cascading water. Silvara, her wet hair falling over her like a silver gown, stood but a few feet from him now.

"Silvara," Gilthanas said, his voice shaking, "there was another reason I left my people. You know what it is."

He extended his hand, palm up, toward her.

Silvara drew back, shaking her head. Her breath came faster.

Gilthanas took another step nearer. "Silvara, I love you," he said softly. "You seem so alone, as alone as I am. Please, Silvara, you will never be alone again. I swear it. . . ."

Hesitantly, Silvara lifted her hand toward his. With a sudden move, Gilthanas grabbed her arm and pulled her across the water. Catching her as she stumbled, he lifted her onto the rock beside him.

Too late the wild doe realized she was trapped. Not by the man's arms, she could easily have broken free of his embrace. It was her own love for this man that had ensnared her. That his love for her was deep and tender sealed their fate. He was trapped as well.

Gilthanas could feel her body trembling, but he knew now—as he looked into her eyes—that she trembled with passion, not fear. Cupping her face in his hands, he kissed her tenderly. Silvara still held the blanket clasped around her body with one hand, but he felt her other hand close around his. Her lips were soft and eager. Then, Gilthanas tasted a salty tear on his lips. He drew back, amazed to see her crying.

"Silvara, don't. I'm sorry— " He released her.

"No!" she whispered, her voice husky. "My tears are not because I am frightened of your love. They are only for myself. You cannot understand."

Reaching out, she shyly put one hand around his neck and drew him near. And then, as he kissed her, he felt her other hand, the hand that had been clasping the blanket around her body, move up to caress his face.

Silvara's blanket slipped unnoticed into the stream and was borne away by the silver water.

6

Pursuit. A desperate plan.

t noon the next day, the companions were forced to abandon the
boats, having reached the river's headwaters, where it flowed down
out of the mountains. Here the water was shallow and frothy white
from the tumbling rapids ahead. Many Kaganesti boats were drawn up on
the bank. Dragging their boats ashore, the companions were met by a group
of Kaganesti elves coming out of the woods. They carried with them the
bodies of two young elven warriors. Some drew weapons and would have
attacked had not Theros Ironfeld and Silvara hurried to talk with them.

The two spoke long with the Kaganesti, while the companions kept an
uneasy watch downriver. Though they had been awake before dawn,
starting as early as the Kaganesti felt was safe to travel through the swift
water, they had, more than once, caught glimpses of the black boats pursuing them.

When Theros returned, his dark face was somber. Silvara's was flushed
with anger.

"My people will do nothing to help us," Silvara reported. "They have
been attacked by lizardmen twice in the last two days. They blame the
coming of this new evil on humans who, they say, brought them here in a
white-winged ship—"

"That's ridiculous!" Laurana snapped. "Theros, didn't you tell them about these draconians?"

"I tried," the blacksmith stated. "But I am afraid the evidence is against you. The Kaganesti saw the white dragon above the ship, but they did not, apparently, see you drive her off. At any rate, they have finally agreed to let us pass through their lands, but they will give us no aid. Silvara and I both pledged our lives for your good conduct."

"What are the draconians doing here?" Laurana asked, memories haunting her. "Is it an army? Is Southern Ergoth being invaded? If so, perhaps we should go back—"

"No, I think not," Theros said thoughtfully. "If the armies of the Dragon Highlords were ready to take this isle, they would do so with flights of dragons and thousands of troops. These appear to be small patrols sent out to make this bad situation deteriorate further. The Highlords probably hope the elves will save them the trouble of a war by destroying each other first."

"The Dragon High Command is not ready to attack Ergoth," Derek said. "They haven't got a firm hold on the north yet. But it is only a matter of time. That is why it is imperative we get the dragon orb to Sancrist and call a meeting of the Council of Whitestone to determine what to do with it."

Gathering their supplies, the companions set out for the high country. Silvara led them along a trail beside the splashing silver river that ran from the hills. They could feel the unfriendly eyes of the Kaganesti follow them out of sight.

The land began rising almost immediately. Theros soon told them they had traveled into regions where he had never been before; it was up to Silvara to guide them. Laurana was not altogether pleased with this situation. She guessed something had happened between her brother and the girl when she saw them share a sweet, secret smile.

Silvara had found time, among her people, to change her clothing. She was now dressed as a Kaganesti woman, in a long leather tunic over leather breeches, covered by a heavy fur cloak. With her hair washed and combed, all of them could see how she had come by her name. Her hair, a strange, metallic silver color, flowed from a peak on her forehead to fall about her shoulders in radiant beauty.

Silvara turned out to be an exceptionally good guide, pushing them along at a rapid pace. She and Gilthanas walked side by side, talking together in elven. Shortly before sundown, they came to a cave.

"Here we can spend the night," Silvara said. "We should have left the pursuit behind us. Few know these mountains as well as I do. But we dare not light a fire. Dinner will be cold, I'm afraid."

Exhausted by the day's climb, they ate a cheerless meal, then made their beds in the cave. The companions, huddled in their blankets and every piece of clothing they owned, slept fitfully. They set the watch, Laurana and Silvara both insisting on taking turns. The night passed quietly, the only sound they heard was the wind howling among the rocks.

But the next morning Tasslehoff, squeezing out through a crack in the cave's hidden entrance to take a look around, suddenly hurried back inside. Putting his finger to his lips, Tas motioned them to follow him outdoors. Theros pushed aside the huge boulder they had rolled across the mouth of the cave, and the companions crept after Tas. He led them to a stop not twenty feet from the cave and pointed grimly at the white snow.

On it were footprints, fresh enough that the blowing, drifting snow had not quite covered them. The light, delicate tracks had not sunk deeply into the snow. No one spoke. There was no need. Everyone recognized the crisp, clear outline of elven boots.

"They must have passed by us in the night," Silvara said. "But we dare not stay here any longer. Soon they will discover they have lost the trail and will backtrack. We must be gone."

"I don't see that it will make much difference," Flint grumbled in disgust. He pointed at their own, highly visible tracks. Then he looked up at the clear, blue sky. "We might as well just sit and wait for them. Save them time and save us bother. There's no way we can hide our trail!"

"Maybe we cannot hide our trail," said Theros, "but we can gain some miles on them, perhaps."

"Perhaps," Derek repeated grimly. Reaching down, he loosened his sword in its scabbard, then he walked back to the cave.

Laurana caught hold of Sturm. "It must not come to bloodshed!" she whispered frantically, alarmed by Derek's action.

The knight shook his head as they followed the others. "We cannot allow your people to stop us from taking the orb to Sancrist."

"I know!" Laurana said softly. Bowing her head, she entered the cave in silent misery.

The rest were ready within moments. Then Derek stood, fuming in the doorway, watching Laurana impatiently.

"Go ahead," she told him, unwilling to let him see her cry. "I'll be along."

Derek left immediately. Theros, Sturm, and the others trudged out more slowly, glancing uneasily at Laurana.

"Go ahead." She gestured. She needed a moment to be by herself. But all she could think of was Derek's hand on his sword. "No!" she told herself sternly. "I will not fight my people. The day that happens is the day the dragons have won. I will lay down my own sword first—"

She heard movement behind her. Whirling around, her hand going reflexively to her sword, Laurana stopped.

"Silvara?" she said in astonishment, seeing the girl in the shadows. "I thought you had gone. What are you doing?"

Laurana walked swiftly to where Silvara had been kneeling in the darkness, her hands busy with something on the cavern floor. The Wilder elf rose quickly to her feet.

"N-nothing," Silvara murmured. "Just gathering my things."

Behind Silvara, on the cold floor of the cave, Laurana thought she saw the dragon orb, its crystal surface shining with a strange swirling light. But before she could look more closely, Silvara swiftly dropped her cloak over the orb. As she did so, Laurana noticed she kept standing in front of whatever it was she had been handling on the floor.

"Come, Laurana," Silvara said, "we must hurry. I am sorry if I was slow—"

"In a moment," Laurana said sternly. She started to walk past the Wilder elf. Silvara's hand clutched at her.

"We must hurry!" she said, and there was an edge of steel in her low voice. Her grip on Laurana's arm was painful, even through the thick fur of Laurana's heavy cloak.

"Let go of me," Laurana said coldly, staring at the girl, her green eyes showing neither fear nor anger. Silvara let fall her hand, lowering her eyes.

Laurana walked to the back of the shallow cave. Looking down, however, she could see nothing that made any sense. There was a tangle of twigs and bark and charred wood, some stones, but that was all. If it was a sign, it was a clumsy one. Laurana kicked at it with her booted foot, scattering the stones and sticks. Then she turned and took Silvara's arm.

"There," Laurana said, speaking in even, quiet tones. "Whatever message you left for your friends will be difficult to read."

Laurana was prepared for almost any reaction from the girl—anger, shame at being discovered. She even half-expected her to attack. But Silvara began to tremble. Her eyes—as she stared at Laurana—were pleading, almost sorrowful. For a moment, Silvara tried to speak, but she couldn't. Shaking her head, she jerked away from Laurana's grasp and ran outside.

"Hurry up, Laurana!" Theros called gruffly.

"I'm coming!" she answered, glancing back at the debris on the cave floor. She thought of taking a moment longer to investigate further, but she knew she dare not take the time.

Perhaps I *am* being too suspicious of the girl, and for no reason, Laurana thought with a sigh as she hurried out of the cave. Then about halfway up the trail, she stopped so abruptly that Theros, walking rear-guard, slammed into her. He caught her arm, steadying her.

"You all right?" he asked.

"Y-yes," Laurana answered, only half-hearing him.

"You look pale. Did you see something?"

"No. I'm fine," Laurana said hurriedly, and she started up the rocky cliff again, slipping in the snow. What a fool she'd been!

What fools they'd all been! Once again, she could see clearly in her mind's eye Silvara rising to her feet, dropping her cloak over the dragon orb. The dragon orb that was shining with a strange light!

She started to ask Silvara about the orb when suddenly her thoughts were scattered. An arrow zinged through the air and thudded into a tree near Derek's head.

"Elves! Brightblade, attack!" the knight cried, drawing his sword.

"No!" Laurana ran forward, grabbing his sword arm. "We will not fight! There will be no killing!"

"You're mad!" Derek shouted. Angrily breaking loose of Laurana's grip, he shoved her backward into Sturm.

Another arrow flew by.

"She's right!" Silvara pleaded, hurrying back. "We cannot fight them. We must reach the pass! There we can stop them."

Another arrow, nearly spent, struck the chain-mail vest Derek wore over his leather tunic. He brushed it away irritably.

"They're not aiming to kill," Laurana added. "If they were, you would be dead by now. We must run for it. We can't fight here, anyhow." She gestured at the thick woods. "We can defend the pass better."

"Put your sword away, Derek," Sturm said, drawing his blade. "Or you'll fight me first."

"You're a coward, Brightblade!" Derek shouted, his voice shaking with fury. "You're running from the enemy!"

"No," Sturm answered coolly, "I'm running from my friends." The knight kept his sword drawn. "Get moving, Crownguard, or the elves will find they have arrived too late to take you prisoner."

Another arrow flew past, lodging in a tree near Derek. The knight, his face splotched with fury, sheathed his sword and, turning, plunged ahead up the trail. But not before he had cast Sturm a look of such intense enmity that Laurana shuddered.

"Sturm—" she began, but he only grabbed her by the elbow and hustled her forward too fast to talk. They climbed rapidly. Behind her, she could hear Theros crashing through the snow, occasionally stopping to send a boulder bouncing down after them. Soon it sounded like the entire side of the mountain was sliding down the steep trail, and the arrows ceased.

"But it's only temporary," the smith puffed, catching up with Sturm and Laurana. "That won't stop them for long."

Laurana couldn't answer. Her lungs were on fire. Blue and gold stars burst before her eyes. She was not the only one suffering. Sturm's breath rasped in his throat. His grasp on her arm was weak and his hand shook. Even the strong smith was blowing like a winded horse. Rounding a boulder, they found the dwarf on his knees, Tasslehoff trying vainly to lift him.

"Must . . . rest . . ." Laurana said, her throat aching. She started to sit down, but strong hands grabbed her.

"No!" Silvara said urgently. "Not here! Just a few more feet! Come on! Keep going!"

The Wilder elf dragged Laurana forward. Dimly she was aware of Sturm helping Flint to his feet, the dwarf groaning and swearing. Between them, Theros and Sturm dragged the dwarf up the trail. Tasslehoff stumbled behind, too tired even to talk.

Finally they came to the top of the pass. Laurana slumped into the snow, past caring what happened to her. The rest sank down beside her, all except Silvara who was staring below them.

Where does she get the strength? Laurana thought through a bleak haze of pain. But she was too exhausted to question. At the moment, she was too tired to care whether the elves found her or not. Silvara turned to face them.

"We must split up," she said decisively.

Laurana stared at her, uncomprehending.

"No," Gilthanas began, trying without success to get to his feet.

"Listen to me!" Silvara said urgently, kneeling down. "The elves are too close. They will catch us for certain, then we must either fight or surrender."

"Fight," Derek muttered savagely.

"There is a better way," Silvara hissed. "You, knight, must take the dragon orb to Sancrist alone! We will draw off the pursuit."

For a moment no one spoke. Everyone stared silently at Silvara, considering this new possibility. Derek lifted his head, his eyes gleaming. Laurana flashed a look of alarm at Sturm.

"I do not think one person should be charged with such a grave responsibility," Sturm said, his breath coming haltingly. "Two of us should go—at least."

"Meaning yourself, Brightblade?" Derek asked angrily.

"Yes, of course, Sturm should go," Laurana said, "if anyone."

"I can draw a map through the mountains," Silvara said eagerly. "The way is not difficult. The outpost of the knights is only a two-day journey from here."

"But we can't fly," Sturm protested. "What about our tracks? Surely the elves will see we've split up."

"An avalanche," Silvara suggested. "Theros throwing the boulders down behind us gave me the idea." She glanced up. They followed her gaze. Snow-covered peaks towered above them, the snow hanging over the edges.

"I can cause an avalanche with my magic," Gilthanas said slowly. "It will obliterate everyone's tracks."

"Not entirely," cautioned Silvara. "We must allow ours to be found once again—though not too obviously. After all, we want them to follow us."

"But where will we go?" asked Laurana. "I don't intend to wander aimlessly through the wilderness."

"I—I know a place."Silvara faltered, her gaze dropping to the ground. "It is secret, known only to my people. I will take you there."She clasped her hands together. "Please, we must hurry. There isn't much time!"

"I will take the orb to Sancrist," Derek said, "and I will go alone. Sturm should go with your group. You'll need a fighter."

"We have fighters," Laurana said. "Theros, my brother, the dwarf. I, myself, have seen my share of battle—"

"And me," piped Tasslehoff.

"And the kender," Laurana added grimly. "Besides, it will not come to bloodshed." Her eyes saw Sturm's troubled face and wondered what he was thinking. Her voice softened. "The decision is up to Sturm, of course. He must do as he believes best, but I think he should accompany Derek."

"I agree," muttered Flint. "After all, we're not the ones who are going to be in danger. We'll be safer without the dragon orb. It's the orb the elves want."

"Yes," agreed Silvara, her voice soft. "We'll be safer without the orb. It is you who will be in danger."

"Then my way is clear," Sturm said. "I will go with Derek."

"And if I order you to stay behind?" Derek demanded.

"You have no authority over me," Sturm said, his brown eyes dark."Have you forgotten? I am not a knight."

There was a painful, profound silence. Derek stared at Sturm intently.

"No," he said, "and if I have my way, you never will be!"

Sturm flinched, as if Derek had struck him a physical blow. Then he stood up, sighing heavily.

Derek had already begun to gather his gear. Sturm moved more slowly, picking up his bedroll with thoughtful deliberation. Laurana pulled herself to her feet and went to Sturm.

"Here," she said, reaching into her pack. "You'll need food—"

"You could come with us," Sturm said in low tones as she divided up their supplies. "Tanis knows we were going to Sancrist. He will come there, too, if possible."

"You're right," Laurana said, her eyes brightening. "Perhaps that would be a good idea—" Then her eyes went to Silvara. The Wilder elf held the dragon orb, still shrouded in its cloak. Silvara's eyes were closed, almost as if she were communing with some unseen spirit. Sighing, Laurana shook her head. "No, I've got to stay with her, Sturm," she said softly. "Something's not right. I don't understand—" she broke off, unable to articulate her thoughts. "What about Derek?" she asked instead. "Why is he so insistent on going alone? The dwarf's right about the danger. If the elves capture you, without us, they won't hesitate to kill you."

Sturm's face was drawn, bitter. "Can you ask? Lord Derek Crown-guard returns alone out of horrifying dangers, bearing with him the coveted dragon orb—" Sturm shrugged.

"But there's so much at stake," Laurana protested.

"You're right, Laurana," Sturm said harshly. "There's a lot at stake. More than you know—the leadership of the Knights of Solamnia. I can't explain it now. . . ."

"Come along, Brightblade, if you're coming!" Derek snarled.

Sturm took the food, stowing it in his pack. "Farewell, Laurana," he said, bowing to her with the quiet gallantry that marked all his actions.

"Farewell, Sturm, my friend," she whispered, putting her arms around the knight.

He held her closely, then kissed her gently on the forehead.

"We will give the orb to the wise men to study. The Council of White-stone will meet soon," he said. "The elves will be invited to attend, since they are advisory members. You must come to Sancrist as soon as possible, Laurana. Your presence will be needed."

"I'll be there, the gods willing," Laurana said, her eyes going to Sil-vara, who was handing Derek the dragon orb. An expression of inexpressible relief flitted over Silvara's face when Derek turned to go.

Sturm said good-bye, then he plunged into the snow after Derek. The companions saw a flash of light as his shield caught the sun.

Suddenly Laurana took a step forward. "Wait!" she cried. "I've got to stop them. They should take the dragonlance, too."

"No!" Silvara shouted, running to block Laurana's path.

Angrily, Laurana reached out to shove the girl aside, then she saw Sil-vara's face and her hand stopped.

"What are you doing, Silvara?" Laurana asked. "Why did you send them off? Why were you so eager to split us up? Why give them the orb and not the lance—"

Silvara didn't answer. She simply shrugged and stared at Laurana with eyes bluer than midnight. Laurana felt her will being drained by those blue, blue eyes. She was reminded terrifyingly of Raistlin.

Gilthanas, too, stared at Silvara with a perplexed and worried expression. Theros stood grim and stern, glancing at Laurana as if beginning to share her doubts. But they were not able to move. They were completely under Silvara's control—yet what had she done to them? They could only stand and stare at the Wilder elf as she walked calmly over to where Laurana had wearily let fall her pack. Bending down, Silvara unwrapped the broken piece of splintered wood. Then she raised it in the air.

Sunlight flashed on Silvara's silver hair, mimicking the flash from Sturm's shield.

"The dragonlance stays with me," Silvara said. Glancing swiftly around the spellbound group, she added, "As do you."

7

Dark journey.

 ehind them, the snow rumbled and toppled over the side of the mountain. Cascading down in white sheets, blocking and choking the pass, it obliterated their presence. The echoes of Gilthanas's magical thunder still resounded in the air, or perhaps it was the booming of the rocks as they bounded down the slopes. They could not be certain.

The companions, led by Silvara, traveled the trails east slowly and cautiously, walking where it was rocky, avoiding the snowy patches if at all possible. They walked through each other's footsteps so that the pursuing elves would never know for certain how many were in their party. They were so careful, in fact, that Laurana grew worried.

"Remember, we want them to find *us*," she said to Silvara as they crept across the top of a rocky defile.

"Do not be upset. They will have no trouble finding us," answered Silvara.

"What makes you so certain?" Laurana started to ask, then she slipped and fell to her hands and knees. Gilthanas helped her stand. Grimacing with pain, she stared at Silvara in silence. None of them, including Theros, trusted the sudden change that had come over the Wilder elf since their parting with the knights. But they had no choice except to follow her.

"Because they know our destination," Silvara answered. "You were clever to think I left a sign to them in the cave. I did. Fortunately, you did not find it. Below those sticks you so kindly scattered for me I had drawn a crude map. When they find it, they will think I drew it to show you our destination. You made it look most realistic, Laurana."Her voice was defiant until she met Gilthanas's eyes.

The elflord turned away from her, his face grave. Silvara faltered. Her voice became pleading. "I did it for a reason, a good reason. I knew then, when I saw the tracks, we would have to split up. You must believe me!"

"What about the dragon orb? What were you doing with it?" Laurana demanded.

"N-nothing," Silvara stammered. "You must trust me!"

"I don't see why," Laurana returned coldly.

"I have done you no harm—" Silvara began.

"Unless you have sent the knights and the dragon orb into a death-trap!" Laurana cried.

"No!" Silvara wrung her hands. "I haven't! Believe me. They will be safe. That has been my plan all along. Nothing must happen to the dragon orb. Above all, it must not fall into the hands of the elves. That is why I sent it away. That is why I helped you escape!" She glanced around, seeming to sniff the air like an animal. "Come! We have lingered too long."

"If we go with you at all!" Gilthanas said harshly. "What do you know about the dragon orb?"

"Don't ask me!" Silvara's voice was suddenly deep and filled with sadness. Her blue eyes stared into Gilthanas's with such love that he could not bear to face her. He shook his head, avoiding her gaze. Silvara caught hold of his arm. "Please, *shalori*, beloved, trust me! Remember what we talked about, at the pool. You said you had to do these things—defy your people, become an outcast, because of what you believed in your heart. I said that I understood, that I had to do the same. Didn't you believe me?"

Gilthanas stood a moment, his head bowed. "I believed you," he said softly. Reaching out, he pulled her to him, kissing her silver hair. "We'll go with you. Come on, Laurana." Arms around each other, the two trudged off through the snow.

Laurana looked blankly at the others. They avoided her eyes. Then Theros came up to her.

"I've lived in this world nearly fifty years, young woman," he said gently. "Not long to you elves, I know. But we humans live those years, we don't just let them drift by. And I'll tell you this—that girl loves your brother as truly as I've ever seen woman love man. And he loves her. Such love cannot come to evil. For the sake of their love alone, I'd follow them into a dragon's den."

The smith walked after the two.

"For the sake of my cold feet, I'd follow them into a dragon's den, if he'd warm my toes!" Flint stamped on the ground. "Come on, let's go." Grabbing the kender, he dragged Tas along after the blacksmith.

Laurana remained standing, alone. That she would follow was settled. She had no choice. She wanted to trust Theros's words. One time, she would have believed the world ran that way. But now she knew much she had believed in was false. Why not love?

All she could see in her mind were the swirling colors of the dragon orb.

The companions traveled east, into the gloom of gathering night. Descending from the high mountain pass, they found the air easier to breathe. The frozen rocks gave way to scraggly pines, then the forests closed in around them once more. Silvara confidently led them at last into a fog-shrouded valley.

The Wilder elf no longer seemed to care about covering their tracks. All that concerned her now was speed. She pushed the group on, as if racing the sun across the sky. When night fell, they sank into the tree-rimmed darkness, too tired even to eat. But Silvara allowed them only a few hours of restless, aching sleep. When the moons rose, the silver and the red, nearing their fullness now, she urged the companions on.

When anyone questioned, wearily, why they hurried, she only answered, "They are near. They are very near."

Each assumed she meant the elves, though Laurana had long ago lost the feeling of dark shapes trailing them.

Dawn broke, but the light was filtered through fog so thick Tasslehoff thought he might grab a handful and store it in one of his pouches. The companions walked close together, even holding hands to avoid being separated. The air grew warmer. They shed their wet and heavy cloaks as they stumbled along a trail that seemed to materialize beneath their feet, out of the fog. Silvara walked before them. The faint light shining from her silver hair was their only guide.

Finally the ground grew level at their feet, the trees cleared, and they walked on smooth grass, brown with winter. Although none of them could see more than a few feet in the gray fog, they had the impression they were in a wide clearing.

"This is Foghaven Vale," Silvara replied in answer to their questions. "Long years ago, before the Cataclysm, it was one of the most beautiful places upon Krynn . . . so my people say."

"It might still be beautiful," Flint grumbled, "if we could see it through this confounded mist."

"No," said Silvara sadly. "Like much else in this world, the beauty of Foghaven has vanished. Once the fortress of Foghaven floated above the mist as if floating on a cloud. The rising sun colored the mists pink in the morning, burned them off at midday so that the soaring spires of the fortress could be seen for miles. In the evening, the fog returned to cover the fortress like a blanket. By night, the silver and the red moons shone on the mists with a shimmering light. Pilgrims came, from all parts of Krynn—" Silvara stopped abruptly. "We will make camp here tonight."

"What pilgrims?" Laurana asked, letting her pack fall.

Silvara shrugged. "I do not know," she said, averting her face. "It is only a legend of my people. Perhaps it is not even true. Certainly no one comes here now."

She's lying, thought Laurana, but she said nothing. She was too tired to care. And even Silvara's low, gentle voice seemed unnaturally loud and jarring in the eerie stillness. The companions spread their blankets in silence. They ate in silence, too, nibbling without appetite on the dried fruit in their packs. Even the kender was subdued. The fog was oppressive, weighing them down. The only thing they could hear was a steady drip, drip, drip of water plopping onto the mat of dead leaves on the forest floor below.

"Sleep now," said Silvara softly, spreading her blanket near Gilthanas's, "for when the silver moon has neared its zenith, we must leave."

"What difference will that make?" The kender yawned. "We can't see it anyway."

"Nonetheless, we must go. I will wake you."

"When we return from Sancrist—after the Council of Whitestone—we can be married," Gilthanas said softly to Silvara as they lay together, wrapped in his blanket.

The girl stirred in his arms. He felt her soft hair rub against his cheek. But she did not answer.

"Don't worry about my father," Gilthanas said, smiling, stroking the beautiful hair that shone even in the darkness. "He'll be stern and grim for a while, but I am the younger brother, no one cares what becomes of me. Porthios will rant and rave and carry on. But we'll ignore him. We don't have to live with my people. I'm not sure how I'd fit in with yours, but I could learn. I'm a good shot with a bow. And I'd like our children to grow up in the wilderness, free and happy . . . what . . . Silvara, why—you're crying!"

Gilthanas held her close as she buried her face in his shoulder, sobbing bitterly. "There, there," he whispered soothingly, smiling in the darkness. Women were such funny creatures. He wondered what he'd said. "Hush, Silvara," he murmured. "It will be all right." And Gilthanas fell asleep, dreaming of silver-haired children running in the green woods.

"It is time. We must leave."

Laurana felt a hand on her shoulder, shaking her. Startled, she woke from a vague, frightening dream that she could not remember to find the Wilder elf kneeling above her.

"I'll wake the others," Silvara said, and disappeared.

Feeling more tired than if she hadn't slept, Laurana packed her things by reflex and stood waiting, shivering, in the darkness. Next to her, she heard the dwarf groan. The damp air was making his joints ache painfully. This journey had been hard on Flint, Laurana realized. He was, after all, what—almost one hundred and fifty years old? A respectable age for a dwarf. His face had lost some of its color during his illness on the voyage. His lips, barely visible beneath the beard, had a bluish tinge, and occasionally he pressed his hand against his chest. But he always stoutly insisted he was fine and kept up with them on the trail.

"All set!" cried Tas. His shrill voice echoed weirdly in the fog, and he had the distinct feeling he'd disturbed something. "I'm sorry," he said, cringing. "Gee," he muttered to Flint, "it's like being in a temple."

"Just shut up and start moving!" the dwarf snapped.

A torch flared. The companions started at the sudden, blinding light that Silvara held.

"We must have light," she said before any could protest. "Do not fear. The vale we are in is sealed shut. Long ago, there were two entrances: one led to human lands where the knights had their outpost, the other led east into the lands of the ogres. Both passes were lost during the Cataclysm. We need have no fear. I have led you by a way known only to myself."

"And to your people," Laurana reminded her sharply.

"Yes—my people . . ." Silvara said, and Laurana was surprised to see the girl grow pale.

"Where are you taking us?" Laurana insisted.

"You will see. We will be there within the hour."

The companions glanced at each other, then all of them looked at Laurana.

Damn them! she thought. "Don't look to me for answers!" she said angrily. "What do you want to do? Stay out here, lost in the fog—"

"I won't betray you!" Silvara murmured despondently. "Please, just trust me a little further."

"Go ahead," said Laurana tiredly. "We'll follow."

The fog seemed to close around them more thickly, until all that kept the darkness at bay was the light of Silvara's torch.

No one had any idea of the direction they traveled. The landscape did not change. They walked through tall grass. There were no trees.

Occasionally a large boulder loomed out of the darkness, but that was all. Of night birds or animals, there was no sign. There was a sense of urgency that increased as they walked until all of them felt it, and they hurried their steps, keeping ever within the light of the torch.

Then, suddenly, without warning, Silvara stopped.

"We are here," she said, and she held the torch aloft. The torch's light pierced the fog. They could all see a shadowy something beyond. At first, it was so ghostly materializing out of the fog that the companions could not recognize it.

Silvara drew closer. They followed her, curious, fearful.

Then the silence of the night was broken by bubbling sounds like water boiling in a giant kettle. The fog grew denser, the air was warm and stifling.

"Hot springs!" said Theros in sudden understanding. "Of course, that explains the constant fog. And this dark shape—"

"The bridge which leads across them," Silvara replied, shining the torchlight upon what they could see was a glistening stone bridge spanning the water boiling in the streams below them, filling the night air with its warm, billowing fog.

"We're supposed to cross that!" Flint exclaimed, staring at the black, boiling water in horror. "We're supposed to cross—"

"It is called the Bridge of Passage," said Silvara.

The dwarf's only answer was a strangled gulp.

The Bridge of Passage was a long, smooth arch of pure white marble. Along its sides—carved in vivid relief—long columns of knights walked symbolically across the bubbling streams. The span was so high that they could not see the top through the swirling mists. And it was old, so old that Flint, reverently touching the worn rock with his hand, could not recognize the craftsmanship. It was not dwarven, not elven, not human. Who had done such marvelous work?

Then he noticed there were no hand-rails, nothing but the marble span itself, slick and glistening with the mist rising constantly from the bubbling springs beneath.

"We cannot cross that," said Laurana, her voice trembling. "And now we are trapped—"

"We *can* cross," Silvara said. "For we have been summoned."

"Summoned?" Laurana repeated in exasperation. "By what? Where?"

"Wait," commanded Silvara.

They waited. There was nothing left for them to do. Each stood staring around in the torchlight, but they saw only the mist rising from the streams, heard only the gurgling water.

"It is the time of Solinari," Silvara said suddenly, and—swinging her arm—she hurled her torch into the water.

Darkness swallowed them. Involuntarily, they crept closer together. Silvara seemed to have vanished with the light. Gilthanas called for her, but she did not answer.

Then the mist turned to shimmering silver. They could see once more, and now they could see Silvara, a dark, shadowy outline against the silvery mist. She stood at the foot of the bridge, staring up into the sky. Slowly she raised her hands, and slowly the mists parted. Looking up, the companions saw the mists separate like long, graceful fingers to reveal the silver moon, full and brilliant in the starry sky.

Silvara spoke strange words, and the moonlight poured down upon her, bathing her in its light. The moon's light shone upon the bubbling waters, making them come alive, dancing with silver. It shone upon the marble bridge, giving life to the knights who spent eternity crossing the stream.

But it was not these beautiful sights that caused the companions to clasp each other with shaking hands or to hold each other closely. The moon's light on the water did not cause Flint to repeat the name of Reorx in the most reverent prayer he ever uttered, or cause Laurana to lean her head against her brother's shoulder, her eyes dimmed with sudden tears, or cause Gilthanas to hold her tightly, overwhelmed by a feeling of fear and awe and reverence.

Soaring high above them, so tall its head might have torn a moon from the sky, was the figure of a dragon, carved out of a mountain of rock, shining silver in the moonlight.

"Where are we?" Laurana asked in a hushed voice. "What is this place?"

"When you cross the Bridge of Passage, you will stand before the Monument of the Silver Dragon," answered Silvara softly. "It guards the Tomb of Huma, Knight of Solamnia."

8

The Tomb of Huma.

n Solinari's light, the Bridge of Passage across the bubbling streams of Foghaven Vale gleamed like bright pearls threaded on a silver chain.

"Do not fear," Silvara said again. "The crossing is difficult only for those who seek to enter the Tomb for evil purposes."

But the companions remained unconvinced. Fearfully they climbed the few stairs leading them up to bridge itself. Then, hesitantly, they stepped upon the marble arch that rose before them, glistening wet with the steam from the springs. Silvara crossed first, walking lightly and with ease. The rest followed her more cautiously, keeping to the very center of the marble span.

Across from them, on the other side of the bridge, loomed the Monument of the Dragon. Even though they knew they must watch their footing, their eyes seemed constantly drawn up to it. Many times, they were forced to stop and stare in awe, while below them the hot springs boiled and steamed.

"Why—I bet that water's so hot you could cook meat in it!" Tasslehoff said. Lying flat on his stomach, he peered over the edge of the highest part of the arched bridge.

"I'll b-bet it c-could c-cook you," stuttered the terrified dwarf, crawl-ing across on his hands and knees.

"Look, Flint! Watch. I've got this piece of meat in my pack. I'll get a string and we'll lower it in the water—"

"Get moving!" Flint roared. Tas sighed and closed his pouch.

"You're no fun to take anywhere," he complained, and he slid down the other side of the span on the seat of his pants.

But for the rest of the companions, it was a terrifying journey, and all of them sighed in heartfelt relief when they came down off the marble bridge onto the ground below.

None of them had spoken to Silvara as they crossed, their minds being too occupied with getting over the Bridge of Passage alive. But when they reached the other side, Laurana was the first to ask questions.

"Why have you brought us here?"

"Do you not trust me yet?" Silvara asked sadly.

Laurana hesitated. Her gaze went once again to the huge stone dragon, whose head was crowned with stars. The stone mouth was open in a silent cry, and the stone eyes stared fiercely. The stone wings were carved out of the sides of the mountain. A stone claw stretched forth, as massive as the trunks of a hundred vallenwood trees.

"You send the dragon orb away, then bring us to a monument dedi-cated to a dragon!" Laurana said after a moment, her voice quivering. "What am I to think? And you bring us to this place you *call* Huma's Tomb. We do not even know if Huma lived, or if he was legend. What is to prove this is his resting place? Is his body within?"

"N-no," Silvara faltered. "His body disappeared, as did—"

"As did what?"

"As did the lance he carried, the Dragonlance he used to destroy the Dragon of All Colors and of None." Silvara sighed and lowered her head. "Come inside," she begged, "and rest for the night. In the morning, all will be made clear, I promise."

"I don't think—" Laurana began.

"We're going inside!" Gilthanas said firmly. "You're behaving like a spoiled child, Laurana! Why would Silvara lead us into danger? Surely, if there was a dragon living here, everyone on Ergoth would know it! It could have destroyed everyone on the island long ago. I sense no evil about this place, only a great and ancient peace. And it's a perfect hiding place! Soon the elves will receive word that the orb has reached Sancrist safely. They'll quit searching, and we can leave. Isn't that right, Silvara? Isn't that why you brought us here?"

"Yes," Silvara said softly. "Th-that was my plan. Now, come, come quickly, while the silver moon still shines. For only then can we enter."

Gilthanas, his hand holding Silvara's hand, walked into the shim-mering silver fog. Tas skipped ahead of them, his pouches bouncing.

Flint and Theros followed more slowly, Laurana more slowly still. Her fears were not eased by Gilthanas's glib explanation, nor by Silvara's reluctant agreement. But there was no place else to go and—as she admitted—she was intensely curious.

The grass on the other side of the bridge was smooth and flat with the steamy clouds of moisture, but the ground began to rise as they approached the body of the dragon carved out of the cliff. Suddenly Tasslehoff's voice floated back to them from the mist where he had run far ahead of the group.

"Raistlin!" they heard him cry in a strangled voice. "He's turned into a giant!"

"The kender's gone mad," Flint said with gloomy satisfaction. "I always knew it—"

Running forward, the companions found Tas jumping up and down and pointing. They stood by his side, panting for breath.

"By the beard of Reorx," gasped Flint in awe. "It *is* Raistlin!"

Looming out of the swirling mist, rising nine feet in the air, stood a stone statue carved in a perfect likeness of the young mage. Accurate in every detail, it even captured his cynical, bitter expression and the carven eyes with their hourglass pupils.

"And there's Caramon!" Tas cried.

A few feet away stood another statue, this time shaped like the mage's warrior twin.

"And Tanis . . ." Laurana whispered fearfully. "What evil magic is this?"

"Not evil," Silvara said, "unless you bring evil to this place. In that case, you would see the faces of your worst enemies within the stone statues. The horror and fear they generate would not allow you to pass. But you see only your friends, and so you may pass safely."

"I wouldn't exactly count Raistlin among my friends," muttered Flint.

"Nor I," Laurana said. Shivering, she walked hesitantly past the cold image of the mage. The mage's obsidian robes gleamed black in the moons' light. Laurana remembered vividly the nightmare of Silvanesti, and she shuddered as she entered what she saw now was a ring of stone statues—each of them bearing a striking, almost frightening resemblance to her friends. Within that silent ring of stone stood a small temple.

The simple rectangular building thrust up into the fog from an octagonal base of shining steps. It, too, was made of obsidian, and the black structure glistened wet with the perpetual fog. Each feature stood as if it had been carved only days before; no sign of wear marred the sharp, clean lines of the carving. Its knights, each bearing the dragonlance, still charged huge monsters. Dragons screamed silently in frozen death, pierced by the long, delicate shafts.

"Inside this temple, they placed Huma's body," Silvara said softly as she led them up the stairs.

Cold bronze doors swung open on silent hinges to Silvara's touch. The companions stood uncertainly on the stairs that encircled the columned temple. But, as Gilthanas had said, they could sense no evil coming from this place. Laurana remembered vividly the Tomb of the Royal Guard in the Sla-Mori and the terror generated by the undead guards left to keep eternal watch over their dead king, Kith-Kanan. In this temple, however, she felt only sorrow and loss, tempered by the knowledge of a great victory—a battle won at terrible cost, but bringing with it eternal peace and sweet restfulness.

Laurana felt her burden ease, her heart become lighter. Her own sorrow and loss seemed diminished here. She was reminded of her own victories and triumphs. One by one, all the companions entered the tomb. The bronze doors swung shut behind them, leaving them in total darkness.

Then light flared. Silvara held a torch in her hand, apparently taken from the wall. Laurana wondered briefly how she had managed to light it. But the trivial question left her mind as she stood gazing around the tomb in awe.

It was empty except for a bier carved out of obsidian, which stood in the center of the room. Chiseled images of knights supported the bier, but the body of the knight that was supposed to have rested upon it was gone. An ancient shield lay at the foot, and a sword, similar to Sturm's, lay near the shield. The companions gazed at these artifacts in silence. It seemed a desecration to the sorrowful serenity of the place to speak, and none touched them, not even Tasslehoff.

"I wish Sturm could be here," murmured Laurana, looking around, tears coming to her eyes. "This *must* be Huma's resting place . . . yet—"

She couldn't explain the growing sense of uneasiness that was creeping over her. Not fear, it was more like the sensation she had felt upon entering the vale—a sense of urgency.

Silvara lit more torches along the wall, and the companions walked past the bier, gazing around the tomb curiously. It was not large. The bier stood in the center and stone benches lined the walls, presumably for the mourners to rest upon while paying their respects. At the far end stood a small stone altar. Carved in its surface were the symbols of the orders of the Knights, the crown, the rose, the kingfisher. Dried rose petals and herbs lay scattered on the top, their fragrance still lingering sweetly in the air after hundreds of years. Below the altar, sunk into the stone floor, was a large iron plate.

As Laurana stared curiously at this plate, Theros came over to stand beside her.

"What do you suppose this is?" she wondered. "A well?"

"Let's see," grunted the smith. Bending over, he lifted the ring on top of the plate in his huge, silver hand and pulled. At first nothing happened. Theros placed both hands on the ring and heaved with all his strength. The iron plate gave a great groan and slid across the floor with a scraping, squeaking sound that set their teeth on edge.

"What have you done?" Silvara, who had been standing near the tomb regarding it sadly, whirled to face them.

Theros stood up in astonishment at the shrill sound of her voice. Laurana involuntarily backed away from the gaping hole in the floor. Both of them stared at Silvara.

"Do not go near that!" Silvara warned, her voice shaking. "Stand clear! It is dangerous!"

"How do you know?" Laurana said coolly, recovering herself. "No one's come here for hundreds of years. Or have they?"

"No!" Silvara said, biting her lip. "I—I know from the . . . legends of my people . . ."

Ignoring the girl, Laurana stepped to the edge of the hole and peered inside. It was dark. Even holding the torch Flint brought her from the wall, she could see nothing down there. A faint musty odor drifted from the hole, but that was all.

"I don't think it's a well," said Tas, crowding to see.

"Stay away from it! Please!" Silvara begged.

"She's right, little thief!" Theros grabbed Tas and pulled him away from the hole. "If you fell in there, you might tumble through to the other side of the world."

"Really?" asked Tasslehoff breathlessly. "Would I really fall through to the other side, Theros? I wonder what it would be like? Would there be people there? Like us?"

"Not like kenders hopefully!" Flint grumbled. "Or they'd all be dead of idiocy by now. Besides, everyone knows that the world rests on the Anvil of Reorx. Those falling to the other side are caught between his hammer blows and the world still being forged. People on the other side indeed!" He snorted as he watched Theros unsuccessfully try to replace the plate. Tasslehoff was still staring at it curiously. Finally Theros was forced to give up, but he glared at the kender until Tas heaved a sigh and wandered away to the stone bier to stare with longing eyes at the shield and sword.

Flint tugged Laurana's sleeve.

"What is it?" she asked absently, her thoughts elsewhere.

"I know stonework," the dwarf said softly, "and there's something strange about all this." He paused, glancing to see if Laurana might laugh. But she was paying serious attention to him. "The tomb and the statues built outside are the work of men. It is old. . . ."

"Old enough to be Huma's tomb?" Laurana interrupted.

"Every bit of it." The dwarf nodded emphatically. "But yon great beast outside"—he gestured in the direction of the huge stone dragon—"was never built by the hands of man or elf or dwarf."

Laurana blinked, uncomprehending.

"And it is older still," the dwarf said, his voice growing husky. "So old it makes this"—he waved his hand at the tomb—"modern."

Laurana began to understand. Flint, seeing her eyes widen, nodded slowly and solemnly.

"No hand of any being that walks upon Krynn with two legs carved the side out of that cliff," he said.

"It must have been a creature with awesome strength, " Laurana murmured. "A huge creature—"

"With wings—"

"With wings," Laurana murmured.

Suddenly she stopped talking, her blood chilled in fear as she heard words being chanted, words she recognized as the strange, spidery language of magic.

"No!" Turning, she lifted her hand instinctively to ward off the spell, knowing as she did so that it was futile.

Silvara stood beside the altar, crumbling rose petals in her hand, chanting softly.

Laurana fought the enchanted drowsiness that crept over her. She fell to her knees, cursing herself for a fool, clinging to the stone bench for support. But it did no good. Lifting her sleep-glazed eyes, she saw Theros topple over and Gilthanas slump to the ground. Beside her, the dwarf was snoring even before his head hit the bench.

Laurana heard a clattering sound, the sound of a shield crashing to the floor, then the air was filled with the fragrance of roses.

9

The kender's startling discovery.

asslehoff heard Silvara chanting. Recognizing the words of a magic spell, he reacted instinctively, grabbed hold of the shield that lay on the bier, and pulled. The heavy shield fell on top of him, striking the floor with a ringing clang, flattening the kender. The shield covered Tas completely.

He lay still beneath it until he heard Silvara finish her chant. Even then, he waited a few moments to see if he was going to turn into a frog or go up in flames or something interesting like that. He didn't—rather to his disappointment. He couldn't even hear Silvara. Finally, growing bored lying in the darkness on the cold stone floor, Tas crept out from beneath the heavy shield with the silence of a falling feather.

All his friends were asleep! So that was the spell she cast. But where was Silvara? Gone somewhere to get a horrible monster to come back and devour them?

Cautiously, Tas raised his head and peered over the bier. To his astonishment, he saw Silvara crouched on the floor, near the tomb entrance. As Tas watched, she rocked back and forth, making small, moaning sounds.

"How can I go through with it?" Tas heard her say to herself. "I've brought them here. Isn't that enough? No!" She shook her head in misery.

"No, I've sent the orb away. They don't know how to use it. I must break the oath. It is as you said, sister—the choice is mine. But it is hard! I love him—"

Sobbing, muttering to herself like one possessed, Silvara buried her face in her knees. The tender-hearted kender had never seen such sorrow, and he longed to go comfort her. Then he realized what she was talking about didn't sound good. "Choice is a hard one, break the oath . . ."

No, Tas thought, I better find a way out of here before she realizes her spell didn't work on me.

But Silvara blocked the entrance to the tomb. He might try to sneak past her. . . . Tas shook his head. Too risky.

The hole! He brightened. He'd wanted to examine it more carefully anyway. He just hoped the lid was still off.

The kender tiptoed around the bier until he came to the altar. There was the hole, still gaping open. Theros lay beside it, sound asleep, his head pillowed upon his silver arm. Glancing back at Silvara, Tas sneaked silently to the edge.

It would certainly be a better place to hide than where he was now. There were no stairs, but he could see handholds on the wall. A deft kender—such as himself—should have no trouble at all climbing down. Perhaps it led outside. Suddenly Tas heard a noise behind him. Silvara sighing and stirring. . . .

Without another thought, Tas lowered himself silently into the hole and began his descent. The walls were slick with moisture and moss, the handholds were spaced far apart. Built for humans, he thought irritably. No one ever considered little people!

He was so preoccupied that he didn't notice the gems until he was practically on top of them.

"Reorx's beard!" he swore. (He was fond of this oath, having borrowed it from Flint.) Six beautiful jewels—each as big around as his hand—were spaced in a horizontal ring around the walls of the shaft. They were covered with moss, but Tas could tell at a glance how valuable they were.

"Now why would anyone put such wonderful jewels down here?" he asked aloud. "I'll bet it was some thief. If I can pry them loose, I'll return them to their rightful owner." His hand closed over a jewel.

A tremendous blast of wind filled the shaft, pulling the kender off the wall as easily as a winter gale rips a leaf off a tree. Falling, Tas looked back up, watching the light at the top of the shaft grow smaller and smaller. He wondered briefly just how big the Hammer of Reorx was, and then he stopped falling.

For a moment, the wind tumbled him end over end. Then it switched directions, blowing him sideways. I'm not going to the other side of the world after all, he thought sadly. Sighing, he sailed along through another tunnel. Then he suddenly felt himself start to rise! A great wind was wafting him up the shaft! It was an unusual sensation, quite exhilarating. Instinctively, he spread his arms to see if he could touch the sides of whatever it was he was in. As he spread his arms, he noticed that he rose faster, borne gently upward on swift currents of air.

Perhaps I'm dead, Tas thought. I'm dead and now I'm lighter than air. How can I tell? Putting his arms down, he felt frantically for his pouches. He wasn't certain, the kender had very vague ideas as to the afterlife—but he had a feeling they wouldn't let him take his things with him. No, everything was there. Tas breathed a sigh of relief that turned into a gulp when he discovered himself slowing down and even starting to fall!

What? he thought wildly, then realized he had pulled both his arms in close to his body. Hurriedly he thrust his arms out again and, sure enough, he began to rise. Convinced that he wasn't dead, he gave himself up to enjoying the flight.

Fluttering his hands, the kender rolled over on his back in midair, and stared up to see where he was going.

Ah, there was a light far above him, growing brighter and brighter. Now he could see that he was in a shaft, but it was much longer than the shaft he had tumbled down.

"Wait until Flint hears about this!" he said wistfully. Then he caught a glimpse of six jewels, like the ones he'd seen in the other shaft. The rushing wind began to lessen.

Just as he decided that he could really enjoy taking up flying as a way of life, Tas reached the top of the shaft. The air currents held him even with the stone floor of a torch-lit chamber. Tas waited a moment to see if he might start flying again, and he even flapped his arms a bit to help, but nothing happened. Apparently his flight had ended.

I might as well explore while I'm up here, the kender thought with a sigh. Jumping out of the air currents, he landed lightly on the stone floor, then began to look around.

Several torches flared on the walls, illuminating the chamber with a bright white radiance. This room was certainly much larger than the tomb! He was standing at the bottom of a great curving staircase. The huge flagstones of each step—as well as all the other stones in the room—were pure white, much different from the black stone of the tomb. The staircase curved to the right, leading up to what appeared to be another level of the chamber. Above him, he could see a railing overlooking the stairs, apparently there was some sort of balcony up there. Nearly breaking his neck trying to see, Tas thought he could make out swirls and splotches of bright colors shining in the torchlight from the opposite wall.

Who lit the torches, he wondered? What is this place? Part of Huma's tomb? Or did I fly up into the Dragon Mountain? Who lives here? Those torches didn't light themselves!

At that thought—just to be safe—Tas reached into his tunic and drew out his little knife. Holding it in his hand, he climbed the grand stairs and came out onto the balcony. It was a huge chamber, but he could see little of it in the flickering torchlight. Gigantic pillars supported the massive ceiling overhead. Another great staircase rose from this balcony level to yet another floor. Tas turned around, leaning against the railing to look at the walls behind him.

"Reorx's beard!" he said softly. "Look at *that!*"

That was a painting. A mural, to be more precise. It began opposite where Tas was standing, at the head of the stairs, and extended on around the balcony in foot after foot of shimmering color. The kender was not much interested in artwork, but he couldn't recall ever seeing anything quite so beautiful. Or had he? Somehow, it seemed familiar. Yes, the more he looked at it, the more he thought he'd seen it before.

Tas studied the painting, trying to remember. On the wall directly across from him was pictured a horrible scene of dragons of every color and description descending upon the land. Towns blazed in flames—like Tarsis—buildings crumbled, people were fleeing. It was a terrible sight, and the kender hurried past it.

He continued walking along the balcony, his eyes on the painting. He had just reached the central portion of the mural when he gasped.

"The Dragon Mountain! That's it—there, on the wall!" he whispered to himself and was startled to hear his whisper come echoing back to him. Glancing around hastily, he crept closer to the other edge of the balcony. Leaning over the rail, he stared closely at the painting. It indeed showed the Dragon Mountain, where he was now. Only this showed a view of the mountain as if some giant sword had chopped it completely in half vertically!

"How wonderful!" The map-loving kender sighed. "Of course," he said. "It *is* a map! And that's where I am! I've gone up into the mountain." He looked around the room in sudden realization. "I'm in the throat of the dragon. That's why this room is such a funny shape." He turned back to the map. "There's the painting on the wall and there's the balcony I'm standing on. And the pillars . . ." He turned completely around. "Yes, there's the grand staircase." He turned back. "It leads up into the head! And there's how I came up. Some sort of wind chamber. But who built this . . . and why?"

Tasslehoff continued on around the balcony, hoping to find a clue in the painting. On the right-hand side of the gallery, another battle was portrayed. But this one didn't fill him with horror. There were red dragons, and black, and blue, and white—breathing fire and ice—but fighting them were other dragons, dragons of silver and of gold. . . .

"I remember!" shouted Tasslehoff.

The kender begin jumping up and down, yelling like a wild thing. "I remember! I remember! It was in Pax Tharkas. Fizban showed me. There are *good* dragons in the world. They'll help us fight the evil ones! We just have to find them. And there are the dragonlances!"

"Confound it!" snarled a voice below the kender. "Can't a person get some sleep? What is all this racket? You're making noise enough to wake the dead!"

Tasslehoff whirled around in alarm, his knife in his hand. He could have sworn he was alone up here. But no. Rising up off a stone bench that stood in a shadowy area out of the torchlight was a dark, robed figure. It shook itself, stretched, then got up and began to climb the stairs, moving swiftly toward the kender. Tas could not have gotten away, even if he had wanted to, and the kender found himself intensely curious about who was up here. He opened his mouth to ask this strange creature what it was and why it had chosen the throat of a Dragon Mountain to nap in, when the figure emerged into the light. It was an old man. It was—

Tasslehoff's knife clattered to the floor. The kender sagged back against the railing. For the first, last, and only time in his life, Tasslehoff Burrfoot was struck speechless.

"F-F-F . . ." Nothing came out of his throat, only a croak.

"Well, what is it? Speak up!" snapped the old man, looming over him. "You were making enough noise a minute ago. What's the matter? Something go down the wrong way?"

"F-F-F . . ." stuttered Tas weakly.

"Ah, poor boy. Afflicted, eh? Speech impediment. Sad, sad. Here—" The old man fumbled in his robes, opening numerous pouches while Tasslehoff stood trembling before him.

"There," the figure said. Drawing forth a coin, he put it in the kender's numb palm and closed his small, lifeless fingers over it. "Now, run along. Find a cleric . . ."

"Fizban!" Tasslehoff was finally able to gasp.

"Where?" The old man whirled around. Raising his staff, he peered fearfully into the darkness. Then something seemed to occur to him. Turning back around, he asked Tas in a loud whisper, "I say, are you sure you saw this Fizban? Isn't he dead?"

"I know *I* thought so . . . " Tas said miserably.

"Then he shouldn't be wandering around, scaring people!" the old man declared angrily. "I'll have a talk with him. Hey, you!" he began to shout.

Tas reached out a trembling hand and tugged at the old man's robe. "I— I'm not sure, b-but I think *you're* Fizban."

"No, really?" the old man said, taken aback. "I was feeling a bit under the weather this morning, but I had no idea it was as bad as all that." His shoulders sagged. "So I'm dead. Done for. Bought the farm. Kicked the bucket." He staggered to a bench and plopped down. "Was it a nice funeral?" he asked. "Did lots of people come? Was there a twenty-one gun salute? I always wanted a twenty-one gun salute."

"I—uh," Tas stammered, wondering what a gun was. "Well, it was . . . more of a . . . memorial service you might say. You see, we—uh—couldn't find your—how shall I put this?"

"Remains?" the old man said helpfully.

"Uh . . . remains." Tas flushed. "We looked, but there were all these chicken feathers . . . and a dark elf . . . and Tanis said we were lucky to have escaped alive. . . ."

"Chicken feathers!" said the old man indignantly. "What have chicken feathers got to do with my funeral?"

"We—uh—you and me and Sestun. Do you remember Sestun, the gully dwarf? Well, there was that great, huge chain in Pax Tharkas. And that big red dragon. We were hanging onto the chain and the dragon breathed fire on it and the chain broke and we were falling"—Tas was warming up to his story; it had become one of his favorites—"and I knew it was all over. We were going to die. There must have been a seventy-foot drop" (this increased every time Tas told the tale) "and you were beneath me and I heard you chanting a spell—"

"Yes, I'm quite a good magician, you know."

"Uh, right," Tas stammered, then continued hurriedly. "You chanted this spell, Featherfall or something like that. Anyway, you only said the first word, 'feather' and suddenly"—the kender spread his hands, a look of awe on his face as he remembered what happened then—"there were millions and millions and millions of chicken feathers. . . ."

"So what happened next?" the old man demanded, poking Tas.

"Oh, uh, that's where it gets a bit—uh—muddled," Tas said. "I heard a scream and a thump. Well, it was more like a splatter actually, and I f-f-figured the splatter was you."

"Me?" the old man shouted. "Splatter!" He glared at the kender furiously. "I never in my life *splattered!*"

"Then Sestun and I tumbled down into the chicken feathers, along with the chain. I looked—I really did." Tas's eyes filled with tears as he remembered his heartbroken search for the old man's body. "But there were too many feathers . . . and there was this terrible commotion outside where the dragons were fighting. Sestun and I made it to the door, and then we found Tanis, and I wanted to go back to look for you some more, but Tanis said no . . ."

"So you left me buried under a mound of chicken feathers?"

"It was an *awfully* nice memorial service," Tas faltered. "Goldmoon spoke, and Elistan. You didn't meet Elistan, but you remember Goldmoon, don't you? And Tanis?"

"Goldmoon . . ." the old man murmured. "Ah, yes. Pretty girl. Big, stern-looking chap in love with her."

"Riverwind!" said Tas in excitement. "And Raistlin?"

"Skinny fellow. Damn good magician," the old man said solemnly, "but he'll never amount to anything if he doesn't do something about that cough."

"You *are* Fizban!" Tas said. Jumping up gleefully, he threw his arms around the old man and hugged him tight.

"There, there," Fizban said, embarrassed, patting Tas on the back."That's quite enough. You'll crumple my robes. Don't sniffle. Can't abide it. Need a hankie?"

"No, I've got one—"

"Now, that's better. Oh, I say, I believe that handkerchief's mine. Those are my initials, "

"Is it? You must have dropped it."

"I remember you now!" the old man said loudly. "You're Tassle—Tassle-something-or-other."

"Tasslehoff. Tasslehoff Burrfoot," the kender replied.

"And I'm—" The old man stopped. "What did you say the name was?"

"Fizban."

"Fizban. Yes . . ." The old man pondered a moment, then he shook his head. "I sure thought he was dead. . . ."

10

Silvara's secret.

 ow *did* you survive?" Tas asked, pulling some dried fruit from a pouch to share with Fizban.

The old man appeared wistful. "I really didn't think I did," he said apologetically. "I'm afraid I haven't the vaguest notion. But, come to think of it, I haven't been able to eat a chicken since. Now"—he stared at the kender shrewdly—"what are you doing here?"

"I came with some of my friends. The rest are wandering around somewhere, if they're still alive." He sniffed again.

"They are. Don't worry." Fizban patted him on the back.

"Do you think so?" Tas brightened. "Well, anyway, we're here with Silvara—"

"Silvara!" The old man leaped to his feet, his white hair flying out wildly. The vague look faded from his face.

"Where is she?" the old man demanded sternly. "And your friends, where are they?"

"D-downstairs," stammered Tas, startled at the old man's transformation. "Silvara cast a spell on them!"

"Ah, she did, did she?" the old man muttered. "We'll see about that. Come on." He started off along the balcony, walking so rapidly, Tas had to run to keep up.

"Where'd you say they were?" the old man asked, stopping near the stairs. "Be specific," he snapped.

"Uh—the tomb! Huma's tomb! I think it's Huma's tomb. That's what Silvara said."

"Humpf. Well, at least we don't have to walk."

Descending the stairs to the hole in the floor Tas had come up through, the old man stepped out into its center. Tas, gulping a little, joined him, clutching at the old man's robes. They hung suspended over nothing but darkness, feeling cool air waft up around them.

"Down," the old man stated.

They began to rise, drifting toward the ceiling of the upper gallery. Tas felt the hair stand up on his head.

"I said *down!*" the old man shouted furiously, waving his staff menacingly at the hole below him.

There was a slurping sound and both of them were sucked into the hole so rapidly that Fizban's hat flew off. It's just like the hat he lost in the red dragon's lair, Tas thought. It was bent and shapeless, and apparently possessed of a mind of its own. Fizban made a wild grab for it, but missed. The hat, however, floated down after them, about fifty feet above.

Tasslehoff peered down, fascinated, and started to ask a question, but Fizban shushed him. Gripping his staff, the old mage began whispering to himself, making an odd sign in the air.

Laurana opened her eyes. She was lying on a cold stone bench, staring at a black, glistening ceiling. She had no idea where she was. Then memory returned. Silvara!

Sitting up swiftly, she flashed a glance around the room. Flint was groaning and rubbing his neck. Theros blinked and looked around, puzzled. Gilthanas, already on his feet, stood at the end of Huma's tomb, gazing down at something by the door. As Laurana walked over to him, he turned around. Putting his finger to his lips, he nodded in the direction of the doorway.

Silvara sat there, her head in her arms, sobbing bitterly.

Laurana hesitated, the angry words on her lips dying. This certainly wasn't what she had expected. What had she expected? she asked herself. Never to wake again, most likely. There had to be an explanation. She started forward.

"Silvara—" she began.

The girl leaped up, her tear-stained face white with fear.

"What are you doing awake? How did you free yourself from my spell?" she gasped, falling back against the wall.

"Never mind that!" Laurana answered, though she hadn't any idea how she had wakened. "Tell us—"

"It was *my* doing!" announced a deep voice. Laurana and the rest turned around to see a white-bearded old man in mouse-colored robes rise up solemnly out of the hole in the floor.

"Fizban!" whispered Laurana in disbelief.

There was a clunk and a thud. Flint toppled over in a dead faint. No one even looked at him. They simply stared at the old mage in awe. Then, with a shrill shriek, Silvara flung herself flat on the cold stone floor, shivering and whimpering softly.

Ignoring the stares of the others, Fizban walked across the floor of the tomb, past the bier, past the comatose dwarf, to come to Silvara. Behind him, Tasslehoff scrambled up out of the hole.

"Look who *I* found," the kender said proudly. "Fizban! And I flew, Laurana. I jumped into the hole and just flew straight up into the air. And there's a painting up there with gold dragons, and then Fizban sat up and yelled at me and—I must admit I felt really queer there for a while. My voice was gone and . . . what happened to Flint?"

"Hush, Tas," Laurana said weakly, her eyes on Fizban. Kneeling down, he shook the Wilder elfmaid.

"Silvara, what have you done?" Fizban asked sternly. Laurana thought then that perhaps she had made a mistake—this must be some other old man dressed in the old magician's clothes. This stern-faced, powerful man was certainly not the befuddled old mage she remembered. But no, she'd recognize that face anywhere, to say nothing of the hat!

Watching the two of them—Silvara and Fizban—before her, Laurana felt great and awesome power like silent thunder surging between the two. She had a terrible longing to run out of this place and keep running until she dropped with exhaustion. But she couldn't move. She could only stare.

"What have you done, Silvara?" Fizban demanded. "You have broken your oath!"

"No!" The girl moaned, writhing on the ground at the old mage's feet. "No, I haven't. Not yet—"

"You have walked the world in another body, meddling in the affairs of men. That alone would be sufficient. But you brought them here!"

Silvara's tear-stained face was twisted in anguish. Laurana felt her own tears sliding unchecked down her cheeks.

"All right then!" Silvara cried defiantly. "I broke my oath, or at least I intended to. I brought them here. I had to! I've seen the misery and the suffering. Besides"—her voice fell, her eyes stared far away—"they had an orb . . ."

"Yes," said Fizban softly. "A dragon orb. Taken from Ice Wall Castle. It fell into your possession. What have you done with it, Silvara? Where is it now?"

"I sent it away . . ." Silvara said almost inaudibly.

Fizban seemed to age. His face grew weary. Sighing deeply, he leaned heavily upon his staff. "Where did you send it, Silvara? Where is the dragon orb now?"

"St-Sturm has it," Laurana interrupted fearfully. "He took it to Sancrist. What does this mean? Is Sturm in danger?"

"Who?" Fizban peered around over his shoulder. "Oh, hullo there, my dear." He beamed at her. "So nice to see you again. How's your father?"

"My father—" Laurana shook her head, confused. "Look, old man, never mind my father! Who—"

"And your brother." Fizban extended a hand to Gilthanas. "Good to see you, son. And you, sir." He bowed to an astonished Theros. "Silver arm? My, my"—he stole a look back at Silvara—"what a coincidence. Theros Ironfeld, isn't it? Heard a lot about you. And my name is . . ." The old magician paused, his brow furrowed.

"My name is . . ."

"Fizban," supplied Tasslehoff helpfully.

"Fizban." The old man nodded, smiling.

Laurana thought she saw the old magician cast a warning glance at Silvara. The girl lowered her head as if to acknowledge some silent, secret signal passed between them.

But before Laurana could sort out her whirling thoughts, Fizban turned back to her again. "And now, Laurana, you wonder who Silvara is? It is up to Silvara to tell you. For I must leave you now. I have a long journey ahead of me."

"Must I tell them?" Silvara asked softly. She was still on her knees and, as she spoke, her eyes went to Gilthanas. Fizban followed her gaze. Seeing the elflord's stricken face, his own face softened. Then he shook his head sadly.

Silvara raised her hands to him in a pleading gesture. Fizban walked over to her. Taking her hands, he raised her to her feet. She threw her arms around him, and he held her close.

"No, Silvara," he said, his voice kind and gentle, "you do not have to tell them. The choice is yours that was your sister's. You can make them forget they were ever here."

Suddenly the only color left in Silvara's face was the deep blue of her eyes. "But, that will mean—"

"Yes, Silvara," he said. "It is up to you." He kissed the girl on the forehead. "Farewell, Silvara."

Turning, he looked back at the rest. "Good-bye, good-bye. Nice seeing you again. I'm a bit miffed about the chicken feathers, but—no hard feelings." He waited impatiently a minute, glaring at Tasslehoff. "Are you coming? I haven't got all night!"

"Coming? With you?" Tas cried, dropping Flint's head back onto the stone floor with a thunk. The kender stood up. "Of course, let me get my pack . . ." Then he stopped, glancing down at the unconscious dwarf. "Flint—"

"He'll be fine," Fizban promised. "You won't be parted from your friends long. We'll see them"—he frowned, muttering to himself—"seven days, add three, carry the one, what's seven times four? Oh well, around Famine Time. That's when they'll hold the Council meeting. Now, come along. I've got work to do. Your friends are in good hands. Silvara will take care of them, won't you, my dear?" He turned to the Wilder elf.

"I will tell them," she promised sadly, eyes on Gilthanas.

The elflord was staring at her and at Fizban, his face pale, fear spreading through his soul.

Silvara sighed. "You are right. I broke the oath long ago. I must finish what I set out to do."

"As you think best." Fizban laid his hand upon Silvara's head, stroking her silver hair. Then he turned away.

"Will I be punished?" she asked, just as the old man stepped into the shadows.

Fizban stopped. Shaking his head, he looked back over his shoulder "Some would say you are being punished right now, Silvara," he said softly. "But what you do, you do out of love. As the choice was up to you, so is your punishment."

The old man stepped into the darkness. Tasslehoff ran after him, his pouches bouncing behind him. "Good-bye, Laurana! Good-bye, Theros! Take care of Flint!" In the silence that followed, Laurana could hear the old man's voice.

"What was that name again? Fizbut, Furball—"

"Fizban!" said Tas shrilly.

"Fizban . . . Fizban . . ." muttered the old man.

All eyes turned to Silvara.

She was calm now, at peace with herself. Although her face was filled with sorrow, it was not the tormented, bitter sorrow they had seen earlier. This was the sorrow of loss, the quiet, accepting sorrow of one who has nothing to regret. Silvara walked toward Gilthanas. She took hold of his hands and looked up into his face with so much love that Gilthanas felt blessed, even as he knew she was going to tell him good-bye.

"I am losing you, Silvara," he murmured in broken tones. "I see it in your eyes. But I don't know why! You love me—"

"I love you, elflord," Silvara said softly. "I loved you when I saw you lying injured upon the sand. When you looked up and smiled at me, I knew that the fate which had befallen my sister was to be mine, too." She sighed. "But it is a risk we take when we choose this form. For though we bring our strength into it, the form inflicts its weaknesses upon us. Or is it a weakness? To love . . ."

"Silvara, I don't understand!" Gilthanas cried.

"You will," she promised, her voice soft. Her head bowed.

Gilthanas took her in his arms, holding her. She buried her face in his chest. He kissed her beautiful silver hair, then clasped her with a sob.

Laurana turned away. This grief seemed too sacred for her eyes to intrude upon. Swallowing her own tears, she looked around and then remembered the dwarf. She took some water from his waterskin and sprinkled it on Flint's face.

His eyes fluttered, then opened. The dwarf stared up at Laurana for a moment and reached out a trembling hand.

"Fizban!" the dwarf whispered hoarsely.

"I know," Laurana said, wondering how the dwarf would take the news about Tas's leaving.

"Fizban's *dead!*" Flint gasped. "Tas said so! In a pile of chicken feathers!" The dwarf struggled to sit up. "Where is that rattle-brained kender?"

"He's gone, Flint," Laurana said. "He went with Fizban."

"Gone?" The dwarf looked around blankly. "You let him go? With that old man?"

"I'm afraid so—"

"You let him go with a dead old man?"

"I really didn't have much choice." Laurana smiled. "It was his decision. He'll be fine—"

"Where'd they go?" Flint stood and shouldered his pack.

"You can't go after them," Laurana said. "Please, Flint." She put her arm around the dwarf's shoulders. "I need you. You're Tanis's oldest friend, my advisor—"

"But he's gone without me," Flint said plaintively. "How could he leave? I didn't see him go."

"You fainted—"

"I did no such thing!" the dwarf roared.

"You—you were out cold," Laurana stammered.

"I never faint!" stated the dwarf indignantly. "It must have been a recurrence of that deadly disease I caught on board that boat—" Flint dropped his pack and slumped down beside it. "Idiot kender. Running off with a dead old man."

Theros came over to Laurana, drawing her to one side. "Who was that old man?" he asked curiously.

"It's a long story." Laurana sighed. "And I'm not certain I could answer that question anyway."

"He seems familiar." Theros frowned and shook his head. "But I can't remember where I've seen him before, though he puts me in mind of Solace and the Inn of the Last Home. And he knew me . . ."The blacksmith stared at his silver hand. "I felt a shock go through me when he looked at me, like lightning striking a tree." The big blacksmith shivered, then he glanced over at Silvara and Gilthanas. "And what of this?"

"I think we're finally about to find out," Laurana said.

"You were right," Theros said. "You didn't trust her—"

"But not for the right reasons," Laurana admitted guiltily.

With a small sigh, Silvara pushed herself away from Gilthanas's embrace. The elflord let her go reluctantly.

"Gilthanas," she said, drawing a shuddering breath, "take a torch off the wall and hold it up before me."

Gilthanas hesitated. Then, almost angrily, he followed her directions.

"Hold the torch there . . ." she instructed, guiding his hand so that the light blazed right before her. "Now—look at my shadow on the wall behind me," she said in trembling tones.

The tomb was silent, only the sputtering of the flaming torch made any sound. Silvara's shadow sprang into life on the cold stone wall behind her. The companions stared at it and—for an instant—none of them could say a word.

The shadow Silvara cast upon the wall was not the shadow of a young elfmaid.

It was the shadow of a dragon.

"*You're* a dragon!" Laurana said in shocked disbelief. She laid her hand on her sword, but Theros stopped her.

"No!" he said suddenly. "I remember. That old man—" He looked at his arm. "Now I remember. He used to come into the Inn of the Last Home! He was dressed differently. He wasn't a mage, but it was him! I'll swear it! He told stories to the children. Stories about good dragons. Gold dragons and—"

"Silver dragons," Silvara said, looking at Theros. "I am a silver dragon. My sister was the Silver Dragon who loved Huma and fought the final great battle with him—"

"No!" Gilthanas flung the torch to the ground. It lay flickering for a moment at his feet, then he stamped on it angrily, putting out its light. Silvara, watching him with sad eyes, reached out her hand to comfort him.

Gilthanas shrank from her touch, staring at her in horror.

Silvara lowered her hand slowly. Sighing gently, she nodded. "I understand," she murmured. "I'm sorry."

Gilthanas began to shake, then doubled over in agony. Putting his strong arms around him, Theros led Gilthanas to a bench and covered him with his cloak.

"I'll be all right," Gilthanas mumbled. "Just leave me alone, let me think. This is madness! It's all a nightmare. A dragon!" He closed his eyes tightly as if he could blot out their sight forever. "A dragon . . ." he whispered brokenly. Theros patted him gently, then returned to the others.

"Where are the rest of the good dragons?" Theros asked. "The old man said there were many. Silver dragons, gold dragons—"

"There are many of us," Silvara answered reluctantly.

"Like the silver dragon we saw in Ice Wall!" Laurana said. "It was a good dragon. If there are many of you, band together! Help us fight the evil dragons!"

"No!" Silvara cried fiercely. Her blue eyes flared, and Laurana fell back a pace before her anger.

"Why not?"

"I cannot tell you." Silvara's hands clenched nervously.

"It has something to do with that oath!" Laurana persisted. "Doesn't it? The oath you've broken. And the punishment you asked Fizban about—"

"I cannot tell you!" Silvara spoke in a low, passionate voice. "What I have done is bad enough. But I had to do something! I could no longer live in this world and see the suffering of innocent people! I thought perhaps I could help, so I took elven form, and I did what I could. I worked long, trying to get the elves to join together. I kept them from war, but matters were growing worse. Then you came, and I saw that we were in great peril, greater than any of us had ever imagined. For you brought with you—" Her voice faltered.

"The dragon orb!" Laurana said suddenly.

"Yes." Silvara's fists clenched in misery. "I knew then I had to make a decision. You had the orb, but you also had the lance. The lance and the orb coming to me! Both, together! It was a sign, I thought, but I didn't know what to do. I decided to bring the orb here and keep it safe forever. Then, as we traveled, I realized the knights would never allow it to remain here. There would be trouble. So, when I saw my chance, I sent it away." Her shoulders sagged. "That was apparently the wrong decision. But how was I to know?"

"Why?" Theros asked severely. "What does the orb do? Is it evil? Have you sent those knights to their doom?"

"Great evil," Silvara murmured. "Great good. Who can say? Even I do not understand the dragon orbs. They were forged long ago by the most powerful of magic-users."

"But the book Tas read said they could be used to control dragons!"Flint stated. "He read it with some kind of glasses. Glasses of true seeing, he called 'em. He said they don't lie—"

"No," said Silvara sadly. "That is true. It is too true, as I fear you friends may discover to their bitter regret."

The companions, fear closing around them, sat together in silence broken only by Gilthanas's choking sobs. The torches sent shadows dodging and dancing around the quiet tomb like undead spirits. Laurana remembered Huma and the Silver Dragon. She thought of that final, terrible battle— the skies filled with dragons, the land erupting in flame and in blood.

"Why have you brought us here, then?" Laurana asked Silvara quietly. "Why not just let us all take the orb away?"

"Can I tell them? Do I have the strength?" Silvara whispered to an unseen spirit.

She sat quietly for a long time, her face expressionless, her hands twisting in her lap. Her eyes closed, her head bowed, her lips moved. She covered her face with her hands and sat quite still. Then, shuddering, she made her decision.

Rising to her feet, Silvara walked over to Laurana's pack. Kneeling down, she slowly and carefully unwrapped the broken shaft of wood that the companions had carried such a long and weary distance. Silvara stood, her face once more filled with peace. But now there was also pride and strength. For the first time, Laurana began to believe this girl was something as powerful and magnificent as a dragon. Walking proudly, her silver hair glistening in the torchlight, Silvara walked over to stand before Theros Ironfeld.

"To Theros of the Silver Arm," she said, "I give the power to forge the dragonlance."

Book III

I

The Red Wizard and His

Wonderful Illusions!

hadows crept across the dusty tables of the Pig and Whistle tavern. The sea breeze off the Bay of Balifor made a shrill whistling sound as it blew through the ill-fitting front windows, that distinctive whistle giving the inn the last part of its name. Any guesses as to how the tavern got the first part ended on sight of the innkeeper. A jovial, kind-hearted man, William Sweetwater had been cursed at birth (so town legend went) when a wandering pig overturned the baby's cradle, so frightening young William that the mark of the pig was forever imprinted on his face.

This unfortunate resemblance had certainly not impaired William's temper, however. A sailor by trade until he had retired to fulfill a lifelong ambition of keeping an inn, there was not a more respected or well-liked man in Port Balifor than William Sweetwater. No one laughed more heartily at pig jokes than did William. He could even grunt quite realistically and often did pig imitations for the amusement of his customers. (But no one ever—after the untimely death of Peg-Leg Al—called William by the name "Piggy.")

William rarely grunted for his customers these days. The atmosphere of the Pig and Whistle was dark and gloomy. The few old customers that came sat huddled together, talking in low voices. For Port Balifor was an occupied town—overrun by the armies of the highlords, whose ships had recently sailed into the Bay, disgorging troops of the hideous dragonmen.

The people of Port Balifor—mostly humans—felt extremely sorry for themselves. They had no knowledge of what was going on in the outside world, of course, or they would have counted their blessings. No dragons came to burn their town. The draconians generally left the citizens alone. The Dragon Highlords were not particularly interested in the eastern part of the Ansalon continent. The land was sparsely populated: a few poor, scattered communities of humans and Kendermore, the homeland of the kenders. A flight of dragons could have leveled the countryside, but the Dragon Highlords were concentrating their strength in the north and the west. As long as the ports remained opened, the Highlords had no need to devastate the lands of Balifor and Goodlund.

Although not many old customers came to the Pig and Whistle, business had improved for William Sweetwater. The draconian and goblin troops of the Highlord were well paid, and their one weakness was strong drink. But William had not opened his tavern for money. He loved the companionship of old friends and new. He did *not* enjoy the companionship of the Highlord's troops. When they came in, his old customers left. Therefore, William promptly raised his prices for draconians to three times higher than in any other inn in town. He also watered the ale. Consequently, his bar was nearly deserted except for a few old friends. This arrangement suited William fine.

He was talking to a few of these friends—sailors mostly, with brown, weathered skin and no teeth—on the evening that the strangers entered his tavern. William glared at them suspiciously for a moment, as did his friends. But, seeing road-weary travelers and not the Highlord's soldiers, he greeted them cordially and showed them to a table in the corner.

The strangers ordered ale all around—except for a red-robed man who ordered nothing but hot water. Then, after a subdued discussion centering around a worn leather purse and the number of coins therein, they asked William to bring them bread and cheese.

"They're not from these parts," William said to his friends in a low voice as he drew the ale from a special keg he kept beneath the bar (not the keg for draconians). "And poor as a sailor after a week ashore, if I make my guess."

"Refugees," said his friend, eyeing them speculatively.

"Odd mixture, though," added the other sailor. "Yon red-bearded fellow's a half-elf, if ever I saw one. And the big one's got weapons enough to take on the Highlord's whole army."

"I'll wager he's stuck a few of them with that sword, too," William grunted. "They're on the run from something, I'll bet. Look at the way that bearded fellow keeps his eyes on the door. Well, we can't help them fight the Highlord, but I'll see they don't want for anything." He went to serve them.

"Put your money away," William said gruffly, plunking down not only bread and cheese but also a tray full of cold meats as well. He shoved the coins away. "You're in trouble of some kind, that's plain as this pig's snout upon my face."

One of the women smiled at him. She was the most beautiful woman William had ever seen. Her silver-gold hair gleamed from beneath a fur hood, her blue eyes were like the ocean on a calm day. When she smiled at him, William felt the warmth of fine brandy run through his body. But a stern-faced, dark-haired man next to her shoved the coins back to the innkeeper.

"We'll not accept charity," the tall, fur-cloaked man said.

"We won't?" asked the big man wistfully, staring at the smoked meat with longing eyes.

"Riverwind," the woman remonstrated, putting a gentle hand on his arm. The half-elf, too, seemed about to interpose when the red-robed man, who had ordered the hot water, reached out and picked up a coin from the table.

Balancing the coin on the back of his bony, metallic-colored hand, the man suddenly and effortlessly sent it dancing along his knuckles. William's eyes opened wide. His two friends at the bar came closer to see better. The coin flickered in and out of the red-robed man's fingers, spinning and jumping. It vanished high in the air, only to reappear above the mage's head in the form of six coins, spinning around his hood. With a gesture, he sent them to spin around William's head. The sailors watched in open-mouthed wonder.

"Take one for your trouble," said the mage in a whisper.

Hesitantly, William tried to grab the coins that whirled past his eyes, but his hand went right through them! Suddenly all six coins disappeared. One only remained now, resting in the palm of the red-robed mage.

"I give you this in payment," the mage said with a sly smile, "but be careful. It may burn a hole in your pocket."

William accepted the coin gingerly. Holding it between two fingers, he gazed at it suspiciously. Then the coin burst into flame! With a startled yelp, William dropped it to the floor, stomping on it with his foot. His two friends burst out laughing. Picking up the coin, William discovered it to be perfectly cold and undamaged.

"That's worth the meat!" the innkeeper said, grinning.

"And a night's lodgings," added his friend, the sailor, slapping down a handful of coins.

"I believe," said Raistlin softly, glancing around at the others, "that we have solved our problems."

Thus was born The Red Wizard and His Wonderful Illusions, a traveling road show that is still talked of today as far south as Port Balifor and as far north as the Ruins.

The very next night the red-robed mage began to perform his tricks to an admiring audience of William's friends. The word spread rapidly. After the mage had performed in the Pig and Whistle for about a week, Riverwind—at first opposed to the whole idea—was forced to admit that Raistlin's act seemed likely to solve not only their financial problems but other, more pressing problems as well.

The shortage of money was the most urgent. The companions might have been able to live off the land—even in the winter, both Riverwind and Tanis being skilled hunters. But they needed money to buy passage on a ship to take them to Sancrist. Once they had the money, they needed to be able to travel freely through enemy-occupied lands.

In his youth, Raistlin had often used his considerable talents at sleight of hand to earn bread for himself and his brother. Although this was frowned on by his master, who threatened to expel the young mage from his school, Raistlin had become quite successful. Now his growing powers in magic gave him a range not possible before. He literally kept his audiences spellbound with tricks and phantasms.

At Raistlin's command, white-winged ships sailed up and down the bar at the Pig and Whistle, birds flew out of soup tureens, while dragons peered through the windows, breathing fire upon the startled guests. In the grand finale, the mage—resplendent in red robes sewn by Tika—appeared to be totally consumed in raging flames, only to walk in through the front door moments later (to tumultuous applause) and calmly drink a glass of white wine to the health of the guests.

Within a week, the Pig and Whistle did more business than William had done in a year. Better still—as far as he was concerned—his friends were able to forget their troubles. Soon, however, unwanted guests began to arrive. At first, he had been angered by the appearance of draconians and goblins in the crowd, but Tanis placated him, and William grudgingly permitted them to watch.

Tanis was, in fact, pleased to see them. It worked out well from the half-elf's point of view and solved their second problem. If the Highlord's troops enjoyed the show and spread the word, the companions could travel the countryside unmolested.

It was their plan—after consulting with William—to make for Flotsam, a city north of Port Balifor, located on the Blood Sea of Istar. Here they hoped to find a ship. No one in Port Balifor would give them passage, William explained. All the local shipowners were in the employ of (or their vessels had been confiscated by) the Dragon Highlords. But Flotsam was a known haven for those more interested in money than politics.

The companions stayed at the Pig and Whistle for a month. William provided free room and board and even allowed them to keep all the money they made. Though Riverwind protested this generosity, William stated firmly that all he cared about was seeing his old customers come back.

During this time, Raistlin refined and enlarged his act which, at first consisted only of his illusions. But the mage tired rapidly, so Tika offered to dance and give him time to rest between acts. Raistlin was dubious, but Tika sewed a costume for herself that was so alluring Caramon was—at first—totally opposed to the scheme. But Tika only laughed at him. Her dancing was a success and increased the money they collected dramatically. Raistlin added her immediately to the act.

Finding the crowds enjoyed this diversion, the mage thought of others. Caramon—blushing furiously—was persuaded to perform feats of strength, the highlight coming when he lifted stout William over his head with one hand. Tanis amazed the crowd with his elven ability to "see" in the dark. But Raistlin was startled one day when Goldmoon came to him as he was counting the money from the previous night's performance.

"I would like to sing in the show tonight," she said.

Raistlin looked up at her incredulously. His eyes flicked to Riverwind. The tall Plainsman nodded reluctantly.

"You have a powerful voice," Raistlin said, sliding the money into a pouch and drawing the string tightly. "I remember quite well. The last song I heard you sing in the Inn of the Last Home touched off a riot that nearly got us killed."

Goldmoon flushed, remembering the fateful song that had introduced her to the group. Scowling, Riverwind laid his hand on her shoulder.

"Come away!" he said harshly, glaring at Raistlin. "I warned you—"

But Goldmoon shook her head stubbornly, lifting her chin in a familiar, imperious gesture. "I will sing," she said coolly, "and Riverwind will accompany me. I have written a song."

"Very well," the mage snapped, slipping the money pouch into his robes. "We will try it this evening."

The Pig and Whistle was crowded that night. It was a diverse audience—small children and their parents, sailors, draconians, goblins, and several kender, who caused everyone to keep an eye on his belongings. William and two helpers bustled about, serving drinks and food. Then the show began.

The crowd applauded Raistlin's spinning coins, laughed when an illusory pig danced upon the bar, and scrambled out of their chairs in terror when a giant troll thundered in through a window. Bowing, the mage left to rest. Tika came on.

The crowd, particularly the draconians, cheered Tika's dancing, banging their mugs on the table.

Then Goldmoon appeared before them, dressed in a gown of pale blue.

Her silver-gold hair flowed over her shoulders like water shimmering in the moonlight. The crowd hushed instantly. Saying nothing, she sat down in a chair on the raised platform William had hastily constructed. So beautiful was she that not a murmur escaped the crowd. All waited expectantly.

Riverwind sat upon the floor at her feet. Putting a hand-carved flute to his lips, he began to play and, after a few moments, Goldmoon's voice blended with the flute. Her song was simple, the melody sweet and harmonious, yet haunting. But it was the words that caught Tanis's attention, causing him to exchange worried glances with Caramon. Raistlin, sitting next to him, grasped hold of Tanis's arm.

"I feared as much!" the mage hissed. "Another riot!"

"Perhaps not," Tanis said, watching. "Look at the audience."

Women leaned their heads onto their husband's shoulders, children were quiet and attentive. The draconians seemed spellbound, as a wild animal will sometimes be held by music. Only the goblins shuffled their flapping feet, seemingly bored but so in awe of the draconians that they dared not protest.

Goldmoon's song was of the ancient gods. She told how the gods had sent the Cataclysm to punish the Kingpriest of Istar and the people of Krynn for their pride. She sang of the terrors of that night and those that followed. She reminded them of how the people, believing themselves abandoned, had prayed to false gods. Then she gave them a message of hope: the gods had not abandoned them. The true gods were here, waiting only for someone to listen to them.

After her song ended, and the plaintive wailing of the flute died, most in the crowd shook their heads, seeming to wake from a pleasant dream. When asked what the song had been about, they couldn't say. The draconians shrugged and called for more ale. The goblins shouted for Tika to dance again. But, here and there, Tanis noticed a face still holding the wonder it had worn during the song. And he was not surprised to see a young, dark-skinned woman approach Goldmoon shyly.

"I ask your pardon for disturbing you, my lady," Tanis overheard the woman say, "but your song touched me deeply. I—I want to learn of the ancient gods, to learn their ways."

Goldmoon smiled. "Come to me tomorrow," she said, "and I shall teach you what I know."

And thus, slowly, word of the ancient gods began to spread. By the time they left Port Balifor, the dark-skinned woman, a soft-voiced young man, and several other people wore the blue medallion of Mishakal, Goddess of Healing. Secretly they went forth, bringing hope to the dark and troubled land.

By the end of the month, the companions were able to buy a wagon, horses to pull it, horses to ride, and supplies. What was left went toward purchase of ship's passage to Sancrist. They planned to add to their money by performing in the small farming communities between Port Balifor and Flotsam.

When the Red Wizard left Port Balifor shortly before the Yuletide season, his wagon was seen on its way by enthusiastic crowds. Packed with their costumes, supplies for two months, and a keg of ale (provided by William), the wagon was big enough for Raistlin to sleep and travel inside. It also held the multi-colored, striped tents in which the others would live.

Tanis glanced around at the strange sight they made, shaking his head. It seemed that—in the midst of everything else that had happened to them—this was the most bizarre. He looked at Raistlin sitting beside his brother, who drove the wagon. The mage's red-sequined robes blazed like flame in the bright winter sunlight. Shoulders hunched against the wind, Raistlin stared straight ahead, wrapped in a show of mystery that delighted the crowd. Caramon, dressed in a bearskin suit (a present of William's), had pulled the head of the bear over his own, making it look as though a bear drove the wagon. The children cheered as he growled at them in mock ferocity.

They were nearly out of town when a draconian commander stopped them. Tanis, his heart caught in his throat, rode forward, his hand pressed against his sword. But the commander only wanted to make certain they passed through Bloodwatch where draconian troops were located. The draconian had mentioned the show to a friend. The troops were looking forward to seeing it. Tanis, inwardly vowing not to set foot near the place, promised faithfully that they would certainly appear.

Finally they reached the city gates. Climbing down from their mounts, they bid farewell to their friend. William gave them each a hug, starting with Tika and ending with Tika. He was going to hug Raistlin, but the mage's golden eyes widened so alarmingly when William approached that the innkeeper backed away precipitously.

The companions climbed back onto their horses. Raistlin and Caramon returned to the wagon. The crowd cheered and urged them to return for the spring Harrowing celebration. The guards opened the gates, bidding them a safe journey, and the companions rode through. The gates shut behind them.

The wind blew chill. Gray clouds above them began to spit snow fitfully. The road, which they were assured was well traveled, stretched before them, bleak and empty. Raistlin began to shiver and cough. After awhile, he said he would ride inside the wagon. The rest pulled their hoods up over their heads and clutched their fur cloaks more closely about them.

Caramon, guiding the horses along the rutted, muddy road, appeared unusually thoughtful.

"You know, Tanis," he said solemnly above the jingling of the bells Tika had tied to the horses' manes, "I'm more thankful than I can tell that none of our friends saw this. Can you hear what Flint would say? That grumbling old dwarf would never let me live this down. And can you imagine Sturm!" The big man shook his head, the thought being beyond words.

Yes, Tanis sighed. I can imagine Sturm. Dear friend, I never realized how much I depended on you—your courage, your noble spirit. Are you alive, my friend? Did you reach Sancrist safely? Are you now the knight in body that you have always been in spirit? Will we meet again, or have we parted never to meet in this life—as Raistlin predicted?

The group rode on. The day grew darker, the storm wilder. Riverwind dropped back to ride beside Goldmoon. Tika tied her horse behind the wagon and crawled up to sit near Caramon. Inside the wagon, Raistlin slept.

Tanis rode alone, his head bowed, his thoughts far away.

2

The Knights Trials.

nd—finally," said Derek in a low and measured voice, "I accuse Sturm Brightblade of cowardice in the face of the enemy."

A low murmur ran through the assemblage of knights gathered in the castle of Lord Gunthar. Three knights, seated at the massive black oak table in front of the assembly, leaned their heads together to confer in low tones.

Long ago, the three seated at this Knights Trials—as prescribed by the Measure—would have been the Grand Master, the High Clerist, and the High Justice. But at this time there was no Grand Master. There had not been a High Clerist since the time of the Cataclysm. And while the High Justice—Lord Alfred MarKenin—was present, his hold on that position was tenuous at best. Whoever became the new Grand Master had leave to replace him.

Despite these vacancies in the Head of the Order, the business of the Knights must continue. Though not strong enough to claim the coveted position of Grand Master, Lord Gunthar Uth Wistan was strong enough to act in that role. And so he sat here today, at the beginning of the Yuletide season, in judgment on this young squire, Sturm Brightblade. To his right sat Lord Alfred, to his left, young Lord Michael Jeoffrey, filling in as High Clerist.

Facing them, in the Great Hall of Castle Uth Wistan, were twenty other Knights of Solamnia who had been hastily gathered from all parts of Sancrist to sit as witnesses to this Knights Trials—as prescribed by the Measure. These now muttered and shook their heads as their leaders conferred.

From a table directly in front of the three Knights Seated in Judgment, Lord Derek rose and bowed to Lord Gunthar. His testimony had reached its end. There remained now only the Knight's Answer and the Judgment itself. Derek returned to his place among the other knights, laughing and talking with them.

Only one person in the hall was silent. Sturm Brightblade sat unmoving throughout all of Lord Derek Crownguard's damning accusations. He had heard charges of insubordination, failure to obey orders, masquerading as a knight—and not a word or murmur had escaped him. His face was carefully expressionless, his hands were clasped on the top of the table.

Lord Gunthar's eyes were on Sturm now, as they had been throughout the Trials. He began to wonder if the man was even still alive, so fixed and white was his face, so rigid his posture. Gunthar had seen Sturm flinch only once. At the charge of cowardice, a shudder convulsed the man's body. The look on his face . . . well, Gunthar recalled seeing that same look once previously—on a man who had just been run through by a spear. But Sturm quickly regained his composure.

Gunthar was so interested in watching Brightblade that he nearly lost track of the conversation of the two knights next to him. He caught only the end of Lord Alfred's sentence.

" . . . not allow Knight's Answer."

"Why not?" Lord Gunthar asked sharply, though keeping his voice low. "It is his right according to the Measure."

"We have never had a case like this," Lord Alfred, Knight of the Sword, stated flatly. "Always before, when a squire has been brought up before the Council of the Order to attain his knighthood, there have been witnesses, many witnesses. He is given an opportunity to explain his reasons for his actions. No one ever questions that he committed the acts. But Brightblade's only defense—"

"Is to tell us that Derek lies," finished Lord Michael Jeoffrey, Knight of the Crown. "And that is unthinkable. To take the word of a squire over a Knight of the Rose."

"Nonetheless, the young man will have his say," Lord Gunthar said, glancing sternly at each of the men. "That is the Law according to the Measure. Do either of you question it?"

"No . . ."

"No, of course not. But—"

"Very well." Gunthar smoothed his moustaches and, leaning forward, tapped gently on the wooden table with the hilt of the sword—Sturm's sword—that lay upon it. The other two knights exchanged looks behind his back, one raising his eyebrows, the other shrugging slightly. Gunthar was aware of this, as he was aware of all the covert scheming and plotting now pervasive in the Knighthood. He chose to ignore it.

Not yet strong enough to claim the vacant position of Grand Master, but still the strongest and most powerful of the knights currently seated on the Council, Gunthar had been forced to ignore a great deal of what he would have—in another day and age—quashed without hesitation. He expected this disloyalty of Alfred MarKenin—the knight had long been in Derek's camp—but he was surprised at Michael, whom he had thought loyal to him. Apparently Derek had gotten to him, too.

Gunthar watched Derek Crownguard as the knights returned to their places. Derek was the only rival with the money and backing capable of claiming the rank of Grand Master. Hoping to earn additional votes, Derek had eagerly volunteered to undertake the perilous quest in search of the legendary dragon orbs. Gunthar was given little choice but to agree. If he had refused, he would appear frightened of Derek's growing power. Derek was undeniably the most qualified—if one strictly followed the Measure. But Gunthar, who had known Derek a long time, would have prevented his going if he could have—not because he feared the knight but because he truly did not trust him. The man was vainglorious and power-hungry, and—when it came down to it—Derek's first loyalties lay to Derek.

And now it appeared that Derek's successful return with a dragon orb had won the day. It had brought many knights into his camp who had been heading that direction anyway and actually enticed away some in Gunthar's own faction. The only ones who opposed him still were the younger knights in the lowest order of the Knighthood—Knights of the Crown.

These young men had little use for the strict and rigid interpretation of the Measure that was life's blood to the older knights. They pushed for change—and had been severely chastened by Lord Derek Crownguard. Some came close to losing their knighthood. These young knights were firmly behind Lord Gunthar. Unfortunately, they were few in number and, for the most part, had more loyalty than money. The young knights had, however, adopted Sturm's cause as their own.

But this was Derek Crownguard's master stroke, Gunthar thought bitterly. With one slice of his sword, Derek was going to get rid of a man he hated and his chief rival as well.

Lord Gunthar was a well-known friend of the Brightblade family, a friendship that traced back generations. It was Gunthar who had advanced Sturm's claim when the young man appeared out of nowhere five years before to seek his father and his inheritance. Sturm had been able, with letters from his mother, to prove his right to the Brightblade name. A few insinuated this had been accomplished on the wrong side of the sheets, but Gunthar quickly squelched those rumors. The young man was obviously the son of his old friend—that much could be seen in Sturm's face. By backing Sturm, however, the lord was risking a great deal.

Gunthar's gaze went to Derek, walking among the knights, smiling and shaking hands. Yes, this trial was making him—Lord Gunthar Uth Wistan—appear a fool.

Worse still, Gunthar thought sadly, his eyes returning to Sturm, it was probably going to destroy the career of what he believed to be a very fine man, a man worthy of walking his father's path.

"Sturm Brightblade," Lord Gunthar said when silence descended on the hall, "you have heard the accusations made against you?"

"I have, my lord," Sturm answered. His deep voice echoed eerily in the hall. Suddenly a log in the huge fireplace behind Gunthar split, sending a flare of heat and a shower of sparks up the chimney. Gunthar paused while the servants hustled in efficiently to add more wood. When the servants were gone, he continued the ritual questioning.

"Do you, Sturm Brightblade, understand the charges made against you, and do you further understand that these are grievous charges and could cause this Council to find you unfit for the knighthood?"

"I do," Sturm started to reply. His voice broke. Coughing, he repeated more firmly, "I do, my lord."

Gunthar smoothed his moustaches, trying to think how to lead into this, knowing that anything the young man said against Derek was going to reflect badly upon Sturm himself.

"How old are you, Brightblade?" Gunthar asked.

Sturm blinked at this unexpected question.

"Over thirty, I believe?" Gunthar continued, musing.

"Yes, my lord," Sturm answered.

"And, from what Derek tells us about your exploits in Ice Wall Castle, a skilled warrior—"

"I never denied that, my lord," Derek said, rising to his feet once again. His voice was tinged with impatience.

"Yet you accuse him of cowardice," Gunthar snapped. "If my memory serves me correctly, you stated that when the elves attacked, he refused to obey your order to fight."

Derek's face was flushed. "May I remind your lordship that I am not on trial—"

"You charge Brightblade with cowardice in the face of the enemy," Gunthar interrupted. "It has been many years since the elves were our enemies."

Derek hesitated. The other knights appeared uncomfortable. The elves were members of the Council of Whitestone, but they were not allowed a vote. Because of the discovery of the dragon orb, the elves would be attending the upcoming Council, and it would never do to have word get back to them that the knights considered them enemies.

"Perhaps 'enemy' is too strong a word, my lord." Derek recovered smoothly. "If I am at fault, it is simply that I am being forced to go by what is written in the Measure. At the time I speak of, the elves—though not our enemies in point of fact—were doing everything in their power to prevent us from bringing the dragon orb to Sancrist. Since this was my mission— and the elves opposed it—I therefore am forced to define them as 'enemies'—according to the Measure."

Slick bastard, Gunthar thought grudgingly.

With a bow to apologize for speaking out of turn, Derek sat down again. Many of the older knights nodded in approval.

"It also says in the Measure," Sturm said slowly, "that we are not to take life needlessly, that we fight only in defense—either our own or the defense of others. The elves did not threaten our lives. At no time were we in actual physical danger."

"They were shooting arrows at you, man!" Lord Alfred struck the table with his gloved hand.

"True, my lord," Sturm replied, "but all know the elves are expert marksmen. If they had wanted to kill us, they would not have been hitting trees!"

"What do you believe would have happened if you had attacked the elves?" Gunthar questioned.

"The results would have been tragic in my view, my lord," Sturm said, his voice soft and low. "For the first time in generations, elves and humans would be killing each other. I think the Dragon Highlords would have laughed."

Several of the young knights applauded.

Lord Alfred glared at them, angry at this serious breach of the Measure's rules of conduct. "Lord Gunthar, may I remind you that Lord Derek Crownguard is not on trial here. He has proven his valor time and again upon the field of battle. I think we may safely take his word for what is an enemy action and what isn't. Sturm Brightblade, do you say that the charges made against you by Lord Derek Crownguard are false?"

"My lord," Sturm began, licking his lips which were cracked and dry, "I do not say the knight has lied. I say, however, that he has misrepresented me."

"To what purpose?" Lord Michael asked.

Sturm hesitated. "I would prefer not to answer that, my lord," he said so quietly that many knights in the back row could not hear and called for Gunthar to repeat the question. He did so and received the same reply— this time louder.

"On what grounds do you refuse to answer that question, Brightblade?" Lord Gunthar asked sternly.

"Because—according to the Measure—it impinges on the honor of the Knighthood," Sturm replied.

Lord Gunthar's face was grave. "That is a serious charge. Making it, you realize you have no one to stand with you in evidence?"

"I do, my lord," Sturm answered, "and that is why I prefer not to respond."

"If I command you to speak?"

"That, of course, would be different."

"Then speak, Sturm Brightblade. This is an unusual situation, and I do not see how we can make a fair judgment without hearing everything. Why do you believe Lord Derek Crownguard misrepresents you?"

Sturm's face flushed. Clasping and unclasping his hands, he raised his eyes and looked directly at the three knights who sat in judgment on him. His case was lost, he knew that. He would never be a knight, never attain what had been dearer to him than life itself. To have lost it through fault of his own would have been bitter enough, but to lose it like this was a festering wound. And so he spoke the words that he knew would make Derek his bitter enemy for the rest of his days.

"I believe Lord Derek Crownguard misrepresents me in an effort to further his own ambition, my lord."

Tumult broke out. Derek was on his feet. His friends restrained him forcibly, or he would have attacked Sturm in the Council Hall. Gunthar banged the sword hilt for order and eventually the assembly quieted down, but not before Derek had challenged Sturm to test his honor in the field.

Gunthar stared at the knight coldly.

"You know, Lord Derek, that in this—a declared time of war—the contests of honor are forbidden! Come to order or I'll have you expelled from this assembly."

Breathing heavily, his face splotched with red, Derek relapsed back into his seat.

Gunthar gave the Assembly a few more moments to settle down, then resumed. "Have you anything more to say in your defense, Sturm Brightblade?"

"No, my lord," Sturm said.

"Then you may withdraw while this matter is considered."

Sturm rose and bowed to the lords. Turning, he bowed to the Assembly. Then he left the room, escorted by two knights who led him to an antechamber. Here, the two knights, not unkindly, left Sturm to himself. They stood near the closed door, talking softly of matters unrelated to the trial.

Sturm sat on a bench at the far end of the chamber. He appeared composed and calm, but it was all an act. He was determined not to let these knights see the tumult in his soul. It was hopeless, he knew. Gunthar's grieved expression told him that much. But what would the judgment be? Exile, being stripped of lands and wealth? Sturm smiled bitterly. He had nothing they could take from him. He had lived outside of Solamnia so long, exile would be meaningless. Death? He would almost welcome that. Anything was better than this hopeless existence, this dull throbbing pain.

Hours passed. The murmur of three voices rose and fell from within the corridors around the Hall, sometimes angrily. Most of the other knights had gone out, since only the three as Heads of the Council could pass judgment. The other knights were split into differing factions.

The young knights spoke openly of Sturm's noble bearing, his acts of courage, which even Derek could not suppress. Sturm was right in not fighting the elves. The Knights of Solamnia needed all the friends they could get these days. Why attack needlessly, and so forth. The older knights had only one answer—the Measure. Derek had given Sturm an order. He had refused to obey. The Measure said this was inexcusable. Arguments raged most of the afternoon.

Then, near evening, a small silver bell rang.

"Brightblade," said one of the knights.

Sturm raised his head. "Is it time?"

The knight nodded.

Sturm bowed his head for a moment, asking Paladine for courage. Then he rose to his feet. He and his guards waited for the other knights to reenter and be seated. He knew that they were learning the verdict as soon as they entered.

Finally, the two knights detailed as escort opened the door and motioned for Sturm to enter. He walked into the Hall, the knights following behind. Sturm's gaze went at once to the table before Lord Gunthar.

The sword of his father—a sword that legend said was passed down from Berthel Brightblade himself, a sword that would break only if its master broke—lay on the table. Sturm's eyes went to the sword. His head dropped to hide the burning tears in his eyes.

Wreathed around the blade was the ancient symbol of guilt, black roses.

"Bring the man, Sturm Brightblade, forward," called Lord Gunthar.

The man, Sturm Brightblade, not *the knight!* thought Sturm in despair. Then he remembered Derek. His head came up swiftly, proudly, as he blinked away his tears. Just as he would have hidden his pain from his enemy on the field of battle, so he was determined to hide it now from Derek. Throwing back his head defiantly, his eyes on Lord Gunthar and on no one else, the disgraced squire walked forward to stand before the three officers of the Order to await his fate.

"Sturm Brightblade, we have found you guilty. We are prepared to render judgment. Are you prepared to receive it?"

"Yes, my lord," Sturm said tightly.

Gunthar tugged his moustaches, a sign that the men who had served with him recognized. Lord Gunthar always tugged his moustaches just before riding into battle.

"Sturm Brightblade, it is our judgment that you henceforth cease wearing any of the trappings or accoutrements of a Knight of Solamnia."

"Yes, my lord," Sturm said softly, swallowing.

"And, henceforth, you will not draw pay from the coffers of the Knights, nor obtain any property or gift from them. . . ."

The knights in the hall shifted restlessly. This was ridiculous! No one had drawn pay in the service of the Order since the Cataclysm. Something was up. They smelled thunder before the storm.

"Finally—" Lord Gunthar paused. He leaned forward, his hands toying with the black roses that graced the antique sword. His shrewd eyes swept the Assembly, gathering up his audience, allowing the tension to build. By the time he spoke, even the fire behind him had ceased to crackle.

"Sturm Brightblade. Assembled Knights. Never before has a case such as this come before the Council. And that, perhaps, is not as odd as it may seem, for these are dark and unusual days. We have a young squire—and I remind you that Sturm Brightblade is young by all standards of the Order—a young squire noted for his skill and valor in battle. Even his accuser admits that. A young squire charged with disobeying orders and cowardice in the face of the enemy. The young squire does not deny this charge, but states that he has been misrepresented.

"Now, by the Measure, we are bound to accept the word of a tried and tested knight such as Derek Crownguard over the word of a man who has not yet won his shield. But the Measure also states that this man shall be able to call witnesses in his own behalf. Due to the unusual circumstances occasioned by these dark times, Sturm Brightblade is not able to call witnesses. Nor, for that matter, was Derek Crownguard able to produce witnesses to support his own cause. Therefore, we have agreed on the following, slightly irregular, procedure."

Sturm stood before Gunthar, confused and troubled. What was happening? He glanced at the other two knights. Lord Alfred was not bothering to conceal his anger. It was obvious, therefore, that this "agreement" of Gunthar's had been hard won.

"It is the judgment of this Council," Lord Gunthar continued, "that the young man, Sturm Brightblade, be accepted into the lowest order of the knights—the Order of the Crown—*on my honor . . .*"

There was a universal gasp of astonishment.

"And that, furthermore, he be placed as third in command of the army that is due to set sail shortly for Palanthas. As prescribed by the Measure, the High Command must have a representative from each of the Orders. Therefore, Derek Crownguard will be High Commander, representing the Order of the Rose. Lord Alfred MarKenin will represent the Order of the Sword, and Sturm Brightblade will act—on my honor—as commander for the Order of the Crown."

Amid the stunned silence, Sturm felt tears course down his cheeks, but now he need hide them no longer. Behind him, he heard the sound of someone rising, of a sword rattling in anger. Derek stalked furiously out of the Hall, the other knights of his faction following him. There were scattered cheers, too. Sturm saw through his tears that about half the knights in the room—particularly the younger knights, the knights he would command—were applauding. Sturm felt swift pain well deep from inside his soul. Though he had won his victory, he was appalled by what the knighthood had become, divided into factions by power-hungry men. It was nothing more than a corrupt shell of a once-honored brotherhood.

"Congratulations, Brightblade," Lord Alfred said stiffly. "I hope you realize what Lord Gunthar has done for you."

"I do, my lord," Sturm said, bowing, "and I swear by my father's sword"—he laid his hand upon it—"that I will be worthy of his trust."

"See to it, young man," Lord Alfred replied and left. The younger lord, Michael, accompanied him without a word to Sturm.

But the other young knights came forward then, offering their enthusiastic congratulations. They pledged his health in wine and would have stayed for an all-out drinking bout if Gunthar had not sent them on their way.

When the two of them were alone in the Hall, Lord Gunthar smiled expansively at Sturm and shook his hand. The young knight returned the handshake warmly, if not the smile. The pain was too fresh.

Then, slowly and carefully, Sturm took the black roses from his sword. Laying them on the table, he slid the blade back in the scabbard at his side. He started to brush the roses aside, but paused, then picked up one and thrust it into his belt.

"I must thank you, my lord," Sturm began, his voice quivering.

"You have nothing to thank me for, son," Lord Gunthar said. Glancing around the room, he shivered. "Let's get out of this place and go somewhere warm. Mulled wine?"

The two knights walked down the stone corridors of Gunthar's ancient castle, the sounds of the young knights leaving drifting up from below—horses's hooves clattering on the cobblestone, voices shouting, some even raising in a military song.

"I must thank you, my lord," Sturm said firmly. "The risk you take is very great. I hope I will prove worthy—"

"Risk! Nonsense, my boy." Rubbing his hands to restore the circulation, Gunthar led Sturm into a small room decorated for the approaching Yule celebration—red winter roses, grown indoors, kingfisher feathers, and tiny, delicate golden crowns. A fire blazed brightly. At Gunthar's command, servants brought in two mugs of steaming liquid that gave off a warm, spicy odor. "Many were the times your father threw his shield in front of me and stood over me, protecting me when I was down."

"And you did the same for him," Sturm said. "You owe him nothing. Pledging your honor for me means that, if I fail, you will suffer. You will be stripped of your rank, your title, your lands. Derek would see to that," he added gloomily.

As Gunthar took a deep drink of his wine, he studied the young man before him. Sturm merely sipped at his wine out of politeness, holding the mug with a hand that trembled visibly. Gunthar laid his hand kindly on Sturm's shoulder, pushing the young man down gently into a chair.

"Have you failed in the past, Sturm?" Gunthar asked.

Sturm looked up, his brown eyes flashing. "No, my lord," he answered. "I have not. I swear it!"

"Then I have no fear for the future," Lord Gunthar said, smiling. He raised his mug. "I pledge your good fortune in battle, Sturm Brightblade."

Sturm shut his eyes. The strain had been too much. Dropping his head on his arm, he wept—his body shaking with painful sobs. Gunthar gripped his shoulder.

"I understand . . ." he said, his eyes looking back to a time in Solamnia when this young man's father had broken down and cried that same way— the night Lord Brightblade had sent his young wife and infant son on a journey into exile—a journey from which he would never see them return.

Exhausted, Sturm finally fell asleep, his head lying on the table. Gunthar sat with him, sipping the hot wine, lost in memories of the past, until he, too, drifted into slumber.

The few days left before the army sailed to Palanthas passed swiftly for Sturm. He had to find armor—used; he couldn't afford new. He packed his father's carefully, intending to carry it since he had been forbidden to wear it. Then there were meetings to attend, battle dispositions to study, information on the enemy to assimilate.

The battle for Palanthas would be a bitter one, determining control of the entire northern part of Solamnia. The leaders were agreed upon their strategy. They would fortify the city walls with the city's army. The knights themselves would occupy the High Clerist's Tower that stood blocking the pass through the Vingaard Mountains. But that was all they agreed upon. Meetings between the three leaders were tense, the air chill.

Finally the day came for the ships to sail. The knights gathered on board. Their families stood quietly on the shore. Though faces were pale, there were few tears, the women standing as tight-lipped and stern as their men. Some wives wore swords buckled around their own waists. All knew that, if the battle in the north was lost, the enemy would come across the sea.

Gunthar stood upon the pier, dressed in his bright armor, talking with the knights, bidding farewell to his sons. He and Derek exchanged a few ritual words as prescribed by the Measure. He and Lord Alfred embraced perfunctorily. At last, Gunthar sought out Sturm. The young knight, clad in plain, shabby armor, stood apart from the crowd.

"Brightblade," Gunthar said in a low voice as he came near him, "I have been meaning to ask this but never found a moment in these last few days. You mentioned that these friends of yours would be coming to Sancrist. Are there any who could serve as witnesses before the Council?"

Sturm paused. For a wild moment the only person he could think of was Tanis. His thoughts had been with his friend during these last trying days. He'd even had a surge of hope that Tanis might arrive in Sancrist. But the hope had died. Wherever Tanis was, he had his own problems, he faced his own dangers. There was another person, too, whom he had hoped against hope he might see. Without conscious thought, Sturm placed his hand over the Starjewel that hung around his neck against his breast. He could almost feel its warmth, and he knew—without knowing how—that though far away, Alhana was with him. Then—

"Laurana!" he said.

"A woman?" Gunthar frowned.

"Yes, but daughter of the Speaker of the Suns, a member of the royal household of the Qualinesti. And there is her brother, Gilthanas. Both would testify for me."

"The royal household . . ." Gunthar mused. His face brightened. "That would be perfect, especially since we have received word that the Speaker himself will attend the High Council to discuss the dragon orb. If that happens, my boy, somehow I'll get word to you, and you can put that armor back on! You'll be vindicated! Free to wear it without shame!"

"And you will be free of your pledge," Sturm said, shaking hands with the knight gratefully.

"Bah! Don't give that a thought." Gunthar laid his hand on Sturm's head, as he had laid his hand on the heads of his own sons. Sturm knelt before him reverently. "Receive my blessing, Sturm Brightblade, a father's blessing I give in the absence of your own father. Do your duty, young man, and remain your father's son. May Lord Huma's spirit be with you."

"Thank you, my lord," Sturm said, rising to his feet. "Farewell."

"Farewell, Sturm," Gunthar said. Embracing the young knight swiftly, he turned and walked away.

The knights boarded the ships. It was dawn, but no sun shone in the winter sky. Gray clouds hung over a lead-gray sea. There were no cheers, the only sounds were the shouted commands of the captain and the responses of his crew, the creaking of the winches, and the flapping of the sails in the wind.

Slowly the white-winged ships weighed anchor and sailed north. Soon the last sail was out of sight, but still no one left the pier, not even when a sudden rain squall struck, pelting them with sleet and icy drops, drawing a fine gray curtain across the chill waters.

3

The dragon orb.

Caramon's pledge.

aistlin stood in the small doorway of the wagon, his golden eyes peering into the sunlit woods. All was quiet. It was past Yuletide. The countryside was held fast in the grip of winter. Nothing stirred in the snow-blanketed land. His companions were gone, busy about various tasks. Raistlin nodded grimly. Good. Turning, he went back inside the wagon and shut the wooden doors firmly.

The companions had been camped here for several days, on the outskirts of Kendermore. Their journey was nearing an end. It had been unbelievably successful. Tonight they would leave, traveling to Flotsam under the cover of darkness. They had money enough to hire a ship, plus some left over for supplies and payment for a week's lodging in Flotsam. This afternoon had been their final performance.

The young mage made his way through the clutter to the back of the wagon. His gaze lingered on the shimmering red robe that hung on a nail. Tika had started to pack it away, but Raistlin had snarled at her viciously. Shrugging, she let it remain, going outside to walk in the woods, knowing Caramon—as usual—would find her.

Raistlin's thin hand reached out to touch the robe, the slender fingers stroking the shining, sequined fabric wistfully, regretting that this period in his life was over.

"I have been happy," he murmured to himself. "Strange. There have not been many times in my life I could make that claim. Certainly not when I was young, nor in these past few years, after they tortured my body and cursed me with these eyes. But then I never expected happiness. How paltry it is, compared to my magic! Still . . . still, these last few weeks have been weeks of peace. Weeks of happiness. I don't suppose any will come again. Not after what I must do—"

Raistlin held the robe a moment longer, then, shrugging, he tossed it in a corner and continued on to the back of the wagon which he had curtained off for his own private use. Once inside, he pulled the curtains securely together.

Excellent. He would have privacy for several hours, until nightfall, in fact. Tanis and Riverwind had gone hunting. Caramon had, too, supposedly, though everyone knew this was just an excuse for him to find time alone with Tika. Goldmoon was preparing food for their journey. No one would bother him. The mage nodded to himself in satisfaction.

Sitting down at the small drop-leaf table Caramon had constructed for him, Raistlin carefully withdrew from the very innermost pocket of his robes an ordinary-looking sack, the sack that contained the dragon orb. His skeletal fingers trembled as he tugged on the drawstring. The bag opened. Reaching in, Raistlin grasped the dragon orb and brought it forth. He held it easily in his palm, inspecting it closely to see if there had been any change.

No. A faint green color still swirled within. It still felt as cold to the touch as if he held a hailstone. Smiling, Raistlin clasped the orb tightly in one hand while he fumbled through the props beneath the table. He finally found what he sought—a crudely carved, three-legged wooden stand. Lifting it up, Raistlin set it on the table. It wasn't much to look at—Flint would have scoffed. Raistlin had neither the love nor the skill needed to work wood. He had carved it laboriously, in secret, shut up inside the jouncing wagon during the long days on the road. No, it was not much to look at, but he didn't care. It would suit his purpose.

Placing the stand upon the table, he set the dragon orb on it. The marble-sized orb looked ludicrous, but Raistlin sat back, waiting patiently. As he had expected, soon the orb began to grow. Or did it? Perhaps *he* was shrinking. Raistlin couldn't tell. He knew only that suddenly the orb was the right size. If anything was different, it was he that was too small, too insignificant to even be in the same room with the orb.

The mage shook his head. He must stay in control, he knew, and he was immediately aware of the subtle tricks the orb was playing to undermine that control. Soon these tricks would not be subtle. Raistlin felt his throat tighten. He coughed, cursing his weak lungs. Drawing a shuddering breath, he forced himself to breathe deeply and easily.

Relax, he thought. I must relax. I do not fear. I am strong. Look what I have done! Silently he called upon the orb: Look at the power I have attained! Witness what I did in Darken Wood. Witness what I did in Silvanesti. I am strong. I do not fear.

The orb's colors swirled softly. It did not answer.

The mage closed his eyes for a moment, blotting the orb from sight. Regaining control, he opened them again, regarding the orb with a sigh. The moment approached.

The dragon orb was now back to its original size. He could almost see Lorac's wizened hands grasping it. The young mage shuddered involuntarily. No! Stop it! he told himself firmly, and immediately banished the vision from his mind.

Once more he relaxed, breathing regularly, his hourglass eyes focused on the orb. Then—slowly—he stretched forth his slender, metallic-colored fingers. After a moment's final hesitation, Raistlin placed his hands upon the cold crystal of the dragon orb and spoke the ancient words.

"Ast bilak moiparalan/Suh akvlar tantangusar." How did he know what to say? How did he know what ancient words would cause the orb to understand him, to be aware of his presence? Raistlin did not know. He knew only that—somehow, somewhere—inside of him, he *did* know the words! The voice that had spoken to him in Silvanesti? Perhaps. It didn't matter. Again he said the words aloud.

"Ast bilak moiparalan/Suh akvlar tantangusar!" Slowly the drifting green color was submerged in a myriad of swirling, gliding colors that made him dizzy to watch. The crystal was so cold beneath his palms that it was painful to touch. Raistlin had a terrifying vision of pulling away his hands and leaving the flesh behind, frozen to the orb. Gritting his teeth, he ignored the pain and whispered the words again.

The colors ceased to swirl. A light glowed in the center, a light neither white nor black, all colors, yet none. Raistlin swallowed, fighting the choking phlegm that rose in his throat.

Out of the light came two hands! He had a desperate urge to withdraw his own, but before he could move, the two hands grasped his in a grip both strong and firm. The orb vanished! The room vanished! Raistlin saw nothing around him. No light. No darkness. Nothing! Nothing . . . but two hands, holding his. Out of sheer terror, Raistlin concentrated on those hands.

Human? Elven? Old? Young? He could not tell. The fingers were long and slender, but their grip was the grip of death. Let go and he would fall into the void to drift until merciful darkness consumed him. Even as he clung to those hands with strength lent him by fear, Raistlin realized the hands were slowly drawing him nearer, drawing him into . . . into . . .

Raistlin came to himself suddenly, as if someone had dashed cold water in his face. No! he told the mind that he sensed controlled the hands. I will not go! Though he feared losing that saving grip, he feared even more being dragged where he did not want to go. He would not let loose. I *will* maintain control, he told the mind of the hands savagely. Tightening his own grip, the mage summoned all of his strength, all of his will, and pulled the hands toward him!

The hands stopped. For a moment, the two wills vied together, locked in a life-or-death contest. Raistlin felt the strength ebb from his body, his hands weakened, the palms began to sweat. He felt the hands of the orb begin to pull him again, ever so slightly. In agony, Raistlin summoned every drop of blood, focused every nerve, sacrificed every muscle in his frail body to regain control.

Slowly . . . slowly . . . just when he thought his pounding heart would burst from his chest or his brain explode in fire—Raistlin felt the hands cease their tug. They still maintained their firm grip on him—as he maintained his firm grip on them. But the two were no longer in contest. His hands and the hands of the dragon orb remained locked together, each conceding respect, neither seeking dominance.

The ecstasy of the victory, the ecstasy of the magic flowed through Raistlin and burst forth, wrapping him in a warm, golden light. His body relaxed. Trembling, he felt the hands hold him gently, support him, lend him strength.

What are you? he questioned silently. Are you good? Evil?

I am neither. I am nothing. I am everything. The essence of dragons captured long ago is what I am.

How do you work? Raistlin asked. How do you control the dragons?

At your command, I will call them to me. They cannot resist my call. They will obey.

Will they turn upon their masters? Will they fall under my command?

That depends on the strength of the master and the bond between the two. In some instances, this is so strong that the master can maintain control of the dragon. But most will do what you ask of them. They cannot help themselves.

I must study this, Raistlin murmured, feeling himself growing weaker. I do not understand. . . .

Be easy. I will aid you. Now that we have joined, you may seek my help often. I know of many secrets long forgotten. They can be yours.

What secrets? . . . Raistlin felt himself losing consciousness. The strain had been too much. He struggled to keep his hold on the hands, but he felt his grip slipping.

The hands held onto him gently, as a mother holds a child.

Relax, I will not let you fall. Sleep. You are weary.

Tell me! I must know! Raistlin cried silently.

This only I will tell you, then you must rest. In the library of Astinus of Palanthas are books, hundreds of books, taken there by the mages of old in the days of the Lost Battle. To all who look at these books, they seem nothing more than encyclopedias of magic, dull histories of mages who died in the caverns of time.

Raistlin saw darkness creeping toward him. He clutched at the hands. What do the books really contain? he whispered.

Then he knew, and with the knowledge, darkness crashed over him like the wave of an ocean.

In a cave near the wagon, hidden by shadows, warmed by the heat of their passion, Tika and Caramon lay in each other's arms. Tika's red hair clung around her face and forehead in tight curls, her eyes were closed, her full lips parted. Her soft body clad in her gaily-colored skirt and puffy-sleeved white blouse pressed against Caramon. Her legs twined around his, her hand caressed his face, her lips brushed his.

"Please, Caramon," she whispered. "This is torture. We want each other. I'm not afraid. Please love me!"

Caramon closed his eyes. His face shone with sweat. The pain of his love seemed impossible to bear. He could end it, end it all in sweet ecstasy. For a moment he hesitated. Tika's fragrant hair was in his nostrils, her soft lips on his neck. It would be so easy . . . so wonderful. . . .

Caramon sighed. Firmly he closed his strong hands around Tika's wrists. Firmly he drew them away from his face and pushed the girl from him.

"No," he said, his passion choking him. Rolling over, he stood up. "No," he repeated. "I'm sorry. I didn't mean to . . . to let things get this far."

"Well, I did!" Tika cried. "I'm *not* frightened! Not anymore."

No, he thought, pressing his hands against his pounding head. I feel you trembling in my hands like a snared rabbit. Tika began to tie the string on her white blouse. Unable to see it through her tears, she jerked at the drawstring so viciously it snapped.

"Now! See there!" She hurled the broken silken twine across the cave. "I've ruined my blouse! I'll have to mend it. They'll all know what happened, of course! Or think they know! I—I . . . Oh, what's the use!" Weeping in frustration, Tika covered her face with her hands, rocking back and forth.

"I don't care what they think!" Caramon said, his voice echoing in the cave. He did not comfort her. He knew if he touched her again, he would yield to his passion. "Besides, they don't think anything at all. They are our friends. They care for us—"

"I know!" Tika cried brokenly. "It's Raistlin, isn't it? He doesn't approve of me. He *hates* me!"

"Don't say that, Tika." Caramon's voice was firm. "If he did and if he were stronger, it wouldn't matter. I wouldn't care what anyone said or thought. The others want us to be happy. They don't understand why we—we don't become—er—lovers. Tanis even told me to my face I was a fool—"

"He's right." Tika's voice was muffled by tear-damp hair.

"Maybe. Maybe not."

Something in Caramon's voice made the girl quit crying. She looked up at him as Caramon turned around to face her.

"You don't know what happened to Raist in the Towers of High Sorcery. None of you know. None of you ever will. But *I* know. I was there. I saw. They *made* me see!" Caramon shuddered, putting his hands over his face. Tika held very still. Then, looking at her again, he drew a deep breath. "They said, 'His strength will save the world.' What strength? Inner strength? I'm his outer strength! I—I don't understand, but Raist said to me in the dream that we were one whole person, cursed by the gods and put into two bodies. We need each other—right now at least." The big man's face darkened. "Maybe someday that will change. Maybe some day he'll find the outer strength—"

Caramon fell silent. Tika swallowed and wiped her hand across her face. "I—" she began, but Caramon cut her off.

"Wait a minute," he said. "Let me finish. I love you, Tika, as truly as any man loves any woman in this world. I want to make love to you. If we weren't involved in this stupid war, I'd make you mine today. This minute. But I can't. Because if I did, it would be a commitment to you that I would dedicate my life to keeping. You must come first in all my thoughts. You deserve no less than that. But I can't make that commitment, Tika. My first commitment is to my brother." Tika's tears flowed again—this time not for herself, but for him. "I must leave you free to find someone who can—"

"Caramon!" A call split the afternoon's sweet silence. "Caramon, come quickly!" It was Tanis.

"Raistlin!" said the big man, and without another word, ran out of the cave.

Tika stood a moment, watching after him. Then, sighing, she tried to comb her damp hair into place.

"What is it?" Caramon burst into the wagon. "Raist?"

Tanis nodded, his face grave.

"I found him like this." The half-elf drew back the curtain to the mage's small apartment. Caramon shoved him aside.

Raistlin lay on the floor, his skin white, his breathing shallow. Blood trickled from his mouth. Kneeling down, Caramon lifted him in his arms.

"Raistlin?" he whispered. "What happened?"

"That's what happened," Tanis said grimly, pointing.

Caramon glanced up, his gaze coming to rest on the dragon orb—now grown to the size Caramon had seen in Silvanesti. It stood on the stand Raistlin had made for it, its swirling colors shifting endlessly as he watched. Caramon sucked in his breath in horror. Terrible visions of Lorac flooded his mind. Lorac insane, dying . . .

"Raist!" he moaned, clutching his brother tightly.

Raistlin's head moved feebly. His eyelids fluttered, and he opened his mouth.

"What?" Caramon bent low, his brother's breath cold upon his skin."What?"

"Mine . . ." Raistlin whispered. "Spells . . . of the ancients . . . mine . . . Mine . . ." The mage's head lolled, his words died. But his face was calm, placid, relaxed. His breathing grew regular.

Raistlin's thin lips parted in a smile.

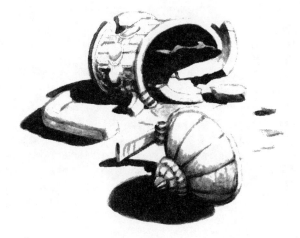

4

Yuletide Guests.

t took Lord Gunthar several days of hard riding to reach his home in time for Yule following the departure of the knights for Palanthas. The roads were knee-deep in mud. His horse foundered more than once, and Gunthar, who loved his horse nearly as well as his sons, walked whenever necessary. By the time he returned to his castle, therefore, he was exhausted, drenched, and shivering. The stableman came out to take charge of the horse personally.

"Rub him down well," Gunthar said, dismounting stiffly. "Hot oats and—" He proceeded with his instructions, the stableman nodding patiently, as if he'd never cared for a horse before in his life. Gunthar was, in fact, on the point of walking his horse to the stables himself when his ancient retainer came out in search of him.

"My lord." Wills drew Gunthar to one side in the entryway. "You have visitors. They arrived just a few hours ago."

"Who?" Gunthar asked without much interest, visitors being nothing new, especially during Yule. "Lord Michael? He could not travel with us, but I asked him to stop on his way home—"

"An old man, my lord," Wills interrupted, "and a kender."

"A kender?" Gunthar repeated in some alarm.

"I'm afraid so, my lord. But don't worry," the retainer added hastily. "I've locked the silver in a drawer, and your lady wife has taken her jewelry to the cellar."

"You'd think we were under siege!" Gunthar snorted. He did, however, go through the courtyard faster than usual.

"You can't be too careful around those critters, my lord," Wills mumbled, trotting along behind.

"What are these two, then? Beggars? Why did you let them in?" Gunthar demanded, beginning to get irritated. All he wanted was his mulled wine, warm clothes, and one of his wife's backrubs. "Give them some food and money, and send them on their way. Search the kender first, of course."

"I was going to, my lord," Wills said stubbornly. "But there's something about them—the old man in particular. He's crackers, if you ask me, but he's a smart crackers, for all that. Knows something, and it may be more than's good for him—or us either."

"What do you mean?"

The two had just opened the huge, wooden doors leading into the living quarters of the castle proper. Gunthar stopped and stared at Wills, knowing and respecting his retainer's keen power of observation. Wills glanced around, then leaned close.

"The old man said I was to tell you he had urgent news regarding the dragon orb, my lord!"

"The dragon orb!" Gunthar murmured. The orb was secret, or he presumed it was. The Knights knew of it, of course. Had Derek told anyone else? Was this one of his maneuvers?

"You acted wisely, Wills, as always," Gunthar said finally. "Where are they?"

"I put them in your war room, my lord, figuring they could cause little mischief there."

"I'll change clothes before I catch my death, then see them directly. Have you made them comfortable?"

"Yes, my lord," Wills replied, hurrying after Gunthar, who was on the move again. "Hot wine, a bit of bread and meat. Though I trust the kender's lifted the plates by now—"

Gunthar and Wills stood outside the door of the war room for a moment, eavesdropping on the visitors' conversation.

"Put that back!" ordered a stern voice.

"I won't! It's mine! Look, it was in my pouch."

"Bah! I saw you put it there not five minutes ago!"

"Well, you're wrong," protested the other voice in wounded tones. "It's mine! See, there's my name engraved—"

" 'To Gunthar, my beloved husband on the Day of Life-Gift,' " said the first voice.

There was a moment's silence in the room. Wills turned pale. Then the shrill voice spoke, more subdued this time.

"I guess it must have fallen into my pack, Fizban. That's it! See, my pack was sitting under that table. Wasn't that lucky? It would have broken if it had hit the floor—"

His face grim, Lord Gunthar flung open the door.

"Merry Yuletide to you, sirs," he said. Wills popped in after him, his eyes darting quickly around the room.

The two strangers whirled around, the old man holding a crockery mug in his hand. Wills made a leap for the mug, whisking it away. With an indignant glance at the kender, he placed it upon the mantlepiece, high above the kender's reach.

"Will there be anything else, my lord?" Wills asked, glaring meaningfully at the kender. "Shall I stay and keep an eye on things?"

Gunthar opened his mouth to reply, but the old man waved a negligent hand.

"Yes, thank you, my good man. Bring up some more ale. And don't bring any of that rotgut stuff from the servants' barrels, either!" The old man looked at Wills sternly. "Tap the barrel that's in the dark corner by the cellar stairs. You know—the one that's all cobwebby."

Wills stared at him, open-mouthed.

"Well, go on. Don't stand there gaping like a landed fish! A bit dim-witted, is he?" the old man asked Gunthar.

"N-no," Gunthar stammered. "That's all right, Wills. I—I believe I'll have a mug, too—of—of the ale from the cask by the—uh—stairs. How did *you* know?" He demanded of the old man suspiciously.

"Oh, he's a magic-user," the kender said, shrugging and sitting down without being invited.

"A magic-user?" The old man peered around. "Where?"

Tas whispered something, poking the old man.

"Really? Me?" he said. "You don't say! How remarkable. Now you know, come to think of it, I do seem to remember a spell . . . Fireball. How did it go?"

The old mage began to speak the strange words. Alarmed, the kender leaped out of his seat and grabbed the old man.

"No, Old One!" he said, tugging him back into a chair. "Not now!"

"I suppose not," the old man said wistfully. "Wonderful spell, though . . ."

"I'm certain," murmured Gunthar, absolutely mystified. Then he shook his head, regaining his sternness. "Now, explain yourselves. Who are you? Why are you here? Wills said something about a dragon orb—"

"I'm—" The mage stopped, blinking.

"Fizban," said the kender with a sigh. Standing, he extended his small hand politely to Gunthar. "And I am Tasslehoff Burrfoot." He started to sit down. "Oh," he said, popping up again. "A Merry Yuletide to you, too, sir knight."

"Yes, yes," Gunthar shook hands, nodding absently. "Now about the dragon orb?"

"Ah, yes, the dragon orb!" The befuddled look left Fizban's face. He stared at Gunthar with shrewd, cunning eyes. "Where is it? We've come a long way in search of it."

"I'm afraid I can't tell you," Gunthar said coolly. "If, indeed, such a thing were ever here—"

"Oh, it was here," Fizban replied. "Brought to you by a Knight of the Rose, one Derek Crownguard. And Sturm Brightblade was with him."

"They're friends of mine," explained Tasslehoff, seeing Gunthar's jaw go slack. "I helped get the orb, in fact," the kender added modestly. "We took it away from an evil wizard in a palace made of ice. It's the most wonderful story—" He sat forward eagerly. "Do you want to hear it?"

"No," said Gunthar, staring at them both in amazement. "And if I believed this swimming bird tale—wait—" He sank back in his chair. "Sturm did say something about a kender. Who were the others in your party?"

"Flint the dwarf, Theros the blacksmith, Gilthanas and Laurana—"

"It must be!" Gunthar exclaimed, then he frowned. "But he never mentioned a magic-user. . . ."

"Oh, that's because I'm dead," Fizban stated, propping his feet upon the table.

Gunthar's eyes opened wide, but before he could reply, Wills came in. Glaring at Tasslehoff, the retainer set mugs down on the table in front of his lordship.

"*Three mugs,* here, my lord. And one on the mantle makes four. And there better be *four* when I come back!"

He walked out, shutting the door with a thud.

"I'll keep an eye on them," Tas promised solemnly. "Do you have a problem with people stealing mugs?" he asked Gunthar.

"I—no. . . . Dead?" Gunthar felt he was rapidly losing his grip on the situation.

"It's a long story," said Fizban, downing the liquid in one swallow. He wiped the foam from his lips with the tip of his beard. "Ah, excellent. Now, where was I?"

"Dead," said Tas helpfully.

"Ah, yes. A long story. Too long for now. Must get the orb. Where is it?"

Gunthar stood up angrily, intending to order this strange old man and this kender from his chamber and his castle. He was going to call his guards to extract them. But, instead, he found himself caught by the old man's intense gaze.

The Knights of Solamnia have always feared magic. Though they had not taken part in the destruction of the Towers of High Sorcery—that would have been against the Measure—they had not been sorry to see magic-users driven from Palanthas.

"Why do you want to know?" Gunthar faltered, feeling a cold fear seep into his blood as he felt the old man's strange power engulf him. Slowly, reluctantly, Gunthar sat back down.

Fizban's eyes glittered. "I keep my own counsel," he said softly. "Let it be enough for you to know that I have come seeking the orb. It was made by magic-users, long ago! I know of it. I know a great deal about it."

Gunthar hesitated, wrestling with himself. After all, there were knights guarding the orb, and if this old man really did know something about it, what harm could there be in telling him where it was? Besides, he really didn't feel like he had any choice in the matter.

Fizban absently picked up his empty mug again and started to drink. He peered inside it mournfully as Gunthar answered.

"The dragon orb is with the gnomes."

Fizban dropped his mug with a crash. It broke into a hundred pieces that went skittering across the wooden floor.

"There, what'd I tell you?" Tas said sadly, eyeing the shattered mug.

The gnomes had lived in Mount Nevermind for as long as they could remember—and since they were the only ones who cared, they were the only ones who counted. Certainly they were there when the first knights arrived in Sancrist, traveling from the newly created kingdom of Solamnia to build their keeps and fortress along the westernmost part of their border.

Always suspicious of outsiders, the gnomes were alarmed to see a ship arriving upon their shores, bearing hordes of tall, stern-faced, warlike humans. Determined to keep what they considered a mountain paradise secret from the humans, the gnomes launched into action. Being the most technologically minded of the races on Krynn (they are noted for having invented the steam-powered engine and the coiled spring), the gnomes first thought of hiding within their mountain caverns, but then had a better idea. Hide the mountain itself!

After several months of unending toil by their greatest mechanical geniuses, the gnomes were prepared. Their plan? They were going to make their mountain disappear!

It was at this juncture that one of the members of the gnomish Philosopher's Guild asked if it wasn't likely that the knights would have already noticed the mountain, the tallest on the island. Might not the sudden disappearance of the mountain create a certain amount of curiosity in the humans?

This question threw the gnomes into turmoil. Days were spent in discussion. The question soon divided the Philosopher gnomes into two factions: those who believed that if a tree fell in a forest and no one heard it, it still made a crashing sound; and those who believed it didn't. Just what this had to do with the original question was brought up on the seventh day, but was promptly referred to committee.

Meanwhile, the Mechanical Engineers, in a huff, decided to set off the device anyhow.

And thus occurred the day that is still remembered in the annals of Sancrist (when almost everything else was lost during the Cataclysm) as the Day of Rotten Eggs.

On that day an ancestor of Lord Gunthar woke up wondering sleepily if his son had fallen through the roof of the hen house again. This had happened only a few weeks before. The boy had been chasing a rooster.

"You take him down to the pond," Gunthar's ancestor told his wife sleepily, rolling over in bed and drawing the covers up over his head.

"I can't!" she said drowsily. "The chimney's smoking!"

It was then that both fully woke up, realizing that the smoke filling the house was not coming from the chimney and that the ungodly odor was not coming from the hen house.

Along with every other resident of the new colony, the two rushed outside, choking and gagging with the smell that grew worse by the minute. They could see nothing, however. The land was covered with a thick yellow smoke, redolent of eggs that had been sitting in the sun for three days.

Within hours, everyone in the colony was deathly sick from the smell. Packing up blankets and clothes, they headed for the beaches. Breathing the fresh salt breezes thankfully, they wondered if they could ever go back to their homes.

While discussing this and watching anxiously to see if the yellow cloud on the horizon might lift, the colonists were considerably startled to see what appeared to be an army of short, brown creatures stagger out of the smoke to fall almost lifeless at their feet.

The kindly people of Solamnia immediately went to the aid of the poor gnomes, and thus did the two races of people living on Sancrist meet.

The meeting of the gnomes and the knights turned out to be a friendly one. The Solamnic people had a high regard for four things: individual honor, the Code, the Measure, and technology. They were vastly impressed with the labor-saving devices the gnomes had invented at this time, which included the pulley, the shaft, the screw, and the gear.

It was during this first meeting that Mount Nevermind got its name as well.

The knights soon discovered that, while gnomes appeared to be related to the dwarves—being short and stocky—all similarity ended there. The gnomes were a skinny people with brown skin and pale white hair, highly nervous and hot-tempered. They spoke so rapidly that the knights at first thought they were speaking a foreign language. Instead, it turned out to be Common spoken at an accelerated pace. The reason for this became obvious when an elder made the mistake of asking the gnomes the name of their mountain.

Roughly translated, it went something like this: A Great, Huge, Tall Mound Made of Several Different Strata of Rock of Which We Have Identified Granite, Obsidian, Quartz With Traces of Other Rock We Are Still Working On, That Has Its Own Internal Heating System Which We Are Studying In Order to Copy Someday That Heats the Rock Up to Temperatures That Convert It Into Both Liquid and Gaseous States Which Occasionally Come to the Surface and Flow Down the Side of the Great, Huge, Tall Mound—

"Nevermind," the elder said hastily.

Nevermind! The gnomes were impressed. To think that these humans could reduce something so gigantic and marvelous into something so simple was wonderful beyond belief. And so, the mountain was called Mount Nevermind from that day forth, to the vast relief of the gnomish Map-Makers Guild.

The knights on Sancrist and the gnomes lived in harmony after that, the knights bringing the gnomes any questions of a technological nature that needed solving, the gnomes providing a steady flood of new inventions.

When the dragon orb arrived, the knights needed to know how the thing worked. They gave it into the keeping of the gnomes, sending along two young knights to guard it. The thought that the orb might be magic did not occur to them.

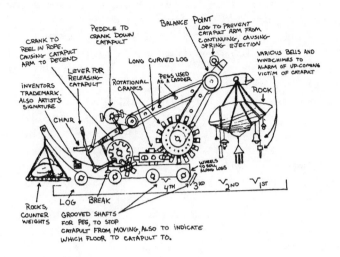

CRANK TO
REEL IN ROPE.
CAUSING CATAPULT
ARM TO DECEND

PEDDLE TO
CRANK DOWN
CATAPULT

BALANCE POINT

LOG TO PREVENT
CATAPULT ARM FROM
CONTINUING, CAUSING
SPRING EJECTION

LONG CURVED LOG

VARIOUS BELLS AND
WINDCHIMES TO
ALARM OF UP-COMING
VICTIM OF CATAPULT

LEVER FOR
RELEASING
CATAPULT

PEGS USED
AS A LADDER

INVENTORS
TRADEMARK.
ALSO ARTIST'S
SIGNATURE

ROTATIONAL
CRANKS

ROCK

CHAIR

WHEELS
TO ROLL
ALONG LOGS

4TH   3RD   2ND   1ST

ROCKS,
COUNTER
WEIGHTS

LOG   BREAK

GROOVED SHAFTS
FOR PEG, TO STOP
CATAPULT FROM MOVING, ALSO TO INDICATE
WHICH FLOOR TO CATAPULT TO.

5

GNOMEFLINGERS.

ow remember. No gnome living or dead ever in his life completed a sentence. The only way you get anywhere is to interrupt them. Don't worry about being rude. They expect it."

The old mage himself was interrupted by the appearance of a gnome dressed in long brown robes, who came up to them and bowed respectfully.

Tasslehoff studied the gnome with excited curiosity, the kender had never seen a gnome before, although old legends concerning the Graygem of Gargath indicated that the two races were distantly connected. Certainly there was something kenderish in the young gnome, his slender hands, eager expression, and sharp, bright eyes intent on observing everything. But here the resemblance ended. There was nothing of the kender's easy-going manner. The gnome was nervous, serious, and businesslike.

"Tasslehoff Burrfoot," said the kender politely, extending his hand. The gnome took Tas's hand, peered at it intently, then, finding nothing of interest—shook it limply. "And this—" Tas started to introduce Fizban, but stopped when the gnome reached out and calmly took hold of the kender's hoopak.

"Ah . . ." the gnome said, his eyes shining as he grasped the weapon. "SendforamemberoftheWeaponsGuild—"

The guard at the ground-level entrance to the great mountain did not wait for the gnome to finish. Reaching up, he pulled a lever and a shriek sounded. Certain that a dragon had landed behind him, Tas whirled around, ready to defend himself.

"Whistle," said Fizban. "Better get used to it."

"Whistle?" repeated Tas, intrigued. "I never heard one like that before. Smoke comes out of it! How does it wor—Hey! Come back! Bring back my hoopak!" he cried as his staff went speeding down the corridor, carried by three eager gnomes.

"Examinationroom," said the gnome, "uponSkimbosh—"

"What?"

"Examination Room," Fizban translated. "I missed the rest. You really must speak slower," he said, shaking his staff at the gnome.

The gnome nodded, but his bright eyes were fixed on Fizban's staff. Then, seeing it was just plain, slightly battered wood, the gnome returned his attention to the mage and kender.

"Outsiders," he said. "I'lltryand'member . . . I will try and remember, so do not worry because"—he now spoke slowly and distinctly—"your weapon will not be harmed since we are merely going to render a drawing—"

"Really," interrupted Tas, rather flattered. "I could give you a demonstration of how it works, if you like."

The gnome's eyes brightened. "Thatwouldbemuch—"

"And now," interrupted the kender again, feeling pleased that he was learning to communicate, "what is your name?"

Fizban made a quick gesture, but too late.

"Gnoshoshallamarionininillisyylphanitdisdisslishxdie—"

He paused to draw a breath.

"Is that your *name*?" Tas asked, astounded.

The gnome let his breath out. "Yes," he snapped, a bit disconcerted."It's my first name, and now if you'll let me proceed—"

"Wait!" cried Fizban. "What do your friends call you?"

The gnome sucked in a breath again. "Gnoshoshallamarioninillis—"

"What do the knights call you?"

"Oh"—the gnome seemed downcast—"Gnosh, if you—

"Thank you," snapped Fizban. "Now, Gnosh, we're in rather a hurry. War going on and all that. As Lord Gunthar stated in his communique, we must see this dragon orb."

Gnosh's small, dark eyes glittered. His hands twisted nervously. "Of course, you may see the dragon orb since Lord Gunthar has requested it, but, if I might ask, what is your interest in the orb besides normalcuri—?"

"I am a magic-user—" Fizban began.

"Magicuser!" the gnome stated, forgetting, in his excitement, to speak slowly. "Comethiswayimmediatelytothe Examinationroomsincethedragonorbwasmadebymagicuser—"

Both Tas and Fizban blinked uncomprehendingly.

"Oh, just come—" the gnome said impatiently.

Before they quite knew what was happening, the gnome, still talking, hustled them through the mountain's entrance, setting off an inordinate number of bells and whistles.

"Examination Room?" Tas said in an undertone to Fizban as they hurried after Gnosh. "What does that mean? They wouldn't have hurt it, would they?"

"I don't think so," Fizban muttered, his bushy white eyebrows coming together in an ominous V-shape over his nose. "Gunthar sent knights to guard it, remember."

"Then what are you worried about?" Tas asked.

"The dragon orbs are strange things. Very powerful. My fear," said Fizban more to himself than to Tas, "is that they may try to *use* it!"

"But the book I read in Tarsis said the orb could control dragons!" Tas whispered. "Isn't that good? I mean, the orbs aren't evil, are they?"

"Evil? Oh, no! Not evil." Fizban shook his head. "That's the danger. They're not good, not evil. They're not *anything!* Or perhaps I should say, they're *everything.*"

Tas saw he would probably never get a straight answer out of Fizban, whose mind was far away. In need of diversion, the kender turned his attention to their host.

"What does your name mean?" Tas asked.

Gnosh smiled happily. "In The Beginning, The Gods Created the Gnomes, and One of the First They Created Was Named Gnosh I and these are the Notable Events Which Occurred in His Life: He Married Marioninillis . . ."

Tas had a sinking feeling. "Wait—" he interrupted. "How long is your name?"

"It fills a book this big in the library," Gnosh said proudly, holding his hands out, "because we are a very old family as you will see when I contin—"

"That's all right," Tas said quickly. Not watching where he was going, he stumbled over a rope. Gnosh helped him to his feet. Looking up, Tas saw the rope led up into a nest of ropes connected to each other, snaking out in all directions. He wondered where they led. "Perhaps another time."

"But there are some very good parts," Gnosh said as they walked toward a huge steel door, "and I could skip to those, if you like, such as the part where great-great-great-grandmother Gnosh invented boiling water—"

"I'd love to hear it." Tas gulped. "But, no time—"

"Yes, I suppose so," Gnosh said, "and anyway, here we are at the entrance to the main chamber, so if you'll excuse me—"

Still talking, he reached up and pulled a cord. A whistle blew. Two bells and a gong rang out. Then, with a tremendous blast of steam that nearly parboiled all of them, two huge steel doors located in the interior of the mountain began to slide open. Almost immediately, the doors stuck, and within minutes the place was swarming with gnomes, yelling and pointing and arguing about whose fault it was.

Tasslehoff Burrfoot had been making plans in the back of his mind as to what he would do after this adventure had ended and all the dragons were slain (the kender tried to maintain a positive outlook). The first thing he had planned to do was to go and spend a few months with his friend, Sestun, the gully dwarf in Pax Tharkas. The gully dwarves led interesting lives, and Tas knew he could settle there quite happily, as long as he didn't have to eat their cooking.

But the moment Tas entered Mount Nevermind, he decided the first thing he would do was come back and live with the gnomes. The kender had never seen anything quite so wonderful in his entire life. He stopped dead in his tracks.

Gnosh glanced at him. "Impressive, isn't it?" he asked.

"Not quite the word I'd use," Fizban muttered. They stood in the central portion of the gnome city. Built within an old shaft of a volcano, it was hundreds of yards across and miles high. The city was constructed in levels around the shaft. Tas stared up . . . and up . . . and up. . . .

"How many levels are there?" the kender asked, nearly falling over backward trying to see.

"Thirty-five and—"

"Thirty-five!" Tas repeated in awe. "I'd hate to live on that thirty-fifth level. How many stairs do you have to climb?"

Gnosh sniffed. "Primitive devices we improved upon long ago and now"—he gestured—"view someofthemarvelsoftechnologywehavein-operat—"

"I can see," said Tas, lowering his eyes to ground level. "You must be preparing for a great battle. I never saw so many catapults in my life . . ."

The kender's voice died. Even as he watched, a whistle sounded, a catapult went off with a twang, and a gnome went sailing through the air. Tas wasn't looking at machines of war, he was looking at the devices that had replaced stairs!

The bottom floor of the chamber was filled with catapults, every type of catapult ever conceived by gnomes. There were sling catapults, crossbow catapults, willow-sprung catapults, steam-driven catapults (still experimental—they were working on adjusting the water temperature).

Surrounding the catapults, over the catapults, under the catapults, and through the catapults were strung miles and miles of rope which operated a crazed assortment of gears and wheels and pulleys, all turning and squeaking and cranking. Out of the floor, out of the machines themselves, and thrusting out from the sides of the walls were huge levers which scores of gnomes were either pushing or pulling or sometimes both at once.

"I don't suppose," Fizban asked in a hopeless tone, "that the Examination Room would be on the ground level?"

Gnosh shook his head. "Examination Room on level fifteen—"

The old mage heaved a heart-rending sigh.

Suddenly there was a horrible grinding sound that set Tas's teeth on edge.

"Ah, they're ready for us. Come along, " Gnosh said.

Tas leaped after him gleefully as they approached a giant catapult. A gnome gestured at them irritably, pointing to a long line of gnomes waiting their turn. Tas jumped into the seat of the huge sling catapult, staring eagerly up into the shaft. Above him, he could see gnomes peering down at him from various balconies, all of them surrounded by great machines, whistles, ropes, and huge, shapeless things hanging from the sides of the wall like bats. Gnosh stood beside him, scolding.

"Elders first, young man, so get outoftherethisinstantandlet"—he dragged Tasslehoff out of the seat with remarkable strength—"themagic-usergofirst—"

"Uh, that's quite all right," Fizban protested, stumbling backward into a pile of rope. "I—I seem to recall a spell of mine that will take me right to the top. Levitate. How did that g-go? Just give me a moment."

"*You* were the one in a hurry—" Gnosh said severely, glaring at Fizban. The gnomes standing in line began to shout rudely, pushing and shoving and jostling.

"Oh, very well," the old mage snarled, and he climbed into the seat,with Gnosh's help.

The gnome operating the lever that launched the catapult yelled something at Gnosh which sounded like "whalevel?"

Gnosh pointed up, yelling back. *"Skimbosh!"*

The chief walked over to stand in front of the first of a series of five levers. An inordinate number of ropes stretched upward into infinity. Fizban sat miserably in the seat of the catapult, still trying to recall his spell.

"Now," yelled Gnosh, drawing Tas closer so he could have the advantage of an excellent view, "in just a moment, the chief will give the signal— yes, there it is—"

The chief pulled on one of the ropes.

"What does that do?" Tas interrupted.

"The rope rings a bell on *Skimbosh,* er, level fifteen, telling them to expect an arrival—"

"What if the bell doesn't ring?" Fizban demanded loudly.

"Then a second bell rings telling them that the first bell didn't—"

"What happens down here if the bell didn't ring?"

"Nothing. It's Skimbosh'sproblemnotyours—"

"It's my problem if they don't know I'm coming!" Fizban shouted."Or do I just drop in and surprise them!"

"Ah," Gnosh said proudly, "you see—"

"I'm getting out . . ." stated Fizban.

"No, wait," Gnosh said, talking faster and faster in his anguish, "they're ready—"

"Who's ready?" Fizban demanded irritably.

"Skimbosh! With the net tocatchyou,yousee—"

"Net!" Fizban turned pale. "That does it!" He flung a foot over the edge.

But before he could move, the chief reached out and pulled on the first lever. The grinding sound started again as the catapult began pivoting in its mooring. The sudden motion threw Fizban back, knocking his hat over his eyes.

"What's happening?" Tas shouted.

"They're getting him in position," Gnosh yelled. "The longitude and latitude have been precalculated and the catapult set to come into the correct location to send the passenger—"

"What about the net?" Tas yelled.

"The magician flies up to Skimbosh—oh, quite safely, I assure you—we've done studies, in fact, proving that flying is safer than walking—and just when he's at the height of his trajectory, beginning to drop a bit, Skimbosh throws a net out underneath him, catching him just like this"—Gnosh demonstrated with his hand, making a snapping motion like catching a fly—"and hauls him—"

"What incredible timing that must take!"

"The timing is ingenious since it all depends on a certain hook we've developed, though"—Gnosh pursed his lips, his eyebrows drawing together—"something is throwing the timing off a bit, but there's a committee—"

The gnome pulled down on the lever and Fizban—with a shriek—went sailing through the air.

"Oh dear," said Gnosh, staring, "it appears—"

"What? What?" Tas yelled, trying to see.

"The net's opened too soon again"—Gnosh shook his head—"and that's the second time today that's happened on Skimbosh alone andthisdefinitelywillbebroughtupatthe nextmeetingoftheNet Guild—"

Tas stared, open-mouthed, at the sight of Fizban whizzing through the air, propelled from below by the tremendous force of the catapult, and suddenly the kender saw what Gnosh was talking about. The net on level fifteen—instead of opening *after* the mage had flown past and then catching him as he started to fall—opened *before* the mage reached level fifteen. Fizban hit the net and was flattened like a squashed spider. For a moment he clung there precariously—arms and legs akimbo, then he fell.

Instantly bells and gongs rang out.

"Don't tell me," Tas guessed miserably. "That's the alarm which means the net failed."

"Quite, but don't be alarmed (small joke)," Gnosh chuckled, "because the alarms trip a device to open the net on level thirteen, just in time, oops—a bit late, well, there's still level twelve—"

"Do something!" Tas shrieked.

"Don't get so worked up!" Gnosh said angrily. "And I'll finishwhatI-wasabouttosayaboutthefinal emergencybackupsystem andthatis, oh, here-itgoes—"

Tas watched in amazement as the bottoms dropped out of six huge barrels hanging from the walls on level three, sending thousands of sponges tumbling down onto the floor in the center of the chamber.This was done—apparently—in case all the nets on every level failed. Fortunately, the net on level nine actually worked, spreading out beneath the mage just in time. Then it folded up around him and whisked him over to the balcony where the gnomes, hearing the mage cursing and swearing inside, appeared reluctant to let him out.

"Sonoweverything'sfineandit'syourturn," said Gnosh.

"Just one last question!" Tas yelled at Gnosh as he sat down in the seat. "What happens if the emergency backup system with the sponges fails?"

"Ingenious—" said Gnosh happily, "because you see if the sponges come down a little too late, the alarm goes off, releasing a huge barrel of water into the center, and, since the sponges are there already, its easy to clean up the mess—"

The chief pulled the lever.

Tas had been expecting all sorts of fascinating things in the Examination Room, but he found it—to his surprise—nearly empty. It was lighted by a hole drilled through the face of the mountain which admitted the sunlight. (This simple but ingenious device had been suggested to the gnomes by a visiting dwarf who called it a 'window;' the gnomes were quite proud of it.) There were three tables, but little else. On the central table, surrounded by gnomes, rested the dragon orb and his hoopak.

It was back to its original size, Tas noted with interest. It looked the same—still a round piece of crystal, with a kind of milky colored mist swirling around inside. A young Knight of Solamnia with an intensely bored expression on his face stood near the orb, guarding it. His bored expression changed sharply at the approach of strangers.

"Quiteallright," Gnosh told the knight reassuringly, "these are the two Lord Gunthar sent word about—" Still talking, Gnosh hustled them over to the central table. The gnome's eyes were bright as he regarded the orb. "A dragon orb," he murmured happily, "after all these years—"

"What years?" Fizban snapped, stopping at some distance from the table.

"You see," Gnosh explained, "each gnome has a Life Quest assigned to him at birth, and from then on his only ambition in life is to fulfill that Life Quest, and it was my Life Quest to study the dragon orb since—"

"But the dragon orbs have been missing for hundreds of years!" Tas said incredulously. "No one knew about them! How could it be your Life Quest?"

"Oh, we knew about them," Gnosh answered, "because it was my grandfather's Life Quest, and then my father's Life Quest. Both of them died without ever seeing a dragon orb. I feared I might, too, but now finally, one has appeared, and I can establish our family's place in the afterlife—"

"You mean you can't get to the—er—afterlife until you complete the Life Quest?" Tas asked. "But your grandfather and your father—"

"Probably most uncomfortable," Gnosh said, looking sad, "wherever they are—My goodness!"

A remarkable change had come over the dragon orb. It began to swirl and shimmer with many different colors—as if in agitation.

Muttering strange words, Fizban walked to the orb and set his hand upon it. Instantly, it went black. Fizban cast a glance around the room, his expression so severe and frightening that even Tas fell back before him. The knight sprang forward.

"Get out!" the mage thundered. "All of you!"

"I was ordered not to leave and I'm not—" The knight reached for his sword, but Fizban whispered a few words. The knight slumped to the floor.

The gnomes vanished from the room instantly, leaving only Gnosh, wringing his hands, his face twisted in agony.

"Come on, Gnosh!" Tas urged. "I've never seen him like this. We better do as he says. If we don't, he's liable to turn us into gully dwarves or something icky like that!"

Whimpering, Gnosh allowed Tas to lead him out of the room. As he stared back at the dragon orb, the door slammed shut.

"My Life Quest . . ." the gnome moaned.

"I'm sure it will be all right," Tas said, although he wasn't sure, not in the least. He hadn't liked the look on Fizban's face. In fact, it hadn't even seemed to be Fizban's face at all—or anyone Tas wanted to know!

Tas felt chilled and there was a tight knot in the pit of his stomach. The gnomes muttered among themselves and cast baleful glances at him. Tas swallowed, trying to get a bitter taste out of his mouth. Then he drew Gnosh to one side.

"Gnosh, did you discover anything about the orb when you studied it?" Tas asked in a low voice.

"Well," Gnosh appeared thoughtful, "I did find out that there's something inside of it, or seems to be, because I'd stare at it and stare at it without seeing anything for the longest time then, right when I was ready to quit, I'd see words swirling about in the mist—"

"Words?" Tas interrupted eagerly. "What did they say?"

Gnosh shook his head. "I don't know," he said solemnly, "because I couldn't read them; no one could, not even a member of the Foreign Language Guild—"

"Magic, probably," Tas muttered to himself.

"Yes," Gnosh said miserably, "that's what I decided—"

The door blew open, as if something had exploded.

Gnosh whirled around, terrified. Fizban stood in the doorway, holding a small black bag in one hand, his staff and Tasslehoff's hoopak in the other. Gnosh sprang past him.

"The orb!" he screeched, so upset he actually completed a sentence. "You've got it!"

"Yes, Gnosh," said Fizban.

The mage's voice sounded tired, and Tas, looking at him closely, saw that he was on the verge of exhaustion. His skin was gray, his eyelids drooped. He leaned heavily on his staff. "Come with me, my boy," he said to the gnome. "And do not worry. Your Life Quest will be fulfilled. But now the orb must be taken before the Council of Whitestone."

"Come with you," Gnosh repeated in astonishment, "to the Council"—he clasped his hands together in excitement—"where perhaps I'll be asked to make a report, do you think—"

"I wouldn't doubt it in the least," Fizban answered.

"Right away, just give me time to pack, where's my papers—"

Gnosh dashed off. Fizban whipped around to face the other gnomes who had been sneaking up behind him, reaching out eagerly for his staff. He scowled so alarmingly that they stumbled backward and vanished into the Examination Room.

"What did you find out?" Tas asked, hesitantly approaching Fizban. The old mage seemed surrounded by darkness. "The gnomes didn't do anything to it, did they?"

"No, no." Fizban sighed. "Fortunately for them. For it is still active and very powerful. Much will depend on the decisions a few make—perhaps the fate of the world."

"What do you mean? Won't the Council make the decisions?"

"You don't understand, my boy," Fizban said gently. "Stop a moment, I must rest." The mage sat down, leaning against a wall. Shaking his head, he continued. "I concentrated my will on the orb, Tas. Oh, not to control dragons," he added, seeing the kender's eyes widen. "I looked into the future."

"What did you see?" Tas asked hesitantly, not certain from the mage's somber expression that he wanted to know.

"I saw two roads stretching before us. If we take the easiest, it will appear the best at the beginning, but darkness will fall at the end, never to be lifted. If we take the other road, it will be hard and difficult to travel. It could cost the lives of some we love, dear boy. Worse, it might cost others their very souls. But only through these great sacrifices will we find hope." Fizban closed his eyes.

"And this involves the orb?" Tas asked, shivering.

"Yes."

"Do you know what must be done to . . . to take the d-dark road?"Tas dreaded the answer.

"I do," Fizban replied in a low voice. "But the decisions have not been left in my hands. That will be up to others."

"I see," Tas sighed. "Important people, I suppose. People like kings and elflords and knights." Then Fizban's words echoed in his mind. *The lives of some we love . . .*

Suddenly a lump formed in Tas's throat, choking him. His head dropped into his hands. This adventure was turning out all wrong! Where was Tanis? And dear old Caramon? And pretty Tika? He had tried not to think about them, particularly after that dream.

And Flint—I shouldn't have gone without him, Tas thought miserably. He might die, he might be dead right now! *The lives of some you love!* I never thought about any of us dying—not really. I always figured that if we were together we could beat anything! But now, we've gotten scattered somehow. And things are going all wrong!

Tas felt Fizban's hand stroke his topknot, his one great vanity. And for the first time in his life, the kender felt very lost and alone and frightened. The mage's grip tightened around him affectionately. Burying his face in Fizban's sleeve, Tas began to cry.

Fizban patted him gently. "Yes," the mage repeated, "important people."

6

The Council of Whitestone.

An important person.

he Council of Whitestone met upon the twenty-eighth day of December, a day known as Famine Day in Solamnia, for it commemorated the suffering of the people during the first winter following the Cataclysm. Lord Gunthar thought it fitting to hold the Council meeting on this day, which was marked by fasting and meditation.

It had been over a month since the armies sailed for Palanthas. The news Gunthar received from that city was not good. A report had arrived early on the morning of the twenty-eighth, in fact. Reading it twice over, he sighed heavily, frowned, and tucked the paper into his belt.

The Council of Whitestone had met once before within the recent past, a meeting precipitated by the arrival of the refugee elves in Southern Ergoth and the appearance of the dragonarmies in northern Solamnia. This Council meeting was several months in the planning, and so all members—either seated or advisory—were represented. Seated members, those who could vote, included the Knights of Solamnia, the gnomes, the hill dwarves, the dark-skinned, sea-faring people of Northern Ergoth, and a representative of the Solamnic exiles living on Sancrist. Advisory members were the elves, the mountain dwarves, and the kender. These members were invited to express their opinions, but they could not vote.

The first Council meeting, however, had not gone well. Some of the old feuds and animosities between the races represented burst into flame. Arman Kharas, representative of the mountain dwarves, and Duncan Hammerrock, of the hill dwarves, had to be physically restrained at one point, or blood from that ancient feud might have flowed again. Alhana Starbreeze, representative of the Silvanesti in her father's absence, refused to speak a word during the entire session. Alhana had come only because Porthios of the Qualinesti was there. She feared an alliance between the Qualinesti and the humans and was determined to prevent it.

Alhana need not have worried. Such was the distrust between humans and elves, that they spoke to each other only out of politeness. Not even Lord Gunthar's impassioned speech in which he had declared, "Our unity begins peace; our division ends hope!" made an impression.

Porthios's answer to this had been to blame the dragons' reappearance on the humans. The humans, therefore, could extricate themselves from this disaster. Shortly after Porthios made his position clear, Alhana rose haughtily and left, leaving no one with any doubts about the position of the Silvanesti.

The mountain dwarf, Arman Kharas, had declared that his people would be willing to help, but that until the Hammer of Kharas was found, the mountain dwarves could not be united. No one knew at the time that the companions would soon return the Hammer, so Gunthar was forced to discount the aid of the dwarves. The only person, in fact, who offered help was Kronin Thistleknott, chief of the kender. Since the last thing any sane country wanted was the "aid" of an army of kenders, this gesture was received with polite smiles, while the members exchanged horrified looks behind Kronin's back.

The first Council disbanded, therefore, without accomplishing much of anything.

Gunthar had higher hopes for this second Council meeting. The discovery of the dragon orb, of course, put everything in a much brighter light. Representatives from both elven factions had arrived. These included the Speaker of the Suns, who brought with him a human claiming to be a cleric of Paladine. Gunthar had heard a great deal about Elistan from Sturm, and he looked forward to meeting him. Just who would represent the Silvanesti, Gunthar wasn't certain. He assumed it was the lord who had been declared regent following Alhana Starbreeze's mysterious disappearance.

The elves had arrived on Sancrist two days ago. Their tents stood out in the fields, gaily colored silk flags fluttering in brilliant contrast to the gray, stormy sky. They were the only other race to attend. There had not been time to send a message to the mountain dwarves, and the hill dwarves were reported to be fighting for their lives against the dragonarmies; no messenger could reach them.

Gunthar hoped this meeting would unite the humans and the elves in the great fight to drive the dragonarmies from Ansalon. But his hopes were dashed before the meeting began.

After scanning the report from the armies in Palanthas, Gunthar left his tent, preparing to make a final tour of the Glade of the Whitestone to see that everything was in order. Wills, his retainer, came dashing after him.

"My lord," the old man puffed, "return immediately."

"What is it?" Gunthar asked. But the old retainer was too much out of breath to reply.

Sighing, the Solamnic lord went back to his tent where he found Lord Michael, dressed in full armor, pacing nervously.

"What's the matter?" Gunthar said, his heart sinking as he saw the grave expression on the young lord's face.

Michael advanced quickly, seizing Gunthar by the arm. "My lord, we have received word that the elves will demand the return of the dragon orb. If we won't return it, they are prepared to go to war to recover it!"

"What?" Gunthar demanded incredulously. "War! Against us! That's ludicrous! They can't—Are you certain? How reliable is this information?"

"Very reliable, I'm afraid, Lord Gunthar."

"My lord, I present Elistan, cleric of Paladine," Michael said. "I beg pardon for not introducing him earlier, but my mind has been in a turmoil since he first brought me this news."

"I have heard a great deal about you, sir," Lord Gunthar said, extending his hand to the man.

The knight's eyes studied Elistan curiously. Gunthar hardly knew what he had expected to see in a purported cleric of Paladine, perhaps a weak-eyed aesthetic, pale and lean from study. Gunthar was not prepared for this tall, well-built man who might have ridden to battle with the best of the knights. The ancient symbol of Paladine—a platinum medallion engraved with a dragon—hung about his neck.

Gunthar reviewed all he had heard from Sturm concerning Elistan, including the cleric's intention to try and convince the elves to unite with the humans. Elistan smiled wearily, as if aware of every thought passing through Gunthar's mind. They were the thoughts he answered.

"Yes, I have failed," Elistan admitted. "It was all I could do to persuade them to attend the Council meeting, and they have come here only, I fear, to give you an ultimatum: return the orb to the elves or fight to retain it."

Gunthar sank into a chair, gesturing weakly with his hand for the others to be seated. Before him, on a table, were spread maps of the lands of Ansalon, showing in shades of darkness, the insidious advance of the dragonarmies. Gunthar's gaze rested on the maps, then suddenly he swept them to the floor.

"We might as well give up right now!" he snarled. "Send a message to the Dragon Highlords: 'Don't bother to come and wipe us out. We're managing quite nicely on our own.' "

Angrily, he hurled on the table the message he had received."There! That's from Palanthas. The people have insisted the knights leave the city. The Palanthians are negotiating with the Dragon Highlords, and the presence of the knights 'seriously compromises their position.' They refuse to give us any aid. And so an army of a thousand Palanthians sits idle!"

"What is Lord Derek doing, my lord?" Michael asked.

"He and the knights and a thousand footmen, refugees from the occupied lands in Throtyl, are fortifying the High Clerist's tower, south of Palanthas," Gunthar said wearily. "It guards the only pass through the Vingaard Mountains. We'll protect Palanthas for a time, but if the dragonarmies get through . . ." He fell silent. "Damn it," he whispered, beating his fist gently upon the table, "we could hold that pass with two thousand men! The fools! And now this!" He waved his hand in the direction of the elven tents.

Gunthar sighed, letting his head fall into his hands. "Well, what do you counsel, cleric?"

Elistan was quiet for a moment, before he answered. "It is written in the Disks of Mishakal that evil, by its very nature, will always turn in upon itself. Thus it becomes self-defeating." He laid his hand upon Gunthar's shoulder. "I do not know what may come of this meeting. My gods have kept this secret from me. It could be they themselves do not know; that the future of the world stands in balance, and what we decide here will determine it. I do know this: Do not enter with defeat in your heart, for that will be the first victory of evil."

So saying, Elistan rose and left the tent quietly.

Gunthar sat in silence after the cleric had gone. It seemed that the whole world was silent, in fact, he thought. The wind had died during the night. The storm clouds hung low and heavy, muffling sound so that even the clarion trumpet's call marking day's dawning seemed flat. A rustling broke his concentration. Michael was slowly gathering up the spilled maps.

Gunthar raised his head, rubbing his eyes.

"What do you think?"

"Of what? The elves?"

"That cleric," Gunthar said, staring out the tent opening.

"Certainly not what I would have expected," Michael answered, his gaze following Gunthar's. "More like the stories we've heard of the clerics of old, the ones that guided the Knights in the days before the Cataclysm. He's not much like these charlatans we've got now. Elistan is a man who would stand beside you on the field of battle, calling down Paladine's blessing with one hand while wielding his mace with the other. He wears the medallion that none have seen since the gods abandoned us. But is he a true cleric?" Michael shrugged. "It will take a lot more than a medallion to convince me."

"I agree." Gunthar rose to his feet and began to walk toward the tent flap. "Well, it is nearly time. Stay here, Michael, in case any more reports come in." Starting to leave, he paused at the entrance to the tent. "How odd it is, Michael," he murmured, his eyes following Elistan, now no more than a speck of white in the distance. "We have always been a people who looked to the gods for our hope, a people of faith, who distrusted magic. Yet now we look to magic for that hope, and when a chance comes to renew our faith, we question it."

Lord Michael made no answer. Gunthar shook his head and, still pondering, made his way to the Glade of the Whitestone.

As Gunthar said, the Solamnic people had always been faithful followers of the gods. Long ago, in the days before the Cataclysm, the Glade of the Whitestone had been one of the holy centers of worship. The phenomenon of the white rock had attracted the attention of the curious longer than anyone remembered. The Kingpriest of Istar himself had blessed the huge white rock that sat in the middle of a perpetually green glade, declaring it sacred to the gods and forbidding any mortal being to touch it.

Even after the Cataclysm, when belief in the old gods died, the Glade remained a sacred place. Perhaps that was because not even the Cataclysm had affected it. Legend held that when the fiery mountain fell from the sky, the ground around the Whitestone cracked and split apart, but the Whitestone remained intact.

So awesome was the sight of the huge white rock that even now none dared either approach or touch it. What strange powers it possessed, none could say. All they knew was that the air around the Whitestone was always springlike and warm. No matter how bitter the winter, the grass in Whitestone Glade was always green.

Though his heart was heavy, Gunthar relaxed as he stepped inside the glade and breathed the warm, sweet air. For a moment, he felt once again the touch of Elistan's hand upon his shoulder, imparting a feeling of inner peace.

Glancing around quickly, he saw all in readiness. Massive wooden chairs with ornately carved backs had been placed on the green grass. Five for the voting members of the Council stood to the left side of the Whitestone, three for the advisory members stood on the right. Polished benches for the witnesses to the proceedings as demanded by the Measure, sat facing the Whitestone and the Council members.

Some of the witnesses had already begun arriving, Gunthar noticed. Most of the elven party traveling with the Speaker and the Silvanesti lord were taking their seats. The two estranged elven races sat near each other, apart from the humans who were filing in as well. Everyone sat quietly, some in remembrance of Famine Day; others, like the gnomes, who did not celebrate that holiday, in awe of their surroundings. Seats in the front row were reserved for honored guests or for those with leave to speak before the Council.

Gunthar saw the Speaker's stern-faced son, Porthios, enter with a retinue of elven warriors. They took their seats in the front. Gunthar wondered where Elistan was. He'd intended to ask him to speak. He had been impressed with the man's words (even if he was a charlatan) and hoped he would repeat them.

As he searched in vain for Elistan, he saw three strange figures enter and seat themselves in the front row: it was the old mage in his bent and shapeless hat, his kender friend, and a gnome they had brought back with them from Mount Nevermind. The three had arrived back from their journey only last night.

Gunthar was forced to turn his attention back to the Whitestone. The advisory Council members were entering. There were only two, Lord Quinath of the Silvanesti, and the Speaker of the Suns. Gunthar looked at the Speaker curiously, knowing he was one of the few beings on Krynn to still remember the horrors of the Cataclysm.

The Speaker was so stooped that he seemed almost crippled. His hair was gray, his face haggard. But as he took his seat and turned his gaze to the witnesses, Gunthar saw the elf's eyes were bright and arresting. Lord Quinath, seated next to him, was known to Gunthar, who considered him as arrogant and proud as Porthios of the Qualinesti, but lacking in the intelligence Porthios possessed.

As for Porthios, Gunthar thought he could probably come to like the Speaker's eldest son quite well. Porthios had every characteristic the knights admired, with one exception, his quick temper.

Gunthar's observations were interrupted, for now it was time for the voting Council members to enter and Gunthar had to take his place. First came Mir Kar-thon of Northern Ergoth, a dark complexioned man with iron-gray hair and the arms of a giant. Next came Serdin MarThasal, representing the Exiles on Sancrist, and finally Lord Gunthar, Knight of Solamnia.

Once seated, Gunthar glanced around a final time. The huge Whitestone glistened behind him, casting its own strange radiance, for the sun would not shine today. On the other side of the Whitestone sat the Speaker, next to him Lord Quinath. Across from them, facing the Council, sat the witnesses upon their benches. The kender was sitting subdued, swinging his short legs on his tall bench. The gnome shuffled through what looked like a ream of paper; Gunthar shuddered, wishing there'd been time to ask for a condensed report. The old magician yawned and scratched his head, peering around vaguely.

All was ready. At Gunthar's signal, two knights entered, bearing a golden stand and a wooden chest. A silence that was almost deathlike descended on the crowd as they watched the entrance of the dragon orb.

The knights came to a halt, standing directly in front of the Whitestone. Here, one of the knights placed the golden stand upon the ground. The other set down the chest, unlocked it, and carefully brought forth the orb that was back to its original size, over two feet in diameter.

A murmur went through the crowd. The Speaker of the Suns shifted uncomfortably, scowling. His son, Porthios, turned to say something to an elflord near him. All of the elves, Gunthar noted, were armed. Not a good sign, from what little he knew of elven protocol.

He had no choice but to proceed. Calling the meeting to order, Lord Gunthar Uth Wistan announced, "Let the Council of Whitestone begin."

After about two minutes, it was obvious to Tasslehoff that things were in a real mess. Before Lord Gunthar had even concluded his speech of welcome, the Speaker of the Suns rose.

"My talk will be brief," the elven leader stated in a voice that matched the steely gray of the storm clouds above him. "The Silvanesti, the Qualinesti, and the Kaganesti met in council shortly after the orb was removed from our camp. It is the first time the members of the three communities have met since the Kinslayer wars." He paused, laying a heavy emphasis on those last words. Then he continued.

"We have decided to set aside our own differences in our perfect agreement that the dragon orb belongs in the hands of the elves, not in the hands of humans or any other race upon Krynn. Therefore, we come before the Council of Whitestone and ask that the dragon orb be given over to us forthwith. In return, we guarantee that we will take it to our lands and keep it safe until such time—if ever—it be needed."

The Speaker sat down, his dark eyes sweeping over the crowd, its silence broken now by a murmur of soft voices. The other Council members, sitting next to Lord Gunthar, shook their heads, their faces grim. The dark-skinned leader of the Northern Ergoth people whispered to Lord Gunthar in a harsh voice, clenching his fist to emphasize his words.

Lord Gunthar, after listening and nodding for several minutes, rose to his feet to respond. His speech was cool, calm, complimentary to the elves. But it said—between the lines—that the Knights would see the elves in the Abyss before they gave them the dragon orb.

The Speaker, understanding perfectly the message of steel couched in the pretty phrases, rose to reply. He spoke only one sentence, but it brought the crowd of witnesses to their feet.

"Then, Lord Gunthar," the Speaker said, "the elves declare that, from this time on—we are at war!"

Humans and elves both headed for the dragon orb that sat upon its golden stand, its milky white insides swirling gently within the crystal. Gunthar shouted for order time and again, banging the hilt of his sword upon the table. The Speaker spoke a few words sharply in elven, staring hard at his son, Porthios, and finally order was restored.

But the atmosphere snapped like the air before a storm. Gunthar talked. The Speaker answered. The Speaker talked. Gunthar answered. The dark-skinned mariner lost his temper and made a few cutting remarks about elves. The lord of the Silvanesti reduced him to quivering anger with his sarcastic rejoinders. Several of the knights left, only to return armed to the teeth. They came to stand near Gunthar, their hands on their weapons. The elves, led by Porthios, rose to surround their own leaders.

Gnosh, his report held fast in his hand, began to realize he wasn't going to be asked to give it.

Tasslehoff looked around despairingly for Elistan. He kept hoping desperately the cleric would come. Elistan could calm these people down. Or maybe Laurana. Where was she? There'd been no word of his friends, the elves had told the kender coldly. She and her brother had apparently vanished in the wilderness. I shouldn't have left them, Tas thought. I shouldn't be here. Why, why did this crazy old mage bring me? I'm useless! Maybe Fizban could do something? Tas looked at the mage hopefully, but Fizban was sound asleep!

"Please, wake up!" Tas begged, shaking him. "Somebody's got to do something!"

At that moment, he heard Lord Gunthar yell, "The dragon orb is *not* yours by right! Lady Laurana and the others were bringing it to *us* when they were shipwrecked! You tried to keep it on Ergoth by force, and your own daughter—"

"Mention not my daughter!" the Speaker said in a deep, harsh voice. "I do not have a daughter."

Something broke within Tasslehoff. Confused memories of Laurana fighting desperately against the evil wizard who guarded the orb, Laurana battling draconians, Laurana firing her bow at the white dragon, Laurana ministering to him so tenderly when he'd been near death. To be cast off by her own people when she was working so desperately to save them, when she had sacrificed so much. . . .

"Stop this!" Tasslehoff heard himself yelling at the top of his voice. "Stop this right now and listen to me!"

Suddenly he saw, to his astonishment, that everyone had stopped talking and was staring at him.

Now that he had his audience, Tas realized he didn't have any idea what to say to all of these important people. But he knew he had to say something. After all, he thought, this is my fault—I read about these damn orbs. Gulping, he slid off his bench and walked toward the Whitestone and the two hostile groups clustered around it. He thought he saw—out of the corner of his eye—Fizban grinning from under his hat.

"I—I . . ." The kender stammered, wondering what to say. He was saved by a sudden inspiration.

"I demand the right to represent my people," Tasslehoff said proudly, "and take my place on the advisory council."

Flipping his tassle of brown hair over his shoulder, the kender came to stand right in front of the dragon orb. Looking up, he could see the Whitestone towering over it and over him. Tas stared at the stone, shivering, then quickly turned his gaze from the rock to Gunthar and the Speaker of the Suns.

And then Tasslehoff knew what he had to do. He began to shake with fear. He—Tasslehoff Burrfoot—who'd never been afraid of anything in his life! He'd faced dragons without trembling, but the knowledge of what he was going to do now appalled him. His hands felt as if he'd been making snowballs without gloves on. His tongue seemed to belong in some larger person's mouth. But Tas was resolute. He just had to keep them talking, keep them from guessing what he planned.

"You've never taken us kenders very seriously, you know," Tas began, his voice sounding too loud and shrill in his own ears, "and I can't say I blame you much. We don't have a strong sense of responsibility, I guess, and we are probably too curious for own good—but, I ask you, how are you going to find out anything if you're not curious?"

Tas could see the Speaker's face turn to steel, even Lord Gunthar was scowling. The kender edged nearer the dragon orb.

"We cause lots of trouble, I suppose, without meaning to, and occasionally some of us do happen to acquire certain things which aren't ours. But one thing the kender know is—"

Tasslehoff broke into a run. Quick and lithe as a mouse, he slipped easily through the hands that tried to catch him, reaching the dragon orb within a matter of seconds. Faces blurred around him, mouths opened, shrieking and yelling at him. But they were too late.

In one swift, smooth movement, Tasslehoff hurled the dragon orb at the huge, gleaming Whitestone.

The round, gleaming crystal—its insides swirling in agitation—hung suspended in the air for long, long seconds. Tas wondered if the orb had the power to halt its flight. But it was just a fevered impression in the kender's mind.

The dragon orb struck the rock and shattered, bursting into a thousand sparkling pieces. For an instant, a ball of milky white smoke hung in the air, as if trying desperately to hold itself together. Then the warm, springlike breeze of the glade caught it and swept it apart.

There was intense, awful silence.

The kender stood, looking calmly down at the shattered dragon orb.

"We know," he said in a small voice that dropped into the dreadful silence like a tiny drop of rain, "we should be fighting dragons. Not each other."

No one moved. No one spoke. Then there was a thump.

Gnosh had fainted.

The silence broke—almost as shattering as the breaking of the orb. Lord Gunthar and the Speaker both lunged at Tas. One caught hold of the kender's left shoulder, one his right.

"What have you done?" Lord Gunthar's face was livid, his eyes wild as he gripped the kender with trembling hands.

"You have brought death upon us all!" The Speaker's fingers bit into Tas's flesh like the claws of a predatory bird. "You have destroyed our only hope!"

"And for that, he himself will be the first to die!"

Porthios—tall, grim-faced elflord—loomed above the cowering kender, his sword glistening in his hand. The kender stood his ground between the elven king and the knight, his small face pale, his expression defiant. He had known when he committed his crime that death would be the penalty.

Tanis will be unhappy over what I've done, Tas thought sadly. But at least he'll hear that I died bravely.

"Now, now, now . . ." said a sleepy voice. "No one's going to die! At least not at this moment. Quit waving that sword around, Porthios! Someone'll get hurt."

Tas peered out from under a heaving sea of arms and shining armor to see Fizban, yawning, step over the inert body of the gnome and totter toward them. Elves and humans made way for him to pass, as if compelled to do so by an unseen force.

Porthios whirled to face Fizban, so angry that saliva bubbled on his lips and his speech was nearly incoherent.

"Beware, old man, or you will share in the punishment!"

"I said quit waving that sword around," Fizban snapped irritably, wiggling a finger at the sword.

Porthios dropped his weapon with a wild cry. Clutching his stinging, burning hand, he stared down at the sword in astonishment—the hilt had grown thorns! Fizban came to stand next to the elflord and regarded him angrily.

"You're a fine young man, but you should have been taught some respect for your elders. I said to put that sword down and I meant it! Maybe you'll believe me next time!" Fizban's baleful gaze switched to the Speaker. "And you, Solostaran, were a good man about two hundred years ago. Managed to raise three fine children—*three* fine children, I said. Don't give me any of this nonsense about not having a daughter. You have one, and a fine girl she is. More sense than her father. Must take after her mother's side. Where was I? Oh, yes. You brought up Tanis Half-Elven, too. You know, Solostaran, between the four of these young people, we might save this world yet.

"Now I want everyone to take his seat. Yes, you, too, Lord Gunthar.

Come along, Solostaran, I'll help. We old men have to stick together. Too bad you're such a damn fool."

Muttering into his beard, Fizban led the astounded Speaker to his chair. Porthios, his face twisted in pain, stumbled back to his seat with the help of his warriors.

Slowly the assembled elves and knights sat down, murmuring among themselves—all casting dark looks at the shattered dragon orb that lay beneath the Whitestone.

Fizban settled the Speaker in his seat, glowered at Lord Quinath, who thought he had something to say but quickly decided he didn't. Satisfied, the old mage came back to the front of the Whitestone where Tas stood, shaken and confused.

"You," Fizban looked at the kender as if he'd never seen him before, "go and attend to that poor chap." He waved a hand at the gnome, who was still out cold.

Feeling his knees tremble, Tasslehoff walked slowly over to Gnosh and knelt down beside him, glad to look at something other than the angry, fear-filled faces.

"Gnosh," he whispered miserably, patting the gnome on the cheek, "I'm sorry. I truly am. I mean about your Life Quest and your father's soul and everything. But there just didn't seem to be anything else to do."

Fizban turned around slowly and faced the assembled group, pushing his hat back on his head. "Yes, I'm going to lecture you. You deserve it, every one of you—so don't sit there looking self-righteous. That kender"— he pointed at Tasslehoff, who cringed—"has more brains beneath that ridiculous topknot of his than the lot of you have put together. Do you know what would have happened to you if the kender hadn't had the guts to do what he did? Do you? Well, I'll tell you. Just let me find a seat here. . . ." Fizban peered around vaguely. "Ah, yes, there . . ." Nodding in satisfaction, the old mage toddled over and sat down on the ground, leaning his back against the sacred Whitestone!

The assembled knights gasped in horror. Gunthar leaped to his feet, appalled at this sacrilege.

"No mortal can touch the Whitestone!" he yelled, striding forward.

Fizban slowly turned his head to regard the furious knight. "One more word," the old mage said solemnly, "and I'll make your moustaches fall off. Now sit down and shut up!"

Sputtering, Gunthar was brought up short by an imperious gesture from the old man. The knight could do nothing but return to his seat.

"Where was I before I was interrupted?" Fizban scowled. Glancing around, his gaze fell on the broken pieces of the orb. "Oh, yes. I was about to tell you a story. One of you would have won the orb, of course. And you would have taken it—either to keep it 'safe' or to 'save the world.' And, yes, it is capable of saving the world, but only if you know how to use it.

Who of you has this knowledge? Who has the strength? The orb was created by the greatest, most powerful mages of old. *All* the most powerful—do you understand? It was created by those of the White Robes and those of the Black Robes. It has the essence of both evil and good. The Red Robes brought both essences together and bound them with their force. Few there are now with the power and strength to understand the orb, to fathom its secrets, and to gain mastery over it. Few indeed"—Fizban's eyes gleamed—"and none who sit here!"

Silence had fallen now, a profound silence as they listened to the old mage, whose voice was strong and carried above the rising wind that was blowing the storm clouds from the sky.

"One of you would have taken the orb and used it, and you would have found that you had hurled yourself upon disaster. You would have been broken as surely as the kender broke the orb. As for hope being shattered, I tell you that hope was lost for a time, but now it has been new born—"

A sudden gust of wind caught the old mage's hat, blowing it off his head and tossing it playfully away from him. Snarling in irritation, Fizban crawled forward to pick it up.

Just as the mage leaned over, the sun broke through the clouds.There was a blazing flash of silver, followed by a splintering, deafening crack as though the land itself had split apart.

Half-blinded by the flaring light, people blinked and gazed in fear and awe at the terrifying sight before their eyes.

The Whitestone had been split asunder.

The old magician lay sprawled at its base, his hat clutched in his hand, his other arm flung over his head in terror. Above him, piercing the rock where he had been sitting, was a long weapon made of gleaming silver. It had been thrown by the silver arm of a black man, who walked over to stand beside it. Accompanying him were three people: an elven woman dressed in leather armor, an old, white-bearded dwarf, and Elistan.

Amid the stunned silence of the crowd, the black man reached out and lifted the weapon from the splintered remains of the rock. He held it high above his head, and the silver barbed point glittered brightly in the rays of the midday sun.

"I am Theros Ironfeld," the man called out in a deep voice, "and for the last month I have been forging these!" He shook the weapon in his hand. "I have taken molten silver from the well hidden deep within the heart of the Monument of the Silver Dragon. With the silver arm given me by the gods, I have forged the weapon as legend foretold. And this I bring to you—to all the people of Krynn—that we may join together and defeat the great evil that threatens to engulf us in darkness forever.

"I bring you—the Dragonlance!"

With that, Theros thrust the weapon deep into the ground. It stood, straight and shining, amid the broken pieces of the dragon orb.

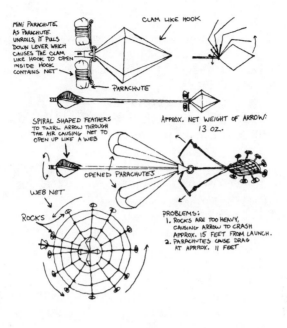

MINI PARACHUTE.
AS PARACHUTE.
UNROLLS, IT PULLS
DOWN LEVER WHICH
CAUSES THE CLAM
LIKE HOOK TO OPEN
INSIDE HOOK
CONTAINS NET

CLAM LIKE HOOK

PARACHUTE

SPIRAL SHAPED FEATHERS
TO TWIRL ARROW THROUGH
THE AIR CAUSING NET TO
OPEN UP LIKE A WEB

APPROX. NET WEIGHT OF ARROW:
13 OZ.

OPENED PARACHUTES

WEB NET

ROCKS

PROBLEMS:
1. ROCKS ARE TOO HEAVY,
CAUSING ARROW TO CRASH
APPROX. 15 FEET FROM LAUNCH.
2. PARACHUTES CAUSE DRAG
AT APPROX. 11 FEET

7

AN UNEXPECTED JOURNEY.

nd now my task is finished," Laurana said. "I am free to leave."

"Yes," Elistan said slowly, "and I know why you leave"—Laurana flushed and lowered her eyes—"but where will you go?"

"Silvanesti," she replied. "The last place I saw him."

"Only in a dream—"

"No, that was more than a dream," Laurana replied, shuddering. "It was real. He was there. He is alive and I must find him."

"Surely, my dear, you should stay here, then," Elistan suggested. "You say that in the dream he had found a dragon orb. If he has it, he will come to Sancrist."

Laurana did not answer. Unhappy and irresolute, she stared out the window of Lord Gunthar's castle where she, Elistan, Flint, and Tasslehoff were staying as his guests.

She should have been with the elves. Before they left Whitestone Glade, her father had asked her to come back with them to Southern Ergoth. But Laurana refused. Although she did not say it, she knew she would never live among her people again.

Her father had not pressed her, and—in his eyes—she saw that he heard her unspoken words. Elves aged by years, not by days, as did humans. For her father, it seemed as if time had accelerated and he was changing even as she watched. She felt as though she were seeing him through Raistlin's hourglass eyes, and the thought was terrifying. Yet the news she brought him only increased his bitter unhappiness.

Gilthanas had not returned. Nor could Laurana tell her father where his beloved son had gone, for the journey he and Silvara made was dark and fraught with peril. Laurana told her father only that Gilthanas was not dead.

"You know where he is?" the Speaker asked after a pause.

"I do," Laurana answered, "or rather—I know where he goes."

"And you cannot speak of this, even to me, his father?"

Laurana shook her head steadfastly. "No, Speaker, I cannot. Forgive me, but we agreed when the decision was made to undertake this desperate action that those of us who knew would tell no one. No one," she repeated.

"So you do not trust me—"

Laurana sighed. Her eyes went to the shattered Whitestone. "Father," she said, "you nearly went to war . . . with the only people who can help save us. . . ."

Her father had not replied, but—in his cool farewell and in the way he leaned upon the arm of his elder child—he made it clear to Laurana that he now had only *one* child.

Theros went with the elves. Following his dramatic presentation of the dragonlance, the Council of Whitestone had voted unanimously to make more of these weapons and unite all races in the fight against the dragonarmies.

"At present," Theros announced, "we have only those few lances I was able to forge by myself within a month's time, and I bring several ancient lances the silver dragons hid at the time the dragons were banished from the world. But we'll need more, many more. I need men to help me!"

The elves agreed to provide men to help make the dragonlances, but whether or not they would help fight—

"That remains a matter we must discuss," the Speaker said.

"Don't discuss it too long," Flint Fireforge snapped, "or you might find yourself discussing it with a Dragon Highlord."

"The elves keep their own counsel and ask for no advice from dwarves," the Speaker replied coldly. "Besides, we do not even know if these lances work! The legend said they were to be forged by one of the Silver Arm, that is certain. But it also says that the Hammer of Kharas was needed in the forging. Where is the Hammer now?" he asked Theros.

"The Hammer could not be brought here in time, even if it could be kept from the dragonarmies. The Hammer of Kharas was required in days of old, because man's skill was not sufficient by itself to produce the lances. Mine is," he added proudly. "You saw what the lance did to that rock."

"We shall see what it does to dragons," the Speaker said, and the Second Council of Whitestone drew to a close. Gunthar proposed at the last that the lances Theros had brought with him be sent to the knights in Palanthas.

These thoughts passed through Laurana's mind as she stared out across the bleak winter landscape. It would be snowing in the valley soon, Lord Gunthar said.

I cannot stay here, Laurana thought, pressing her face against the chill glass. I shall go mad.

"I've studied Gunthar's maps," she murmured, almost speaking to herself, "and I've seen the location of the dragonarmies. Tanis will never reach Sancrist. And if he does have the orb, he may not know the danger it poses. I must warn him."

"My dear, you're not talking sensibly," Elistan said mildly. "If Tanis cannot reach Sancrist safely, how will you reach him? Think logically, Laurana—"

"I don't want to think logically!" Laurana cried, stomping her foot and glaring angrily at the cleric. "I'm sick of being sensible! I'm tired of this whole war. I've done my part—more than my part. I just want to find Tanis!"

Seeing Elistan's sympathetic face, Laurana sighed. "I'm sorry, my dear friend. I know what you say is true," she said, ashamed. "But I can't stay here and do nothing!"

Though Laurana didn't mention it, she had another concern. That human woman, that Kitiara. Where was she? Were they together as she had seen in the dream? Laurana realized now, suddenly, that the remembered image of Kitiara standing with Tanis's arm around her was more disturbing than the image she had seen of her own death.

At that moment, Lord Gunthar suddenly entered the room.

"Oh!" he said, startled, seeing Elistan and Laurana. "I'm sorry, I hope I am not disturbing—"

"Please, no, come in," Laurana said quickly.

"Thank you," Gunthar said, stepping inside and carefully shutting the door, first glancing down the hallway to make certain no one was near. He joined them at the window. "Actually I needed to talk to you both, anyway. I sent Wills looking for you. This is best, however. No one knows we're speaking."

More intrigue, Laurana thought wearily. Throughout their journey to Gunthar's castle, she had heard about nothing but the political infighting that was destroying the Knighthood.

Shocked and outraged at Gunthar's story of Sturm's trial, Laurana had gone before a Council of Knights to speak in Sturm's defense. Although the appearance of a woman at a Council was unheard of, the knights were impressed by this vibrant, beautiful young woman's eloquent speech on Sturm's behalf. The fact that Laurana was a member of the royal elven household, and that she had brought the dragonlances, also spoke highly in her favor.

Even Derek's faction—those that remained—were hard-pressed to fault her. But the knights had been unable to reach a decision. The man appointed to stand in Lord Alfred's place was strongly in Derek's tent—as the phrase went—and Lord Michael had vacillated to such a degree that Gunthar had been forced to throw the matter to an open vote. The knights demanded a period of reflection and the meeting was adjourned. They had reconvened this afternoon. Apparently, Gunthar had just come from this meeting.

Laurana knew, from the look on Gunthar's face, that things had gone favorably. But if so, why the maneuvering?

"Sturm's been pardoned?" she asked.

Gunthar grinned and rubbed his hands together. "Not pardoned, my dear. That would have implied his guilt. No. He has been completely vindicated! I pushed for that. Pardon would not have suited us at all. His knighthood is granted. He has his command officially bestowed upon him. And Derek is in serious trouble!"

"I am happy, for Sturm's sake," Laurana said coolly, exchanging worried looks with Elistan. Although she liked what she had seen of Lord Gunthar, she had been brought up in a royal household and knew Sturm was being made a game piece.

Gunthar caught the edge of ice in her voice, and his face became grave. "Lady Laurana," he said, speaking more somberly, "I know what you are thinking—that I am dangling Sturm from puppet strings. Let us be brutally frank, lady. The Knights are divided, split into two factions—Derek's and my own. And we both know what happens to a tree split in two: both sides wither and die. This battle between us must end, or it will have tragic consequences. Now, lady and Elistan, for I have come to trust and rely on your judgment, I leave this in your hands. You have met me and you have met Lord Derek Crownguard. Who would you choose to head the Knights?"

"You, of course, Lord Gunthar," Elistan said sincerely.

Laurana nodded her head. "I agree. This feud is ruinous to the Knighthood. I saw that myself, in the Council meeting. And—from what I've heard of the reports coming from Palanthas—it is hurting our cause there as well. My first concern must be for my friend, however."

"I quite understand, and I am glad to hear you say so," Gunthar said approvingly, "because it makes the very great favor I am about to ask of you easier." Gunthar took Laurana's arm. "I want you to go to Palanthas."

"What? Why? I don't understand!"

"Of course not. Let me explain. Please sit down. You, too, Elistan. I'll pour some wine—"

"I think not," Laurana said, sitting near the window.

"Very well." Gunthar's face became grave. He laid his hand over Laurana's. "We know politics, you and I, lady. So I am going to arrange all my game pieces before you. Ostensibly you will be traveling to Palanthas to teach the knights to use the dragonlances. It is a legitimate reason. Without Theros, you and the dwarf are the only ones who understand their usage. And—let's face it—the dwarf is too short to handle one."

Gunthar cleared his throat. "You will take the lances to Palanthas. But more importantly, you will carry with you a Writ of Vindication from the Council fully restoring Sturm's honor. That will strike the death's blow to Derek's ambition. The moment Sturm puts on his armor, all will know I have the Council's full support. I shouldn't wonder if *Derek* won't go on trial when he returns."

"But why me?" Laurana asked bluntly. "I can teach anyone—Lord Michael, for example—to use a dragonlance. He can take them to Palanthas. He can carry the Writ to Sturm—"

"Lady"—Lord Gunthar gripped her hand hard, drawing near and speaking barely above a whisper—"you still do not understand! I cannot trust Lord Michael! I cannot—I dare not trust any one of the knights with this! Derek has been knocked from his horse—so to speak—but he hasn't lost the tourney yet. I need someone I can trust implicitly! Someone who knows Derek for what he is, who has Sturm's best interests at heart!"

"I *do* have Sturm's interests at heart," Laurana said coldly. "I put them above the interests of the Knighthood."

"Ah, but remember, Lady Laurana," Gunthar said, rising to his feet and bowing as he kissed her hand, "Sturm's *only* interest is the Knighthood. What would happen to him, do you think, if the Knighthood should fall? What will happen to him if Derek seizes control?"

In the end, of course, Laurana agreed to go to Palanthas, as Gunthar had known she must. As the time of her departure drew nearer, she began to dream almost nightly of Tanis arriving on the island just hours after she left. More than once she was on the verge of refusing to go, but then she thought of facing Tanis, of having to tell him she had refused to go to Sturm to warn him of this peril. This kept her from changing her mind. This—and her regard for Sturm.

It was during the lonely nights, when her heart and her arms ached for Tanis and she had visions of him holding that human woman with the dark, curly hair, flashing brown eyes, and the charming, crooked smile, that her soul was in turmoil.

Her friends could give her little comfort. One of them, Elistan, left when a messenger arrived from the elves, requesting the cleric's presence, and asking that an emissary from the knights accompany him.There was little time for farewells. Within a day of the arrival of the elven messenger, Elistan and Lord Alfred's son, a solemn, serious young man named Douglas, began their journey back to Southern Ergoth. Laurana had never felt so alone as she bid her mentor good-bye.

Tasslehoff faced a sad parting as well.

In the midst of the excitement over the dragonlance, everyone forgot poor Gnosh and his Life Quest, which lay in a thousand sparkling pieces on the grass. Everyone but Fizban. The old magician rose from where he lay cowering on the ground before the shattered Whitestone and went to the stricken gnome, who was staring woefully at the shattered dragon orb.

"There, there, my boy," said Fizban, "this isn't the end of everything!"

"It isn't?" asked Gnosh, so miserable he finished a sentence.

"No, of course not! You've got to look at this from the proper perspective. Why, now you've got a chance to study a dragon orb from the inside out!"

Gnosh's eyes brightened. "You're right," he said after a short pause, "and, in fact, I bet I could glue—"

"Yes, yes," Fizban said hurriedly, but Gnosh lunged forward, his speech growing faster and faster.

"We could tag the pieces, don'tyousee,andthendrawadiagramof-whereeachpiece waslyingontheground,which—"

"Quite, quite," Fizban muttered.

"Step aside, step aside," Gnosh said importantly, shooing people away from the orb. "Mind where you walk, Lord Gunthar, and, yes, we're going to study it from the inside out now, and I should have a report in a matter of weeks—"

Gnosh and Fizban cordoned off the area and set to work. For the next two days, Fizban stood on the broken Whitestone making diagrams, supposedly marking the exact location of each piece before it was picked up. (One of Fizban's diagrams accidentally ended up in the kender's pouch. Tas discovered later that it was actually a game known as "x's and zeroes" which the mage had been playing against himself and apparently—lost.)

Gnosh, meanwhile, crawled happily around on the grass, sticking bits of parchment adorned with numbers on pieces of glass smaller than the bits of parchment. He and Fizban finally collected the 2,687 pieces of dragon orb in a basket and transported them back to Mount Nevermind.

Tasslehoff had been offered the choice of staying with Fizban or going to Palanthas with Laurana and Flint. The choice was simple. The kender knew two such innocents as the elfmaid and the dwarf could not survive without him. But it was hard leaving his old friend. Two days before the ship sailed, he paid a final visit to the gnomes and to Fizban.

After an exhilarating ride in the catapult, he found Gnosh in the Examination Room. The pieces of the broken dragon orb—tagged and numbered—were spread out across two tables.

"Absolutelyfascinating," Gnosh spoke so fast he stuttered, "because wehaveanalyzedtheglass, curiousmaterial, unlikenothingwe'veeverseen, greatestdiscovery, thiscentury—"

"So your Life Quest is over?" Tas interrupted. "Your father's soul—"

"Restingcomfortably!" Gnosh beamed, then returned to his work."Andsogladyoucouldstopbyandifyou'reeverintheneighborhoodcomebyandseeusagain—"

"I will," Tas said, smiling.

Tas found Fizban two levels down. (A fascinating journey—he simply yelled out the name of his level, then leaped into the void. Nets flapped and fluttered, bells went off, gongs sounded and whistles blew. Tas was finally caught one level above the ground, just as the area was being inundated with sponges.)

Fizban was in Weapons Development, surrounded by gnomes, all gazing at him with unabashed admiration.

"Ah, my boy!" he said, peering vaguely at Tasslehoff. "You're just in time to see the testing of our new weapon. Revolutionize warfare. Make the dragonlance obsolete."

"Really?" Tas asked in excitement.

"A fact!" Fizban confirmed. "Now, you stand over here—" He motioned to a gnome who leaped to do his bidding, running to stand in the middle of the cluttered room.

Fizban picked up what looked, to the kender's confused mind, like a crossbow that had been attacked by an enraged fisherman. It was a crossbow all right. But instead of an arrow, a huge net dangled from a hook on the end. Fizban, grumbling and muttering, ordered the gnomes to stand behind him and give him room.

"Now, you are the enemy," Fizban told the gnome in the center of the room. The gnome immediately assumed a fierce, warlike expression. The other gnomes nodded appreciatively.

Fizban aimed, then let fly. The net sailed out into the air, got snagged on the hook at the end of crossbow, and snapped back like a collapsing sail to engulf the magician.

"Confounded hook!" Fizban muttered.

Between the gnomes and Tas, they got him disentangled.

"I guess this is good-bye," Tas said, slowly extending his small hand.

"It is?" Fizban looked amazed. "Am I going somewhere? No one told me! I'm not packed—"

"*I'm* going somewhere," Tas said patiently, "with Laurana. We're taking the lances and—oh, I don't think I'm supposed to be telling anyone," he added, embarrassed.

"Don't worry. Mum's the word," Fizban said in a hoarse whisper that carried clearly through the crowded room. "You'll love Palanthas. Beautiful city. Give Sturm my regards. Oh, and Tasslehoff"—the old magician looked at him shrewdly—"you did the right thing, my boy!"

"I did?" Tas said hopefully. "I'm glad." He hesitated. "I wondered . . . about what you said—the dark path. Did I—?"

Fizban's face grew grave as he gripped Tas firmly on the shoulder "I'm afraid so. But you have the courage to walk it."

"I hope so," Tas said with a small sigh. "Well, good-bye. I'll be back. Just as soon as the war's over."

"Oh, I probably won't be here," Fizban said, shaking his head so violently his hat slid off. "Soon as the new weapon's perfected, I'll be leaving for—" he paused. "Where was that I was supposed to go? I can't seem to recall. But don't worry. We'll meet again. At least you're not leaving me buried under a pile of chicken feathers!" he muttered, searching for his hat.

Tas picked it up and handed it to him.

"Good-bye," the kender said, a choke in his voice.

"Good-bye, good-bye!" Fizban waved cheerfully. Then—giving the gnomes a hunted glance—he pulled Tas over to him. "Uh, I seem to have forgotten something. What was my name again?"

Someone else said good-bye to the old magician, too, although not under quite the same circumstances.

Elistan was pacing the shore of Sancrist, waiting for the boat that would take him back to Southern Ergoth. The young man, Douglas, walked along beside him. The two were deep in conversation, Elistan explaining the ways of the ancient gods to a rapt and attentive listener.

Suddenly Elistan looked up to see the old, befuddled magician he had seen at the Council meeting. Elistan had tried for days to meet the old mage, but Fizban always avoided him. Thus it was with astonishment Elistan saw the old man come walking toward them now along the shoreline. His head was bowed, he was muttering to himself. For a moment, Elistan thought he would pass by without noticing them, when suddenly the old mage raised his head.

"Oh, I say! Haven't we met?" he asked, blinking.

For a moment Elistan could not speak. The cleric's face turned deathly white beneath its weathered tan. He was finally able to answer the old mage, his voice was husky. "Indeed we have, sir. I did not realize it before now. And though we were but lately introduced, I feel that I have known you a long, long time."

"Indeed?" The old man scowled suspiciously. "You're not making some sort of comment on my age, are you?"

"No, certainly not!" Elistan smiled.

The old man's face cleared.

"Well, have a pleasant journey. And a safe one. Farewell."

Leaning on a bent and battered staff, the old man toddled on past them. Suddenly he stopped and turned around. "Oh, by the way, the name's Fizban."

"I'll remember," Elistan said gravely, bowing. "Fizban."

Pleased, the old magician nodded and continued on his way along the shoreline while Elistan, suddenly thoughtful and quiet, resumed his walk with a sigh.

8

The Perechon

Memories of long ago.

his is crazy, I hope you realize that!" Caramon hissed.

"We wouldn't be here if we were sane, would we?" Tanis responded, gritting his teeth.

"No," Caramon muttered. "I suppose you're right."

The two men stood in the shadows of a dark alleyway, in a town where generally the only things ever found in alleyways were rats, drunks, and dead bodies.

The name of the wretched town was Flotsam, and it was well named, for it lay upon the shores of the Blood Sea of Istar like the wreckage of a broken vessel tossed upon the rocks. Peopled by the dregs of most of the races of Krynn, Flotsam was, in addition, an occupied town now, overrun with draconians, goblins, and mercenaries of all races, attracted to the Highlords by high wages and the spoils of war.

And so, "like the other scum," as Raistlin observed, the companions floated along upon the tides of war and were deposited in Flotsam. Here they hoped to find a ship that would take them on the long, treacherous journey around the northern part of Ansalon to Sancrist—or wherever—

Where they were going was a point that had been much in contention lately—ever since Raistlin's recovery from his illness. The companions had anxiously watched him following his use of the dragon orb, their concern not completely centered on his health. What had happened when he used the orb? What harm might he have brought upon them?

"You need not fear," Raistlin told them in his whispering voice. "I am not weak and foolish like the elven king. I gained control of the orb. It did not gain control of me."

"Then what does it do? How can we use it?" Tanis asked, alarmed by the frozen expression on the mage's metallic face.

"It took all my strength to gain control of the orb," Raistlin replied, his eyes on the ceiling above his bed. "It will require much more study before I learn how to use it."

"Study . . ." Tanis repeated. "Study of the orb?"

Raistlin flicked him a glance, then resumed staring at the ceiling. "No," he replied. "The study of books, written by the ancient ones who created the orb. We must go to Palanthas, to the library of one Astinus, who resides there."

Tanis was silent for a moment. He could hear the mage's breath rattle in his lungs as he struggled to draw breath.

What keeps him clinging to this life? Tanis wondered silently.

It had snowed that morning, but now the snow had changed to rain. Tanis could hear it drumming on the wooden roof of the wagon. Heavy clouds drifted across the sky. Perhaps it was the gloom of the day, but as he looked at Raistlin, Tanis felt a chill creep through his body until the cold seemed to freeze his heart.

"Was this what you meant, when you spoke of ancient spells?" Tanis asked.

"Of course. What else?" Raistlin paused, coughing, then asked,"When did I speak of . . . ancient spells?"

"When we first found you," Tanis answered, watching the mage closely. He noticed a crease in Raistlin's forehead and heard tension in his shattered voice.

"What did I say?"

"Nothing much," Tanis replied warily. "Just something about ancient spells, spells that would soon be yours."

"That was all?"

Tanis did not reply immediately. Raistlin's strange, hourglass eyes focused on him coldly. The half-elf shivered and nodded. Raistlin turned his head away. His eyes closed. "I will sleep now," he said softly. "Remember, Tanis. Palanthas."

Tanis was forced to admit he wanted to go to Sancrist for purely selfish reasons. He hoped against hope that Laurana and Sturm and the others would be there. And it was where he had promised he would take the dragon orb. But against this, he had to weigh Raistlin's steady insistence that they must go to the library of this Astinus to discover how to use the orb.

His mind was still in a quandary when they reached Flotsam. Finally, he decided they would set about getting passage on a ship going north first and decide where to land later.

But when they reached Flotsam, they had a nasty shock. There were more draconians in that city than they had seen on their entire journey from Port Balifor north. The streets were crawling with heavily armed patrols, taking an intense interest in strangers. Fortunately, the companions had sold their wagon before entering the town, so they were able to mingle with the crowds on the streets. But they hadn't been inside the city gates five minutes before they saw a draconian patrol arrest a human for "questioning."

This alarmed them, so they took rooms in the first inn they came to—a run-down place at the edge of town.

"How are we going to even get to the harbor, much less buy passage on a ship?" Caramon asked as they settled into their shabby rooms. "What's going on?"

"The innkeeper says a Dragon Highlord is in town. The draconians are searching for spies or something," Tanis muttered uncomfortably. The companions exchanged glances.

"Maybe they're searching for *us*," Caramon said.

"That's ridiculous!" Tanis answered quickly—too quickly. "We're getting spooked. How could anyone know we're here? Or know what we carry?"

"I wonder . . ." Riverwind said grimly, glancing at Raistlin.

The mage returned his glance coolly, not deigning to answer. "Hot water for my drink," he instructed Caramon.

"There's only one way I can think of," Tanis said, as Caramon brought his brother the water as ordered. "Caramon and I will go out tonight and waylay two of the dragonarmy soldiers. We'll steal their uniforms. Not the draconians—" he said hastily, as Caramon's brow wrinkled in disgust. "The human mercenaries. Then we can move around Flotsam freely."

After some discussion, everyone agreed it was the only plan that seemed likely to work. The companions ate dinner without much appetite—dining in their rooms rather than risk going into the common room.

"You'll be all right?" Caramon asked Raistlin uneasily when the two were alone in the room they shared.

"I am quite capable of taking care of myself," Raistlin replied. Rising to his feet, he had picked up a spellbook to study, when a fit of coughing doubled him over.

Caramon reached out his hand, but Raistlin flinched away.

"Be gone!" the mage gasped. "Leave me be!"

Caramon hesitated, then he sighed. "Sure, Raist," he said, and left the room, shutting the door gently behind him.

Raistlin stood for a moment, trying to catch his breath. Then he moved slowly across the room, setting down the spellbook. With a trembling hand, he picked up one of the many sacks that Caramon had placed on the table beside his bed. Opening it, Raistlin carefully withdrew the dragon orb.

Tanis and Caramon—the half-elf keeping his hood pulled low over his face and ears—walked the streets of Flotsam, watching for two guards whose uniforms might fit them. This would have been relatively easy for Tanis, but finding a guard whose armor fit the giant Caramon was more difficult.

They both knew they had better find something quickly. More than once, draconians looked them over suspiciously. Two draconians even stopped them, insisting roughly on knowing their business. Caramon replied in the crude mercenary dialect that they were seeking employment in the Dragon Highlord's army, and the draconians let them go. But both men knew it was only a matter of time before a patrol caught them.

"I wonder what's going on?" Tanis muttered worriedly.

"Maybe the war's heating up for the Highlords," Caramon began. "There, look, Tanis. Going into that bar—"

"I see. Yeah, he's about your size. Duck into that alley. We'll wait until they come out, then—" The half-elf made a motion of wringing a neck. Caramon nodded. The two slipped through the filthy streets and vanished into the alley, hiding where they could keep on eye on the front door of the bar.

It was nearly midnight. The moons would not rise tonight. The rain had ceased, but clouds still obscured the sky. The two men crouched in the alley were soon shivering, despite their heavy cloaks. Rats skittered across their feet, making them cringe in the darkness. A drunken hobgoblin took a wrong turn and lurched past them, falling headfirst into a pile of garbage. The hobgoblin did not get back up again and the stench nearly made Tanis and Caramon sick, but they dared not leave their vantage point.

Then they heard welcome sounds—drunken laughter and human voices speaking Common. The two guards they had been waiting for lurched out of the bar and staggered toward them.

A tall iron brazier stood on the sidewalk, lighting the night. The mercenaries lurched into its light, giving Tanis a close look at them. Both were officers in the dragonarmy, he saw. Newly promoted, he guessed, which may have been what they were celebrating. Their armor was shining new, relatively clean, and undented. It was good armor, too, he saw with satisfaction. Made of blue steel, it was fashioned after the style of the Highlords' own dragon-scale armor.

"Ready?" Caramon whispered. Tanis nodded.

Caramon drew his sword. "Elven scum!" he roared in his deep, barrel-chested bass. "I've found you out, and now you'll come with me to the Dragon Highlord, spy!"

"You'll never take me alive!" Tanis drew his own sword.

At the sound of their voices, the two officers staggered to a stop, peering bleary-eyed into the dark alley.

The officers watched with growing interest as Caramon and Tanis made a few passes at each other, maneuvering themselves into position. When Caramon's back was to the officers and Tanis was facing them, the half-elf made a sudden move. Disarming Caramon, he sent the warrior's sword flying.

"Quick! Help me take him!" Caramon bellowed. "There's a reward out for him—dead or alive!"

The officers never hesitated. Fumbling drunkenly for their weapons, they headed for Tanis, their faces twisted into expressions of cruel pleasure.

"That's it! Nail 'im!" Caramon urged, waiting until they were past him. Then—just as they raised their swords—Caramon's huge hands encircled their necks. He slammed their heads together, and the bodies slumped to the ground.

"Hurry!" Tanis grunted. He dragged one body by the feet away from the light. Caramon followed with the other. Quickly they began to strip off the armor.

"Phew! This one must have been half-troll," Caramon said, waving his hand to clear the air of the foul smell.

"Quit complaining!" Tanis snapped, trying to figure out how the complex system of buckles and straps worked. "At least you're used to wearing this stuff. Give me a hand with this, will you?"

"Sure." Caramon, grinning, helped to buckle Tanis into the armor. "An elf in plate armor. What's the world coming to?"

"Sad times," Tanis muttered. "When are we supposed to meet that ship captain William told you about?"

"He said we could find her on board around daybreak."

"The name's Maquesta Kar-thon," said the woman, her expression cool and businesslike. "And—let me guess—you're *not* officers in the dragonarmy. Not unless they're hiring elves these days."

Tanis flushed, slowly drawing off the helm of the officer. "Is it that obvious?"

The woman shrugged. "Probably not to anyone else. The beard is very good—perhaps I should say half-elf, of course. And the helm hides your ears. But unless you get a mask, those pretty, almond shaped eyes of yours are a dead give-away. But then, not many draconians are apt to look into your pretty eyes, are they?" Leaning back in her chair, she put a booted foot on a table, and regarded him coolly.

Tanis heard Caramon chuckle, and felt his skin burn.

They were on board the *Perechon,* sitting in the captain's cabin, across from the captain herself. Maquesta Kar-thon was one of the dark-skinned race living in Northern Ergoth. Her people had been sailors for centuries and, it was popularly believed, could speak the languages of seabirds and dolphins. Tanis found himself thinking of Theros Ironfeld as he looked at Maquesta. The woman's skin was shining black, her hair tightly curled and bound with a gold band around her forehead. Her eyes were brown and shining as her skin. But there was the glint of steel from the dagger at her belt, and the glint of steel in her eyes.

"We're here to discuss business, Captain Maque—" Tanis stumbled over the strange name.

"Sure you are," the woman said. "And call me Maq. Easier for both of us. It's well you have this letter from Pig-faced William, or I wouldn't have even talked to you. But he says you're square and your money's good, so I'll listen. Now, where're you bound?"

Tanis exchanged glances with Caramon. That was the question. Besides, he wasn't certain he wanted either of their destinations known. Palanthas was the capital city of Solamnia, while Sancrist was a well-known haven of the Knights.

"Oh, for the love of—" Maq snapped, seeing them hesitate. Her eyes flared. Removing her foot from the table, she stared at them grimly. "You either trust me or you don't!"

"Should we?" Tanis asked bluntly.

Maq raised an eyebrow. "How much money do you have?"

"Enough," Tanis said. "Let's just say that we want to go north, around the Cape of Nordmaar. If, at that point, we still find each other's company agreeable, we'll go on. If not, we'll pay you off, and you put us in a safe harbor."

"Kalaman," said Maq, settling back. She seemed amused. "That's a safe harbor. As safe as any these days. Half your money now. Half at Kalaman. Any farther is negotiable."

"*Safe* delivery to Kalaman," Tanis amended.

"Who can promise?" Maq shrugged. "It's a rough time of year to travel by sea." She rose languidly, stretching like a cat. Caramon, standing up quickly, stared at her admiringly.

"It's a deal," she said. "Come on. I'll show you the ship."

Maq led them onto the deck. The ship seemed fit and trim as far as Tanis, who knew nothing about ships, could tell. Her voice and manner had been cold when they first talked to her, but when she showed them around her ship, she seemed to warm up. Tanis had seen the same expression, heard the same warm tones Maq used in talking about her ship that Tika used when talking about Caramon. The *Perechon* was obviously Maq's only love.

The ship was quiet, empty. Her crew was ashore, along with her first mate, Maq explained. The only other person Tanis saw on board was a man sitting by himself, mending a sail. The man looked up as they passed, and Tanis saw his eyes widen in alarm at the sight of the dragon armor.

"*Nocesta,* Berem," Maq said to him soothingly as they passed. She made a slashing motion with her hand, gesturing to Tanis and Caramon. "*Nocesta.* Customers. Money."

The man nodded and went back to his work.

"Who is he?" Tanis asked Maq in a low voice as they walked toward her cabin once more to conclude their business.

"Who? Berem?" she asked, glancing around. "He's the helmsman. Don't know much about him. He came around a few months back, looking for work. Took him on as a deckswab. Then my helmsman was killed in a small altercation with—well, never mind. But this fellow turned out to be a damn good hand at the wheel, better than the first, in fact. He's an odd one, though. A mute. Never speaks. Never goes ashore, if he can help it. Wrote his name down for me in the ship's book, or I wouldn't have known that much about him. Why?" she asked, noticing Tanis studying the man intently.

Berem was tall, well-built. At first sight, one might guess him to be middle-aged, by human terms. His hair was gray; his face was clean shaven, deeply tanned, and weathered from months spent on board ship. But his eyes were youthful, clear, and bright. The hands that held the needle were smooth and strong, the hands of a young man. Elven blood, perhaps, Tanis thought, but if so it wasn't apparent in any of his features.

"I've seen him somewhere," Tanis murmured. "How about you, Caramon? Do you remember him?"

"Ah, come on," said the big warrior. "We've seen hundreds of people this past month, Tanis. He was probably in the audience at one of our shows.

"No." Tanis shook his head. "When I first saw him, I thought of Pax Tharkas and Sturm. . . ."

"Hey, I got a lot of work to do, half-elf," Maquesta said. "You coming, or you gonna gawk at a guy stitching a sail?"

She climbed down the hatch. Caramon followed clumsily, his sword and armor clanking. Reluctantly, Tanis went after them. But he turned for one final look at the man, and caught the man regarding him with a strange, penetrating gaze.

"All right, you go back to the inn with the others. I'll buy the supplies. We sail when the ship's ready. Maquesta says about four days."

"I wish it was sooner," muttered Caramon.

"So do I," said Tanis grimly. "There's too damn many draconians around here. But we've got to wait for the tide or some such thing. Go back to the inn and keep everyone inside. Tell your brother to lay in a store of that herb stuff he drinks—we'll be at sea a long time. I'll be back in a few hours, after I get the supplies."

Tanis walked down the crowded streets of Flotsam, no one giving him a second glance in his dragon armor. He would be glad to take it off. It was hot, heavy and itchy. And he had trouble remembering to return the salutes of draconians and goblins. It was beginning to occur to him— as he saw the respect his uniform commanded—that the humans they stole the uniforms from must have held a high rank. The thought was not comforting. Any moment now, someone might recognize his armor.

But he couldn't do without it, he knew. There were more draconians in the streets than ever today. The air of tension in Flotsam was high. Most of the town's citizens were staying home, and most of the shops were closed—with the exception of the taverns. In fact, as he passed one closed shop after another, Tanis began to worry about where he was going to buy supplies for the long ocean voyage.

Tanis was musing on this problem as he stared into a closed shop window, when a hand suddenly wrapped around his boot and yanked him to the ground.

The fall knocked the breath from the half-elf's body. He struck his head heavily on the cobblestones and—for a moment—was groggy with pain. Instinctively he kicked out at whatever had him by the feet, but the hands that grasped him were strong. He felt himself being dragged into a dark alley.

Shaking his head to clear it, he strained to look at his captor. It was an elf! His clothes filthy and torn, his elven features distorted by grief and hatred, the elf stood above him, a spear in his hand.

"Dragon man!" the elf snarled in Common. "Your foul kind slaughtered my family—my wife and my children! Murdered them in their beds, ignoring their pleas for mercy. This is for them!" The elf raised his spear.

"*Shak! It mo dracosali!*" Tanis cried desperately in elven, struggling to pull off his helmet. But the elf, driven insane by grief, was beyond hearing or understanding. His spear plunged downward. Suddenly the elf's eyes grew wide, riveted in shock. The spear fell from his nerveless fingers as a sword punctured him from behind. The dying elf fell with a shriek, landing heavily upon the pavement.

Tanis looked up in astonishment to see who had saved his life. A Dragon Highlord stood over the elf's body.

"I heard you shouting and saw one of my officers in trouble. I guessed you needed some help," said the Highlord, reaching out a gloved hand to help Tanis up.

Confused, dizzy with pain and knowing only that he mustn't give himself away, Tanis accepted the Highlord's hand and struggled to his feet. Ducking his face, thankful for the dark shadows in the alley, Tanis mumbled words of thanks in a harsh voice. Then he saw the Highlord's eyes behind the mask widen.

"Tanis?"

The half-elf felt a shudder run through his body, a pain as swift and sharp as the elven spear. He could not speak, he could only stare as the Highlord swiftly removed the blue and gold dragonmask.

"Tanis! It *is* you!" the Highlord cried, grasping him by the arms. Tanis saw bright brown eyes, a crooked, charming smile.

"Kitiara . . ."

9

Tanis captured.

o, Tanis! An officer, and in my own command. I should review my troops more often!" Kitiara laughed, sliding her arm through his. "You're shaking. You took a nasty fall. Come on. My rooms aren't far from here. We'll have a drink, patch up that wound, then . . . talk."

Dazed—but not from the head wound—Tanis let Kitiara lead him out of the alley onto the sidewalk. Too much had happened too fast. One minute he had been buying supplies and now he was walking arm in arm with a Dragon Highlord who had just saved his life and who was also the woman he had loved for so many years. He could not help but stare at her, and Kitiara—knowing his eyes were on her—returned his gaze from beneath her long, sooty-black eyelashes.

The gleaming, night-blue dragon-scale armor of the Highlords suited her well, Tanis caught himself thinking. It was tight-fitting, emphasizing the curves of her long legs.

Draconians swarmed around them, hoping for even a brief nod from the Highlord. But Kitiara ignored them, chatting breezily with Tanis as if it were only an afternoon since they had parted, instead of five years. He could not absorb her words, his brain was still fumbling to make sense of this, while his body was reacting—once again—to her nearness.

The mask had left her hair somewhat damp, the curls clung to her face and forehead. Casually she ran her gloved hand through her hair, shaking it out. It was an old habit of hers and that small gesture brought back memories—

Tanis shook his head, struggling desperately to pull his shattered world together and attend to her words. The lives of his friends depended on what he did now.

"It's hot beneath that dragon helm!" she was saying. "I don't need the frightful thing to keep my men in line. Do I?" she asked, winking.

"N-no," Tanis stammered, feeling himself flush.

"Same old Tanis," she murmured, pressing her body against his."You still blush like a schoolboy. But you were never like the others, never. . ." she added softly. Pulling him close, she put her arms around him. Closing her eyes, her moist lips brushed his. . . .

"Kit—" Tanis said in a strangled voice, wrenching backward. "Not here! Not in the street," he added lamely.

For a moment Kitiara regarded him angrily, then—shrugging, she dropped her hand down to clasp his arm again. Together they continued along the street, the draconians leering and joking.

"Same Tanis," she said again, this time with a little, breathless sigh."I don't know why I let you get away with it. Any other man who refused me like that would have died on my sword. Ah, here we are."

She entered the best inn in Flotsam, the Saltbreeze. Built high on a cliff, it overlooked the Blood Sea of Istar, whose waves broke on the rocks below. The innkeeper hurried forward.

"Is my room made up?" Kit asked coolly.

"Yes, Highlord," the innkeeper said, bowing again and again. As they ascended the stairs, the innkeeper hustled ahead of them to make certain that all was in order.

Kit glanced around. Finding everything satisfactory, she casually tossed the dragonhelm on a table and began pulling off her gloves. Sitting down in a chair, she raised her leg with sensual and deliberate abandon.

"My boots," she said to Tanis, smiling.

Swallowing, giving her a weak smile in return, Tanis gripped her leg in his hands. This had been an old game of theirs, him taking off her boots. It had always led to—Tanis tried to keep himself from thinking about that!

"Bring us a bottle of your finest wine," Kitiara told the hovering innkeeper, "and two glasses." She raised her other leg, her brown eyes on Tanis. "Then leave us alone."

"But—my lord—" the innkeeper said hesitantly, "there have been messages from Dragon Highlord Ariakas. . . ."

"If you show your face in this room—*after* you bring the wine—I'll cut off your ears," Kitiara said pleasantly. But, as she spoke, she drew a gleaming dagger from her belt.

The innkeeper turned pale, nodded, and left hurriedly.

Kit laughed. "There!" she said, wiggling her toes in their blue silken hose. "Now, I'll take off your boots—"

"I—I really must go," Tanis said, sweating beneath his armor. "My c-company commander will be missing me . . ."

"But *I'm* commander of your company!" Kit said gaily. "And tomorrow *you'll* be commander of your company. Or higher, if you like. Now, sit down."

Tanis could do nothing but obey, knowing, however, that in his heart he *wanted* to do nothing but obey.

"It's so good to see you," Kit said, kneeling before him and tugging at his boot. "I'm sorry I missed the reunion in Solace. How is everyone? How is Sturm? Probably fighting with the Knights, I suppose. I'm not surprised you two separated. That was one friendship I never could understand—"

Kitiara talked on, but Tanis ceased to listen. He could only look at her. He had forgotten how lovely she was, how sensual, inviting. Desperately he concentrated on his own danger. But all he could think of were nights of bliss spent with Kitiara.

At that moment, Kit looked up into his eyes. Caught and held by the passion she saw in them, she let his boot slip from her hands. Involuntarily, Tanis reached out and drew her near. Kitiara slid her hand around his neck and pressed her lips against his.

At her touch, the desires and longings that had tormented Tanis for five years surged through his body. Her fragrance, warm and womanly—mingled with the smell of leather and steel. Her kiss was like flame. The pain was unbearable. Tanis knew only one way to end it.

When the innkeeper knocked on the door, he received no answer. Shaking his head in admiration—this was the third man in as many days—he set the wine upon the floor and left.

"And now," Kitiara murmured sleepily, lying in Tanis's arms. "Tell me about my little brothers. Are they with you? The last I saw them, you were escaping from Tarsis with that elf woman."

"That was you!" Tanis said, remembering the blue dragons.

"Of course!" Kit cuddled nearer. "I like the beard," she said, stroking his face. "It hides those weak elvish features. How did you get into the army?"

How indeed? thought Tanis frantically.

"We . . . were captured in Silvanesti. One of the officers convinced me I was a fool to fight the D-Dark Queen."

"And my little brothers?"

"We—we were separated," Tanis said weakly.

"A pity," Kit said with a sigh. "I'd like to see them again. Caramon must be a giant by now. And Raistlin—I hear he is quite a skilled mage. Still wearing the Red Robes?"

"I—I guess," Tanis muttered. "I haven't seen him—"

"That won't last long," Kit said complacently. "He's like me. Raist always craved power . . ."

"What about you?" Tanis interrupted quickly. "What are you doing here, so far from the action? The fighting's north—"

"Why, I'm here for the same reason you are," Kit answered, opening her eyes wide. "Searching for the Green Gemstone Man, of course."

"That's where I've seen him before!" Tanis said, memories flooding his mind. The man on the *Perechon*! The man in Pax Tharkas, escaping with poor Eben. The man with the green gemstone embedded in the center of his chest.

"You've found him!" Kitiara said, sitting up eagerly. "Where, Tanis? Where?" Her brown eyes glittered.

"I'm not sure," Tanis said, faltering. "I'm not sure it was him. I—we were just given a rough description. . . ."

"He looks about fifty in human years," Kit said in excitement, "but he has strange, young eyes, and his hands are young. And in the flesh of his chest is a green gemstone. We had reports he was sighted in Flotsam. That's why the Dark Queen sent me here. He's the key, Tanis! Find him—and no force on Krynn can stop us!"

"Why?" Tanis made himself ask calmly. "What's he got that's so essential to—uh—our side winning this war?"

"Who knows?" Shrugging her slender shoulders, Kit lay back in Tanis's arms. "You're shivering. Here, this will warm you." She kissed his neck, running her hands over his body. "We were just told the most important thing we could do to end this war in one swift stroke is to find this man."

Tanis swallowed, feeling himself warming to her touch.

"Just think," Kitiara whispered in his ear, her breath hot and moist against his skin, "if we found him—you and I—we would have all of Krynn at our feet! The Dark Queen would reward us beyond anything we ever dreamed! You and I, together always, Tanis. Let's go now!"

Her words echoed in his mind. The two of them, together, forever. Ending the war. Ruling Krynn. No, he thought, feeling his throat constrict. This is madness! Insanity! My people, my friends. . . . Yet, haven't I done enough? What do I owe any of them, humans or elves? Nothing! They are the ones who have hurt me, derided me! All these years, a cast-out. Why think about them? *Me!* It's time I thought about *me* for a change! This is the woman I've dreamed of for so long. And she can be mine! Kitiara . . . so beautiful, so desirable . . .

"No!" Tanis said harshly, then, "No," he said more gently. Reaching out his hand, he pulled her back near him. "Tomorrow will do. If it was him, he isn't going anywhere. I know. . . ."

Kitiara smiled and, with a sigh, lay back down. Tanis, bending over her, kissed her passionately. Far away, he could hear the waves of the Blood Sea of Istar crashing on the shore.

10

The High Clerist's Tower.

The knighting.

y morning, the storm over Solamnia had blown itself out. The sun rose, a disk of pale gold that warmed nothing. The knights who stood watch upon the battlements of the Tower of the High Clerist went thankfully to their beds, talking of the wonders they had seen during the awful night, for such a storm as this had not been known in the lands of Solamnia since the days after the Cataclysm. Those who took over the watch from their fellow knights were nearly as weary; no one had slept.

Now they looked out upon a plain covered with snow and ice. Here and there the landscape was dotted with flickering flames where trees, blasted by the jagged lightning that had streaked out of the sky during the blizzard, burned eerily. But it was not to those strange flames the eyes of the knights turned as they ascended the battlements. It was to the flames that burned upon the horizon—hundreds and hundreds of flames, filling the clear, cold air with their foul smoke.

The campfires of war. The campfires of the dragonarmies.

One thing stood between the Dragon Highlord and victory in Solamnia. That "thing" (as the Highlord often referred to it) was the Tower of the High Clerist. Built long ago by Vinas Solamnus, founder of the Knights, in the only pass through the snow-capped, cloud-shrouded Vingaard Mountains, the Tower protected Palanthas, capital city of Solamnia, and the harbor known as the Gates of Paladine. Let the Tower fall, and Palanthas would belong to the dragonarmies. It was a soft city—a city of wealth and beauty, a city that had turned its back upon the world to gaze with admiring eyes into its own mirror.

With Palanthas in her hands and the harbor under her control, the Highlord could easily starve the rest of Solamnia into submission and then wipe out the troublesome Knights.

The Dragon Highlord, called the Dark Lady by her troops, was not in camp this day. She was gone on secret business to the east. But she had left loyal and able commanders behind her, commanders who would do anything to win her favor.

Of all the Dragon Highlords, the Dark Lady was known to sit highest in the regard of her Dark Queen. And so the troops of draconians, goblins, hobgoblins, ogres, and humans sat around their campfires, staring at the Tower with hungry eyes, longing to attack and earn her commendation.

The Tower was defended by a large garrison of Knights of Solamnia who had marched out from Palanthas only a few weeks ago. Legend recalled that the Tower had never fallen while men of faith held it, dedicated as it was to the High Clerist—that position which, second only to the Grand Master, was most revered in the Knighthood.

The clerics of Paladine had lived in the High Clerist's Tower during the Age of Dreams. Here young knights had come for their religious training and indoctrination. There were still many traces of the clerics' presence left behind.

It wasn't only fear of the legend that forced the dragonarmies to sit idle. It didn't take a legend to tell their commanders that taking this tower was going to be costly.

"Time is in our favor," stated the Dark Lady before she left. "Our spies tell us the knights have received little help from Palanthas. We've cut off their supplies from Vingaard Keep to the east. Let them sit in their tower and starve. Sooner or later their impatience and their stomachs will cause them to make a mistake. When they do, we will be ready."

"We could take it with a flight of dragons," muttered a young commander. His name was Bakaris, and his bravery in battle and his handsome face had done much to advance him in the Dark Lady's favor. She eyed him speculatively, however, as she prepared to mount her blue dragon, Skie.

"Perhaps not," she said coolly. "You've heard the reports of the discovery of the ancient weapon—the dragonlance?"

"Bah! Children's stories!" The young commander laughed as he assisted her onto Skie's back. The blue dragon stood glaring at the handsome commander with fierce, fiery eyes.

"Never discount children's stories," the Dark Lady said, "for these were the same tales that were told of dragons." She shrugged. "Do not worry, my pet. If my mission to capture the Green Gemstone Man is successful, we will not need to attack the Tower, for its destruction will be assured. If not, perhaps I will bring you that flight of dragons you ask for."

With that, the giant blue lifted his wings and sailed off toward the east, heading for a small and wretched town called Flotsam on the Blood Sea of Istar.

And so the dragonarmies waited, warm and comfortable around their fires, while—as the Dark Lady had predicted—the knights in their Tower starved. But far worse than the lack of food was the bitter dissension within their own ranks.

The young knights under Sturm Brightblade's command had grown to revere their disgraced leader during the hard months that followed their departure from Sancrist. Although melancholy and often aloof, Sturm's honesty and integrity won him his men's respect and admiration. It was a costly victory, causing Sturm a great deal of suffering at Derek's hands. A less noble man might have turned a blind eye to Derek's political maneuvers, or at least kept his mouth shut (as did Lord Alfred), but Sturm spoke out against Derek constantly—even though he knew it worsened his own cause with the powerful knight.

It was Derek who had completely alienated the people of Palanthas. Already distrustful, filled with old hatreds and bitterness, the people of the beautiful, quiet city were alarmed and angered by Derek's threats when they refused to allow the Knights to garrison the city. It was only through Sturm's patient negotiations that the knights received any supplies at all.

The situation did not improve when the knights reached the High Clerist's Tower. The disruption among the knights lowered the morale of the footmen, already suffering from a lack of food. Soon the Tower itself became an armed camp—the majority of knights who favored Derek were now openly opposed by those siding with Lord Gunthar, led by Sturm. It was only because of the knights' strict obedience to the Measure that fights within the Tower itself had not yet broken out. But the demoralizing sight of the dragonarmies camped nearby, as well as the lack of food, led to frayed tempers and taut nerves.

Too late, Lord Alfred realized their danger. He bitterly regretted his own folly in supporting Derek, for he could see clearly now that Derek Crownguard was going insane.

The madness grew on him daily; Derek's lust for power ate away at him and deprived him of his reason. But Lord Alfred was powerless to act. So locked into their rigid structure were the knights that it would take—according to the Measure—months of Knights Councils to strip Derek of his rank.

News of Sturm's vindication struck this dry and crackling forest like a bolt of lightning. As Gunthar had foreseen, this completely shattered Derek's hopes. What Gunthar had not foreseen was that this would sever Derek's tenuous hold on sanity.

On the morning following the storm, the eyes of the guards turned for a moment from their vigilance over the dragonarmies to look down into the courtyard of the Tower of the High Clerist. The sun filled the gray sky with a chill, pale light that was reflected in the coldly gleaming armor of the Knights of Solamnia as they assembled in the solemn ceremony awarding knighthood.

Above them, the flags with the Knight's Crest seemed frozen upon the battlements, hanging lifeless in the still, cold air. Then a trumpet's pure notes split the air, stirring the blood. At that clarion call, the knights lifted their heads proudly and marched into the courtyard.

Lord Alfred stood in the center of a circle of knights. Dressed in his battle armor, his red cape fluttering from his shoulders, he held an antique sword in an old, battered scabbard. The kingfisher, the rose, and the crown—ancient symbols of the Knighthood—were entwined upon the scabbard. The lord cast a swift, hopeful gaze around the assembly, but then lowered his eyes, shaking his head.

Lord Alfred's worst fears were realized. He had hoped bleakly that this ceremony might reunite the knights. But it was having the opposite effect. There were great gaps in the Sacred Circle, gaps that the knights in attendance stared at uncomfortably. Derek and his entire command were absent.

The trumpet call sounded twice more, then silence fell upon the assembled knights. Sturm Brightblade, dressed in long, white robes, stepped out of the Chapel of the High Clerist where he had spent the night in solemn prayer and meditation as prescribed by the Measure. Accompanying him was an unusual Guard of Honor.

Beside Sturm walked an elven woman, her beauty shining in the bleakness of the day like the sun dawning in the spring. Behind her walked an old dwarf, the sunlight bright on his white hair and beard. Next to the dwarf came a kender dressed in bright blue leggings.

The circle of knights opened to admit Sturm and his escorts. They came to a halt before Lord Alfred. Laurana, holding his helm in her hands, stood on his right. Flint, carrying his shield, stood on his left, and after a poke in the ribs from the dwarf—Tasslehoff hurried forward with the knight's spurs.

Sturm bowed his head. His long hair, already streaked with gray though he was only in his early thirties, fell about his shoulders. He stood a moment in silent prayer, then, at a sign from Lord Alfred, fell reverently to his knees.

"Sturm Brightblade," Lord Alfred declared solemnly, opening a sheet of paper, "the Knights Council, on hearing testimony given by Lauralanthalasa of the royal family of Qualinesti and further testimony by Flint Fireforge, hill dwarf of Solace township, has granted you Vindication from the charges brought against you. In recognition of your deeds of bravery and courage as related by these witnesses, you are hereby declared a Knight of Solamnia." Lord Alfred's voices softened as he looked down upon the knight. Tears streamed unchecked down Sturm's gaunt cheeks. "You have spent the night in prayer, Sturm Brightblade," Alfred said quietly. "Do you consider yourself worthy of this great honor?"

"No, my lord," Sturm answered, according to ancient ritual, "but I most humbly accept it and vow that I shall devote my life to making myself worthy." The knight lifted his eyes to the sky. "With Paladine's help," he said softly, "I shall do so."

Lord Alfred had been through many such ceremonies, but he could not recall such fervent dedication in a man's face.

"I wish Tanis were here," Flint muttered gruffly to Laurana, who only nodded briefly.

She stood tall and straight, wearing armor specially made for her in Palanthas at Lord Gunthar's command. Her honey-colored hair streamed from beneath a silver helm. Intricate gold designs glinted on her breastplate, her soft black leather skirt—slit up the side to allow freedom of movement—brushed the tips of her boots. Her face was pale and grim, for the situation in Palanthas and in the Tower itself was dark and seemingly without hope.

She could have returned to Sancrist. She had been ordered to, in fact. Lord Gunthar had received a secret communique from Lord Alfred relating the desperate straits the knights were in, and he had sent Laurana orders to cut short her stay.

But she had chosen to remain, at least for a while. The people of Palanthas had received her politely—she was, after all, of royal blood and they were charmed with her beauty. They were also quite interested in the dragonlance and asked for one to exhibit in their museum. But when Laurana mentioned the dragonarmies, they only shrugged and smiled.

Then Laurana found out from a messenger what was happening in the High Clerist's Tower. The knights were under siege. A dragonarmy numbering in the thousands waited upon the field. The knights needed the dragonlances, Laurana decided, and there was no one but her to take the lances to the knights and teach them their use. She ignored Lord Gunthar's command to return to Sancrist.

The journey from Palanthas to the Tower was nightmarish. Laurana started out accompanying two wagons filled with meager supplies and the precious dragonlances. The first wagon bogged down in snow only a few miles outside of the city. Its contents were redistributed between the few knights riding escort, Laurana and her party, and the second wagon. It, too, foundered. Time and again they dug it out of the snow drifts until, finally, it was mired fast. Loading the food and the lances onto their horses, the knights and Laurana, Flint, and Tas walked the rest of the way. Theirs was the last group to make it through. After the storm of last night, Laurana knew, as did everyone in the Tower, no more supplies would be coming. The road to Palanthas was now impassable.

Even by strictest rationing, the knights and their footmen had food enough for only a few days. The dragonarmies seemed prepared to wait for the rest of the winter.

The dragonlances were taken from the weary horses who had borne them and, by Derek's orders, were stacked in the courtyard. A few of the knights looked at them curiously, then ignored them. The lances seemed clumsy, unwieldy weapons.

When Laurana timidly offered to instruct the knights in the use of the lances, Derek snorted in derision. Lord Alfred stared out the window at the campfires burning on the horizon. Laurana turned to Sturm to see her fears confirmed.

"Laurana," he said gently, taking her cold hand in his, "I don't think the Highlord will even bother to send dragons. If we cannot reopen the supply lines, the Tower will fall because there will be only the dead left to defend it."

So the dragonlances lay in the courtyard, unused, forgotten, their bright silver buried beneath the snow.

II

A kender's curiosity.

The Knights ride forth.

turm and Flint walked the battlements the night of Sturm's knighting, reminiscing.

"A well of pure silver—shining like a jewel—within the heart of the Dragon Mountain," Flint said, awe his voice. "And it was from that silver Theros forged the dragonlances."

"I should have liked—above all things—to have seen Huma's Tomb," Sturm said quietly. Staring out at the campfires on the horizon, he stopped, resting his hand on the ancient stone wall. Torchlight from a nearby window shone on his thin face.

"You will," said the dwarf. "When this is finished, we'll go back. Tas drew a map, not that it's likely to be any good—"

As he grumbled on about Tas, Flint studied his other old friend with concern. The knight's face was grave and melancholy—not unusual for Sturm. But there was something new, a calmness about him that came not from serenity, but from despair.

"We'll go there together," he continued, trying to forget about his hunger. "You and Tanis and I. And the kender, too, I suppose, plus Caramon and Raistlin. I never thought I'd miss that skinny mage, but a magicuser might be handy now. It's just as well Caramon's not here. Can you

---

315

imagine the belly-aching we'd hear about missing a couple of meals?"

Sturm smiled absently, his thoughts far away. When he spoke, it was obvious he hadn't heard a word the dwarf said.

"Flint," he began, his voice soft and subdued, "we need only one day of warm weather to open the road. When that day comes, take Laurana and Tas and leave. Promise me."

"We should all leave if you ask me!" the dwarf snapped. "Pull the knights back to Palanthas. We could hold that town against even dragons, I'll wager. Its buildings are good solid stone. Not like this place!" The dwarf glanced around the human-built Tower with scorn. "Palanthas could be defended."

Sturm shook his head. "The people won't allow it. They care only for their beautiful city. As long as they think it can be saved, they won't fight. No, we must make our stand here."

"You don't have a chance," Flint argued.

"Yes, we do," Sturm replied, "if we can just hold out until the supply lines can be firmly established. We've got enough manpower. That's why the dragonarmies haven't attacked—"

"There's another way," came a voice.

Sturm and Flint turned. The torchlight fell on a gaunt face, and Sturm's expression hardened.

"What way is that, Lord Derek?" Sturm asked with deliberate politeness.

"You and Gunthar believe you have defeated me," Derek said, ignoring the question. His voice was soft and shaking with hatred as he stared at Sturm. "But you haven't! By one heroic act, I will have the Knights in my palm"—Derek held out his mailed hand, the armor flashing in the firelight—"and you and Gunthar will be finished!" Slowly, he clenched his fist.

"I was under the impression our war was out there, with the dragonarmies," Sturm said.

"Don't give me that self-righteous twaddle!" Derek snarled. "Enjoy your knighthood, Brightblade. You paid enough for it. What did you promise the elfwoman in return for her lies? Marriage? Make a respectable woman of her?"

"I cannot fight you—according to the Measure—but I do not have to listen to you insult a woman who is as good as she is courageous," Sturm said, turning upon his heel to leave.

"Don't you ever walk away from me!" Derek cried. Leaping forward, he grabbed Sturm's shoulder. Sturm whirled in anger, his hand on his sword. Derek reached for his weapon as well, and it seemed for a moment that the Measure might be forgotten. But Flint laid a restraining hand on his friend. Sturm drew a deep breath and lifted his hand away from the hilt.

"Say what you have to say, Derek!" Sturm's voice quivered.

"You're finished, Brightblade. Tomorrow I'm leading the knights onto the field. No more skulking in this miserable rock prison. By tomorrow night, my name will be legend!"

Flint looked up at Sturm in alarm. The knight's face had drained of blood. "Derek," Sturm said softly, "you're mad! There are thousands of them! They'll cut you to ribbons!"

"Yes, that's what you'd like to see, isn't it?" Derek sneered. "Be ready at dawn, Brightblade."

That night, Tasslehoff—cold, hungry, and bored—decided that the best way to take his mind off his stomach was to explore his surroundings. *There are plenty of places to hide things here,* thought Tas. *This is one of the strangest buildings I've ever seen.*

The Tower of the High Clerist sat solidly against the west side of the Westgate Pass, the only canyon pass that crossed the Habbakuk Range of mountains separating eastern Solamnia from Palanthas. As the Dragon Highlord knew, anyone trying to reach Palanthas other than by this route would have to travel hundreds of miles around the mountains, or through the desert, or by sea. And ships entering the Gates of Paladine were easy targets for the gnomes' fire-throwing catapults.

The High Clerist's Tower had been built during the Age of Might. Flint knew a lot about the architecture of this period—the dwarves having been instrumental in designing and building most of it. But they had not built or designed this Tower. In fact, Flint wondered who had—figuring the person must have been either drunk or insane.

An outer curtain wall of stone formed an octagon as the Tower's base. Each point of the octagonal wall was surmounted by a turret. Battlements ran along the top of the curtain wall between turrets. An inner octagonal wall formed the base of a series of towers and buttresses that swept gracefully upward to the central Tower itself.

This was fairly standard design, but what puzzled the dwarf was the lack of internal defense points. Three great steel doors breached the outer wall, instead of one door—as would seem most reasonable, since three doors took an incredible number of men to defend. Each door opened into a narrow courtyard at the far end of which stood a portcullis leading directly into a huge hallway. Each of these three hallways met in the heart of the Tower itself!

"Might as well invite the enemy inside for tea!" the dwarf had grumbled. "Stupidest way to build a fortress I ever saw."

No one entered the Tower. To the knights, it was inviolate. The only one who could enter the Tower was the High Clerist himself, and since there was no High Clerist, the knights would defend the Tower walls with their lives, but not one of them could set foot in its sacred halls.

Originally the Tower had merely guarded the pass, not blocked it. But the Palanthians had later built an addition to the main structure that sealed off the pass. It was in this addition that the knights and the footmen were living. No one even thought of entering the Tower itself.

No one except Tasslehoff.

Driven by his insatiable curiosity and his gnawing hunger, the kender made his way along the top of the outer wall. The knights on guard duty eyed him warily, gripping their swords in one hand, their purses in the other. But they relaxed as soon as he passed, and Tas was able to slip down the steps and into the central courtyard.

Only shadows walked down here. No torches burned, no guard was posted. Broad steps led up to the steel portcullis. Tas padded up the stairs toward the great, yawning archway and peered eagerly through the bars. Nothing. He sighed. The darkness beyond was so intense he might have been staring into the Abyss itself.

Frustrated, he pushed up on the portcullis, more out of habit than hope, for only Caramon or ten knights would have the strength necessary to raise it.

To the kender's astonishment, the portcullis began to rise, making the most god-awful screeching! Grabbing for it, Tas dragged it slowly to a halt. The kender looked fearfully up at the battlements, expecting to see the entire garrison thundering down to capture him. But apparently the knights were listening only to the growlings of their empty stomachs.

Tas turned back to the portcullis. There was a small space open between the sharp iron spikes and the stone work, a space just big enough for a kender. Tas didn't waste any time or stop to consider the consequences. Flattening himself, he wriggled beneath the spikes.

He found himself in a large, wide hall, nearly fifty feet across. He could see just a short distance. There were old torches on the wall, however. After a few jumps, Tas reached one and lit it from Flint's tinder box he found in his pouch.

Now Tas could see the gigantic hall clearly. It ran straight ahead, right into the heart of the Tower. Strange columns ranged along either side, like jagged teeth. Peering behind one, he saw nothing but an alcove.

The hall itself was empty. Disappointed, Tas continued walking down it, hoping to find something interesting. He came to a second portcullis, already raised, much to his chagrin. "Anything easy is more trouble than it's worth," was an old kender saying. Tas walked beneath that portcullis into a second hallway, narrower than the first—only about ten feet wide— but with the same strange, toothlike columns on either side.

Why build a tower so easy to enter? Tas wondered. The outer wall was formidable, but once past that, five drunken dwarves could take this place. Tas peered up. And why so huge? The main hall was thirty feet high!

Perhaps the knights back in those days had been giants, the kender speculated with interest as he crept down the hall, peering into open doors and poking into corners.

At the end of the second hallway, he found a third portcullis. This one was different from the other two, and as strange as the rest of the Tower. This portcullis had two halves, which slid together to join in the center. Oddest of all, there was a large hole cut right through the middle of the doors!

Crawling through this hole, Tas found himself in a smaller room. Across from him stood two huge steel doors. Pushing on them casually, he was startled to find them locked. None of the portcullises had been locked. There was nothing to protect.

Well, at least here was something to keep him occupied and make him forget about his empty stomach. Climbing onto a stone bench, Tas stuck his torch into a wall sconce, then began to fumble through his pouches. He finally discovered the set of lock-picking devices that are a kender's birthright—"Why insult the door's purpose by locking it?" is a favorite kender expression.

Quickly Tas selected the proper tool and set to work. The lock was simple. There was a slight click, and Tas pocketed his tools with satisfaction as the door swung inward. The kender stood a moment, listening carefully. He could hear nothing. Peering inside, he could see nothing. Climbing up on the bench again, he retrieved his torch and crept carefully through the steel doors.

Holding his torch aloft, he found himself in a great, wide, circular room. Tas sighed. The great room was empty except for a dust-covered object that resembled an ancient fountain standing squarely in the center. This was the end of the corridor, too, for though there were two more sets of double doors leading out of the room, it was obvious to the kender that they only led back up the other two giant hallways. This was the heart of the Tower. This was the sacred place. This was what all the fuss was about.

Nothing.

Tas walked around a bit, shining his torchlight here and there. Finally the disgruntled kender went to examine the fountain in the center of the room before leaving.

As Tas drew closer, he saw it wasn't a fountain at all, but the dust was so thick, he couldn't figure it out. It was about as tall as the kender, standing four feet off the ground. The round top was supported on a slender three-legged stand.

Tas inspected the object closely, then he took a deep breath and blew as hard as he could. Dust flew up his nose and he sneezed violently, nearly dropping the torch. For a moment he couldn't see a thing. Then the dust settled and he could see the object. His heart leaped into his throat.

"Oh, no!" Tas groaned. Diving into another pouch, he pulled out a handkerchief and rubbed the object. The dust came off easily, and he knew now what it was. "Drat!" he said in despair. "I was right. Now what do I do?"

The sun rose red the next morning, glimmering through a haze of smoke hovering above the dragonarmies. In the courtyard of the Tower of the High Clerist, the shadows of night had not yet lifted before activity began. One hundred knights mounted their horses, adjusted the girths, called for shields, or buckled on armor, while a thousand footmen milled around, searching for their proper places in line.

Sturm, Laurana, and Lord Alfred stood in a dark doorway, watching in silence as Lord Derek, laughing and calling out jokes to his men, rode into the courtyard. The knight was resplendent in his armor, the rose glistening on his breastplate in the first rays of the sun. His men were in good spirits, the thought of battle making them forget their hunger.

"You've got to stop this, my lord," Sturm said quietly.

"I can't!" Lord Alfred said, pulling on his gloves. His face was haggard in the morning light. He had not slept since Sturm awakened him in the waning hours of the night. "The Measure gives him the right to make this decision."

In vain had Alfred argued with Derek, trying to convince him to wait just a few more days! Already the wind was starting to shift, bringing warm breezes from the north.

But Derek had been adamant. He would ride out and challenge the dragonarmies on the field. As for being outnumbered, he laughed in scorn. Since when do goblins fight like Knights of Solamnia? The Knights had been outnumbered fifty to one in the Goblin and Ogre warsof the Vingaard Keep one hundred years ago, and they'd routed the creatures with ease!

"But you'll be fighting draconians," Sturm warned. "They are not like goblins. They are intelligent and skilled. They have magic-users among their ranks, and their weapons are the finest in Krynn. Even in death they have the power to kill—"

"I believe we can deal with them, Brightblade," Derek interrupted harshly. "And now I suggest you wake your men and tell them to make ready."

"I'm not going," Sturm said steadily. "And I'm not ordering my men to go, either."

Derek paled with fury. For a moment he could not speak, he was so angry. Even Lord Alfred appeared shocked.

"Sturm," Alfred began slowly, "do you know what you are doing?"

"Yes, my lord," Sturm answered. "We are the only thing standing between the dragonarmies and Palanthas. We dare not leave this garrison unmanned. I'm keeping my command here."

"Disobeying a direct order," Derek said, breathing heavily. "You are a witness, Lord Alfred. I'll have his *head* this time!" He stalked out. Lord Alfred, his face grim, followed, leaving Sturm alone.

In the end, Sturm had given his men a choice. They could stay with him at no risk to themselves—since they were simply obeying the orders of their commanding officer—or they could accompany Derek. It was, he mentioned, the same choice Vinas Solamnus had given his men long ago, when the Knights rebelled against the corrupt Emperor of Ergoth. The men did not need to be reminded of this legend. They saw it as a sign and, as with Solamnus, most of them chose to stay with the commander they had come to respect and admire.

Now they stood watching, their faces grim, as their friends prepared to ride out. It was the first open break in the long history of the Knighthood, and the moment was grievous.

"Reconsider, Sturm," Lord Alfred said as the knight helped him mount his horse. "Lord Derek is right. The dragonarmies have not been trained, not like the Knights. There's every probability we'll route them with barely a blow being struck."

"I pray that is true, my lord," Sturm said steadily.

Alfred regarded him sadly. "If it *is* true, Brightblade, Derek will see you tried and executed for this. There'll be nothing Gunthar can do to stop him."

"I would willingly die that death, my lord, if it would stop what I fear will happen," Sturm replied.

"Damn it, man!" Lord Alfred exploded. "If we are defeated, what will you gain by staying here? You couldn't hold off an army of gully dwarves with your small contingent of men! Suppose the roads do open up? You won't be able to hold the Tower long enough for Palanthas to send reinforcements."

"At the least we can buy Palanthas time to evacuate her citizens, if—"

Lord Derek Crownguard edged his horse between those of his men. Glaring down at Sturm, his eyes glittering from behind the slits in his helm, Lord Derek raised his hand for silence.

"According to the Measure, Sturm Brightblade," Derek began formally, "I hereby charge you with conspiracy and—"

"To the Abyss with the Measure!" Sturm snarled, his patience snapping. "Where has the Measure gotten us? Divided, jealous, crazed! Even our own people prefer to treat with the armies of our enemies! The Measure has failed!"

A deathly hush settled over the knights in the courtyard, broken only by the restless pawing of a horse or the jingle of armor as here and there a man shifted in his saddle.

"Pray for my death, Sturm Brightblade," Derek said softly, "or by the gods I'll slit your throat at your execution myself!" Without another word, he wheeled his horse around and cantered to the head of the column.

"Open the gates!" he called.

The morning sun climbed above the smoke, rising into the blue sky. The winds blew from the north, fluttering the flag flying bravely from the top of the Tower. Armor flashed. There was a clatter of swords against shields and the sound of a trumpet call as men rushed to open the thick wooden gates.

Derek raised his sword high in the air. Lifting his voice in the Knight's salute to the enemy, he galloped forward. The knights behind him picked up his ringing challenge and rode forth out onto the fields where—long ago—Huma had ridden to glorious victory. The footmen marched, their footsteps beating a tattoo upon the stone pavement. For a moment, Lord Alfred seemed about to speak to Sturm and the young knights who stood watching. But he only shook his head and rode away.

The gates swung shut behind him. The heavy iron bar was dropped down to lock them securely. The men in Sturm's command ran to the battlements to watch.

Sturm stood silently in the center of the courtyard, his gaunt face expressionless.

The young and handsome commander of the dragonarmies in the Dark Lady's absence was just waking to breakfast and the start of another boring day when a scout galloped into camp.

Commander Bakaris glared at the scout in disgust. The man was riding through camp wildly, his horse scattering cooking pots and goblins. Draconian guards leaped to their feet, shaking their fists and cursing. But the scout ignored them.

"The Highlord!" he called, sliding off his horse in front of the tent. "I must see the Highlord."

"The Highlord's gone," said the commander's aide.

"I'm in charge," snapped Bakaris. "What's your business?"

The ranger looked around quickly, not wanting to make a mistake. But there was no sign of the dread Dark Lady or the big blue dragon she rode.

"The Knights have taken the field!"

"What?" The commander's jaw sagged. "Are you certain?"

"Yes!" The scout was practically incoherent. "Saw them! Hundreds on horseback! Javelins, swords. A thousand foot."

"She was right!" Bakaris swore softly to himself in admiration. "The fools have made their mistake!"

Calling for his servants, he hurried back to his tent. "Sound the alarm," he ordered, rattling off instructions. "Have the captains here in five minutes for final orders." His hands shook in eagerness as he strapped on his armor. "And send the wyvern to Flotsam with word for the Highlord."

Goblin servants ran off in all directions, and soon blaring horn calls were echoing throughout the camp. The commander cast one last, quick glance at the map on his table, then left to meet with his officers.

"Too bad," he reflected coolly as he walked away. "The fight will probably be over by the time she gets the news. A pity. She would have wanted to be present at the fall of the High Clerist's Tower. Still," he reflected, "perhaps tomorrow night we'll sleep in Palanthas, she and I."

12

Death on the plains.

Tasslehoff's discovery.

he sun climbed high in the sky. The knights stood upon the battlements of the Tower, staring out across the plains until their eyes ached. All they could see was a great tide of black, crawling figures swarming over the fields, ready to engulf the slender spear of gleaming silver that advanced steadily to meet it.

The armies met. The knights strained to see, but a misty gray veil crept across the land. The air became tainted with a foul smell, like hot iron. The mist grew thicker, almost totally obscuring the sun.

Now they could see nothing. The Tower seemed afloat on a sea of fog. The heavy mist even deadened sound, for at first they heard the clash of weapons and the cries of the dying. But even that faded, and all was silent.

The day wore on. Laurana, pacing restlessly in her darkening chamber, lit candles that sputtered and flickered in the foul air. The kender sat with her. Looking down from her tower window, Laurana could see Sturm and Flint, standing on the battlements below her, reflected in ghostly torchlight.

A servant brought her the bit of maggoty bread and dried meat that was her ration for the day. It must be only midafternoon, she realized. Then movement down on the battlements caught her attention. She saw a man dressed in mud-splattered leather approach Sturm. A messenger, she thought. Hurriedly, she began to strap on her armor.

"Coming?" she asked Tas, thinking suddenly that the kender had been awfully quiet. "A messenger's arrived from Palanthas!"

"I guess," Tas said without interest.

Laurana frowned, hoping he wasn't growing weak from lack of food. But Tas shook his head at her concern.

"I'm all right," he mumbled. "Just this stupid gray air."

Laurana forgot about him as she hurried down the stairs.

"News?" she asked Sturm, who peered over the walls in a vain effort to see out onto the field of battle. "I saw the messenger—"

"Oh, yes." He smiled wearily. "Good news, I suppose. The road to Palanthas is open. The snow melted enough to get through. I have a rider standing by to take a message to Palanthas in case we are def—" He stopped abruptly, then drew a deep breath. "I want you to be ready to go back to Palanthas with him."

Laurana had been expecting this and her answer was prepared. But now that the time had come for her speech, she could not give it. The bitter air dried her mouth, her tongue seemed swollen. No, that wasn't it, she chided herself. She was frightened. Admit it. She *wanted* to go back to Palanthas! She wanted to get out of this grim place where death lurked in the shadows. Clenching her fist, she beat her gloved hand nervously on the stone, gathering her courage.

"I'm staying here, Sturm," she said. After pausing to get her voice under control, she continued, "I know what you're going to say, so listen to me first. You're going to need all the skilled fighters you can get. You know my worth."

Sturm nodded. What she said was true. There were few in his command more accurate with a bow. She was a trained swordsman, as well. She was battle-tested—something he couldn't say about many of the young knights under his command. So he nodded in agreement. He meant to send her away anyhow.

"I am the only one trained to use the dragonlance—"

"Flint's been trained," Sturm interrupted quietly.

Laurana fixed the dwarf with a penetrating stare.

Caught between two people he loved and admired, Flint flushed and cleared his throat. "That's true," he said huskily, "but—uh—I—must admit—er, Sturm, that I *am* a bit short."

"We've seen no sign of dragons, anyhow," Sturm said as Laurana flashed him a triumphant glance. "The reports say they're south of us, fighting for control of Thelgaard."

"But you believe the dragons are on the way, don't you?" Laurana returned.

Sturm appeared uncomfortable. "Perhaps," he muttered.

"You can't lie, Sturm, so don't start now. I'm staying. It's what Tanis would do—"

"Damn it, Laurana!" Sturm said, his face flushed. "Live your own life! *You* can't be Tanis! *I* can't be Tanis! He isn't here! We've got to face that!" The knight turned away suddenly. "He isn't here," he repeated harshly.

Flint sighed, glancing sorrowfully at Laurana. No one noticed Tasslehoff, who sat huddled miserably in a corner.

Laurana put her arm around Sturm. "I know I'm not the friend Tanis is to you, Sturm. I can never take his place. But I'll do my best to help you. That's what I meant. You don't have to treat me any differently from your knights—"

"I know, Laurana," Sturm said. Putting his arm around her, he held her close. "I'm sorry I snapped at you." Sturm sighed. "And you know why I must send you away. Tanis would never forgive me if anything happened to you."

"Yes, he would," Laurana answered softly. "He would understand. He told me once that there comes a time when you've got to risk your life for something that means more than life itself. Don't you see, Sturm? If I fled to safety, leaving my friends behind, he would say he understood. But, deep inside, he wouldn't. Because it is so far from what he would do himself. Besides"—she smiled—"even if there were no Tanis in this world, I still could not leave my friends."

Sturm looked into her eyes and saw that no words of his would make any difference. Silently, he held her close. His other arm went around Flint's shoulder and drew the dwarf near.

Tasslehoff, bursting into tears, stood up and flung himself on them, sobbing wildly. They stared at him in astonishment.

"Tas, what is it?" Laurana asked, alarmed.

"It's all my fault! I broke one! Am I doomed to go around the world breaking these things?" Tas wailed incoherently.

"Calm down," Sturm said, his voice stern. He gave the kender a shake. "What are you talking about?"

"I found another one," Tas blubbered. "Down below, in a big empty chamber."

"Another what, you doorknob?" Flint said in exasperation.

"Another dragon orb!" Tas wailed.

Night settled over the Tower like a thicker, heavier fog. The knights lighted torches, but the flame only peopled the darkness with ghosts. The knights kept silent watch from the battlements, straining to hear or see something, anything. . . .

Then, when it was nearly midnight, they were startled to hear, not the victorious shouts of their comrades or the flat, blaring horns of the enemy, but the jingle of harness, the soft whinny of horses approaching the fortress.

Rushing to the edge of the battlements, the knights shone torches down into the fog. They heard the hoofbeats slowly come to a halt. Sturm stood above the gate.

"Who rides to the Tower of the High Clerist?" he called.

A single torch flared below. Laurana, staring down into the misty darkness, felt her knees grow weak and grabbed the stone wall to support herself. The knights cried out in horror.

The rider who held the flaming torch was dressed in the shining armor of an officer in the dragonarmy. He was blonde, his features handsome, cold, and cruel. He led a second horse across which were thrown two bodies—one of them headless, both bloody, mutilated.

"I have brought back your officers," the man said, his voice harsh and blaring. "One is quite dead, as you can see. The other, I believe, still lives. Or he did when I started on my journey. I hope he is still living, so that he can recount for you what took place upon the field of battle today. If you could even call it a battle."

Bathed in the glare of his own torch, the officer dismounted. He began to untie the bodies, using one hand to strip away the ropes binding them to the saddle. Then he glanced up.

"Yes, you could kill me now. I am a fine target, even in this fog. But you won't. You're Knights of Solamnia"—his sarcasm was sharp—"and your honor is your life. You wouldn't shoot an unarmed man returning the bodies of your leaders." He gave the ropes a yank. The headless body slid to the ground. The officer dragged the other body off the saddle. He tossed the torch down into the snow next to the bodies. It sizzled, then went out, and the darkness swallowed him.

"You have a surfeit of honor out there on the field," he called. The knights could hear the leather creak, his armor clang as he remounted his horse. "I'll give you until morning to surrender. When the sun rises, lower your flag. The Dragon Highlord will deal with you mercifully—"

Suddenly there was the twang of a bow, the thunk of an arrow striking into flesh, and the sound of startled swearing from below them. The knights turned around to stare in astonishment at a lone figure standing on the wall, a bow in its hand.

"I am not a knight," Laurana called out, lowering her bow. "I am Lauralanthalasa, daughter of the Qualinesti. We elves have our own code of honor and, as I'm sure you know, I can see you quite well in this darkness. I could have killed you. As it is, I believe you will have some difficulty using that arm for a long time. In fact, you may never hold a sword again."

"Take that as our answer to your Highlord," Sturm said harshly. "We will lie cold in death before we lower our flag!"

"Indeed you will!" the officer said through teeth clenched in pain. The sound of galloping hooves was lost in the darkness.

"Bring in the bodies," Sturm ordered.

Cautiously, the knights opened the gates. Several rushed out to cover the others who gently lifted the bodies and bore them inside. Then the guard retreated back into the fortress and bolted the gates behind them.

Sturm knelt in the snow beside the body of the headless knight. Lifting the man's hand, he removed a ring from the stiff, cold fingers. The knight's armor was battered and black with blood. Dropping the lifeless hand back into the snow, Sturm bowed his head. "Lord Alfred," he said tonelessly.

"Sir," said one of the young knights, "the other is Lord Derek. The foul dragon officer was right—he is still alive."

Sturm rose and walked over to where Derek lay on the cold stone. The lord's face was white, his eyes wide and glittering feverishly. Blood caked his lips, his skin was clammy. One of the young knights supporting him, held a cup of water to his lips, but Derek could not drink.

Sick with horror, Sturm saw Derek's hand was pressed over his stomach, where his life's blood was welling out, but not fast enough to end the agonizing pain. Giving a ghastly smile, Derek clutched Sturm's arm with a bloody hand.

"Victory!" he croaked. "They ran before us and we pursued! It was glorious, glorious! And I—I will be Grand Master!" He choked and blood spewed from his mouth as he fell back into the arms of the young knight, who looked up at Sturm, his youthful face hopeful.

"Do you suppose he's right, sir? Maybe that was a ruse—" His voice died at the sight of Sturm's grim face, and he looked back at Derek with pity. "He's mad, isn't he, sir?"

"He's dying—bravely—like a true knight," Sturm said.

"Victory!" Derek whispered, then his eyes fixed in his head and he gazed sightlessly into the fog.

"No, you mustn't break it," said Laurana.

"But Fizban said—"

"I know what he said," Laurana replied impatiently. "It isn't evil, it isn't good, it's not anything, it's everything. That"—she muttered—"is so like Fizban!"

She and Tas stood in front of the dragon orb. The orb rested on its stand in the center of the round room, still covered with dust except for the spot Tas had rubbed clean. The room was dark and eerily silent, so quiet, in fact, that Tas and Laurana felt compelled to whisper.

Laurana stared at the orb, her brow creased in thought. Tas stared at Laurana unhappily, afraid he knew what she was thinking.

"These orbs have to work, Tas!" Laurana said finally. "They were created by powerful magic-users! People like Raistlin who do not tolerate failure. If only we knew how—"

"I know how," Tas said in a broken whisper.

"What?" Laurana asked. "You know! Why didn't you—"

"I didn't know I knew—so to speak," Tas stammered. "It just came to me. Gnosh—the gnome—told me that he discovered writing inside the orb, letters that swirled around in the mist. He couldn't read them, he said, because they were written in some sort of strange language—"

"The language of magic."

"Yes, that's what I said and—"

"But that won't help us! We can't either of us speak it. If only Raistlin—"

"We don't need Raistlin," Tas interrupted. "I can't speak it, but I can read it. You see, I have these glasses—glasses of true seeing, Raistlin called them. They let me read languages—even the language of magic. I know because he said if he caught me reading any of his scrolls he'd turn me into a cricket and swallow me whole."

"And you think you can read the orb?"

"I can try," Tas hedged, "but, Laurana, Sturm said there probably wouldn't be any dragons. Why should we risk even bothering with the orb? Fizban said only the most powerful magic-users dared use it."

"Listen to me, Tasslehoff Burrfoot," Laurana said softly, kneeling down beside the kender and staring him straight in the eye. "If they bring even one dragon here, we're finished. That's why they gave us time to surrender instead of just storming the place. They're using the extra time to bring in dragons. We must take this chance!"

A dark path and a light path. Tasslehoff remembered Fizban's words and hung his head. *Death of those you love, but you have the courage.*

Slowly Tas reached into the pocket of his fleecy vest, pulled out the glasses, and fit the wire frames over his pointed ears.

13

Che sun rises.

Darkness descends.

he fog lifted with the coming of morning. The day dawned bright and clear—so clear that Sturm, walking the battlements, could see the snow-covered grasslands of his birthplace near Vingaard Keep— lands now completely controlled by the dragonarmies. The sun's first rays struck the flag of the Knights—kingfisher beneath a golden crown, holding a sword decorated with a rose in his claws. The golden emblem glittered in the morning light. Then Sturm heard the harsh, blaring horns.

The dragonarmies marched upon the Tower at dawn.

The young knights—the hundred or so that were left—stood silently on the battlements watching as the vast army crawled across the land with the inexorability of devouring insects.

At first Sturm had wondered about the knight's dying words. "They ran before us!" Why had the dragonarmy run? Then it became clear to him—the dragonmen had used the knights' own vainglory against them in an ancient, yet simple, maneuver. Fall back before your enemy . . . not too fast, just let the front lines show enough fear and terror to be believable. Let them seem to break in panic. Then let your enemy charge after you, overextending his lines. And let your armies close in, surround him, and cut him to shreds.

It didn't need the sight of the bodies—barely visible in the distant trampled, bloody snow—to tell Sturm he had judged correctly. They lay where they had tried desperately to regroup for a final stand. Not that it mattered how they died. He wondered who would look on his body when it was all over.

Flint peered out from a crack in the wall. "At least I'll die on dry land," the dwarf muttered.

Sturm smiled slightly, stroking his moustaches. His eyes went to the east. As he thought about dying, he looked upon the land where he'd been born—a home he had barely known, a father he barely remembered, a country that had driven his family into exile. He was about to give his life to defend that country. Why? Why didn't he just leave and go back to Palanthas?

All of his life he had followed the Code and the Measure. The Code: *Est Sularus oth Mithas*—My Honor Is My Life. The Code was all he had left. The Measure was gone. It had failed. Rigid, inflexible, the Measure had encased the Knights in steel heavier than their armor. The Knights, isolated, fighting to survive, had clung to the Measure in despair—not realizing that it was an anchor, weighing them down.

Why was I different? Sturm wondered. But he knew the answer, even as he listened to the dwarf grumble. It was because of the dwarf, the kender, the mage, the half-elf. . . . They had taught him to see the world through other eyes: slanted eyes, smaller eyes, even hourglass eyes. Knights like Derek saw the world in stark black and white. Sturm had seen the world in all its radiant colors, in all its bleak grayness.

"It's time," he said to Flint. The two descended from the high lookout point just as the first of the enemy's poison-tipped arrows arched over the walls.

With shrieks and yells, the blaring of horns, and clashing of shield and sword, the dragonarmies struck the Tower of the High Clerist as the sun's brittle light filled the sky.

By nightfall, the flag still flew. The Tower stood.

But half its defenders were dead.

The living had no time during the day to shut the staring eyes or compose the contorted, agonized limbs. The living had all they could do to stay alive. Peace came at last with the night, as the dragonarmies withdrew to rest and wait for the morrow.

Sturm paced the battlements, his body aching with weariness. Yet every time he tried to rest, taut muscles twitched and danced, his brain seemed on fire. And so he was driven to pace again—back and forth, back and forth with slow, measured tread. He could not know that his steady pace drove the day's horrors from the thoughts of the young knights who listened. Knights in the courtyard, laying out the bodies of friends and comrades, thinking that tomorrow someone might be doing this for them, heard Sturm's steady pacing and felt their fears for tomorrow eased.

The ringing sound of the knight's footfalls brought comfort to everyone, in fact, except to the knight himself. Sturm's thoughts were dark and tormented: thoughts of defeat; thoughts of dying ignobly, without honor; tortured memories of the dream, seeing his body hacked and mutilated by the foul creatures camped beyond. Would the dream come true? he wondered, shivering. Would he falter at the end, unable to conquer fear? Would the Code fail him, as had the Measure?

Step . . . step . . . step . . . step . . .

Stop this! Sturm told himself angrily. You'll soon be mad as poor Derek. Spinning abruptly on his heel to break his stride, the knight turned to find Laurana behind him. His eyes met hers, and the black thoughts were brightened by her light. As long as such peace and beauty as hers existed in this world there was hope. He smiled at her and she smiled back—a strained smile—but it erased lines of fatigue and worry in her face.

"Rest," he told her. "You look exhausted."

"I tried to sleep," she murmured, "but I had terrible dreams—hands encased in crystal, huge dragons flying through stone hallways." She shook her head, then sat down, exhausted, in a corner sheltered from the chill wind.

Sturm's gaze moved to Tasslehoff, who lay beside her. The kender was fast asleep, curled into a ball. Sturm looked at him with a smile. Nothing bothered Tas. The kender'd had a truly glorious day, one that would live in his memory forever.

"I've never been at a siege before," Sturm had heard Tas confide to Flint just seconds before the dwarf's battle-axe swept off a goblin's head.

"You know we're all going to die," Flint growled, wiping black blood from his axe blade.

"That's what you said when we faced that black dragon in Xak Tsaroth," Tas replied. "Then you said the same thing in Thorbardin, and then there was the boat—"

"This time we're going to die!" Flint roared in a rage. "If I have to kill you myself!"

But they hadn't died—at least not today. There's always tomorrow, Sturm thought, his gaze resting on the dwarf who leaned against a stone wall, carving at a block of wood.

Flint looked up. "When will it start?" he asked.

Sturm sighed, his gaze shifting out to the eastern sky. "Dawn," he replied. "A few hours yet."

The dwarf nodded. "Can we hold?" His voice was matter-of-fact, the hand that held the wood firm and steady.

"We must," Sturm replied. "The messenger will reach Palanthas tonight.

If they act at once, it's still a two-day march to reach us. We must give them two days—"

"If they act at once!" Flint grunted.

"I know . . ." Sturm said softly, sighing. "You should leave," he turned to Laurana, who came out of her reverie with a start. "Go to Palanthas. Convince them of the danger."

"Your messenger must do that," Laurana said tiredly. "If not, no words of mine will sway them."

"Laurana," he began.

"Do you need me?" she asked abruptly. "Am I of use here?"

"You know you are," Sturm answered. He had marveled at the elf-maid's unflagging strength, her courage, and her skill with the bow.'

"Then I'm staying," Laurana said simply. Drawing the blanket up more closely around her, she closed her eyes. "I can't sleep," she whispered. But within a few moments, her breathing became soft and regular as the slumbering kender's.

Sturm shook his head, swallowing a choking thickness in his throat. His glance met Flint's. The dwarf sighed and went back to his carving. Neither spoke, both men thinking the same thing. Their deaths would be bad if the draconians overran the Tower. Laurana's death could be a thing of nightmares.

The eastern sky was brightening, foretelling the sun's approach, when the knights were roused from their fitful slumber by the blaring of horns. Hastily they rose, grabbed their weapons, and stood to the walls, peering out across the dark land.

The campfires of the dragonarmies burned low, allowed to go out as daylight neared. They could hear the sounds of life returning to the horrible body. The knights gripped their weapons, waiting. Then they turned to each other, bewildered.

The dragonarmies were retreating! Although only dimly seen in the faint half-light, it was obvious that the black tide was slowly withdrawing. Sturm watched, puzzled. The armies moved back, just over the horizon. But they were still out there, Sturm knew. He sensed them.

Some of the younger knights began to cheer.

"Keep quiet!" Sturm commanded harshly. Their shouts grated on his raw nerves. Laurana came to stand beside him and glanced at him in astonishment. His face was gray and haggard in the flickering torchlight. His gloved fists, resting atop the battlements, clenched and unclenched nervously His eyes narrowed as he leaned forward, staring eastward.

Laurana, sensing the rising fear within him, felt her own body grow chill. She remembered what she had told Tas.

"Is it what we feared?" she asked, her hand on his arm.

"Pray we are wrong!" he spoke softly, in a broken voice.

Minutes passed. Nothing happened. Flint came to join them, clambering up on a huge slab of broken stone to see over the edge of the wall. Tas woke, yawning.

"When's breakfast?" the kender inquired cheerfully, but no one paid any attention to him.

Still they watched and waited. Now all the knights, each of them feeling the same rising fear, lined the walls, staring eastward without any clear idea why.

"What is it?" Tas whispered. Climbing up to stand beside Flint, he saw the small red sliver of sun burning on the horizon, its orange fire turning the night sky purple, dimming the stars.

"What are we looking at?" Tas whispered, nudging Flint.

"Nothing," Flint grumbled.

"Then why are we looking—" The kender caught his breath with a sharp gulp. "Sturm—" he quavered.

"What is it?" the knight demanded, turning in alarm.

Tas kept staring. The rest followed his gaze, but their eyes were no match for the kender's.

"Dragons . . ." Tasslehoff replied. "Blue dragons."

"I thought as much," Sturm said softly. "The dragonfear. That's why they pulled the armies back. The humans fighting among them could not withstand it. How many dragons?"

"Three," answered Laurana. "I can see them now."

"Three," Sturm repeated, his voice empty, expressionless.

"Listen, Sturm—" Laurana dragged him back away from the wall. "I—we—weren't going to say anything. It might not have mattered, but it does now. Tasslehoff and I know how to use the dragon orb!"

"Dragon orb?" Sturm muttered, not really listening.

"The orb here, Sturm!" Laurana persisted, her hands clutching him eagerly. "The one below the Tower, in the very center. Tas showed it to me. Three long, wide hallways lead to it and—and—" Her voice died. Suddenly she saw vividly, as her subconscious had seen during the night, dragons flying down stone halls. . . .

"Sturm!" she shouted, shaking him in her excitement. "I know how the orb works! I know how to kill the dragons! Now, if we just have the time—"

Sturm caught hold of her, his strong hands grasping her by the shoulders. In all the months he had known her, he could not recall seeing her more beautiful. Her face, pale with weariness, was alight with excitement.

"Tell me, quickly," he ordered. Laurana explained, her words falling over themselves as she painted the picture for him that became clearer to her as she talked. Flint and Tas watched from behind Sturm, the dwarf's face aghast, the kender's face filled with consternation.

"Who'll use the orb?" Sturm asked slowly.

"I will," Laurana replied.

"But, Laurana," Tasslehoff cried, "Fizban said—"

"Tas, shut up!" Laurana said through clenched teeth. "Please, Sturm!" she urged. "It's our only hope. We have the dragonlances—and the dragon orb!"

The knight looked at her, then toward the dragons speeding out of the ever-brightening east.

"Very well," he said finally. "Flint, you and Tas go down and gather the men together in the center courtyard. Hurry!"

Tasslehoff, giving Laurana a last, troubled glance, jumped down from the rock where he and the dwarf had been standing. Flint came after him more slowly, his face somber and thoughtful. Reaching the ground, he walked up to Sturm.

Must you? Flint asked Sturm silently, as their eyes met.

Sturm nodded once. Glancing at Laurana, he smiled sadly. "I'll tell her," he said softly. "Take care of the kender. Good-bye, my friend."

Flint swallowed, shaking his old head. Then, his face a mask of sorrow, the dwarf brushed his gnarled hand across his eyes and gave Tas a shove in the back.

"Get moving!" the dwarf snapped.

Tas turned to look at him in astonishment, then shrugged and ran skipping along the top of the battlements, his shrill voice shouting out to the startled knights.

Laurana's face glowed. "You come, too, Sturm!" she said, tugging at him like a child eager to show a parent a new toy. "I'll explain this to the men if you want. Then you can give the orders and arrange the battle disposition—"

"You're in command, Laurana," Sturm said.

"What?" Laurana stopped, fear replacing the hope in her heart so suddenly the pain made her gasp.

"You said you needed time," Sturm said, adjusting his swordbelt, avoiding her eyes. "You're right. You must get the men in position. You must have time to use the orb. I will gain you that time." He picked up a bow and a quiver of arrows.

"No! Sturm!" Laurana shivered with terror. "You can't mean this! I can't command! I need you! Sturm, don't do this to yourself!" Her voice died to a whisper. "Don't do this to me!"

"You can command, Laurana," Sturm said, taking her head in his hands. Leaning forward, he kissed her gently. "Farewell, elfmaid," he said softly. "Your light will shine in this world. It is time for mine to darken. Don't grieve, dear one. Don't cry." He held her close. "The Forestmaster said to us, in Darken Wood, that we should not mourn those who have fulfilled their destiny. Mine is fulfilled. Now, hurry, Laurana. You'll need every second."

"At least take the dragonlance with you," she begged.

Sturm shook his head, his hand on the antique sword of his father. "I don't know how to use it. Good-bye, Laurana. Tell Tanis—" He stopped, then he sighed. "No," he said with a slight smile. "He will know what was in my heart."

"Sturm . . ." Laurana's tears choked her into silence. She could only stare at him in mute appeal.

"Go," he said.

Stumbling blindly, Laurana turned around and somehow made her way down the stairs to the courtyard below. Here she felt a strong hand grasp hers.

"Flint," she began, sobbing painfully, "he, Sturm . . ."

"I know, Laurana," the dwarf replied. "I saw it in his face. I think I've seen it there for as long as I can remember. It's up to you now. You can't fail him."

Laurana drew a deep breath, then wiped her eyes with her hands, cleaning her tear-streaked face as best she could. Taking another breath, she lifted her head.

"There," she said, keeping her voice firm and steady. "I'm ready. Where's Tas?"

"Here," said a small voice.

"Go on down. You read the words in the orb once before. Read them again. Make absolutely certain you've got it right."

"Yes, Laurana." Tas gulped and ran off.

"The knights are assembled," Flint said. "Waiting your command."

"Waiting my command," Laurana repeated absently.

Hesitating, she looked up. The red rays of the sun flashed on Sturm's bright armor as the knight climbed the narrow stairs that led to a high wall near the central Tower. Sighing, she lowered her gaze to the courtyard where the knights waited.

Laurana drew another deep breath, then walked toward them, the red crest fluttering from her helmet, her golden hair flaming in the morning light.

The cold and brittle sun stained the sky blood red, deepening into the velvet blue-blackness of receding night. The Tower stood in shadow still, though the sun's rays sparkled off the golden threads in the fluttering flag.

Sturm reached the top of the wall. The Tower soared above him. The parapet Sturm stood upon extended a hundred feet or more to his left. Its stone surface was smooth, providing no shelter, no cover.

Looking east, Sturm saw the dragons.

They were blue dragons, and on the back of the lead dragon in the formation sat a Dragon Highlord, the blue-black dragon-scale armor gleaming in the sunlight. He could see the hideous horned mask, the black cape fluttering behind. Two other blue dragons with riders followed the

Dragon Highlord. Sturm gave them a brief, perfunctory glance. They did not concern him. His battle was with the leader, the Highlord.

The knight looked into the courtyard far below him. Sunlight was just climbing the walls. Sturm saw it flicker red off the tips of the silver dragonlances that each man held now in his hand. He saw it burn on Laurana's golden hair. He saw the men look up at him. Grasping his sword, he raised it into the air. Sunlight flashed from the ornately carved blade.

Smiling up at him, though she could barely see him through her tears, Laurana raised her dragonlance into the air in answer—in good-bye.

Comforted by her smile, Sturm turned back to face his enemy.

Walking to the center of the wall, he seemed a small figure poised halfway between land and sky. The dragons could fly past him, or circle around him, but that wasn't what he wanted. They must see him as a threat. They must take time to fight him.

Sheathing his sword, Sturm fit an arrow to his bow and took careful aim at the lead dragon. Patiently he waited, holding his breath. I cannot waste this, he thought. Wait . . . wait . . .

The dragon was in range. Sturm's arrow sped through the morning brilliance. His aim was true. The arrow struck the blue dragon in the neck. It did little damage, bouncing off the dragon's blue scales, but the dragon reared its head in pain and irritation, slowing its flight. Quickly Sturm fired again, this time at the dragon flying directly behind the leader.

The arrow tore into a wing, and the dragon shrieked in rage. Sturm fired once more. This time the lead dragon's rider steered it clear. But the knight had accomplished what he set out to do: capture their attention, prove he was a threat, force them to fight him. He could hear the sound of running footsteps in the courtyard and the shrill squeak of the winches raising the portcullises.

Now Sturm could see the Dragon Highlord rise to his feet in the saddle. Built like a chariot, the saddle could accommodate its rider in a standing position for battle. The Highlord carried a spear in his gloved hand. Sturm dropped his bow. Picking up his shield and drawing his sword, he stood upon the wall, watching as the dragon flew closer and closer, its red eyes flaring, its white teeth gleaming.

Then—far away—Sturm heard the clear, clarion call of a trumpet, its music cold as the air from the snow-covered mountains of his homeland in the distance. Pure and crisp, the trumpet call pierced his heart, rising bravely above the darkness and death and despair that surrounded him.

Sturm answered the call with a wild battle-cry, raising his sword to meet his enemy. The sunlight flashed red on his blade. The dragon swooped in low.

Again the trumpet sounded, and again Sturm answered, his voice rising in a shout. But this time his voice faltered, for suddenly Sturm realized he had heard this trumpet before.

The dream!

Sturm stopped, gripping his sword in a hand that was sweating inside its glove. The dragon loomed above him. Astride the dragon was the Highlord, the horns of his mask flickering blood-red, his spear poised and ready.

Fear knotted Sturm's stomach, his skin grew cold. The horn call sounded a third time. It had sounded three times in the dream, and after the third call he had fallen. The dragon fear was overwhelming him. Escape! his brain screamed.

Escape! The dragons would swoop into the courtyard. The knights could not be ready yet, they would die, Laurana, Flint, and Tas. . . .The Tower would fall.

No! Sturm got hold of himself. Everything else was gone: his ideals, his hopes, his dreams. The Knighthood was collapsing. The Measure had been found wanting. Everything in his life was meaningless. His death must not be so. He would buy Laurana time, buy it with his life, since that was all he had to give. And he would die according to the Code, since that was all he had to cling to.

Raising his sword in the air, he gave the knight's salute to an enemy. To his surprise, it was returned with grave dignity by the Dragon Highlord. Then the dragon dove, its jaws open, prepared to slash the knight apart with its razor-sharp teeth. Sturm swung his sword in a vicious arc, forcing the dragon to rear its head back or risk decapitation. Sturm hoped to disrupt its flight. But the creature's wings held it steady, its rider guiding it with a sure hand while holding the gleaming-tipped spear in the other.

Sturm faced east. Half-blinded by the sun's brilliance, Sturm saw the dragon as a thing of blackness. He saw the creature dip in its flight, diving below the level of the wall, and he realized the blue was going to come up from beneath, giving its rider the room needed to attack. The other two dragon riders held back, watching, waiting to see if their lord required help finishing this insolent knight.

For a moment the sun-drenched sky was empty, then the dragon burst up over the edge of the wall, its horrifying scream splitting Sturm's eardrums, filling his head with pain. The breath from its gaping mouth gagged him. He staggered dizzily but managed to keep his feet as he slashed out with his sword. The ancient blade struck the dragon's left nostril. Black blood spurted into the air. The dragon roared in fury.

But the blow was costly. Sturm had no time to recover.

The Dragon Highlord raised his spear, its tip flaming in the sun. Leaning down, he thrust it deep, piercing through armor, flesh, and bone.

Sturm's sun shattered.

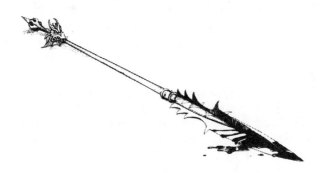

14

DRAGON ORB. DRAGONLANCE.

he knights surged past Laurana into the High Clerist's Tower, taking their places where she had told them. Although at first skeptical, hope dawned as Laurana explained her plan.

The courtyard was empty after the knights' departure. Laurana knew she should hurry. Already she should be with Tas, preparing herself to use the dragon orb. But Laurana could not leave that gleaming, solitary figure standing alone—waiting—upon the wall.

Then, silhouetted in the rising sun, she saw the dragons.

Sword and spear flashed in the brilliant sunlight.

Laurana's world stopped turning. Time slowed to a dream. The sword drew blood. The dragon screamed. The spear held poised for an eternity. The sun stood still.

The spear struck.

A glittering object fell slowly from the top of the wall into the court-yard. The object was Sturm's sword, dropped from his lifeless hand, and it was—to Laurana—the only movement in a static world. The knight's body stood still, impaled upon the spear of the Dragon Highlord. The dragon hovered above, its wings poised. Nothing moved, everything held perfectly still.

Then the Highlord jerked the spear free and Sturm's body crumpled where he stood, a dark mass against the sun. The dragon roared in outrage and a bolt of lightning streaked from the blue's blood-frothed mouth and struck the High Clerist's Tower. With a booming explosion, the stone burst apart. Flames flared, brighter than the sun. The other two dragons dove for the courtyard as Sturm's sword clattered to the pavement with a ringing sound.

Time began.

Laurana saw the dragons diving at her. The ground around her shook as stone and rock rained down upon her and smoke and dust filled the air. Still Laurana could not move. To move would make the tragedy real. Some inane voice kept whispering in her brain—if you stand perfectly still, this will not have happened.

But there lay the sword, only a few feet from her. And as she watched, she saw the Dragon Highlord wave the spear, signaling to the dragon-armies that waited out upon the plains, telling them to attack. Laurana heard the blaring of the horns. In her mind's eye, she could see the dragon-armies surging across the snow-covered land.

Again the ground shook beneath her feet. Laurana hesitated one instant more, bidding a silent farewell to the spirit of the knight. Then she ran forward, stumbling as the ground heaved and the air crackled with terrifying lightning blasts. Reaching down, she grabbed Sturm's sword and raised it defiantly in the air.

"*Soliasi Arath!!*" she cried in elven, her voice ringing above the sounds of destruction in challenge to the attacking dragons.

The dragon riders laughed, shouting their scornful challenges in return. The dragons shrieked in cruel enjoyment of the kill. Two dragons who had accompanied the Highlord plummeted after Laurana into the courtyard.

Laurana ran toward the huge, gaping portcullis, the entryway into the Tower that made so little sense. The stone walls were a blur as she fled past them. Behind her she could hear a dragon swooping after her. She could hear its stertorous breathing, the rush of air past its wings. She heard the dragon rider's command that stopped the dragon from following her right into the Tower. Good! Laurana smiled grimly to herself.

Running through the wide hallway, she sped swiftly past the second portcullis. Knights stood there, poised and ready to drop it.

"Keep it open!" she gasped breathlessly. "Remember!"

They nodded. She sped on. Now she was in the dark, narrower chamber where the oddly shaped, toothlike pillars slanted toward her with razor sharpness. Behind the pillars, she saw white faces beneath gleaming helms. Here and there, light sparkled on a dragonlance. The knights peered at her as she ran past.

"Get back!" she shouted. "Stay behind the pillars."

"Sturm?" one asked.

Laurana shook her head, too exhausted to talk. She ran through the third portcullis—the strange one, the one with a hole in the center. Here stood four knights, along with Flint. This was the key position. Laurana wanted someone here she could depend on. She had no time for more than an exchange of glances with the dwarf, but that was enough. Flint read the story of his friend in her face. The dwarf's head bowed for a moment, his hand covering his eyes.

Laurana ran on. Through this small room, beneath double doors made of solid steel and then into the chamber of the dragon orb.

Tasslehoff had dusted the orb with his handkerchief. Laurana could see inside it now, a faint red mist swirling with a myriad colors. The kender stood before it, staring into it, his magical glasses perched upon his small nose.

"What do I do?" Laurana gasped, out of breath.

"Laurana," Tas begged, "don't do this! I've read—if you fail to control the essence of the dragons within the orb, the dragons will come, Laurana, and take control of you!"

"Tell me what I need to do!" Laurana said firmly.

"Put your hands on the orb," Tas faltered, "and—no—wait, Laurana!"

It was too late. Laurana had already placed both slender hands upon the chill crystal globe. There was a flash of color from inside the orb, so bright Tas had to avert his eyes.

"Laurana!" he cried in his shrill voice. "Listen! You must concentrate, clear your mind of everything except bending the orb to your will! Laurana . . ."

If she heard him, she made no response, and Tas realized she was already caught up in the battle for control of the orb. Fearfully he remembered Fizban's warning, death for those you love, worse—the loss of the soul. Only dimly did he understand the dire words written in the flaming colors of the orb, but he knew enough to realize that Laurana's soul was at balance here.

In agony he watched her, longing to help—yet knowing that he did not dare do anything. Laurana stood for long moments without moving, her hands upon the orb, her face slowly draining of all life. Her eyes stared deep into the spinning, swirling colors. The kender grew dizzy looking at it and turned away, feeling sick. There was another explosion outside. Dust drifted down from the ceiling. Tas stirred uneasily. But Laurana never moved.

Her eyes closed, her head bent forward. She clutched the orb, her hands whitening from the pressure she exerted. Then she began to whimper and shake her head. "No," she moaned, and it seemed as if she were trying desperately to pull her hands away. But the orb held them fast.

Tas wondered bleakly what he should do. He longed to run up and pull her away. He wished he had broken this orb, but there was nothing he could do now. He could only stand and watch helplessly.

Laurana's body gave a convulsive shudder. Tas saw her drop to her knees, her hands still holding fast to the orb. Then Laurana shook her head angrily. Muttering unfamiliar words in elven, she fought to stand, using the orb to drag herself up. Her hands turned white with the strain and sweat trickled down her face. She was exerting every ounce of strength she possessed. With agonizing slowness, Laurana stood.

The orb flared a final time, the colors swirled together, becoming many colors and none. Then a bright, beaming, pure white light poured from the orb. Laurana stood tall and straight before it. Her face relaxed. She smiled.

And then she collapsed, unconscious, to the floor.

In the courtyard of the High Clerist's Tower, the dragons were systematically reducing the stone walls to rubble. The army was nearing the Tower, draconians in the forefront, preparing to enter through the breached walls and kill anything left alive inside. The Dragon Highlord circled above the chaos, his blue dragon's nostril black with dried blood. The Highlord supervised the destruction of the Tower. All was proceeding well when the bright daylight was pierced by a pure white light beaming out from the three huge, gaping entryways into the Tower.

The dragon riders glanced at these light beams, wondering casually what they portended. Their dragons, however, reacted differently. Lifting their heads, their eyes lost all focus. The dragons heard the call.

Captured by ancient magic-users, brought under control by an elf-maiden, the essence of the dragons held within the orb did as it was bound to do when commanded. It sent forth its irresistible call. And the dragons had no choice but to answer that call and try desperately to reach its source.

In vain the startled dragon riders tried to turn their mounts. But the dragons no longer heard the riders' commanding voices, they heard only a single voice, that of the orb. Both dragons swooped toward the inviting portcullises while their riders shouted and kicked wildly.

The white light spread beyond the Tower, touching the front ranks of the dragonarmies, and the human commanders stared as their army went mad.

The orb's call sounded clearly to dragons. But draconians, who were only part dragon, heard the call as a deafening voice shouting garbled commands. Each one heard the voice differently, each one received a different call.

Some draconians fell to their knees, clutching their heads in agony. Others turned and fled an unseen horror lurking in the Tower. Still others dropped their weapons and ran wildly, straight *toward* the Tower. Within moments an organized, well-planned attack had turned into mass confusion as a thousand draconians dashed off shrieking in a thousand directions. Seeing the major part of their force break and run, the goblins promptly fled the battlefield, while the humans stood bewildered amidst the chaos, waiting for orders that were not forthcoming.

The Dragon Highlord's own mount was barely kept in control by the Highlord's powerful force of will. But there was no stopping the other two dragons or the madness of the army. The Highlord could only fume in impotent fury, trying to determine what this white light was and where it was coming from. And—if possible—try to eradicate it.

The first blue dragon reached the first portcullis and sped inside the huge entryway, its rider ducking just in time to avoid having his head taken off by the wall. Obeying the call of the orb, the blue dragon flew easily through the wide stone halls, the tips of her wings just barely brushing the sides.

Through the second portcullis she darted, entering the chamber with the strange, toothlike pillars. Here in this second chamber she smelled human flesh and steel, but she was so in thrall to the orb she paid no attention to them. This chamber was smaller, so she was forced to pull her wings close to her body, letting momentum carry her forward.

Flint watched her coming. In all his one hundred forty-some years, he had never seen a sight like this . . . and he hoped he never would again. The dragonfear broke over the men confined in the room like a stupifying wave. The young knights, lances clutched in their shaking hands, fell back against the walls, hiding their eyes as the monstrous, blue-scaled body thundered past them.

The dwarf staggered back against the wall, his nerveless hand resting feebly on the mechanism that would slide shut the portcullis. He had never been so terrified in his life. Death would be welcome if it would end this horror. But the dragon sped on, seeking only one thing—to reach the orb. Her head glided under the strange portcullis.

Acting instinctively, knowing only that the dragon must not reach the orb, Flint released the mechanism. The portcullis closed around the dragon's neck, holding it fast. The dragon's head was now trapped within the small chamber. Her struggling body lay helpless, wings pressed against her sides, in the chamber where the knights stood, dragonlances ready.

Too late, the dragon realized she was trapped. She howled in such fury the rocks shuddered and cracked as she opened her mouth to blast the dragon orb with her lightning breath. Tasslehoff, trying frantically to revive Laurana, found himself staring into two flaming eyes. He saw the dragon's jaws part, he heard the dragon suck in her breath.

Lightning crackled from the dragon's throat, the concussion knocking the kender flat. Rock exploded into the room and the dragon orb shuddered on its stand. Tas lay on the floor, stunned by the blast. He could not move, did not even want to move, in fact. He just lay there, waiting for the next bolt which he knew would kill Laurana—if she wasn't already dead—and him, too. At this point, he really didn't much care.

But the blast never came.

The mechanism finally activated. The double steel door slammed shut in front of the dragon's snout, sealing the creature's head inside the small room.

At first it was deathly silent. Then the most horrible scream imaginable reverberated through the chamber. It was high-pitched, shrill, wailing, bubbling in agony, as the knights lunged out of their hiding places behind the tooth-like pillars and drove the silver dragonlances into the blue, writhing body of the trapped dragon.

Tas covered his ears with his hands, trying to block out the awful sound. Over and over he pictured the terrible destruction he had seen the dragons wreak on towns, the innocent people they had slaughtered. The dragon would have killed him, too, he knew—killed him without mercy. It had probably already killed Sturm. He kept reminding himself of that, trying to harden his heart.

But the kender buried his head in his hands and wept.

Then he felt a gentle hand touch him.

"Tas," whispered a voice.

"Laurana!" He raised his head. "Laurana! I'm sorry. I shouldn't care what they do to the dragon, but I can't stand it, Laurana! Why must there be killing? I can't stand it!" Tears streaked his face.

"I know," Laurana murmured, vivid memories of Sturm's death mingling with the shrieks of the dying dragon. "Don't be ashamed, Tas. Be thankful you can feel pity and horror at the death of an enemy. The day we cease to care, even for our enemies, is the day we have lost this battle."

The fearful wailing grew even louder. Tas held out his arms and Laurana gathered him close. The two clung to each other, trying to blot out the screams of the dying dragon. Then they heard another sound—the knights calling out a warning. A second dragon had entered the other chamber, slamming its rider into the wall as it struggled to enter the smaller entryway in response to the beaming call of the dragon orb. The knights were sounding the alarm.

At that moment, the Tower itself shuddered from top to foundation, shaken by the violent flailings of the tortured dragon.

"Come on!" Laurana cried. "We've got to get out of here!" Dragging Tas to his feet, she ran stumbling toward a small door in the wall that would lead them out into the courtyard. Laurana yanked open the door, just as the dragon's head burst into the room with the orb. Tas could not help stopping, just a moment, to watch. The sight was so fascinating. He could see the dragon's flaring eyes—mad with rage at the sounds of his dying mate, knowing—too late—that he had flown into the same trap. The dragon's mouth twisted into a vicious snarl, he sucked in his breath. The double steel doors dropped in front of the dragon—but only halfway.

"Laurana, the door's stuck!" Tas shouted. "The dragon orb—"

"Come on!"Laurana yanked at the kender's hand. Lightning flashed, and Tas turned and fled, hearing the room behind him explode into flame. Rock and stone filled the chamber. The white light of the dragon orb was buried in the debris as the Tower of the High Clerist collapsed on top of it.

The shock threw Laurana and Tas off balance, sending them slamming against the wall. Tas helped Laurana to her feet, and the two of them kept going, heading for the bright daylight.

Then the ground was still. The thunder of falling rock ceased. There was only a sharp crack now and again or a low rumble. Pausing a moment to catch their breath, Tas and Laurana looked behind them. The end of the passage was completely blocked, choked by the huge boulders of the Tower.

"What about the dragon orb?" Tas gasped.

"It is better destroyed."

Now that Tas could see Laurana more clearly in the daylight, he was stunned at the sight. Her face was deathly white, even her lips drained of blood. The only color was in her green eyes, and they seemed disturbingly large, shadowed by purple smudges.

"I could not use it again," she whispered, more to herself than to him. "I nearly gave up. Hands . . . I can't talk about it!" Shivering, she covered her eyes.

"Then I remembered Sturm, standing upon the wall, facing his death alone. If I gave in, his death would be meaningless. I couldn't let that happen. I couldn't let him down." She shook her head, trembling. "I forced the orb to obey my command, but I knew I could do it only once. And I can never, never go through that again!"

"Sturm's dead?" Tas's voice quavered.

Laurana looked at him, her eyes softened. "I'm sorry, Tas," she said "I didn't realize you didn't know. He—he died fighting a Dragon Highlord."

"Was it—was it . . ." Tas choked.

"Yes, it was quick," Laurana said gently. "He did not suffer long."

Tas bowed his head, then raised it again quickly as another explosion shook what was left of the fortress.

"The dragonarmies . . ." Laurana murmured. "Our fight is not ended." Her hand went to the hilt of Sturm's sword, which she had buckled around her slender waist. "Go find Flint."

Laurana emerged from the tunnel into the courtyard, blinking in the bright light, almost surprised to see it was still day. So much had happened, it seemed to her years might have passed. But the sun was just lifting over the courtyard wall.

The tall Tower of the High Clerist was gone, fallen in upon itself, a heap of stone rubble in the center of the courtyard. The entryways and halls leading to the dragon orb were not damaged, except where the dragons had smashed into them. The walls of the outer fortress still stood, although breached in places, their stone blackened by the dragons' lightning bolts.

But no armies poured through the breaches. It was quiet, Laurana realized. In the tunnels behind her, she could hear the dying screams of the second dragon, the hoarse shouts of the knights finishing the kill.

What had happened to the army? Laurana wondered, looking around in confusion. They must be coming over the walls. Fearfully she looked up at the battlements, expecting to see the fierce creatures pouring over them.

And then she saw the flash of sunlight shining on armor. She saw the shapeless mass lying on the top of the wall.

Sturm. She remembered the dream, remembered the bloody hands of the draconians hacking at Sturm's body.

It must not happen! she thought grimly. Drawing Sturm's sword, she ran across the courtyard and immediately realized the ancient weapon would be too heavy for her to wield. But what else was there? She glanced around hurriedly. The dragonlances! Dropping the sword, she grabbed one. Then, carrying the lightweight footman's lance easily, she climbed the stairs.

Laurana reached the top of the battlements and stared out across the plain, expecting to see the black tide of the army surging forward. But the plain was empty. There were only a few groups of humans standing, staring vaguely around.

What could it mean? Laurana had no idea, and she was too exhausted to think. Her wild elation died. Weariness descended on her now, as did her grief. Dragging the lance behind her, she stumbled over to Sturm's body lying in the blood-stained snow.

Laurana knelt beside the knight. Putting her hand out, she brushed back the wind-blown hair to look once more upon the face of her friend. For the first time since she had met him, Laurana saw peace in Sturm's lifeless eyes.

Lifting his cold hand, she pressed it to her cheek. "Sleep, dear friend," she murmured, "and let not your sleep be troubled by dragons." Then, as she lay the cold white hand upon the shattered armor, she saw a bright sparkle in the blood-stained snow. She picked up an object so covered with blood she could not see what it was. Carefully Laurana brushed the snow and blood away. It was a piece of jewelry. Laurana stared at it in astonishment.

But before she could wonder how it came to be here, a dark shadow fell over her. Laurana heard the creak of huge wings, the intake of breath into a gigantic body. Fearfully she leaped to her feet and whirled around.

A blue dragon landed upon the wall behind her. Stone gave way as the great claws scrabbled for a hold. The creature's great wings beat the air. From the saddle upon the dragon's back, a Dragon Highlord gazed at Laurana with cold, stern eyes from behind the hideous mask.

Laurana took a step backward as the dragonfear overcame her. The dragonlance slipped from her nerveless hand, and she dropped the jewel into the snow. Turning, she tried to flee, but she could not see where she was going. She slipped and fell into the snow to lie trembling beside Sturm's body.

In her paralyzing fear, all she could think of was the dream! Here she had died—as Sturm had died. Laurana's vision was filled with blue scales as the creature's great neck reared above her.

The dragonlance! Scrambling for it in the blood-wet snow, Laurana's fingers closed over its wooden shaft. She started to rise, intending to plunge it into the dragon's neck.

But a black boot slammed down upon the lance, narrowly missing her hand. Laurana stared at the shining black boot, decorated with gold work that gleamed in the sun. She stared at the black boot standing in Sturm's blood, and she drew a deep breath.

"Touch his body, and you will die," Laurana said softly. "Your dragon will not be able to save you. This knight was my friend, and I will not let his killer defile his body."

"I have no intention of defiling the body," the Dragon Highlord said. Moving with elaborate slowness, the Highlord reached down and gently shut the knight's eyes, which were fixed upon the sun he would see no more.

The Dragon Highlord stood up, facing the elfmaid who knelt in the snow, and removed the booted foot from the dragonlance. "You see, he was my friend, too. I knew—the moment I killed him."

Laurana stared up at the Highlord. "I don't believe you," she said tiredly. "How could that be?"

Calmly, the Dragon Highlord removed the hideous horned dragon mask. "I think you might have heard of me, Lauralanthalasa. That is your name, isn't it?"

Laurana nodded dumbly, rising to her feet.

The Dragon Highlord smiled, a charming, crooked smile. "And my name is—"

"Kitiara."

"How did you know?"

"A dream . . ." Laurana murmured.

"Oh, yes—the dream." Kitiara ran her gloved hand through her dark, curly hair. "Tanis told me about the dream. I guess you all must have shared it. He thought his friends might have." The human woman glanced down at the body of Sturm, lying at her feet. "Odd, isn't it—the way Sturm's death came true? And Tanis said the dream came true for him as well: the part where I saved his life."

Laurana began to tremble. Her face, which had already been white with exhaustion, was so drained of blood it seemed transparent. "Tanis? . . . You've seen Tanis?"

"Just two days ago," Kitiara said. "I left him in Flotsam, to look after matters while I was gone."

Kitiara's cold, calm words drove through Laurana's soul like the High-lord's spear had driven through Sturm's flesh. Laurana felt the stones start to shift from under her. The sky and ground mixed, the pain cleaved her in two. She's lying, Laurana thought desperately. But she knew with despairing certainty that, though Kitiara might lie when she chose—she was not lying now.

Laurana staggered and nearly fell. Only the grim determination not to reveal any weakness before this human woman kept the elfmaiden on her feet.

Kitiara had not noticed. Stooping down, she picked up the weapon Laurana had dropped and studied it with interest.

"So this is the famed dragonlance?" Kitiara remarked.

Laurana swallowed her grief, forcing herself to speak in a steady voice. "Yes," she replied. "If you want to see what it's capable of, go look within the walls of the fortress at what's left of your dragons."

Kitiara glanced down into the courtyard briefly, without a great deal of interest. "It was not these that lured my dragons into your trap," she said, her brown eyes appraising Laurana coolly, "nor scattered my army to the four winds."

Once more Laurana glanced across the empty plains.

"Yes," Kitiara said, seeing the dawning comprehension on Laurana's face. "You have won—today. Savor your victory now, Elf, for it will be short-lived." The Dragon Highlord dexterously flipped the lance in her hand and held it aimed at Laurana's heart. The elfmaid stood unmoving before her, the delicate face empty of expression.

Kitiara smiled. With a quick motion, she reversed the killing stroke "Thank you for this weapon," she said, standing the lance in the snow. "We've received reports of these. Now we can find out if it as formidable a weapon as you claim."

Kitiara made Laurana a slight bow from the waist. Then, replacing the dragonmask over her head, she grasped the dragonlance and turned to go. As she did, her gaze went once more to the body of the knight.

"See that he is given a knight's funeral," Kitiara said. "It will take at least three days to rebuild the army. I give you that time to prepare a ceremony befitting him."

"We will bury our own dead," Laurana said proudly. "We ask you for nothing!"

The memory of Sturm's death, the sight of the knight's body, brought Laurana back to reality like cold water poured on the face of a dreamer. Moving to stand protectively between Sturm's body and the Dragon Highlord, Laurana looked into the brown eyes, glittering behind the dragonmask.

"What will you tell Tanis?" she asked abruptly.

"Nothing," Kit said simply. "Nothing at all." Turning, she walked away.

Laurana watched the Dragon Highlord's slow, graceful walk, the black cape fluttering in the warm breeze blowing from the north. The sun glinted off the prize Kitiara held in her hand. Laurana knew she should get the lance away. There was an army of knights below. She had only to call.

But Laurana's weary brain and her body refused to act. It was an effort just to remain standing. Pride alone kept her from falling to the cold stones.

Take the dragonlance, Laurana told Kitiara silently. Much good it will do you.

Kitiara walked to the giant blue dragon. Down below, the knights had come into the courtyard, dragging with them the head of one of her blue dragons. Skie tossed his own head angrily at the sight, a savage growl rumbling deep within his chest. The knights turned their amazed faces toward the wall where they saw the dragon, the Dragon Highlord, and Laurana. More than one drew his weapon, but Laurana raised her hand to stop them. It was the last gesture she had strength to make.

Kitiara gave the knights a disdainful look and laid her hand upon Skie's neck, stroking him, reassuring him. She took her time, letting them see she was not afraid of them.

Reluctantly, the knights lowered their weapons.

Laughing scornfully, Kitiara swung herself onto the dragon.

"Farewell, Lauralanthalasa," she called.

Lifting the dragonlance in the air, Kitiara commanded Skie to fly. The huge blue dragon spread his wings, rising effortlessly into the air. Guiding him skillfully, Kitiara flew just above Laurana.

The elfmaid looked up into the dragon's fiery red eyes. She saw the wounded, bloodied nostril, the gaping mouth twisted in a vicious snarl. On his back, sitting between the giant wings, was Kitiara, the dragon-scale armor glistening, the sun glinting off the horned mask. Sunlight flashed from the point of the dragonlance.

Then, glittering as it turned over and over, the dragonlance fell from the Dragon Highlord's gloved hand. Clattering on the stones, it landed at Laurana's feet.

"Keep it," Kitiara called to her in a ringing voice. "You're going to need it!"

The blue dragon lifted his wings, caught the air currents, and soared into the sky to vanish into the sun.

The Funeral

Winter's night was dark and starless. The wind had become a gale, bringing driving sleet and snow that pierced armor with the sharpness of arrows, freezing blood and spirit. No watch was set. A man standing upon the battlements of the High Clerist's Tower would have frozen to death at his post.

There was no need for the watch. All day, as long as the sun shone, the knights had stared across the plains, but there was no sign of the dragonarmies' return. Even after darkness fell, the knights could see few campfires on the horizon.

On this winter's night, as the wind howled among the ruins of the crumbled Tower like the shrieks of the slaughtered dragons, the Knights of Solamnia buried their dead.

The bodies were carried into a cavelike sepulcher beneath the Tower. Long ago, it had been used for the dead of the Knighthood. But that had been in ages past, when Huma rode to glorious death upon the fields beyond. The sepulcher might have remained forgotten but for the curiosity of a kender. Once it must have been guarded and well kept, but time had touched even the dead, who are thought to be beyond time. The stone coffins were covered with a fine sifting of thick dust. When it was brushed away, nothing could be read of the writings carved into the stone.

Called the Chamber of Paladine, the sepulcher was a large rectangular room, built far below the ground where the destruction of the Tower did not affect it. A long, narrow staircase led down to it from two huge iron doors marked with the symbol of Paladine—the platinum dragon, ancient symbol of death and rebirth. The knights brought torches to light the chamber, fitting them into rusted iron sconces upon the crumbling stone walls.

The stone coffins of the ancient dead lined the walls of the room. Above each one was an iron plaque giving the name of the dead knight, his family, and the date of his death. A center aisle led between the rows of coffins toward a marble altar at the head of the room. In this central aisle of the Chamber of Paladine, the knights lay their dead.

There was no time to build coffins. All knew the dragonarmies would return. The knights must spend their time fortifying the ruined walls of the fortress, not building homes for those who no longer cared. They carried the bodies of their comrades down to the Chamber of Paladine and laid them in long rows upon the cold stone floor. The bodies were draped with ancient winding sheets which had been meant for the ceremonial wrapping. There was no time for that either. Each dead knight's sword was laid upon his breast, while some token of the enemy—an arrow perhaps, a battered shield, or the claws of a dragon—were laid at his feet.

When the bodies had been carried to the torch-lit chamber, the knights assembled. They stood among their dead, each man standing beside the body of a friend, a comrade, a brother. Then, amid a silence so profound each man could hear his own heart beating, the last three bodies were brought inside. Carried upon stretchers, they were attended by a solemn Guard of Honor.

This should have been a state funeral, resplendent with the trappings detailed by the Measure. At the altar should have stood the Grand Master, arrayed in ceremonial armor. Beside him should have been the High Clerist, clad in armor covered with the white robes of a cleric of Paladine. Here should have stood the High Justice, his armor covered by the judicial robes of black. The altar itself should have been banked with roses. Golden emblems of the kingfisher, the crown, and the sword should have been placed upon it.

But here at the altar stood only an elfmaiden, clad in armor that was dented and stained with blood. Beside her stood an old dwarf, his head bowed in grief, and a kender, his impish face ravaged by sorrow. The only rose upon the altar was a black one, found in Sturm's belt; the only ornament was a silver dragonlance, black with clotted blood.

The Guard carried the bodies to the front of the chamber and reverently laid them before the three friends.

On the right lay the body of Lord Alfred MarKenin, his mutilated, headless corpse mercifully shrouded in white linen. On the left lay Lord Derek Crownguard, his body covered with white cloth to hide the hideous grin death had frozen upon his face. In the center lay the body of Sturm Brightblade. He was not covered by a white sheet. He lay in the armor he had worn at his death: his father's armor. His father's antique sword was clasped in cold hands upon his breast. One other ornament lay upon his shattered breast, a token none of the knights recognized.

It was the Starjewel, which Laurana had found in a pool of the knight's own blood. The jewel was dark, its brilliance fading even as Laurana had held it in her hand. Many things became clear to her later, as she studied the Starjewel. This, then, was how they shared the dream in Silvanesti. Had Sturm realized its power? Did he know of the link that had been forged between himself and Alhana? No, Laurana thought sadly, he had probably not known. Nor could he realize the love it represented. No human could. Carefully she had placed it upon his breast as she thought with sorrow of the dark-haired elven woman, who must know the heart upon which the glittering Starjewel rested was stilled forever.

The Honor Guard stepped back, waiting. The assembled knights stood with heads bowed for a moment, then lifted them to face Laurana.

This should have been the time for proud speeches, for recitals of the dead knights' heroic deeds. But for a moment, all that could be heard was the wheezing sobs of the old dwarf and Tasslehoff's quiet snuffle. Laurana looked down into Sturm's peaceful face, and she could not speak.

For a moment she envied Sturm, envied him fiercely. He was beyond pain, beyond suffering, beyond loneliness. His war had been fought. He was victorious.

You left me! Laurana cried in agony. Left me to cope with this by myself! First Tanis, then Elistan, now you. I can't! I'm not strong enough! I can't let you go, Sturm. Your death was senseless, meaningless! A fraud and a sham! I won't let you go. Not quietly! Not without anger!

Laurana lifted her head, her eyes blazing in the torchlight.

"You expect a noble speech," she said, her voice cold as the air of the sepulcher. "A noble speech honoring the heroic deeds of these men who have died. Well, you won't get it. Not from me!"

The knights glanced at each other, faces dark.

"These men, who should have been united in a brotherhood forged when Krynn was young, died in bitter discord, brought about by pride, ambition, and greed. Your eyes turn to Derek Crownguard, but he was not totally to blame. You are. All of you! All of you who took sides in this reckless bid for power."

A few knights lowered their heads, some paled with shame and anger. Laurana choked with her tears. Then she felt Flint's hand slip into hers, squeezing it comfortingly. Swallowing, she drew a deep breath.

"Only one man was above this. Only one man here among you lived the Code every day of his life. And for most of those days, he was not a knight. Or rather, he was a knight where it meant the most—in spirit, in heart, not in some official list."

Reaching behind her, Laurana took the blood-stained dragonlance from the altar and raised it high over her head. And as she lifted the lance, her spirit was lifted. The wings of darkness that had hovered around her were banished. When she raised her voice, the knights stared at her in wonder. Her beauty blessed them like the beauty of a dawning spring day.

"Tomorrow I will leave this place," Laurana said softly, her luminous eyes on the dragonlance. "I will go to Palanthas. I will take with me the story of this day! I will take this lance and the head of a dragon. I will dump that sinister, bloody head upon the steps of their magnificent palace. I will stand upon the dragon's head and make them listen to me! And Palanthas will listen! They will see their danger! And then I will go to Sancrist and to Ergoth and to every other place in this world where people refuse to lay down their petty hatreds and join together. For until we conquer the evils within ourselves—as this man did—we can never conquer the great evil that threatens to engulf us!"

Laurana raised her hands and her eyes to heaven. "Paladine!" she called out, her voice ringing like the trumpet's call. "We come to you, Paladine, escorting the souls of these noble knights who died in the High

Clerist's Tower. Give us who are left behind in this war-torn world the same nobility of spirit that graces this man's death!"

Laurana closed her eyes as tears spilled unheeded and unchecked down her cheeks. No longer did she grieve for Sturm. Her sorrow was for herself, for missing his presence, for having to tell Tanis of his friend's death, for having to live in this world without this noble friend by her side.

Slowly she laid the lance upon the altar. Then she knelt before it a moment, feeling Flint's arm around her shoulder and Tasslehoff's gentle touch on her hand.

As if in answer to her prayer, she heard the knights' voices rising behind her, carrying their own prayers to the great and ancient god, Paladine.

Return this man to Huma's breast:
Let him be lost in sunlight,
In the chorus of air where breath is translated;
At the sky's border receive him.

Beyond the wild, impartial skies
Have you set your lodgings,
In cantonments of stars, where the sword aspires
In an arc of yearning, where we join in singing.

Grant to him a warrior's rest.
Above our singing, above song itself,
May the ages of peace converge in a day,
May he dwell in the heart of Paladine.

And set the last spark of his eyes
In a fixed and holy place
Above words and the borrowed land too loved
As we recount the ages.

Free from the smothering clouds of war
As he once rose in infancy,
The long world possible and bright before him,
Lord Huma, deliver him.

Upon the torches of the stars
Was mapped the immaculate glory of childhood;
From that wronged and nestling country,
Lord Huma, deliver him.

Let the last surge of his breath
Perpetuate wine, the attar of flowers;

From the vanguard of love, the last to surrender,
Lord Huma, deliver him.

Take refuge in the cradling air
From the heart of the sword descending,
From the weight of battle on battle;
Lord Huma, deliver him.

Above the dreams of ravens where
His dreams first tried a rest beyond changing,
From the yearning for war and the war's ending,
Lord Huma, deliver him.

Only the hawk remembers death
In a late country; from the dusk,
From the fade of the senses, we are thankful that you,
Lord Huma, deliver him.

Then let his shade to Huma rise
Out of the body of death, of the husk unraveling;
From the lodging of mind upon nothing,
  we are thankful that you,
Lord Huma, deliver him.

Beyond the wild, impartial skies
Have you set your lodgings,
In cantonments of stars, where the sword aspires
In an arc of yearning, where we join in singing.

Return this man to Huma's breast
Beyond the wild, impartial skies;
Grant to him a warrior's rest
And set the last spark of his eyes
Free from the smothering clouds of wars
Upon the torches of the stars.
Let the last surge of his breath
Take refuge in the cradling air
Above the dreams of ravens where
Only the hawk remembers death.
Then let his shade to Huma rise
Beyond the wild, impartial skies.

The chant ended. Slowly, solemnly, the knights walked forward one by one to pay homage to the dead, each kneeling for a moment before the altar. Then the Knights of Solamnia left the Chamber of Paladine, returning to their cold beds to try and find some rest before the next day's dawning.

Laurana, Flint, and Tasslehoff stood alone beside their friend, their arms around each other, their hearts full. A chill wind whistled through the open door of the sepulcher where the Honor Guard stood, ready to seal the chamber.

"*Kharan bea Reorx,*" said Flint in dwarven, wiping his gnarled and shaking hand across his eyes. "Friends meet in Reorx." Fumbling in his pouch, he took out a bit of wood, beautifully carved into the shape of a rose. Gently he laid it upon Sturm's breast, beside Alhana's Starjewel.

"Good-bye, Sturm," Tas said awkwardly. "I only have one gift that, that you would approve of. I—I don't think you'll understand. But then again, maybe you do now. Maybe you understand better than I do." Tasslehoff placed a small white feather in the knight's cold hand.

"*Quisalan elevas,*" Laurana whispered in elven. "Our loves-bond eternal." She paused, unable to leave him in this darkness.

"Come, Laurana," Flint said gently. "We've said our good-byes. We must let him go. Reorx waits for him."

Laurana drew back. Silently, without looking back, the three friends climbed the narrow stairs leading from the sepulcher and walked steadfastly into the chill, stinging sleet of the bitter winter's night.

Far away from the frozen land of Solamnia, one other person said good-bye to Sturm Brightblade.

Silvanesti had not changed with the passing months. Though Lorac's nightmare was ended, and his body lay beneath the soil of his beloved country, the land still remembered Lorac's terrible dreams. The air smelled of death and decay. The trees bent and twisted in unending agony. Misshapen beasts roamed the woods, seeking an end to their tortured existence.

In vain Alhana watched from her room in the Tower of the Stars for some sign of change.

The griffons had come back—as she had known they would once the dragon was gone. She had fully intended to leave Silvanesti and return to her people on Ergoth. But the griffons carried disturbing news: war between the elves and humans.

It was a mark of the change in Alhana, a mark of her suffering these past months, that she found this news distressing. Before she met Tanis and the others, she would have accepted war between elves and humans, perhaps even welcomed it. But now she saw that this was only the work of the evil forces in the world.

She should return to her people, she knew. Perhaps she could end this insanity. But she told herself the weather was unsafe for traveling. In reality, she shrank from facing the shock and the disbelief of her people when she told them of the destruction of their land and her promise to her dying father that the elves would return and rebuild—after they had helped the humans fight the Dark Queen and her minions.

Oh, she would win. She had no doubt. But she dreaded leaving the solitude of her self-imposed exile to face the tumult of the world beyond Silvanesti.

And she dreaded—even as she longed—to see the human she loved. The knight, whose proud and noble face came to her in her dreams, whose very soul she shared through the Starjewel. Unknown to him, she stood beside him in his fight to save his honor. Unknown to him, she shared his agony and came to learn the depths of his noble spirit. Her love for him grew daily, as did her fear of loving him.

And so Alhana continually put off her departure. I will leave, she told herself, when I see some sign I may give my people, a sign of hope. Otherwise they will not come back. They will give up in despair. Day after day, she looked from her window.

But no sign came.

The winter nights grew longer. The darkness deepened. One evening Alhana walked upon the battlements of the Tower of the Stars. It was afternoon in Solamnia then, and—on another Tower—Sturm Brightblade faced a sky-blue dragon and a Dragon Highlord called the Dark Lady. Suddenly Alhana felt a strange and terrifying sensation—as though the world had ceased to turn. A shattering pain pierced her body, driving her to the stone below. Sobbing in fear and grief, she clutched the Starjewel she wore around her neck and watched in agony as its light flickered and died.

"So this is my sign!" she screamed bitterly, holding the darkened jewel in her hand and shaking it at the heavens. "There is no hope! There is nothing but death and despair!"

Holding the jewel so tightly that the sharp points bit into her flesh, Alhana stumbled unseeing through the darkness to her room in the Tower. From there she looked out once more upon her dying land. Then, with a shuddering sob, she closed and locked the wooden shutters of her window.

Let the world do what it will, she told herself bitterly. Let my people meet their end in their own way. Evil will prevail. There is nothing we can do to stop it. I will die here, with my father.

That night she made one final journey out into the land. Carelessly she threw a thin cape over her shoulders and headed for a grave lying beneath a twisted, tortured tree. In her hand, she held the Starjewel.

Throwing herself down upon the ground, Alhana began to dig frantically with her bare hands, scratching at the frozen ground of her father's grave with fingers that were soon raw and bleeding. She didn't care. She welcomed the pain that was so much easier to bear than the pain in her heart.

Finally, she had dug a small hole. The red moon, Lunitari, crept into the night sky, tinging the silver moon's light with blood. Alhana stared at the Starjewel until she could no longer see it through her tears, then she cast it into the hole she had dug. She forced herself to quit crying. Wiping the tears from her face, she started to fill in the hole.

Then she stopped.

Her hands trembled. Hesitantly, she reached down and brushed the dirt from the Starjewel, wondering if her grief had driven her mad. No, from it came a tiny glimmer of light that grew even stronger as she watched. Alhana lifted the shimmering jewel from the grave.

"But he's dead," she said softly, staring at the jewel that sparkled in Solinari's silver light.

"I know death has claimed him. Nothing can change that. Yet, why this light—"

A sudden rustling sound startled her. Alhana fell back, fearing that the hideously deformed tree above Lorac's grave might be reaching to grasp her in its creaking branches. But as she watched she saw the limbs of the tree cease their tortured writhing. They hung motionless for an instant, then—with a sigh—turned toward the heavens. The trunk straightened and the bark became smooth and began to glisten in the silver moonlight. Blood ceased to drip from the tree. The leaves felt living sap flow once more through their veins.

Alhana gasped. Rising unsteadily to her feet, she looked around the land. But nothing else had changed. None of the other trees were different—only this one, above Lorac's grave.

I am going mad, she thought. Fearfully she turned back to look at the tree upon her father's grave. No, it was changed. Even as she watched, it grew more beautiful.

Carefully, Alhana hung the Starjewel back in its place over her heart. Then she turned and walked back toward the Tower. There was much to be done before she left for Ergoth.

The next morning, as the sun shed its pale light over the unhappy land of Silvanesti, Alhana looked out over the forest. Nothing had changed. A noxious green mist still hung low over the suffering trees. Nothing would change, she knew, until the elves came back and worked to make it change. Nothing had changed except the tree above Lorac's grave.

"Farewell, Lorac," Alhana called, "until we return."

Summoning her griffon, she climbed onto its strong back and spoke a firm word of command. The griffon spread its feathery wings and soared into the air, rising in swift spirals above the stricken land of Silvanesti. At a word from Alhana, it turned its head west and began the long flight to Ergoth.

Far below, in Silvanesti, one tree's beautiful green leaves stood out in splendid contrast to the black desolation of the forest around it. It swayed in the winter wind, singing soft music as it spread its limbs to shelter Lorac's grave from the winter's darkness, waiting for spring.